Jackson

The DISTANT SHORE

Books by JAN DE HARTOG

THE DISTANT SHORE

THE LOST SEA

The
DISTANT SHORE

A Story of the Sea

by JAN DE HARTOG

HARPER & BROTHERS, PUBLISHERS, NEW YORK

Library of Congress catalog card number: 52-5443

Part I   WAR

Chapter I

WHEN I ARRIVED IN ENGLAND EARLY IN THE WAR, AFTER ESCAPING
from occupied Holland, I was appointed captain of an ocean-
going tugboat on the Western Approaches.

I was amazed by this appointment, for I had been out of the
service for seven years. I had started on ocean-going tugboats
as a boy, worked my way up to mate in eight years' service, then
I had quit and joined the Amsterdam Harbor Police, which
was a nicer job. Dutch ocean-going tugboats are different from
the busy little things one sees scurrying about in harbors, pulling
or pushing the liners about. They are the same sort of vessel but
three times as large, intended for salvaging ships in distress or
towing drydocks and other large material across the oceans. After
a voyage of seventeen months I had called it a day.

When I got my commission in London I told them that I didn't
think myself good enough for it, but they laughed. As any man will
believe it when people tell him that he is too modest, and as there
didn't seem to be room for discussion left after someone had
said, "This is an order," I went to the store, tried on several uniforms, got one that was too tight under the arms, and set out for
my wartime destination with a suitcase.

The destination was Westport, a medium-sized harbor in the
extreme southwest of England. I vaguely remembered it from a
visit ten years before, when I had been a bosun's apprentice. I
remembered a big, noisy port, a restaurant called Lyons, and a
little tattooist's shop with a notice in the window: "Three-colored
mermaids, painless and indelible, 2/6 per square inch." I remembered also an artificial hill in the middle of the town, with a tower

3

on top and a gilt angel on top of the tower. Someone had told me that it was a symbol of the independence of Westport: the hill and the tower had been erected in honor of a man who had not discovered America, and the angel spreading its wings toward the New World faced the wrong way.

When I came back to Westport, one foggy autumn evening in 1941, the things I remembered were still there, but little else; the rest had been bombed out of existence. The center of the town was a waste of dunes of rubble, dotted with broken chimney stacks and twisted girders like tree trunks after a forest fire. There wasn't a single house left standing, but the tower on the artificial hill had survived.

The angel still faced east defiantly, its gilt blistered and one of its wings broken, but the prim little lawns with the heart-shaped flower beds and the evergreen shrubs trimmed to resemble cocks and poodles that I remembered from my visit ten years ago had changed into a nightmarish jungle. In the straggling grass, among the ruins of what once had been ornamental benches, scores of lovers rolled about, as uninhibited as animals. Only the women looked different from one another in the dusk; all the men were in uniform. In the middle of the jungle stood a huge, blistered notice board on thin poles, saying: "Carpet beating strictly forbidden."

My marching orders told me that I was billeted in the Grand Hotel on the Esplanade, and so I started toward the harbor. As I turned a corner I suddenly found myself facing the little tattooist's shop. The top floors of the building had gone, but the basement with the shop was still there. Its window had shrunk to a solitary pane in a shutter of asbestos, and showed a new notice: "Names and hearts removed without a trace." Under the circumstances it seemed a grim joke.

I found the Grand Hotel without much difficulty. It was one of two huge lumps of masonry left standing on the boulevard that skirted the harbor. The first was a block of flats called "Sea-view," then there was half a mile of rubble, and after that the Grand Hotel. I worked my way toward it through a teeming crowd of sailors of many nationalities, British soldiers and R.A.F. men, through which dispatch riders on motor bikes weaved at great speed. When one of them stopped and took off his crash-helmet I saw that they were girls.

The Grand Hotel was a somber three-storied building with a mock-Grecian façade. I expected it to be requisitioned as a naval billet, but when I entered through the swing doors I saw that this could not be true. In the hall sat a crowd of old ladies in wicker chairs, with little doll's coffee sets on wicker tables in front of them, listening to the nine o'clock news. They were an island in a sea of uniformed males, who stood about sipping cocktails, and drowning the bland voice of the B.B.C. announcer with shouts and jokes in a language I hadn't heard for a long time. It was Dutch.

Apart from the last stand of the old ladies, the entire population of the Grand Hotel seemed to be Dutch. I saw only two kinds of uniforms: pilots' and sailors'. The pilots were of the K.L.M., the Royal Dutch Airlines, and the sailors wore the same uniform as I. I carried my suitcase to the desk and was greeted by a surly old porter with the words: "Jesus! Another one!"

By his side sat a lady with glasses, who gave me a motherly smile and said, "Welcome home, Captain; I hope you will be very happy here. Your room is No. 77, very nice and warm because it is just over the Turkish bath." She turned to the old porter and said, "Take the Captain to his room, Francis, and make sure that he gets a towel of his own."

The porter grabbed my suitcase, tried to lift it, said, "Jesus" again, and then, "Follow me," in a tone that made me climb the stairs with apprehension.

The apprehension was right. Room 77 resembled the Black Hole of Calcutta. It had three sets of bunks in three layers, a window consisting almost entirely of asbestos, a cracked washbasin, a mirror with the word "chronometer" written on it with soap, and it was infernally hot. Clothes, shoes, caps, bits of newspaper with the remains of meals, and empty beer bottles lay strewn about. The beds were unmade and the ceiling covered with crude drawings of the female anatomy, obviously made by the occupants of the top berths.

I wondered which one would be mine; the porter helped me out. He dumped my suitcase among the rubble and said, "You're

5

up on top there; Captain Wolters' bunk. He killed himself last week." He turned to go; before he closed the door behind him, he said, "And don't piss in the wash basin, there is a perfectly good lavatory at the top of the stairs."

I said, "Thank you," and fumbled in my pocket for a coin.

He saw it and spat. "Keep the change," he said, "all I want is peace."

I managed a smile, and said, "So do I."

He looked at me with one eye closed, like a photographer, and said, "You'll have it, Captain, before you know what hit you. The average life of you boys is three months." Then he added, enigmatically, "Ask Miss Headland," and shut the door.

I was tired, but very much awake. I took off my jacket as it was hurting me under the arms; then I decided that I might as well undress altogether and go to bed. I had some difficulty in finding room for my clothes; I ended up by putting them on the only chair in the room, which stood in the middle of the floor.

After I had climbed into my bunk and lay down to sleep I saw, on the wall next to my pillow, a poem written by a school-mastery hand:

> There is an old belief
> that on some distant shore
> far from despair and grief
> old friends shall meet once more.

I wondered whether Captain Wolters had written this, and decided he hadn't, for it looked more than three months old.

I remember vaguely the sounds of voices and the splashing of water that half woke me several hours later, but I didn't bother to look down and introduce myself. Not only had the heat doped me, it seemed hardly worth the trouble.

∾

Toward dawn I was woken up by a loud banging on the door, and a voice shouting, "Captain! S.O.S.!" I recognized the voice of the old porter.

Nobody else in the room seemed to have heard it; the hot silence was full of wheezes and snores. The door was opened and

6

the light switched on; the porter came in, muttering, and shook the shoulder of a shape in the middle bunk of the tier opposite me. As the shape did not react, he repeated his call, "Captain! S.O.S.!" then he muttered, "Jesus! drunk as an owl," shuffled out of sight, and there was a sound of water.

He came back with a dripping face towel in his hand, which he rubbed in the shape's neck, calling: "Coo-coo, Captain," and "Wakey-wakey," as if he was in a night nursery. The shape woke up, cursing, kicked off its blankets, and two bare legs were swung out of the bunk. They looked very young.

After the porter had left, their owner came out into the open. He was a fair-haired boy; his tousled hair gave him an almost childish appearance. He groped among the disorderly pile of clothes on the chair until he had found his own; I watched him with amazement. He seemed far too young to be a captain; I thought that he must be an airman until I saw him put on a jacket with four stripes on its sleeves. They looked incongruous on him; in my tugboat days captains had been at least forty-five, he looked as if he had just left naval college. He dressed with an amazing speed considering his condition; when he left the room he had the good grace to switch off the light, and left me wondering in the dark. On my way to Westport I had felt nervous and insecure at the idea of being the captain of a tug-boat; after seeing him I felt like an old hand at the game.

As I tried to fall asleep again I had a curious feeling. It had to do with memories and loneliness, with old standards crumbling and a growing new fear. I felt as if I was about to cross a shadow line; as if for me the war had not yet really started, despite the things that had happened during my escape. I suddenly felt a great sympathy for the unknown boys, wheezing and snoring around me. I remembered the poem on the wall with a sensation of beauty and understanding; as if I had already set out toward that distant shore, as if we already were old friends, before I even knew their names.

I lay in the darkness and heard the town wake up. I heard the distant booming of hooters in the harbor, the growing and dimin-ishing roar of the first motor bikes streaking past. I thought of

7

the girls with the crash-helmets who rode them, the sheltered lives they had left to pin up their hair and put on breeches and roar through the dawn, knowing more about two-cylinder engines and death than they had ever known about algebra and love. I saw the solitary pane in the asbestos window grow pink, and thought of the boy with the four stripes on his jacket. For the first time in my life I felt old, and yet I wasn't even thirty.

∽

Next morning I had breakfast in a huge dining room full of bleary-eyed characters with hangovers, seated untidily at long tables with communal teapots and huge sugar bowls that looked like sand pits after playtime. The only spots of defiant tidiness in that dining room were the little one-man tables at which sat the old ladies reading *The Daily Telegraph* and *The Times*.

During breakfast an airman came in, followed by a tired private carrying a huge bunch of bananas. The airman ripped off a strip of bananas at each of the little tables, offered them to the old lady behind it with a bow and a flowery little speech; then he slumped into a chair at one of the long tables and said, "Hell's bells! They nearly got me this time." Someone asked, "Where?" and the airman answered, "Three hundred miles west of Gib," before he yelled, "Lily! Breakfast!" Nobody commented upon this.

After breakfast I reported at Headquarters, as ordered. I was directed to a small red brick building at the end of a pier, carrying his Britannic Majesty's Coat of Arms and the legend hewn in granite: "H.M. Customs and Excise." On the heavy oak door a piece of three-ply had been nailed, saying: "R.N.A.N., OTWA, R.H.Q., Knock."

I knocked, a voice shouted, "Ja!" and on opening the door I heard a multiple twittering of radio signals, as if I had entered the birds' gallery in a zoo. Three wireless receiving sets were lined up on a bench along the right-hand wall with loud-speakers above them; the left-hand wall was empty but for an enormous desk. Behind it sat an angry old tugboat Captain, faced by a young Lieutenant Commander of the British Navy, who was

8

busy cleaning his nails. I remembered the Captain's face from an earlier occasion: he had been a member of the jury when I passed through the ordeal of the Mate's examination for ocean-going tugboats. I had been frightened by him then; when I told the story of the examination later I had made fun of it, because it consisted mainly of shouting; whoever bellowed the usual tug-boat service commands loudest was sure to pass with praise. Now I was frightened of him again.

He talked to me in a husky voice, and every word seemed to travel across to me on a widening ring of gin fumes. What he said was difficult to understand because of the frantic twittering of the loud-speakers on the opposite wall. I understood that my ship, the *Zeeland*, was at present in dry dock for repairs, and that this was fortunate because it enabled me to acquaint myself again with the service as a guest on one of the active tugboats during the next week. He talked in an angry voice about the noble character of OTWA, calling it at least six times: "The Red Cross of the ocean." Apart from this obviously hackneyed phrase, which he uttered with the impatient boredom of an overworked man, the only thing I understood from all he said was that OTWA was short for "Ocean-going Tugboats Western Approaches." But suddenly one word made me sit up: the name of the Captain on whose ship I would be a guest until the *Zeeland* was put back into service. The name was Dop.

I knew Jan Dop very well indeed. We had gone through the same year of Naval College and sailed together off and on on various trips until I quit. He was a nice chap but a bit wild: when I had thought of him at all since the beginning of the war I had pictured him sitting quietly in some apartment somewhere in Rotterdam or Amsterdam with a girl, planning boyish excursions into the black market. Hearing his name that morning was like seeing a raft swirl past; I asked the old Captain, excitedly, where I could find him. The Captain said, "Wait a minute," and shouted at the radio desk, "Hey! Whereabouts is the *Vlieland*?"

One of the three men sitting with their backs to us answered, without looking round, "Just passed B.R. on his way home, with a tanker in tow."

9

"Bishop Rock," said the Captain. "He'll be back in about four hours; you report here at 11 A.M. Good-by."

᮪

When I came back at eleven I found the old Captain in a rage. He was banging the table and shouting at the top of his voice, but no one paid any attention to him. The loud-speakers twittered; the three men sat underneath them with their backs to him, scribbling; the English officer had finished cleaning his nails and was now carefully filling his lighter. When I came in the old Captain started to shout at me.

"The bastards!" he screamed, "the sneaking sharks! This is the second they have got within two weeks! If from now on my ships don't get fighter cover, or are at least fitted out with guns that can shoot level, I'm quitting this job!" He shouted these last remarks at the British officer opposite him, who didn't look up, but went on filling his lighter. I understood that a tugboat had been sunk by a U-boat, and thought for a moment with a feeling of nausea that it was Jan Dop's. But when I asked the old Captain he answered, "No," in a tone as if he regretted it. It was the *Friesland,* he said, with Captain Daamen, the youngest skipper of the fleet but the best. It was always the best who went first in this bloody war. I realized that Captain Daamen had been the boy I had seen woken up by the porter the night before.

Dop's ship came in half an hour later. I watched her through the steamed windows of the office. She rounded the pier at reckless speed and backed roughly into the row of tugboats opposite; I heard a splintering noise, and saw her mast tremble as her stern hit the quay; in our old days Dop would have been called on the mat for this. His crew was still mooring when I saw him jump ashore off the poop, followed by a man in a gaudy uniform that looked like an admiral's.

When he came into the office he was very noisy and very nervous. When he saw me he fell silent. He looked at me for a moment, his mouth open, and it was a moment of uncanny truth; never since have I seen him show his secret so plainly. He was a man terrified out of his wits.

He recovered in a flash, shouted, "No!" and practically jumped

10

on my neck. He was exactly like the old Dop I had known: happy-go-lucky, breezy, and loud. He completely hid the terror which I had seen. He slapped my shoulders, pulled my hair, thumped my chest, and shouted the curses that are the Dutchman's only expression of strong emotion. Then the old Captain called, "Hey, you two! Go and play outside, don't keep this bird waiting, he has to go on!"

The bird was the man I had taken for an admiral from afar; he turned out to be the captain of a Yugoslav tanker. I remember the strong smell of petrol he brought into the room, and his dazed dark eyes. Dop and he filled out a number of forms, stating what had happened to his ship, where Dop had picked him up, what opposition they had encountered from the enemy, what course they had taken to get here, and how long it had taken them. Dop was very matter-of-fact about it all; it was obvious that he had done this many times before; but the Yugoslav Captain was dazed and went on rubbing his eyebrows, trying to remember exactly, formulating painstaking answers in an English entirely his own. After they had signed the forms and Dop had said, "Well, that's it, Skipper. Be seeing you sometime," the Yugoslav rose solemnly to his feet, put out a grimy hand, and said, "Aye wande zenk yu ver zavink my sheep." Dop shook hands quickly, said, "Any time, Skipper, any time," and whispered to me, "Let's beat it."

The old Captain called after us, "Hey, your pills!" when Dop had already opened the door to go out. He hurried back and grabbed the envelope offered to him. The Captain said, "And no monkey business you two; be either at your flat or in the hotel. I don't want to rouse the whole bloody town again in the middle of the night, trying to hunt down Captain Dop on a binge." Dop said, "O.K., O.K.," good-naturedly, and shut the door.

Outside was a lovely autumn morning. When we stood in the wind Dop grabbed my shoulders, held me at arm's length, and said, "Fancy seeing you here! God, this is wonderful." Then he put his arm round my shoulders and we walked clumsily down the pier. His arm trembled.

It was difficult to choose from all the questions I wanted to ask him and all the things I wanted to say, so after a few moments

11

of silence I asked him what the pills were the old Captain had given him. He said, "Oh, stuff to sleep. They used to give us a tin at a time, but after Wolters swallowed them all at one helping and killed himself, they started handing them out three at a time after each trip." Then he looked at me with a grin and said, "God, I'm glad he did it, the dope, for otherwise you wouldn't have turned up."

I didn't understand this, and he told me that Wolters had been one of the two captains of the *Zeeland,* I was to replace him. Dop was sure he hadn't wanted to commit suicide, but had taken the stuff when he was drunk. When I asked him what he meant by "One of the two captains," he gave me the first concrete information about OTWA I had received so far. Each tugboat had two crews, one took over from the other the moment the ship came in from a trip so that it could sail again instantly if necessary. During the trip no one on board shut an eye, it would be impossible to keep the ships in constant readiness without having two crews. That was why the officers lodged in the Grand Hotel and the crews on an old channel steamer lying in the harbor. No one slept on board.

I thought at first that we were on our way to the Grand Hotel when we walked along the boulevard; but when we got to the door and I stopped he said, "Are you crazy? I've got a flat."

"A flat," I repeated.

"Yes," he said, "didn't you know? I am the only Dutchman in this town who has got a flat of his own. A flat and a girl." When he said this he grinned, with the look of boyish bravado in his eyes that I remembered best about him. It was that look that had made me assume during the past year that he was sure to have found a job in the black market. Seeing him grin like that gave me a feeling of great friendship for him, and I grinned back and slapped his shoulder, and said, "Good old Dop. What is she like?" He winked and said, "You come and have a look, chum. The best peach on the tree."

The flat was on the top floor of the other clump of masonry left standing on the boulevard: the block called "Seaview" which I had passed the night before. There was a lift, but its gate carried a lopsided notice "Out of order," which looked as if it had

12

hung there for years. We climbed ten flights of gritty stairs, two flights to a floor. On each floor were three identical doors with aluminum numbers on them. The top floor was the lightest, for in the ceiling was a broken skylight that had once been covered with asbestos and through which sunlight now poured in. The floor beneath it was stained by rain and soot in an irregular pattern, which looked like a map of Africa. Dop stopped in front of the left hand door, No. 12. The top of the "2" was loose, and the number hung upside down. He pulled a key from his pocket and opened the door. The flat was silent, it felt as if no one was there. The door opened directly into a small kitchen dining room, very tidy, with red checkered curtains on the window. Dop took off his cap, threw it on the table, and called, "Hey, where are you?" Then a door in the far corner of the room opened, and a girl came in.

She looked about twenty-three, and was tall and blonde. She wore her hair loose with a white ribbon in it, and was dressed in a blue dressing gown. She had big blue eyes, very pretty, and a shy, large mouth. I liked her.

"This is Stella," said Dop.

She gave me a smile, but her eyes stayed earnest; she looked at me as children look at people they see for the first time: a look of grave observation, that was entirely unself-conscious.

Dop went across to her, took her in his arms, and gave her a mighty hug. "Did you sleep well?" he asked; and she nodded and kissed him.

Then she asked, "Did you have a nice trip?" Her voice was husky and lower than I had expected it to be.

"Oh, all right," said Dop. "A Yugoslav on fire. He was very cooperative." He kissed her and ruffled her hair; her eyes were so frank that it was almost embarrassing to watch. She was obviously very much in love.

"Well," said Dop, "sit down, chum, and make yourself at home." The girl asked whether I'd like something to eat, and I answered, "No, thank you." Dop said, "Don't be polite, have something to eat while I have a wash. She makes the best beans on toast in the world."

I sat down at the table; Dop left the room by the same door through which the girl had come in, and he left it open. While

13

she was taking out bread from a bin and lighting the gas stove I heard him humming in the next room, and the splashing of water.

She cut the bread into slices and put them under the grill; then she opened a tin of beans, shook the contents into a little pan and put it over the flame. I wondered what else she would do to make the best beans on toast in the world, but she did nothing else. She made the toast, buttered it, and heaped the hot beans on top, that was all. Dop must be very much in love, too.

While she was doing this she asked me a few friendly questions; whether I was new in the service and that sort of thing. Her soft, low voice had a quiet quality which was somehow soothing. I realized this when I felt myself relaxing on that kitchen chair for the first time since I had come to Westport. For the first time I realized how tense I had been, how afraid. I suddenly became conscious again of the tightness of my jacket, and I asked her if she would mind if I took it off, for it pinched under the arms.

As I said that she looked at me again with her grave blue eyes, and said, "Give it to me, perhaps I can alter it for you."

I mumbled something polite, but she didn't listen and I handed her my jacket. She held it up by the shoulders, then looked at me, sizing me up, and said, "You come with me. Perhaps I've got something for you."

I followed her through the door in the corner into a bedroom with a double bed and a wardrobe. Another door into the room stood ajar and I saw Dop, stark naked, bent over a wash basin, washing his face. She put my jacket on the bed and went to the wardrobe. On top of the wardrobe was a big photograph in a leather frame of a young man in uniform; on it was written: "I'll walk beside you."

She opened the wardrobe, looked among a row of suits hanging on a rod inside, took one out, lifted the jacket off the hanger, and said, "Try this." It was a mate's uniform.

I tried it on and it fitted. Dop's voice called, "What are you doing?" from the bathroom; then he came in, in slippers and a dressing gown, drying his hair with a towel.

"I'm trying to find him another jacket," said the girl. "Does that one fit you?"

I said, "Yes," a bit embarrassed for Dop looked as if he didn't

14

like what we were doing, and I suddenly realized that the uniform couldn't be one of his. He was a captain, and much thinner than I.

She said, "If it fits you, I'll change the stripes for you. Are you sure it fits?"

I said, "Yes, perfectly."

"Don't say it does if it doesn't," she said, like a grownup to a child in a shop. "Try the armholes; put your hand inside and see how much room you have."

I did so, and said there was plenty of room. She said, "All right, give it to me." After I had taken it off, she took the two jackets to the kitchen.

When she had gone I whispered to Dop, "Sorry if I . . ." but he didn't let me finish. He whispered, "Ssht. I'll tell you later," and then added, aloud, "Come, let's have some grub!" He shut the doors of the wardrobe; the portrait on top of it wobbled. We went back to the kitchen.

We sat down at the table and ate our beans on toast, while she snipped the stripes off my old jacket with a pair of nail scissors. While we were eating I noticed her hands; they were large and red like a boy's, she fumbled with the tiny scissors clumsily. Somehow this was moving; the best beans on toast in the world out of a tin and the clumsy sewing made me realize that she was an amateur, like all of us. Dop had sailed into the harbor with great gusto as if he was the best sailor in the world, and crashed his stern into the quay; I would soon have to sail a tugboat and make everybody believe that I had done so all my life, while in reality I had no idea any more of the maneuvers and the commands I had bellowed so juicily at my examination, nine years before. We were all amateurs: the drunken boy who had died that morning, the girls on the motor bikes, the angry old Captain in Headquarters; she was one of us. She played at being a good cook and an expert housewife; she was very sweet.

I would have felt at ease with her but for the uniform from the wardrobe and the wobbly portrait on top of it. I think that somehow she frightened me a bit, not as a person but as an enigma. When I had come in she had made me relax, because she had seemed part of the world I knew: one of Dop's girls.

15

Now I realized that she wasn't; she was part of that other world across the shadow line, into which I had not yet entered. She was part of the war.

When she saw that we had nearly finished our beans on toast she got up and made coffee with a percolator. While we sat sipping it Dop told me about OTWA. He was not nervous and loud any more, but matter-of-fact and quiet. He told me that OTWA had three stations along the western seafront; Westport was one of them. Every station had two or three ocean-going tugboats in service, whose task it was to pick up the lame ducks left behind by the big convoys that sailed from America to England on the Western Approaches. "Lame ducks" were ships that had either been hit by bombs from airplanes, or by torpedoes or gunfire from U-boats, and whose engines had been put out of order so that they couldn't keep up to the convoy's speed any longer. As the convoys by now numbered several a day and were steadily increasing in volume, there were a great number of lame ducks about, and it was not unusual for a tugboat to turn around and sail again with its second crew the moment after it had brought someone in. In the beginning it hadn't been so bad, this station; they had started with five tugs, now there were three left, and no replacements had arrived so far.

I asked him what the Royal Dutch Airlines were doing here, and he said that they were operating a service between England and the Near East via Gibraltar. He said it curtly and with a glance at the sewing girl, as if he didn't want to discuss it in her presence. She said suddenly, "You ought to take your pills now," but he answered, "No, I'm going out again."

She looked up from her sewing with alarm in her eyes. "You haven't got to sail again, have you?"

"No," he said, "I'm going out with him. I must introduce him to Van Dam."

She looked at me with a smile, but her eyes were reproachful. "Don't keep him too long," she said, "he must sleep, otherwise he'll go to pieces when he has to sail again, tomorrow."

She said it casually, as if it was a perfectly normal thing to say; if Dop hadn't got angry I wouldn't have thought about it twice. But he got very angry; he shouted at her, "Who the hell

16

is going to pieces? I've never gone to pieces in my life! Don't start mixing me up with someone else! I . . ." He would have said a lot more, if she hadn't got up and kissed him.

It was a curious moment; I don't think I'll ever forget it. I saw his insensate terror dwindle and vanish under her kiss. I was envious of him, although my vague fear was nothing compared to what I had seen in his eyes the first moment I saw him in that office. I had seen it in his eyes again when he started to shout at her, and now I saw it taken away from him by nothing but a kiss.

It worried me, his fear; I had seen many people in action so far, who did things that on the face of it were more dangerous than the work of OTWA, and they hadn't been nearly so jumpy. The R.A.F. boys, swarming out over Germany every night, certainly had more reason to be afraid than we had, and yet from what I knew of them they were in much better shape. There must be something to this OTWA business that was different, something I didn't know yet. But as I thought this I remembered the Dutch airman, who had come into the breakfast room that morning with the bananas, and I realized that he had had the same look in his eyes when he sat down at our table. It was a mystery, and I didn't like it.

Dop got up and went into the bedroom to dress while she finished her sewing. We talked a bit; that is to say, she did the talking. She had the Englishwoman's admirable capacity for making conversation on trivial subjects in awkward circumstances. She talked about how nice the civilians in Westport were; there was a Mrs. Bell who constantly gave little parties for the forces with raffles and soft drinks, and I must ask Jan to take me to the Savage Club one night where sweet old gentlemen sang songs and played snooker, and where anybody from the forces could get up whenever he liked and give a little lecture on his adventures or recite a poem in his native language; that was why the club was called "Savage." It was the kind of chatter that looks silly written down, but is a relief to listen to when you are at a loss what to say new. By the time Dop came back she had finished my jacket.

I put it on, and, after having assured her once more that it

17

fitted, I started taking my things from the old jacket and putting them into the pockets of the new one. As I put my wallet into the inside pocket I noticed a little tab sewn onto the lining with a name on it: H. F. Barger. It struck me like a blow. "Not Henk Barger?" I asked, for we had been friends for three years. We had sailed together first as sailors and finally as mates' assistants on the tugboat *Terschelling*, before we both passed our examination and were commissioned on different ships. Dop said, "Yes, yes," hastily, and nudged me hard. I must have looked rather stupid, for when she turned away to get his coat for him, he whispered, "Don't look like a fool! I'll tell you later."

When I said good-by to her and thanked her for the jacket, she gave me a big smile and said, "Do come and have dinner with us sometime." But by then I knew the English well enough to realize that this meant nothing, unless you agreed upon a date. I concluded that I hadn't been much of a success with her, and that she didn't approve of me barging into Dop's life and keeping him up when he should have been in bed.

It was a pity, for I liked her.

∽

When we got out of the building, Dop took me along the crowded quay and through streets lined with rubble to the cellar of a ruin, that had once been the town hall. In the cellar was a canteen for allied forces called the "Social Center." In it I found hundreds of sailors of all nationalities, dancing in a dense smoke with tired girls to music from three loud-speakers, or sitting at small tables against the wall sipping tea or Coca-Cola. The noise was so deafening that we had to shout; Dop shouted that it was the only spot in Westport where we could talk privately.

I found out that this was indeed true. Once we had found a table and two free chairs in a far corner, and Dop started bellowing at me, it seemed as if after a few moments the infernal noise isolated us completely from our neighbors, who sat so close to us that we rubbed shoulders. We shook our heads to two girls, who came to ask us in deaf-mute language whether we would like a dance, and ordered two Coca-Colas from an overworked waitress

18

who dragged a huge untidy tea-trolley through the crowd; then Dop started to talk.

At first I was so distracted that I didn't really listen; but after a while I forgot that he was shouting and that the whole situation was preposterous. The din and the smoke seemed to isolate his pale, tense face. He looked younger than I had ever seen him, with his cap on the back of his head and his thin hands nervously breaking up a matchbox. His captain's stripes began to look as incongruous on him as they had looked on the boy whom I had watched dressing for death last night. He began by apologizing for shushing me in the flat, when I had begun to talk about Barger. There was nothing mysterious behind it, he said, only he didn't want Stella to get upset by talking about people who had been killed in action. She was a sensitive girl, who before the war had lived quite out of this world; she came from one of the Hebrides. She had volunteered at the beginning of the war and been landed in the air raids and the hell-hole of Westport without any transition. I asked what her job was, and he said that she had been secretary to the Dutch Airlines' Headquarters until she had started to live with him in the flat; now she devoted all her time to looking after him.

I didn't ask about the portrait on top of the wardrobe, but he must have sensed the question in my mind. Perhaps I looked a bit noncommittal when he talked about her as if she was still a Victorian girl keeping a diary on a misty island at the edge of the world. He said the photograph was her brother's; he had been drafted into the army early in the war and was now fighting in the desert. They were devoted to each other and she wrote him a long letter each week.

I began to get a bit fed up with all this talk about Stella; like all people in love he would have talked about nothing else if I had let him. I wanted to know about Barger, and he told me that Barger had been the previous tenant of the flat. Before he died he had given Dop a duplicate of his key, because he had rented the flat for the duration and didn't want it to get out of the hands of the Dutch. He had given the key on condition that Dop in his turn would have a duplicate made, once he moved

19

in, and give that to another Dutchman on whom he was to impose the same condition.

He asked if I had known Barger well; when I said I had he glanced at me, then he looked back at his hands that were brushing the remains of the matchbox into a neat little heap on the table. He hadn't known him very well himself, he said, but he had seemed a nice chap. I asked how he had died; he shrugged his shoulders without looking up and said, "Oh, the usual thing: intercepted and gunned by a U-boat before he got to the duck he was to pick up." I asked why this was usual, and he answered, "The tricky bit is between here and the ship you are going to pick up. Once you get there you're all right; for the duck is armed, and we are not."

I said, "I see," but I didn't, not until a good three minutes later. We sat silently in the infernal noise for a while, Dop brushing the remains of the matchbox into an ever neater heap, while the truth slowly dawned on me. "But surely you've got some sort of cannon on board?" I asked.

"Oh yes," said Dop, "we've got a pom-pom. But it is vintage 1926, and it's not aircraft that are bothering us, it's U-boats. If you want to attack a U-boat with the thing you might as well try a peashooter." He looked up and grinned. "What's more: the thing won't shoot level," he said.

The disheveled waitress passed with her trolley and snatched our empty Coca-Cola bottles away, upsetting the neat little heap Dop had made of his matchbox. "Anything else?" she asked, and we shook our heads. "Let's go and have a drink somewhere," said Dop.

We worked our way through the dancing crowd, our eyes stinging with smoke. When we got outside in the cool dusk and the faint powdery smell of the ruins, I thought of the pilot I had seen come home that morning. I asked, "The planes of the Royal Airlines—aren't they armed either?"

"No," said Dop.

∽

We had a drink in the bar of the Grand Hotel. It was full of Dutchmen; few were sober. After our third drink Dop fumbled in his pocket and took out a key. "Here," he said, "tuck this away somewhere and forget about it until you need it."

I knew instantly what key it was, but to give myself time to think of something to say I asked, "What the hell is this?"

Dop eyed me unsteadily; he was getting drunk. "I promised Barger," he said; "but so far I didn't know anybody here whom I considered good enough for the flat. I'm jolly glad you came; this takes a load off my mind. A promise is a promise. A man ought to stick to his promises. God knows there is little else left to stick to. Here." He closed my fingers over the key; his hand was hot and moist. "Put it away, forget about it, and if anything should happen to me: use it. Promise." His hot hand still held my fist, and he tried to focus his eyes on mine. "Promise that the moment you use it you will have a duplicate made, which you will give to your best friend."

I said, "Don't be silly. If anyone will survive this war it's you."

He shook his head slowly, his eyes closed, with drunken stubbornness. "You put it away and forget about it," he said. "And when you give the duplicate to your best friend, make him promise the same. Let's keep Barger's memory hallowed."

I said, "I don't want your bloody key, you're drunk."

Then he brought his face very close to mine, opened his eyes and asked, "You want me to bash your face in for you?"

I sighed, said, "O.K.," put the key in my pocket, and started trying to take him home.

By the time I succeeded I wasn't sober any more either. We weaved our way through the crowd on the boulevard arm in arm, shaking hands with people. After we had finally reached the house and started climbing the ten flights of stairs, we got out of breath once or twice and sat down, giggling. Dop tried to pick himself up when we stood in front of the door with the inverted "2," but he didn't succeed. I wanted to open the door for him with my key, after I had asked him several times for his. The moment he saw the key he sobered up instantly and slapped my hand. I was angry for a second, until I saw his face. He looked at me with such loathing that I suddenly felt sorry for him.

21

"What the hell do you think you are doing?" he said. "I'm not dead yet!"

He took out his own key, managed to put it in the lock at the third try, giggled, and said, "You'll sail with me for the whole of next week, so we are b-both bloody asses." Then he opened the door and staggered in.

I didn't wait for him to shut it. I went home.

Chapter II

THAT NIGHT I WAS WOKEN UP BY THE OLD PORTER MYSELF. HE SHOOK me by the shoulder and called, "Captain! S.O.S.!" He must have banged on the door and shouted before, but I hadn't heard him.

I swung my legs out of the bunk as I heard a splashing of water in the corner, for I didn't want the wet face-flannel treatment. My head felt as if my brains had got loose; I must have got pretty tight the night before. I dressed as quickly as I could, and managed to pick out my jacket from the heap of clothes on the chair without trying them all on because it had Barger's name on it. When I came down to the hall I saw the old porter sitting behind the desk in his shirt sleeves. On the desk was a glass of water with a set of dentures in it. He gave me a toothless grin and said, "Good luck, Captain"; then he vanished behind the desk. He obviously had a bed there.

When I got out into the open it was pitch dark and cold. The wind had freshened but there must have been a lot of cloud, for I didn't see a single star. I saw nothing at all. I stood there cursing under my breath, when the thin beam of a blacked-out torch darted at me and a voice said, "Looking for something, chum?"

I said, "Yes, the tugboat *Vlieland*."

The spidery beam slid down my sleeve and caught my stripes. "Sorry, sir," said the voice. "Let me take you there, sir."

I said, "Thank you, that's very civil of you," and followed the faint pinpoint of light that the torch made on the pavement in front of my feet. I heard heavy steps of hobnailed boots beside

22

me, but I saw nothing; I had no idea who it was. The voice chatted on the way with a broad cockney accent, warning me when we stepped off the pavement; the torch carefully picked out the obstacles on the pier when we got there. To each sentence the voice added "sir"; by the time we got to the ship and I saw him in the faint mooring light shining down from the poop, I had already realized that he was an M.P. I thanked him, wondering for a moment whether I should shake hands with him; he saluted smartly and I saluted back.

When I got on board ship I was quite prepared to salute some more; I had found that it gave me a nice feeling of authority for which I didn't find any justification inside me. But nobody did; for one thing the shadowy shapes I discerned on the aftdeck hadn't got anything on to salute at. I didn't see a single peaked cap; some of them wore knitted things with a tassel on top, the others nothing but hair which needed cutting. I addressed one of the shapes as it passed close to me, and said, "Would you take me to Captain Dop, please." The shape answered, "Who the hell are you?" and I told him my rank and my name, rather primly. He said, "O.K., keep your shirt on. This way." At that he vanished completely.

I groped my way along the rail, muttering, was whistled at from the darkness, stumbled several times, hurried up by a hissing voice ahead of me; when I finally got to the chartroom, where a dim oil light was burning, I was ready to give him a piece of my mind. He was a small swarthy man in a jersey covered with grease, a dirty towel round his neck. "He'll be around in a minute," he said, "wait here." I asked him whether he was the Admiral, and he answered, "No, the cook" indifferently.

I sat waiting in the chartroom for a good ten minutes before Dop turned up. It was the first tugboat I had been on for seven years, and things seemed to have changed in the meantime. I remembered the chartroom of the tugs I had known as fairly tidy places; this one was in an incredible mess. The chart on the table was scribbled all over with pencil marks and lines, and covered with rings like a pub table. I counted eight empty mugs, cracked and grimy, among the litter on that table; the rest was

23

bottles, candlesticks, socks, crumpled-up signal flags, empty cigarette packs and a moldy rope-soled shoe. The cabin itself looked as if it hadn't been swept for months; the floor was covered with dirt and crushed cigarette stubs; in one corner lay a pile of empty bottles.

When Dop arrived he looked awful. He had dark rings under his eyes, and was unshaven. "God," he said, "we certainly hit it good and proper last night; Stella gave me hell." A boy wearing a sleeveless goatskin jacket over a sweater came in. "What have we got tonight?" he asked.

"A Norwegian in square 686," said Dop, "with a cigar hole in number one hold."

"Tanker?" asked the boy.

"No," said Dop, "wheat."

The boy said, "Good. Ready to go?"

"If everybody is there."

"Everybody but Martens."

"O.K.," said Dop, "the hell with him. Let's go."

When the boy had gone I asked who he was, and Dop said, "My Mate." He threw his cap among the rubble on the table, opened three drawers crammed with junk before he found a pencil; when he found it the point was broken, and he threw it away without looking where it fell. I gave him mine.

He said, "Thanks," and made a cross on the map about sixty miles due west of Bishop Rock. "The duck is here," he said. "It's wheat which will get soaked, that means no fire. The wind is south-southeast, force six, so we can sail the last ten miles if it doesn't get too light."

"Sail?" I asked.

"Yes," he said. "Jerry will be hanging around the wreck, and at night the only means by which he can spot us coming is the sound of our propeller. So if we sail the last bit we'll be able to sneak up on the duck without Jerry knowing we are there, before we have floated our line across."

"You don't shoot your line?" I asked, for that was what we had been used to doing in my days. Each tugboat carried a little cannon like the whalers use for their harpoons, and with it we shot a flare with a thin line attached to it across the deck of the

24

vessel in distress. They hauled in the line and we attached our hawser to the end of it.

Dop said impatiently, "Hell no! The whole point is that Jerry mustn't spot us until we are well within the range of the duck's guns; if we started shooting lines we might as well light ourself up with Bengal fires to help him take aim. We approach the duck to the windward, float a cask with the line attached to it, and when the cask hits the duck's side, she picks it up."

I asked whether the duck knew this, and Dop said, "Of course. Every captain sailing in a convoy gets a set of sealed envelopes before he starts, to be opened in various cases of emergency. Ours is envelope D: "If disabled by enemy action and left behind by the convoy." In it he finds a set of instructions which we composed for him: Don't use your wireless, your position will be reported to base by the convoy's escort. Try to keep your vessel afloat as well as you can, and put out any fires as quickly as possible. Above all: Don't waste your ammunition by having pot shots at any U-boats that may surface around you while you are waiting for the tugboat; don't answer their fire, not even under the severest provocation; the U-boat won't sink you until it can take in the tugboat as well, so save your ammunition until we have made fast, then give them hell."

"What else?" I asked.

"Oh, some blurb about not betraying our presence when they sight us, and not giving wheel unless instructed to do so, and a set of day and night signals," said Dop. "But the wireless and the shooting business are the most important. We don't want the ducks to give the show away and attract all the U-boats in the region, while we are creeping toward them without as much as a slingshot to hit back with." The boy with the goatskin jacket stuck his head in and said, "Ready when you are." Dop said, "O.K.," and we went to the bridge.

In the cold, windy darkness I thought over what Dop had told me downstairs. It wasn't difficult to understand, but I found it hard to stomach. I had never thought of myself as a hero, and never felt any desire of being one; a job that seemed to consist mainly of being shot at without being able to shoot back didn't appeal to me at all. Before we sailed into the open I had the

25

thoughts that must be common to anyone about to go into action for the first time. I thought how the devil I could wangle it so that this would be the last time. I thought of any special qualities which could make me eligible for a safer job; looking at it from Headquarters' point of view I decided that I had none. I thought of having an unfortunate accident, which would crush my foot or my left hand; but even while I thought so I knew that I hadn't got the guts to do it. I tried to bring out my better self by thinking of the others on board and all the boys of OTWA, who were running the same risks as I and didn't squeak about it. When that didn't work either, I stimulated the secret feeling common to all soldiers: that nothing could happen to me; that, if not immortal, I was sure of a long life and would die in bed. I remembered a fortune teller whom I had gone to see before I left Holland; she had predicted many narrow escapes but a long, long life for two guilders. During my escape, whenever I had found myself in a tight corner, the thought of that fortune teller had comforted me; now her prediction seemed as cold as a dead fish.

Perhaps I had too much imagination; I foresaw everything that would happen, down to the minutest detail. Although I had never seen a U-boat in my life, I saw a vivid picture of one, surfacing right beside us. I saw its commando tower, or whatever the thing was called, opened from the inside, and a dozen Fritzes climbing down on to her deck. They uncovered the gun, pointed it at us, and while we were dashing from side to side on a zigzag course, I heard the sharp reports of the shots, the screaming of the shells, and the sickening explosions when they burst all around us, sending up milk-white fountains of water. I didn't get to the actual direct hit which would tear open the ship and fling me into the sea to drown, a dismembered bleeding lump; before I got that far I was already so sick with terror that I had to force my mind on to other things by talking to Dop, or by looking at the dull glint of the piece of rail I could see in the darkness and trying to make out whether it was mahogany or teak.

When the swell got us and the ship started pitching and rolling I got better, for something unexpected happened: I was sea-

26

sick. Somehow I had never foreseen this, although it stood to reason. A tugboat is a lively ship; I had known captains who felt queasy every time they hit the first swell, after as little as two months' shore leave. So far I had been so busy worrying what to do now I was a captain that I had overlooked seasickness.

I stood on the bridge, swallowing and belching, for as long as I could stick it; when I felt that I couldn't any longer, I said to Dop, "I think I'm going to lie down for a minute, call me if anything turns up."

"O.K.," he said, "take the couch in the chartroom."

I vomited over the rail as soon as I got down the stairs from the bridge, realizing too late that I was on the windward side. Somehow the thought that the traces of my seasickness would be visible to anyone looking overboard after daybreak was very humiliating. I even had a mad flicker of a thought: a U-boat captain seeing it through his binoculars. I decided that my imagination had got beyond a joke, and staggered into the chartroom, for a moment disgusted with myself.

I lay on the couch, listening to the shuffling of the oilskins against the wall overhead, feeling so sick that I didn't care any longer whether we were sunk that night or not. The boy with the goatskin jacket came in several times, to look at the chart or to get something; I didn't know which and I was too ill to care. I didn't even care about him seeing me in this condition: a full-grown Captain in parade dress, lolling about on the couch, green in the face. But whatever I may have looked like, he didn't give it a second thought; he didn't even glance at me. When he came in the third or the fourth time, he reached over me to take off a couple of oilskins, dragged the cold cloth across my face, and said, "Sorry." I realized that I hated him, and that it had started to rain.

After that I must have fallen asleep, for several times I half woke up because I thought I heard gunshots in the distance. Once or twice the ship suddenly shuddered and seemed to rise on her hind legs; the seconds after that happened I lay breathless, trying to listen. But nothing happened; we must have hit a white horse.

I was woken up by a sound, or rather a lack of sound. The one

27

pair of oilskins left suddenly shuffled much more loudly against the wall with the rolling of the ship; it took me some time to realize that the engine had been stopped. I got up, put on the oilskins and went to the bridge.

The moment I got into the open a cold hard rain hit me in the face and sobered me up. I didn't feel sick any longer, nor afraid. I felt a brittle excitement which made the whole thing seem almost fun. I had to hold on to the rail of the stairs and the bridge, for despite the fact that I now felt as clean as a whistle I was oddly weak in the knees. A murky dawn was breaking, and in it I saw a sight that almost made me laugh, it was so incongruous: a trawler's sail attached to the mast of a tugboat. It was a clumsy, flapping affair, and didn't seem to do much good; only occasionally it strained in the wind and then it made us heel over with an exhilarating feeling of recklessness. I remembered the feeling from my boyhood, when I had rigged up a bathtub with a sail and messed about in it with a couple of friends in the harbor of our village. I suddenly felt good, better than I had felt ever since I set out for Westport. Despite the rain I wanted to light a cigarette, if only to prove to myself that I had recovered from my seasickness, also because I had a foul taste in my mouth and my tongue and palate felt very dry. The moment I took out my lighter someone put his hand over mine, and said, "Are you crazy?"

It was the boy with the goatskin jacket, now clad in glistening oilskins, his wet hair matted over his dripping forehead. I said, "Sorry," and decided that if he spoke to me again I'd grab him by the scruff of his neck and fling him off the bridge. I was a captain, damn it all; I had been mad to worry whether I could tackle the command of a tugboat after all these years. I could sail any bloody tugboat in the business a hundred times better than any of these louts in their fancy dress.

I felt on top of the world just then; shaky, but on top. Then a whistle chirped twice from the fo'c'sle. I heard Goatskin's voice say, "There she is, abaft the beam on . . ." He may have finished his sentence, I didn't hear it. A frantic whine came whistling at us from the sea, rapidly growing in volume until it sounded like the screaming wheels of a streetcar rounding a

28

corner. I never heard the shot, for the mast and the sail came toppling down with a terrific noise. Dop's voice shouted, "Hard starboard!" I heard the ringing of the engine room telegraph, the rattle of the steering engine. Then another whine came whistling at us, and passed right overhead with a sound that I felt in my teeth. This time I heard the shot: a high metallic twang in the distance, as if someone had hit an iron railing with a stick. Perhaps it wasn't the shot, perhaps it was something else; I had no time to wonder, for at that moment a colossal sound right overhead frightened the life out of me. It was my first moment of fear in face of the real thing; when I realized that it was the ship's siren I burst into a loud laughter, which I managed to check as soon as it occurred to me that it was hysteria.

The siren screamed for minutes on end; then the ship seemed to jump bodily out of the sea and throw herself on her starboard side. My feet slid from under me; I was flung down the full length of the bridge and hit the starboard rail with a sickening thud, that knocked the breath out of me. I lay there gasping for a while, expecting to feel the water, for it seemed impossible that any ship could stand up to this; but I regained my breath and felt the ship right herself. I heard shouting and a loud clatter of iron; then there was a sudden burst of gunfire, very close to. A quiet voice said, "Well, she's handing it out good and proper, the old bird."

It was Goatskin. He stood looking at something over the rail as if he had remained on his feet all the time. Perhaps he had. Perhaps he was God. I dragged myself up to my knees in a praying position and managed to get back on my feet, despite the fact that vital bones in my body seemed to be broken. He glanced at me and asked, "All right?" I nodded, unable to speak, with a lump in my throat and a hot prickly feeling in my eyes. I hated him to tears.

I looked over the rail. The cannonade thundered overhead remorselessly, like five pneumatic drills gone mad. I saw the Norwegian: a dark hull, her bow sunken right up to her fo'c'sle. From her poop and her foredeck spurted the vivid flashes of gunfire. Our siren had stopped screaming when we were flung aside; now it yelped again, two short blasts. The guns on the ship alongside fell silent.

I expected them to start up again any minute while we maneuvered toward her stern and shot a line across; but they didn't. They didn't start up again until a good deal later, when we had already made fast and started towing. I stood looking back at the high stern of the ship when I heard that sickening whine again. The very moment I heard it the siren started screaming again, and was drowned by the thunder of guns abaft. I never knew whether the shell passed overhead or came anywhere near us at all; anyhow, it missed us.

After that nothing else happened in the way of shooting; we just towed the ship home in the growing daylight, that was all. I never saw the U-boat, and I still didn't know whether my picture of the Fritzes climbing out of the commando tower was right. I stayed on the bridge with Dop and Goatskin for the rest of the trip. The cook brought up tea at one time that looked all right, but made me seasick again. I took only a sip or two, and managed to keep them down until we got home, but it was hard work. Only when we sighted the harbor did I realize that I had hardly been afraid.

The moment I thought this, I got it. It started in my calves and crept up to the back of my knees: a trembling, so uncontrollable that I had to cling to the rail to keep myself from sitting down. I thought I was the only one, until I saw Goatskin's face. He was not God any longer, he was green.

Dop took me by the arm, once we had moored, and said, "Well, that's that. Let's nip across to Headquarters and get the form business over with." His hand trembled as his arm had done when he put it around my shoulders the morning before. I remembered someone had told me once that fear came only before and after the danger; I had forgotten who it was, but he was right.

We got the form business over quickly. The Captain of the Norwegian had been brought on board our ship by a British Navy launch, when we handed over his vessel to two small tugs in the outer harbor who would tow her the rest of the way up the coast. He was a quiet man with very blue eyes and very tidy;

30

he looked as if he had come straight out of the barber's after a nice thorough shave. He thanked Dop politely for bringing in his ship and Dop thanked him for putting up such a good show with his guns. The Norwegian raised his eyebrows slightly and asked, "Well, wasn't that what you wanted?" Dop said it was, and we went home feeling a bit silly, as if the Norwegian had told us in so many words not to make such a fuss about a normal operation which had proceeded according to plan.

I took Dop home because he insisted. The flat was there, he said; Stella would be waiting with food anyhow, we had been in this together so we might as well finish it off with some grub and a chat. I knew it was wrong, that she wouldn't want to see me at all. But the prospect of going to bed all alone in that untidy room, after swallowing the pills the old Captain had handed me, made me give in.

When Dop opened the door and we entered the kitchen I was struck by the same uncanny feeling as the day before: a feeling of emptiness, as if no one was there. Dop called again, "Hey, where are you?" The door in the corner opened and she came out exactly as she had done the day before: in her blue dressing gown, a white ribbon in her hair.

But when she looked at me it was different. Her grave blue eyes did not observe me any longer like a child's; she gave me a look of such instant understanding that I suddenly felt my knees again. I grinned at her and said, "Hello, how are you?" in a voice that must have sounded like a parrot's; then I sat down at the kitchen table, fighting a childish desire to drop my head on my arms and cry.

I got over it. I told myself that I was a sentimental fool, a coward who had come home to roost, and I believed it. I sneered at myself as I sat there, making polite conversation and watching her grill the toast and heat up the beans; my knees trembled all the time, although I grasped my knee caps until my knuckles went white.

When the beans on toast were put in front of me by a red hand that looked like a boy's, I knew I wouldn't be able to eat them however much I tried. My eyes filmed over, and I believed it was the steam until I felt a hand on my shoulder and heard her

31

low, soft voice say, "Don't worry, you'll be all right. The first time is the worst."

I felt like screaming "Goddam you!" and bursting into tears. I got up, said in a general way, "Thank you; I think I had better go home now," and managed to get out of the door without making a fool of myself.

I got to the hotel somehow, went upstairs to room 77, took off my clothes, threw them on the chair, and swallowed my pills with a gulp of water from the dirty glass on the washstand; when I finally fell on my back in my bunk I couldn't be bothered to pull up the blankets. My head fell aside, spinning; I saw the poem and closed my eyes with a sour taste contracting my mouth.

I decided then and there that I would not go back to the flat until I had found a woman of my own, to kiss me and take my fear away as Stella had done to Dop. I knew now that that kiss was the only cure. I was jealous.

∾

I sailed with Dop twice more that week. The fear didn't get better, but the seasickness did. The fear had nothing to do with what actually happened, for we weren't gunned at all, but with the thoughts of what was going to happen. Nobody can tell me that he ever got to a point where he was not afraid in action; he may have come to know his fear so well in the end that he could take it for something else. But our fear was worse, because we were powerless. We couldn't hit back.

When I was in London someone told me that at the beginning of the blitz people got very worked up and defeatist because they felt defenseless against the bombs; they almost gave up until a couple of gunboats started pounding shells at the sky which were perfectly pointless, but made a heartening noise. The person who told me this didn't think that any enemy aircraft had ever been hit by those shells, but their effect on the population was tremendous. I wondered whether we would feel better if we started to work our pom-pom in the face of the gunning U-boats, and I asked Dop this. He said it would be pointless, our only hope was our small size and our maneuverability. Even if the pom-pom was modified so that it could shoot level, it was so weak, and

32

so difficult to train as we were tossed about so much, that we might just as well save the manpower and concentrate on zig-zagging. I wondered whether he was right. I was sure that I would have felt a lot better if we had been able to make some noise ourselves even while knowing that it was just noise and nothing else.

Then I began to suspect something: perhaps the men of OTWA didn't want any guns. I was surely not the only one who went weak at the knees when he was being shot at like a helpless rabbit. There must be some thought or some emotion unknown to me, that made these boys so nauseatingly brave and so disdainful of the enemy's sharpshooting.

The one who gave me a possible explanation was Captain Van Dam, my opposite number, with whom I was to share the command of the *Zeeland* after she came out of dock. I went to see him the day before my first command was to start at midnight. He lived in the Grand Hotel in room 50, which he shared with three other Captains. Room 50 was called "The Club," because the four Captains were old compared to the rest of the population of the hotel; none of them was under forty.

When I knocked on the door of room 50 no one answered at first, and I listened with my ear to the crack to hear if there was anyone in. I heard a curious noise, as if someone was sharpening a pencil with a badly oiled machine. I knocked again; a voice called, "Come in"; when I opened the door the first thing I saw was a cage with a canary in it, making the noise. A man sat with his back to me in a low chair, reading a newspaper. He was in shirt sleeves with his waistcoat on, and on the back of his head was a bald spot the size of a guilder. He turned around when he heard me, and I was reminded of the forced visits I had paid to the local police station of our village when I used to scale the wall of the vicarage garden to steal the parson's pears. The man in the chair looked at me exactly as Sergeant Bulters, the head of the local constabulary, had done.

I knew the man was Captain Van Dam, for I recognized him from the photographs. He was an old professional, and before the war he had towed a dry dock from the Clyde to Australia round the Cape of Good Hope which had given him a fortnight's fame.

33

He was one of the best deep-sea-towing experts alive; thinking of him during the preceding week I had felt an awe which I would not have experienced if I hadn't been drafted back into the service. It was the kind of awe I would have felt for him when I was still a mate with aspirations; ten years had fallen out of my life.

I had not been prepared, however, to feel twenty years fall away, and yet that was exactly what happened when the stern regard of his pale blue eyes hit me for the first time. I almost expected him to say, "What? You again?" and to hear myself answer, "No, sir, it wasn't me. I just climbed the wall to see what the others were doing." Instead he said, "Yes?" and I introduced myself. "Good day," he said, without getting up. He folded his newspaper, pointed at a chair underneath the cage with the canary, and said, "Sit down."

I sat down, my cap on my knees, and looked around. The room was spotlessly clean and so tidy that it hurt. On the wall was a calendar with a picture of the Dutch Royal family, and a lithograph of the Monarch of the Glen; the rest were family photographs, concentrated in little clusters over the four beds: matronly woman, fat children, babies on sheepskin rugs and provincial wedding groups. By the side of each bed hung the ghostly shape of a bunch of suits on hangers, covered with a dust sheet; one of the shapes was partly uncovered, and I saw a sleeve with very worn captain's stripes, shiny at the elbow. The sight of that sleeve made me feel as if I was masquerading, a kid playing at being a sailor.

"What can I do for you?"

He looked at me with those pale blue eyes as if he had been watching me for some time and decided that I had gaped enough.

I asked him a few questions about our ship and the routine; he answered them precisely, without any attempt at making conversation. I had the feeling that he disapproved of me, not as a person but as an amateur. I mentioned something about the *Vlieland* being rather untidy, and for a moment he looked as if that would set him talking. He knitted his eyebrows and pursed his thin lips as if he was tasting something bitter, and I waited for him to give a regimental sergeant-major's speech. But he said

34

nothing. His face relaxed; he took a cigar out of the breast pocket of his waistcoat, snipped its tip off with a little surgical instrument hanging from his watch chain, produced a brass lighter which sprang to flame like a torch, and lit the cigar with care. After he had pocketed the lighter again he looked at me through the smoke with one eye closed, the cigar clenched between his teeth, and asked, "Made any sorties yet?"

The word was so old-fashioned that it took me a moment to realize what he meant. Then I answered him that I had made three sorties so far.

"Liked them?" he asked.

I thought I had him taped by then; he was one of our frank boys. Two could play at that game, so I answered, "No."

"Why not?" he asked.

It was such a preposterous question that it took me a moment to decide whether to get up and leave after patting the bald spot on his head, or to carry on this stage dialogue. "I don't like being shot at without being able to shoot back," I said. "It makes me nervous."

He eyed me coldly for a while; then he said, "That is because you have got the wrong approach to your work. Stretcher-bearers on the battlefield can't shoot back either."

I said that was quite a thought, and began planning how to get out of the place quickly. But I had put him on the rails, and pushed him off; now he was running downhill all by himself, nothing would stop him until he reached the terminus. He took the cigar out of his mouth, and addressed it as if it was me he was holding upright in his stubby fingers at a hand's width from his face. War had nothing noble or sensible about it, he said; it was just an epidemic of madness sweeping the people ashore, and anyone who got caught by it deserved to have his eyes gouged out by a fellow patient. He would rather be shot to hell ten times over, trying to bring in a helpless wreck, than join the lunatics by shooting back. "Shooting back!" he snorted, as if I had suggested something stupid in a complicated maneuver; "Be glad; the fact that you cannot shoot back gives you a chance to remain sane among all this murder."

I thought that the word "murder" was the terminus, for he

stuck his cigar back between his teeth. But it wasn't; he took the cigar out again and added, "What's more, if you are a good sailor you won't get hit. The German will be hanging around the wreck; you aim two squares above the one your wreck is in. Pass it for one square, then turn around and close in. Ten to one you are well within the range of the wreck's guns by the time the German spots you. If you aren't and he starts gunning you, don't zigzag, for that is asking to be sunk. When the first shell comes, turn your arse toward the gun and travel backward. They'll plonk about a dozen rounds over your head in front of you, then you'll find there will be a pause. While they are dithering you travel forward again, and so on. Just use your brains. But above all: no drink, and no women."

That was the terminus all right. After he had put his cigar back again, he shut up like a clam. I tried to make him talk a bit more about this idea of remaining sane in an epidemic of madness, for it sounded as if he had got something there. But he just grunted and picked up his newspaper again.

When he started to read it I left.

∾

I met Van Dam again a couple of hours later, when I went to look over the ship. I thought I might as well get an idea what she looked like before I crawled on board in pitch darkness at the first S.O.S. I had expected her to be deserted except for the stoker who was to keep the steam up, but I found her fully manned.

Van Dam was there and he spotted me the moment I stepped on to the poop. He came marching toward me with brisk little steps; he was much shorter than I had thought when I saw him sitting down, and he had a large behind. "Glad you came," he snapped when he got to me. "I'd like to show you the condition I expect to find my ship in when I take over from you at the beginning of each sortie. You may like living in a cabin that looks like a gipsy's caravan after a collision; I don't. So please be good enough to tidy up your mess before you knock off."

I thought of a number of humorous and withering answers I could have given him after that little speech. I thought of them

36

while he was showing me around the ship; they were good but too late.

The ship was in apple pie order. War didn't exist for Captain Van Dam, it stopped at his gunwales. I wouldn't have called her a model of sanity; she seemed to me a model of pernickety and futile tidiness. Every spot of brass was polished to gold, there wasn't a scratch in the varnish on any of the rails; while I followed him around, I spotted an old man with an upturned pipe touching up the varnish on the thresholds. The table in the chartroom was so clean that you could eat off it; the charts were meticulously rolled up, and so neatly stacked in the rack that I was sure someone must have brought the edges into line with a ruler. In the pen tray were three pencils: one red, one blue, one black, sharpened to a point where they began to look dangerous. The leatherette couch looked like a gynecologist's; if it had been covered with a sheet he could have taken anyone into that chartroom and charged five guineas per visit.

When we had finished the tour, he said, "I was told in Headquarters that you were to have the first watch, but I changed this. I know this ship, I want to find out if she is all right after her repairs." I asked him what had been the damage, and he answered, "Superstructure shot away."

I thought this took a bit off the bloom of his advice that morning, which had sounded rather convincing at the time. Perhaps he hadn't thrown his arse round quick enough. He must have suspected my reflections, for he said, "It was Mr. Wolters' contribution." I saw his point, but I thought that all the same he might be a little more lenient toward the amateurs, at least once they were dead.

Before I left he asked me, "Have you briefed your crew yet?" and when I answered, "No, I haven't even met them," he gave me one of those glances that are supposed to kill, and said, "I see." After that he turned briskly round and marched away on his short legs. Seen from the back he looked like a duck.

I met my crew that afternoon. I didn't exactly brief them, I just shook hands with them, chatted a bit with each one, and got their names mixed up. They looked a sensible, competent lot; I particularly liked the chief engineer, who had the nice homely quality about him that results from a single-track mind. To him, war or no war, nothing was more important in the world than engines. I was not so happy with my Mate, a thin nervous youth called Waterman. He seemed to have a lot of good will, but little experience. From what I knew of Wolters, the two of them between them must have had quite some luck, to get through four months of OTWA without anything worse than a super-structure shot away.

It was because of the reactions and the attitude of my crew that I first realized that I no longer considered myself an amateur. I was a professional all right, a bit stiff in the creases after seven years among the mothballs, but one of the old guard. I was surprised at this, for the change had come without my noticing it. But for my two brief encounters with Captain Van Dam I would have approached these boys differently, trying either to please or to impress them. I had done neither; I had just looked them up and down, shaken hands with them and forgotten their names when I got to the next man. When I left they eyed me with a curious relief, as if I had somehow convinced them that my presence on the ship would give them a new chance.

I had dinner in the dining room of the hotel. In the far corner was a table for eight, where the Club used to dine; four captains and four engineers of prewar standing. So far I had eaten with the untidy crowd at the long tables, where pilots and sailors sat down indifferently wherever there happened to be a free chair. As I passed the Club table that night, Van Dam called me. He said, "De Groot here has found something wrong with the auxiliary bilge pump, and he would like to talk to your chief engineer about it. Is he around?"

I answered that I would have a look, and turned to the noisy crowd rather unhappily, for I was sure that even if my chief engineer was there, I wouldn't be able to pick him out. But I had hardly made a move, before someone got up in the distance and called, "Looking for me, Skipper?" He was the homely character, it must have been telepathy. I beckoned to him and he came running, his napkin in his hand. I introduced him to the Club as "Mr. Er . . ." Van Dam asked us to sit down. While we were talking, Lily the waitress put plates in front of us, and before

I noticed what had happened we were eating with the Club, as if we had been tacitly accepted as members.

I could understand that they accepted my chief engineer, for he was indeed a professional; what surprised me was that they included me, after the parting look Van Dam had given me that afternoon.

After we had finished our meal and I had accepted a cigar from one of the bald heads, I left the dining room with the thing between my teeth, feeling somehow fatter. As I went out through the door I saw someone staring at me with unfriendly eyes. It was Goatskin; he obviously had his thoughts at seeing me, the new member of the Club. But whatever his thoughts may have been, I had my little moment.

༄

As Van Dam had taken over the first watch and I had at least twenty-four hours ahead of me with nothing to do, I decided to start by devoting two of them to meditation. There were a couple of things I wanted to work out in my mind before sailing on my first operation, so I went to the only place in Westport where one could think privately.

As I entered the cellar the infernal music from the loud-speakers hit me like a barrage of naval artillery. I worked my way through the dancing crowd, and managed to find a free table underneath one of the loud-speakers. I sat down, shook my head at several girls, ordered a cup of tea, and started thinking.

I put my lighter on the far edge of the table: that was the lame duck. On the edge nearest to me I put my pencil: that was the U-boat. In the center of the table I put a match: that was me.

I put myself there because Dop had told me that U-boats rarely got between the tug and the duck, for fear of drawing the duck's fire. They usually began to close in on you from the rear when you got near the duck. I hadn't quite understood why they should do this; if I was a U-boat captain lusting for a tugboat I'd go to meet her on her probable course, and finish her off in peace. Dop had answered that they were greedy; they didn't want to lose sight of the duck and lay there licking their lips for hours, waiting to kill two birds with one stone.

39

It all sounded rather vague and emotional to me. I was still a bit confused, for I had been living in a sort of daze ever since I sailed with Dop for the first time; but even so I was conscious of something illogical in the whole U-boat–tugboat relationship. Why didn't the U-boat finish off the helpless duck, before the tugboat arrived? Dop had said, because the guns of the U-boat were inferior to those fitted on the Allied merchant ships, and so they stayed out of range. I thought that was odd, but I didn't see any other explanation for the U-boat's behavior. Then, why did the U-boat, instead of closing in on the tugboat once it had spotted her, insist on gunning her from a distance? Surely the Germans must know by now that we weren't armed? Dop had said, because they wanted to stay out of the range of our pom-pom. It seemed silly, for the pom-pom was harmless. Then, why those mysterious bursts of a dozen rounds Van Dam had told me about? Why didn't the U-boat keep up its fire? There was something fishy there; but as I had no means of solving the mystery, I sighed and started working out positions with my toys on the table.

Van Dam's advice had impressed me. His bit of common sense about approaching the duck was obviously sound; and his recipe for dodging gunfire was a cunning idea: the moment you are shot at, turn your stern toward the U-boat, thereby diminishing yourself as a target to your smallest possible size; then travel backward. Dop had told me that U-boat guns had a lot of kick in them, but they were only auxiliary armament; they had none of the elaborate range finders that made surface ships so deadly. It could safely be assumed that no one, staring at a pinpoint in the distance through his binoculars, could make out whether it was traveling ahead or astern; they would naturally suppose that the rabbit was running away from them, and direct their fire accordingly. The idea of a rabbit running backward was a novelty.

But when I started working out Van Dam's idea on the table it looked less convincing. My aim was the lame duck; I had to get into the shelter of its guns as quickly as possible, and I couldn't quite see how to get there by traveling backward away from it. After some thought, under the screams of "You made me love you," I hit upon the idea of traveling backward toward the lame duck instead of away from it, thus facing the U-boat, and making

40

it believe that I was heading for it. It seemed I had got something there, until a teacup was put slap on the match by the waitress's hand. It gave me quite a shock, because it looked like a direct hit; sipping the black tea I concluded that this was probably exactly what would happen. Jerry might be slow witted; he was certainly not stupid. I put my lighter back in my pocket, took out my notebook, and began to work out positions on paper.

I sat in the Social Center till closing time, and drank five cups of tea. When I finally went out into the night air I felt depressed. Upon close scrutiny Van Dam's panacea didn't work; he must have said it just to impress me. The only thing that kept me doubtful was the undeniable fact that he was still alive after six months of OTWA, and so sure of himself that he made people varnish his thresholds.

ᦿ

I slept badly that night, and spent most of the following day hanging around Headquarters waiting for the *Zeeland* to return. She came in toward dusk, a fat Greek in tow with a list of forty-five degrees. As soon as she was moored I asked Headquarters to summon my crew; I wanted to do some drill in the outer harbor while it was still daylight.

My crew reported with a speed that impressed me; the old Captain in the office might be a foghorn, he certainly worked his ropes fast. Van Dam came in with the Greek Captain to deal with the forms as though he had arrested him, and was now going to enter his offense on the charge sheet. When he saw me he said, "She's all right but for that bilge pump; see to it that your C.E. puts it right." I said I would, and asked whether she was lively on her rudder. "Yes," he said, "you'll find that you'll have to give counterwheel the moment you start pulling her around. Anything else?"

I said, "No, thank you, that's all for the moment," and went on board.

I was nervous when I gave my first order; when I pulled the engine-room telegraph on "Slow astern" for the first time I felt as if I was going in for an examination. Not only did my crew watch me critically; I saw faces behind the steamed windows of the office. The first three minutes I cursed the moment I had thought of trying her out; it would have been better to start at night and get the feel of the ship on my way to my first operation; now I was just sticking my neck out. But once we headed toward the open I felt better, for I concentrated on the ship.

She was a lovely ship, lively and very fast. When I pulled the stops for the first time and let her have it, she seemed to lift her bow like a speedboat and trailed a wake that was impressive to see. The boy Waterman, who was with me on the bridge, said she made sixteen knots under top pressure, and I could well believe it. When I stood in the speedwind, and the bloom of the spray settled on my face, I felt an unexpected exhilaration. This was my first command; with a ship like this it was worth making a good job of it.

We maneuvered in the outer harbor until it was dark. When we put in, the Chief came to the bridge, wiping his hands with a wad of cotton waste and his forehead with his sleeve. "Blimey, Skipper," he said, "you certainly kept us busy." I had. I must have swung her round, switching from full ahead to full astern, at least a dozen times. I had made her spin in narrowing circles, until she listed so much that I had heard things in the chartroom slide and the bell had started ringing itself. I had found out that she was indeed a lovely ship; you couldn't expect her to do more and still be called a tugboat. I had found out also that my crew was all right, with the possible exception of the boy Waterman, who was very jumpy. But when we went ashore, after mooring her as if she was a crate of eggs, and set out for the Grand Hotel, he trotted beside me, chippering excitedly as if I was his uncle. Whatever the practical results of that bit of drill might be, it had established me in the eyes of my crew as a methodical man who knew what he was doing.

I had dinner with the Club again, and felt fine and confident. When at last I lay on my bed, the confidence ebbed a bit, as a suspicion grew in me. All I had been doing was trying to convince other people that I was a man who knew his job; I had better watch out not to believe it myself too soon, or I would be sorry.

I had no experience as a captain, and didn't know yet that you

42

are as good as your crew think you are; if they think you stink, you had better change ships or you'll begin to bungle things. I don't know why this should be, but there you are.

ᕱᕲ

When the call came I felt as if I hadn't slept at all; my watch said it was half-past three. I dressed quickly and hurried to Headquarters, finding my way with the torch I had bought the day before.

When I entered the office to get my instructions, I found them waiting for me, written on a memo form. It was an Englishman, 16,000 tons, cargo agricultural machinery, hit by a torpedo in No. 4 hold, rudder and propeller shot away, position square 365. That meant a good hundred miles west of Bishop Rock; a good ten hours' sailing. That meant daylight.

When I got on board, I felt worse than I had ever felt before; I felt like shooting myself. I went to the chartroom and started plotting our course on a chart which Van Dam's slaves had tucked away so neatly that it took me minutes to find it. The pencil had been sharpened so meticulously by the slaves that I broke its point the moment it touched the paper. I closed my eyes tightly to fight back the tears and thought, "God, help me." I thought of my father, and prayed to him to be with me and help me; he had been dead twenty years and wherever he was, it was a long way away. I prayed to my mother, but although she was nearer, smiling anxiously, she seemed helpless with her flowered apron and her frying pan. I must have been a nice heartening spectacle for the boy Waterman to see when he came in. He coughed respectfully, and said, "Skipper?" I opened my eyes but didn't look around. I looked at the chart; Bishop Rock swam in a haze. I said, "Yes?" He said, "Rea—ready when you are." His voice broke on the "ready," and that cured me.

This was the spot where Van Dam had stood forty-eight hours before; and he had made room for Christopher Robin saying his prayers. I don't know where it came from, but I started to hum, "Hush, hush, whisper who dares—Christopher Robin is saying his prayers." It somehow made all the difference; I went to the bridge with a confidence and a calmness that seemed miraculous.

43

I gave my orders in a voice so quiet with authority that I could hardly be heard, and I felt Waterman's presence edging nearer in the darkness, nervously. I was such a center of self-assurance and experience that I even impressed myself. I just was one hell of a good Captain. My crew was lucky that fate had sent me, they had got nothing to worry about. It was a touching sham; I had just slipped into the character the boy Waterman had offered me when his voice broke.

I stayed on the bridge from the moment we sailed: old Captain Ironsides lighting his pipe, and pacing up and down at hiking speed on his sturdy sea dog's legs. A yellow dawn broke through thin cloud and grew into a murky day. The sea was tired, a bored gray swell kept us rocking mechanically. I didn't realize how lucky I was that there was so little wind, as I still hadn't quite got over my seasickness; I even ate the bacon and the mashed potatoes cook brought me without giving it a second thought, and I drank two cups of his coffee. I thought, while pacing, how silly I had been ever to leave the tugboat service; this obviously was the job I was born to do.

The Chief came to the bridge halfway and talked about the bilge pump. He had fixed it. I nodded approvingly without taking my pipe out of my mouth, and he retired, mysteriously satisfied. I saw, every time I turned on my heels on the starboard side, a scratch in the varnish on the rail. After I had seen it about six hundred times without registering, I suddenly noticed it, stopped, rubbed my finger over it like a housewife testing a mantelpiece for dust, whistled the bosun, and told him to put it on his list. He asked, "List?" I frowned. Surely he had a list of minor jobs to be done? He said he hadn't; I ordered him to buy a notebook tomorrow. My bosuns used to have a little notebook to write their jobs in, to be checked as soon as they were done. He could get one at Woolworth's for sixpence; he could add the sixpence to the petty cash account. He left, mysteriously satisfied.

It was the boy Waterman who spotted the U-boat; I was thinking of Stella when he called me. I saw her standing with her back to me at the stove, making beans on toast; her hair looked soft and shiny. Waterman said, "I think there is one, Skipper."

44

I took over his binoculars and saw my first U-boat. A low, gray shape in the haze.

I had a moment of coldness. My cheeks contracted and I felt the quiver in the back of my knees again. At the same time it seemed as if I was watching myself with curiosity: a man who couldn't play chess, but only knew one opening.

I played my opening with a gusto that had an almost humorous edge of complete despair. I called the engine room through the blower and told the Chief that we were in for some quick maneuvering. Then I spun the ship around until she ran away in a straight line from the U-boat, and switched to full speed astern. The moment my hand left the handle of the telegraph, the first shell came whistling at us. It passed so close overhead that I ducked; when the rumble of the explosion sounded thickly ahead I looked up and saw the cauliflower collapse in the wake we had made, about seventy yards in front of our bow. But for Van Dam's little hint, Jerry would have scored a direct hit with his first round.

The boy Waterman didn't know it was Van Dam he had to thank for still being of one piece; nobody knew but me. I realized that when I saw their faces. They looked at old Captain Ironsides with such reverence that I almost turned around to see who was standing behind me; then I slipped back into character.

Captain Ironsides was as cool as a cucumber. He moved his ship about with geometrical precision. The shells and the ship seemed to perform a slow, formal dance, to the accompaniment of whistles and a kettle drum; every move followed a rigid pattern. At first I felt tense, then relaxed, then tense again with the quiver in the back of my knees returning, as the notion dawned on me that this couldn't go on forever. This was just crazy. Then, suddenly, the music stopped. Jerry had spent his dozen rounds.

This was the opening as far as I knew it. I fell back on to my course, full speed ahead, and waited, suspended in a vacuum. The duck we were heading for must be just behind the horizon, but she was not yet in sight. I raced toward her as fast as I could; then I spotted a flash in the haze abaft and switched to full speed astern with a quickness that was purely automatic. The ship quivered, pitched; the bridge was set trembling until everything rattled; then we ploughed back on our wake. The whistle again

45

passed close overhead, again the shell struck ahead of us. The dance started again until the dozen rounds were spent. By then I was sure that Van Dam had it taped. We could go on doing this for as long as our coal lasted, and that was a lot longer than Jerry's ammunition would last. The only thing that amazed me was that Jerry didn't get wise; but he just didn't.

We went through the intricate pattern of our dance four times, and in the end the shells began to strike very close. Then hell broke loose on the horizon. We heard two salvos soar overhead like low flying planes; then four fountains of milk spouted far behind us. Whatever was the matter with that duck, she certainly had good eyes.

That first salvo from the Englishman had an odd effect on me: it dried me up completely. I pulled the telegraph on full speed ahead, but it was no more than a reflex. After that I just stood there on the bridge, grinning like a cretin, feeling my knees turn to jelly.

I leaned back against the rail, trying frantically to think of something to do or to say next, for I hadn't got the faintest idea, I couldn't even think of the names of the most familiar objects, like "line" and "hawser"; I just stood there, speechless, while Captain Ironsides floated away and left me behind: an actor who had forgotten his lines.

When we got alongside the duck I stared at it in a dull panic. This was a job I had tackled at least a hundred times before; I had even passed an examination going through all the moves; I could dream them. But at that moment I just hadn't got a clue. I didn't know whether to attach a rope to her mast and pull, or to put my nose under her smashed tail and push her. Then a cunning thought slid out of the jungle of my confusion, like a snake. I gave the boy Waterman the falsest smile I must ever have produced, and said, "Well, Mate, now let's see what you can do. You take over." He woke up from a sort of daydream, blinked, swallowed, and said, "Aye aye, Skipper." As he started blowing his little whistle and shouting commands with his high piping voice, I tried to light my pipe. I tried three times; then I gave up, for I was sure that by then the shaking of my hands was getting too obvious.

46

I watched the proceedings in a haze. Once or twice I became conscious of Waterman asking something, I had no idea what. I just said, "No, no, you go ahead; this is your show," and went on sucking my dead pipe, looking quizzical.

Whatever the boy Waterman did, he made a job of it. Within twenty minutes we were on our way home with the duck in tow, deafened by the thunder of her guns that went on pounding overhead with exhausting regularity. I remembered at one moment that Dop had done something under similar circumstances, something rather important; but I couldn't for the life of me remember what.

I remembered it a good twelve hours later, when we were nearing home. I was lying on the consultation couch in Van Dam's clinic, when the boy Waterman came in. He seemed anxious to say something, but unable to decide how to begin. I raised my eyebrows in a gross imitation of the absent doctor, and asked, "Well?"

He said, "I'm sorry I forgot the hooter, Skipper. I know I should have signaled them to hold their fire, but I don't know what came over me. I just forgot. I'm sorry."

I gazed at him for a moment from an utter, dizzy emptiness; then I remembered what I had forgotten: the signals with our siren, to direct the duck's fire. One long blast for "Fire" and two short ones for "Hold it." That was why the Englishman had gone on pounding away with all his guns, long after the U-boat had stopped being dangerous; he had stuck to the letter of the instructions in envelope D with religious fervour, waiting until his guns turned red for us to signal him to hold his fire.

It was shocking, and I couldn't think of anything to say. The poor boy had had more reason to forget those signals than I had; he had been pushed into the command of a tugboat while he was staring dreamily across the rail, thinking of flowers. I was about to say something disastrous to my prestige, when suddenly the snake slid out of the jungle again and hissed: *that's quite all right, you didn't do badly.*

I said, "That's quite all right, old man, you didn't do badly."

He said, "Thank you for not ticking me off on the bridge. That—that's what I really came in to say."

47

The snake hissed: *Get along with you*, and I said it, with a fine, fatherly smile.

He went away and left me lying on that couch, stunned. I had fooled myself all my life, until I honestly believed that I had an accurate idea of what I really was like. Fooled was the word, indeed.

∾

The devil knows what was the matter with the last cup of coffee Cook brought up for me as a treat, just before we entered the harbor. It must have sat on his stove boiling for hours. It made me seasick, the moment I had finished it. For the next hour or so I was so busy keeping it down that I hardly registered what happened.

We handed the Englishman over to the Navy tugs; we took her Captain on board, sailed into the harbor, and moored. The Englishman was of the tubby, chatty type; but I was not responsive. I just looked stolid and stern, with my jaws clenching my pipe and my hands clasped behind my back as if they were grafted together. I needed all my concentration to keep myself from throwing up.

When we moored, the tugboat next to us was very lively. It was Dop's, and she was obviously about to leave. I found Dop in the office reading his orders. He asked if I had done all right, and I said I had. He looked curiously happy and excited, and behaved as if he was dying to tell me something. The Englishman said, sportingly, "The nicest piece of dodging I've seen for a long time. I must say you chaps know your job all right." I would have enjoyed this more if I hadn't felt so sick; at the moment all I thought of was how to get the form business over as quickly as possible.

We got through the forms at record speed; the Englishman barely got the chance to mumble the traditional "Thank you for bringing me in." I said he was welcome anytime, and started to hurry out before finishing the phrase; then a voice I hadn't heard before stopped me. It was a very British voice, so bland that I had the momentary delusion that one of the wireless operators sitting with their backs to us had switched on the B.B.C. news. It was the British Lieutenant Commander, whom so far I had only

48

seen cleaning his nails, filling his lighter, and smoking a long pipe. "By the way, Captain!" he called after me. "You didn't get a clear picture of the U-boat, I suppose?" I said no, not very clear; just a long gray shape in the haze. "You said she gave you four bursts of a dozen rounds each; did you notice by any chance whether she dived between those bursts, or did she remain surfaced?" I said I hadn't noticed; I was too sick to ask why the hell he thought she should have dived. He gave me a smile, said, "That will be all, thank you," and I made for the door. I had my hand already on the knob when Dop caught up with me.

He whispered, "We're going to be married!" I said, "Good! When?" He said, "As soon as I come back from this trip. You must be best man." I said, "O.K."; then I just had to get out, and fast. The moment I had shut the door behind me I vomited in the darkness.

The English Captain opened the door again when I had just about finished. I was already feeling relieved that no one had seen me, when I caught sight of a dim shape close to me before the door shut off the light. It had only been a second, but long enough to recognize the shape. It was Stella.

I stumbled home to the Grand Hotel, convincing myself all the way that she had not recognized me. When I entered the hall the old porter rose from his grave behind the counter on hearing the swing doors swish. He narrowed his eyes, recognized my uniform, produced a bottle wrapped in paper and said, "Want a drink, Captain? Canteen price." When I answered, "No, thank you," and hurried on, he called after me, "All right, you stingy bastard; lie down and rot!" He was a curious old boy, he hated our guts. Perhaps it was only the war he hated, because it had upset his nicely organized life just when his sun was setting, and we were the only part of the war he could get hold of to show how he felt about it.

When I lay on my bunk in the darkness, listening to the wheezing and snoring round me, I felt so sick that I hardly dared move. I trembled all over, and had a splitting headache. I thought that I would have to get up and go to the lavatory at the top of the stairs, until I realized that it was not that kind of sickness.

I wanted a kiss, to take my fear away. I wanted a woman, any

49

woman, so badly that it made me groan. It wasn't the coffee; it wasn't even the fear, although I now lay there shaking like a leaf. I was just sick with desire.

When I realized this I was already so drunk with the pills that it struck me as funny. I sniggered, and as that caused another wave of nausea I began to hum. I remember humming: "Onward, Christian Soldiers," and thinking it a wonderful joke. I must have fallen asleep soon afterward.

Chapter III

I WENT TO HEADQUARTERS THE NEXT EVENING TO TELL THEM THAT if anything came up before midnight I would be in the Social Center.

Van Dam wasn't back yet, but Dop had just come in. When I entered the office the Captain of the duck which the *Vlieland* had brought in was being taken through the paper routine. I didn't register what he was like or his nationality; I never looked at him, for it was Goatskin who sat filling out the forms.

I knew instantly that Dop had been killed, even before Goatskin looked up and I saw his face. I didn't feel any particular shock; so much had happened during the ten days since I had met Dop again that my sensitiveness had got a bit blunted. My first thought was not "How terrible," or whatever else one thinks in normal circumstances on realizing that one's friend is dead; my first thought was "What happened?" for it seemed odd that only one man out of an entire crew should have been killed by U-boat gunfire. Perhaps he had fallen overboard.

Goatskin told me that he had. They had been strafed by machine-gun fire from a plane, on their way to the duck. The plane had strafed them twice; Dop had caught it the second time. He had refused to take shelter until the very last moment; when he had tried to duck behind the rail it was too late. The plane came in from starboard, he was standing on the port side of the bridge; he had no time left to run across the bridge for shelter, so he had tried to climb over the rail and sit on the navigation light. At least Goatskin assumed that this had been his train of thought, otherwise it couldn't be explained why he had suddenly tried to climb over the rail. He had been hit when he straddled the rail; he had arched his back, clutched his side and fallen overboard. They had stopped the ship and circled, but there had been no sign of him.

After Goatskin had told this, the old Captain started to bellow again and to thump the table, trying to frighten the British officer opposite him with the threat that he would quit this job unless his ships got fighter cover. The officer listened to him impassively, smoking his long pipe. The old Captain made a mistake when he included, "Guns that could shoot level" with the conditions of his ultimatum, for in this case it did not apply. The officer let it pass; he didn't betray the fact that he had noticed the mistake. Perhaps he was thinking of something else.

I didn't remember the key until I had followed Goatskin outside and heard him say, "I had better go and tell his girl." He didn't sound happy at the thought, so I said, "I'll do that, if you like."

We were walking down the pier; when I said that he stopped and looked at me with the same expression in his eyes I had noticed when I left the dining room after my first meal with the Club. I didn't understand why. "What's the matter?" I asked. "Nothing," he said, and walked on.

I should have let him go; but I caught up with him, feeling rather foolish. Somehow I still had the notion that people had to be comforted after a loss. Although he had told the story of Dop's death so crisply that it had sounded as if he was dictating a cable to his local newspaper, his face looked haggard. He didn't say another word until we got to the bottom of the pier. There he said, "Well, enjoy yourself," and turned briskly away. This time I should have caught up with him, grabbed him by the collar of his goatskin, and asked him what the hell he meant by that. But I let him go.

On my way to the flat I thought of an explanation for his attitude. Perhaps he knew about the key business, and had only realized that Dop had given it to me when I offered to go and see Stella. Perhaps he had expected to be given that key himself; Dop

51

and he had seemed to get on well together. So either he was hurt that Dop had not considered him his best friend, or jealous because he had expected to take over the flat himself.

I didn't think about the flat at all. I thought about Stella and how I was going to break the news to her. I had never told a woman that her husband was dead, and I felt sorry that I hadn't let Goatskin tackle the job when he said he would. When I had climbed the stairs and stood on the map of Africa in front of the door with the inverted "2," I leaned against the wall staring at the lock. I tried to figure out what would be better: to knock or to use my key. I had been climbing the stairs with the key in my hand and it had grown warm by now. I listened at the crack but didn't hear a sound; I knocked once.

It was a feeble knock, and nobody answered it. Even if she was in the flat she could hardly have heard it. I was about to knock for a second time, when I heard steps mounting the stairs, and I decided to wait until they had gone. I heard them shuffle about on each landing, between climbing the flight of stairs; when they got to the floor below me I heard knocks. I decided it must be the milkman; when the steps mounted the last flight and he came into view it was a postman.

He saw me, said, "Good morning. Lovely day, isn't it?" then he shoved a letter under Stella's door, knocked, and turned to go. When he was already descending the stairs, he asked, "Waiting for No. 12?"

I felt embarrassed, and said, "Yes, I don't think she's in."

The postman said, "She's not in? Then it's the first time since I've been on this round. She never goes out, that one." As he turned the corner between the two floors he called, "You try again!" and vanished. I listened to his steps until they were gone; then I put the key in the lock, turned it and opened the door.

The kitchen was empty, the door to the bedroom stood ajar. On the mat lay the white square of the envelope which the postman had pushed in.

I was sure she wasn't there, for the flat had a feeling of emptiness. Then I remembered that it had had that feeling both times I had come in with Dop, and I was not so sure any more.

I coughed, but didn't hear a sound. I thought that she might be

52

out after all; perhaps I had better leave a note on the table asking her to call me when she came in. Of course I was sure all the time that she was in, for if Dop had been still alive he would have come home at this time. But somehow I wanted her to be out so much that I just believed it.

I picked up the letter from the mat to write the note on the back of it. Before I turned it around I read the address. It was a bill from the Southwestern Electricity Board to Captain David de Jong, K.L.M., 12 Seaview, Esplanade, Westport. "K.L.M." were the initials for the Royal Dutch Airlines.

As I stood looking at the letter I heard a sound from the bedroom. A sound as if someone was choking. It gave me a shock; I forgot about my embarrassment and went to the bedroom door.

The bedroom was empty and tidy. The bed was made and covered with a chintz spread. The face in the leather frame on top of the wardrobe smiled at me fixedly. I called, "Stella?" softly, but with an alarm in my voice that I had not intended. Then I heard a sound from the bathroom; the same sound I had heard before. This time I recognized it; it was the sound of vomiting.

I stood there for a moment, motionless, listening. I thought I ought to go in there and help her, but I didn't quite know how. I remembered that when I was sick as a child my mother had held my forehead for me with a quiet cool hand. My hands were hot and sticky, and I didn't know her well enough to be of any comfort to her in such a humiliating position. I really didn't know her at all.

I went back into the kitchen, looked around, and sat down. I took off my cap and put it on the table. I noticed the letter again, and for some reason I got up and put it back on the mat, face downward. Then I went back and sat down again; put my hand on the table and drummed with my fingers. When I took my hand away there was a damp patch on the polished surface; I wiped it off with my sleeve. I remembered that it was she who had sewn on my stripes, how her red boy's hands had fumbled with the nail scissors, how kind and sweet she had been. I felt very sorry for her, and didn't want to go away any longer. I was the only one who could be of any use to her in this, if only by letting myself be talked to. I was the only one who had known Dop as a normal

53

carefree chap, the way she must have known him; Goatskin knew only his tense, noisy side. If I had a girl and someone had to tell her that I had been killed in action, I would hate the idea of the boy Waterman going to see her to break the news, for he had no idea what I really was like. He would come to announce the death of old Captain Ironsides; the poor girl wouldn't know who he was talking about.

As I sat there, waiting, I hardly had any thoughts at all; I just listened. I heard no more sounds from the bathroom, and I wondered what was happening. I wondered why she was sick; perhaps she knew. Perhaps my cough had given me away; perhaps opening the door with my key and not calling, "Hey, where are you?" with Dop's voice had been all that was needed. Then I heard the sound of a toilet being flushed.

At first I thought it might be at the neighbors'. The flats were very noisy; while I sat there waiting I had heard steps and voices on the other side of the kitchen wall, and a blast of music from a radio being tuned in. Then the hissing of the tap filling the cistern suddenly got louder, before it dimmed again. I knew she had come out of the bathroom into the bedroom. I stood up and waited for her to come in.

She took a long time coming in. At first I thought she must be standing there in that room, listening, as I was in the kitchen. Then I heard a soft stroking noise, and a clatter of something being put down on a glass surface. I realized that she had been brushing her hair at her dressing table.

That gave me a moment's doubt whether she knew after all, whether she even knew I was there. When she came in I didn't doubt any longer.

She came in exactly as I had seen her come in twice before. She wore her long blue dressing gown and the white ribbon in her hair. She smiled, but it was not pretty to see. Her face was as white as a sheet, and she had painted herself a bright red mouth which looked horrible. I had never noticed that she used lipstick before, although I think she must have; perhaps she had put on no more than usual this time, but her face was so white that the mouth made her look like a clown.

It was the color of her face that gave her away; her eyes ex-

54

pressed nothing. She looked at me steadily and with a desperate gentleness, and said, "Hello." Her voice was steady, but very soft.

I said, "I'm sorry," and thought of what to say next, but she didn't let me.

She said, "Would you like something to eat?" and I answered, "If you like," for anything else would have sounded sillier. She went to the stove and started going through the routine of making beans on toast.

I remembered Dop telling me she made the best beans on toast in the world, I remembered the time I hadn't been able to eat them. I wanted to tell her how Dop had died, and that he couldn't have had much pain; but I decided to wait until she asked me.

She stood with her back to me for a long time; cutting the bread, putting it under the grill, opening a tin, emptying it into the little pan, putting it over the flame. She said nothing and the silence became so oppressive that I couldn't stand it any longer. I said, "He was killed by m.g. fire from a plane and fell overboard. He can't have felt anything; he must . . ."

Before I had finished she turned around, crying, "Don't talk about it! Don't!" Her face was so haggard that I suddenly felt cold. Then her eyes seemed to fill with that gentleness again, and she added, "Please." She said "please" in exactly the same tone in which she had said, "Don't worry, you'll be all right," and I couldn't bear to look at her any longer. I turned away, and said, "I'm sorry, I know how you feel. Let's have something to eat."

I sat staring at the emblem of my cap on the table until she took it away and put a plate in its stead. I said, "Thank you," and wanted to start eating, but I had nothing to eat with. She put down another plate and sat down herself; then she saw me staring, said, "Oh, I'm sorry," got up and fetched knives and forks.

We sat eating in silence for a while. I concentrated on my plate, but occasionally I glanced at her hands. She was eating too, and I wondered how she managed it. I thought how very English she was, how she must have been brought up in that curious tradition of never showing any feelings in order not to embarrass other people, until it had become engrained in her character. As we ate on I began to feel very alien to her; I wished she had broken down and wept, or just been unable to eat like that. It would somehow have made me feel a lot better.

Halfway through the meal she asked, "When do you want the flat?"

I said, "I don't want it at all. I want you to stay here and carry on until you have made up your mind what to do."

She said, "I wouldn't want that. You promised him that you would take over, otherwise he would never have given you the key. I want you to keep that promise, it's important."

Then I just couldn't stand it any longer. I put down my knife and fork, and said, "Look here. He was my best friend. He was killed this morning. I'm not an Englishman; I cannot just sit here and eat beans on toast and behave as if he never existed. I . . ."

She put her hand over mine and clasped it, hard. Her hand was very cold.

"Don't," she said; when I looked up I saw that she had bent her head, her long hair hung down by the sides of her face. I felt ashamed to think it, but she looked beautiful at that moment. I wanted to look away, but she lifted her head and looked at me with such concentrated strength in her eyes that I couldn't. Her eyes seemed to have the experience of all the generations of sailors' wives of her island behind them. While she sat looking at me I had an odd feeling, as if we had sat like this many times before. As if I had as much experience of bringing messages of doom as she had of receiving them. Perhaps I had gone through this before, in a dream.

It was that feeling that made me accept her attitude as inevitable. I said, "I'm sorry; it was stupid of me. Is there anything I can do?"

She thought for a while, then she answered, "I'd like you to come in after you get home next time, and have a meal with me. Then we can talk about the flat and decide what to do."

I said, "O.K., I'll be seeing you," and left.

∽

I didn't go back to her until a week later. I sailed three times that week; twice I got home between midnight and three in the morning, so tired that I couldn't be bothered. There was of course

56

another reason why I didn't go, but I kept it nicely tucked away, well out of reach of my consciousness.

The first two times we sailed for nothing. We didn't encounter any U-boats, but when we got to the square in which the wreck had been reported, it was gone. Both times my wireless operator came to the bridge, after some pointless circling, to say that Headquarters had reported the wreck lost, and could we please pick up survivors. We cruised about, looking for them, but there weren't any. The first time we found nothing at all, the second time only some wreckage floating about.

The third time, when we neared the appointed spot at day-break, we heard a dull thud behind the horizon, and after a while saw a new cloud slowly rising out of it. When we got nearer we heard the sharp, metallic reports we knew so well; they were shots from a U-boat gun. It somehow seemed a decent thing to do to keep on our course and race to the duck's assistance, although our assistance couldn't amount to much. I ordered the bosun to uncover the pom-pom and bring it to the ready; he looked doubtful when he went to obey this command, as if I had asked him to put the old tricycle from the attic in running order.

We never got near enough to see what had actually happened; before we got there a U-boat surfaced close to us.

This time I saw it very clearly: an ugly gray thing, much smaller than I had expected; water oozed from its nostrils when it came up, and until it was up all the way the gun sticking out of the foredeck seemed to be traveling by itself. Then the lid of its conning tower was opened and a lot of busy little men came tumbling out; when they ran toward the gun I shouted at the bosun, "Fire!" The bosun and a couple of sailors turned what seemed to be an incredible number of wheels, handles and gauges; the thing swung around on its pedestal with screams of rusty iron, then it went off.

It made one hell of a racket. I never saw any bullets get any-where at all. The thing just spat fire and sounded as if it had six barrels instead of two; as far as I could make out from the bridge it was aiming in a general way at the sky. The effect, however, was surprising: the busy little men ran back to the tower as if they were being swept away. One of them went on fumbling

57

heroically with the cover over the gun for a second, then some-body shouted at him from the tower like an angry mother on the beach, and he scurried back. The moment the lid was closed there was a loud curse from my bosun in a sudden silence. He looked at the bridge, made a gesture of helpless rage, and shouted, "The bloody thing's got stuck!" then he turned around and kicked it, after which he grabbed his foot. The U-boat went under with a lot of bubbling noises, and at an astonishing speed; then it vanished completely. I wished I had been sailing an icebreaker instead of a tugboat, for during the minute she was going under I could have rammed her easily.

As it was, we went on at full speed toward the spot where the wreck had been reported. It wasn't difficult to find, for the cloud, although much fainter, still floated over it. I knew the duck had a cargo of agricultural machinery. Judging from the way she had blown up I could imagine what kind of machinery it had been; they couldn't have had any time for lowering lifeboats. We met some wreckage and spotted a raft; when we got nearer we saw it was empty. Sparks came to the bridge and said he had just picked up a signal from Headquarters that the duck had fallen silent after squeaking for a bit, which meant that she had been sunk in action, for according to envelope D a duck was to squeak only when subject to a direct attack. I swung around at full speed and began running for home.

As I had expected, the U-boat surfaced on our course. This time we had no duck to run to for shelter, and although our pom-pom was permanently out of order I decided to put up a show as if it was working. The moment we saw the U-boat surfacing over starboard I headed right at it, even though it was still a long way away. I saw through my binoculars the mannikins tumbling out of the tower, uncovering the gun and pointing it at us. When the first shell came whistling at us and fell short, I took over the wheel myself and started zigzagging. Although the ship was very quick on her wheel I couldn't zigzag fast enough for a good gunner, and while the shells came whistling and splashing ever closer, I became convinced that this time we would buy it. But an amazing thing happened: when they were just about to pot us, they stopped; the mannikins covered the gun and ran back

58

to the tower, the lid was closed, and the U-boat dived. When they did this they were still well beyond the range of our pom-pom even if it had worked and been able to shoot level. I seemed to be lucky that day.

I called the engine room and told them to give her all they could, that if we wanted to get home we had to run faster than a U-boat. I wouldn't have been surprised if my Chief had refused to put up the pressure, for he was that kind of man; he had no notion of what was going on in the world outside his engine room and would rather be blown to bits by a direct hit than by an exploding boiler. But he obeyed; never had I known the *Zeeland* to run faster.

Our speed for some reason put my crew in an exhilarated mood. They stood laughing and slapping each other on the shoulder, looking at the bow wave and the wake; the boy Waterman asked me whether it would be all right if he timed her. When I said, "No," he looked disappointed; he seemed to have forgotten the U-boat in the excitement of going so much faster than God had meant us to.

The U-boat surfaced again, this time behind us. Again she lashed out with a dozen rounds without scoring a hit, although several times I ducked with my heart in my mouth. After the dozen rounds were spent, the mannikins went through the same rigmarole of covering up the gun, running back to the tower, closing the lid and diving, letting us, by this incomprehensible waste of time and opportunity, run away from what was almost certain death.

The U-boat surfaced twice more, before we got out of her reach. Every time she was further away; every time she did the same: surfaced, uncovered the gun, shot a dozen rounds, covered the gun up, and dived. I followed her antics through my binoculars; they left me in a pensive mood. I didn't hit upon any logical explanation for this diving business, but although it had certainly saved our lives I somehow didn't like it. I didn't like it a bit.

We got home about midnight. When I went to the office to report, the old Captain wasn't there; he had obviously gone home when he heard that there was nothing doing. The only ones there were the wireless operator on night shift and the British officer.

59

The W.O. was reading a book with his feet on the radio bench; only one of his loud-speakers twittered faintly, but he didn't seem to be listening to it. The officer was cleaning his pipe, a messy business; while we talked he went on mucking about with soggy cleaners and bits of paper he wormed inside the hole in the pipe's head, and filled the room with the stench of tobacco juice.

I told him that this time I had seen the U-boat close enough to give him a full word picture. While I gave it to him he didn't look up once. He asked, after I had finished, whether she had dived between shooting her rounds; when I answered, "Yes," he looked up with a happy smile as if this was good news. He was then sitting with a soaked cleaner in one hand and a dirty piece of twisted paper in the other, undecided where to put them; I am sure he would have shaken hands with me otherwise. He said, "Splendid! This helps us a lot. I'm sure we have spotted him now."

I asked whether he would mind telling me what he was talking about, as I was rather interested. He said, "Of course, old man, of course. Do sit down."

I sat down, while he wrapped his nasty business in a sheet of typewriting paper, folded it into a neat little parcel, and dropped it in the wastepaper basket. Then he said, "The U-boat that has been pestering us is a very old one, used by the French for gunnery practice, and taken over by the Germans for the same end. Its captain is called Hasenfratz, he's an old instructor and trains crews. Until a week ago he seemed to do only gun training, but it looks now as if he was given a cigar to spend on each trip, for he could never have sunk those ducks by gunfire alone. His gun is too small, he wouldn't have a hope against the stuff most of our merchant ships are fitted out with now. So all he is doing, really, is target shooting."

I asked, "On us, you mean?"

He said, "That's right. You chaps are the perfect target for training. You are small but not too small, slow but not too slow, armed, but insufficiently, and you put up one hell of a fight in the way of dodging fire. Old Hasenfratz could ask for nothing better; but as he is a Jerry, he sticks to the drill, and allows his pupils only a dozen rounds a go. After that they dive and surface

60

again. You didn't notice how long they took between surfacing and firing the first round, did you?" I said that I didn't, but that they were pretty nippy about it. "I had to make a lot of inquiries before I reached my deduction," he said. "I found out from our people that our record time between surfacing and shooting the first round is fifty-five seconds."

I said, "Fancy," and he looked at me for the first time in a way as if he really saw me. "Pretty hard on you chaps," he said, "to realize that you are being used for target practice. I don't think we should make it generally known."

I said, "You might consider filing an application on our behalf for better guns, if you can fit it in."

He said, "No need to get cynical, old man, I'm doing my best. I've been pleading for you ever since I got commissioned here. I am sure that by now they are putting my reports in the waste-paper basket without even reading them, for they are always the same. I think it's a shocking shame to let you chaps face the music with the antique stuff you have got; but now look at it from their point of view. I can't tell you how many convoys come in on the Western Approaches, but you must have a pretty accurate idea yourself from the way you are being kept busy. Out of all the ships making up those convoys a very low percentage gets lost or disabled; in their eyes you just aren't worth bothering about, neither the ducks nor you. The moment a ship gets left behind by a convoy it is written off; if you manage to salvage one or two it is sheer profit. I'll go on pestering them on your behalf until they go black in the face, and transfer me to get rid of the buzz-ing in their ears; but if you ask me my honest opinion: you won't get your guns until every single merchantman in the Allied fleet has been properly fitted out. I'm sorry, but that's how it is."

I looked at him for a while without saying anything. He was not a bad chap after all, and I was sure he had done all he said he did. But somehow I felt like bashing somebody's face in. I said, "So, if I get you right: all we are is just a set of clay pigeons for Captain Hasensomething."

He looked at me the way Stella had looked, when I wanted her to show some reaction to the news of Dop's death. "I'm afraid

61

you are," he said. "But you might care to consider that you are not the only one."

That reply brought me so near to screaming point that I had some difficulty in getting up and going out like a sensible, well-mannered hero. But it made me understand something about the English that I had not realized before, and that explained in a way how they had managed to stick it for so long, alone against overwhelming odds, without flinching. They were merciless toward everybody, including themselves.

∽

When I got out of the office I was in a black rage. I suppose I should have felt a more complicated emotion; but the idea that all we were—with our fears, our hopes, our philosophy, our love —was just a set of clay pigeons for a German artillery instructor, was such a monstrous idea that all I could do to defend myself was to fly into a helpless rage. I stamped along the pier and the Esplanade, my fists in my pockets, muttering, "Hasenfratz!"

By the time I got to the Grand Hotel, I had so much explosiveness bottled up inside me by the sheer repetition of the name "Hasenfratz," that I only realized I hadn't been given any pills that night when the old porter rose from his grave, brandishing a bottle wrapped in paper, and whispering, "Want a drink, Captain? Canteen price." It was the glass with the dentures that reminded me, for it was the same type of glass that was on all the washstands in the hotel, and to me they were associated with gulps of tepid water washing bitter pills down.

I asked him what he had got there. He unwrapped part of the bottle and showed me it was Scotch. I said, "O.K., I'll have it. Canteen price," shoved a pound note across the counter, and went away.

He squeaked, "Hey, hey! It's one pound five!" He shouldn't have said that; I turned slowly round, came back and said, "Listen, Hasenfratz, one more squeak out of you and you'll be sorry for a long, long time."

He eyed me as unflinchingly as a stuffed parrot, and repeated, "That will be one pound five." His eyes had the same strength

62

behind them that Stella's and the officer's had had; God, they were tough, these English.

I said, "How would you like it if I wrung your neck for you?" and he answered, "Fine."

I gave him two sweaty half crowns from my pocket; only then did he blink. It looked as if the lids covered his eyes from the bottom up; he looked more like a parrot than ever. He said, "Good night, Captain, happy dreams," and sank back into his grave.

I stood for a moment in doubt whether I would empty the glass with the dentures on his head; that was the state of mind Captain Hasenfratz had put me in. Then I turned round, groped my way to a corner of the darkened hall, sat down in a twanging club chair, opened the bottle and took a swig. The Scotch tasted foul; I knew instantly that it was some beastly hooch he had concocted himself in the basement and poured into an empty bottle. I thought of a means to prove this, and considered going back to the counter and offering him a drink of his own stuff, then I would know all right. But I couldn't be bothered; I just sat there in that corner, staring across the dark mausoleum of the hall at the dentures on the tombstone, swilling hooch and thinking.

I thought of how the others would take it when they came to know what the U-boat was doing, that had sunk two of our ships and kept us in a state of continuous fear that amounted to neurasthenia. I wondered how Van Dam would feel with his lovely little theory about us being stretcher-bearers on a battlefield; whether he would still be so damned snooty about shooting back if he realized that he was bearing stretchers at the wrong end of a shooting gallery. I wondered whether Captain Hasenfratz's pupils who had bagged Frankendaal and Daamen had got a prize for scoring a hit: a teddy bear, or a bottle of perfume.

I tried to see the whole thing from Hasenfratz's point of view, and as soon as I did this found out that I couldn't hate him any longer. When I was still in Holland during the occupation, British planes had nipped across frequently on little training excursions, bagging trains and bridges; although occasionally a passenger train or a tollkeeper's house had been blown up, we had never taken this in bad grace, we had understood that everybody had

63

got to learn. I could not make light of a tollkeeper's wife and children being blown sky high, and at the same time sulk because someone else was doing some practicing on me. I wasn't even a civilian, I got hooch at canteen price; so what was I whining about.

Now I had solved all the mysteries that had seemed to surround me so thickly when I first got to Westport. I had crossed the shadow line good and proper, and was now one of the initiated in the brotherhood of Christian Soldiers. I didn't blame Captain Hasenfratz for anything, I didn't even blame Headquarters for not giving us guns. After my fifth swig I didn't even blame Van Dam any more, for having found his own little design for dying and being high and mighty about it; if anything I was envious of him, for I could do with one myself. I tried to think of all the arguments for this war being a holy one, that had sounded so convincing when I was still living under the German occupation, and not being shot at by Captain Hasenfratz and his kindergarten. I thought of Hitler's hysterical speeches over the radio, exterminated Jews, defenseless people beaten to death in the concentration camps; but it was not enough to make me get up and brace my shoulders and stride out through those swinging doors, longing to be shot at again by an artillery instructor for the sake of freedom of conscience and democracy.

I might have kidded myself into accepting some sort of higher purpose for being the bull's-eye in a shooting gallery, if I hadn't had so much hooch inside me by then. The hooch didn't make me drunk, it made me objective. I was just a man terrified out of his wits, a coward, trying to sip courage from a bottle. That was the nasty part about it; I knew how I would feel when I had to sail again. I wished the British officer had never told me.

Once I had got to the ugly truth at the bottom of the bottle, I felt so sick with fear that I sat there whimpering; I just had to talk to somebody about it, dilute the concentration of fear in my system by sharing it with someone else. I thought of the people to whom I could talk about it and who would make me feel better by getting frightened themselves; I could think of no one. It wouldn't make the slightest difference to Van Dam, whether he was being shot at by a skilled lunatic or an unskilled one; Goatskin would recognize my fear at a glance and disdainfully brace himself against anything I could tell him. The only one who would be impressed by my story was the boy Waterman; but he was too easy. And as I had to sail with him again tomorrow the idea of having two sets of chattering teeth on my bridge didn't appeal to me. The only one I could think of was Stella.

It was surprising that it should have taken me so long to come to the decision to go to the flat. I had needed a bottle of hooch and Captain Hasenfratz's assistance to get up and face those blue eyes again. I got up, went out, walked through the chilly night air along the crowded boulevard gingerly, convincing myself that I was not drunk by making bee lines at lampposts. I sailed from post to post, keeping my eyes fixed on the guiding lights, until I reached the entrance to Seaview. When I got there I knew that I was lucky not to have broken my neck on the way. I was very drunk.

I climbed the stairs slowly, pausing for breath on each landing. When I got to the top floor I felt as if I had climbed the mast of a windjammer at sea, and I clung to the doorpost. On my way I had made a little plan: I would tell Stella everything about Captain Hasenfratz, fly into an incoherent rage, and she would help me out of it with a kiss. But when I stood there, clinging to that doorpost, I knew I couldn't even get all the syllables of that name out in one breath; it would take me so long to say "Hasenfratz" that I would break down halfway.

I felt very sorry for myself, particularly sorry because I had allowed my little plan to float to the surface of my consciousness, a troubled sea of hooch. If only I had been able to enter that kitchen as a nice, clean, innocent soul, beset by the terrors of a nasty, cruel world, I would have slid into the double bed as if I had never expected such a thing. But as I stood there, clutching the doorpost, the little plan was forced to the surface by hiccups smelling of gas. And that was not all; while I stood wondering with one section of my mind why people ever bothered to put their heads in a gas oven when they could achieve the same end so much more pleasantly by buying a bottle of Scotch at canteen price, another section dealt with the last mysteries of Westport still hidden in the dark. I realized that they hadn't been true mysteries, that I had known the truth all along, but just managed to keep my gaze on heaven.

I had suspected that Stella was a tart when I had seen the photograph on the wardrobe and Barger's name inside the jacket she took from it; I had known it for certain when I found that letter on the mat addressed to Captain David de Jong, K.L.M. De Jong had obviously lived in the flat, so had Barger, so had Dop. Perhaps there had even been others between; Stella had not moved into the flat when Dop took it over: she went with it. I tried to remember the exact moment when I had known this; it had been even before I found that letter on the mat. Although I was thinking of people putting their heads in the gas oven at the same time, and sniggering at the idea of having poured the water with the dentures into the porter's grave, I remembered it all right. Goatskin had told me when he had turned at the end of the pier to leave me on my way to Stella, and said, "Enjoy yourself."

Enjoy yourself, for no one knows what the morrow will bring. I tried to put the key in the lock and succeeded at the third try; just like Dop had done when I had taken him home drunk that night. Perhaps I was Dop; perhaps our fear was so important in all of us, that to her it didn't matter what face or what name it carried. All I was about to do, was to step into a dead man's place in the ranks marching toward Captain Hasenfratz. *Serrez les rangs.*

I opened the door with a fine gesture, ready to find the kitchen empty. But it wasn't; she was sitting at the table under the lamplight, doing nothing. She looked at me the way she had done when I came in with Dop, after my first trip on his ship: with such instant understanding that it almost sobered me. I refused to be sobered, I said, "Here comes the next one!" intending it as a joke, but somehow it didn't come out funny.

She asked, "What has happened?" and the way she asked it almost sobered me again. She looked so sincere, so decent; what a pity she was just a tart. I wanted to answer her question but forgot what it was about. I wanted to say, "Hasenfratz," but knew I couldn't manage, and didn't even try. I decided to tell her the truth; I said, "I'm drunk." After that I felt very weak, as if it had

66

taken all my strength to make that confession. I wanted to go through that doorway into the kitchen and sit down, but I dared not let go of the doorpost.

She got up and came to me. When she got near I smelt her through the hooch: a clean smell of soap. She put her arm around my shoulders and tried to make me let go of the doorpost. I resisted for a while, then I gave in. I felt very weak, walking into the flat, as if my knees bent lower and lower while I walked, like Groucho Marx. I thought we were heading for the table, but she steered me past it. I wanted to turn round and sit down; I wanted to give her a chance to tell me she was not a tart, but a clean English girl, smelling of soap. But she let her chance go by; she steered me into the dark doorway to the bedroom and switched on the light.

I saw the double bed rocking on a lazy sea, a U-boat covered with a chintz spread. I thought of a good joke: I would go down on my knees and look under the bed for Captain Hasenfratz. But when I did, it didn't work out funny; I fell, half on the bed, into a sea of sadness. I thought, "Jesus, I'll never be able to sail again," and wanted to get up; but something kept me down and turned me over; I was as helpless as if I was already a floating corpse, turning into corruption. I saw her face overhead, a vision of tenderness and understanding, and closed my eyes, waiting for the kiss that would turn it into corruption.

It didn't come. Instead I felt someone fumbling at my shoes and realized that she had begun to undress me. I tried to rise on my elbows in protest and despair; even though I was drunk, I didn't want it to happen in that way. I didn't want her to undress me and tuck me in and then undress herself and get into bed beside me; even though I knew that I was just closing the ranks, I did not want that horrible fact to be so callously revealed. I wanted to tell her that I wasn't the cynical character I pretended to be, that in reality I was as sentimental as a spaniel. I thought of myself as a helpless, gentle little boy who had never grown up; when I was on the verge of tears of self-pity and homesickness for the child's cot on which my mother had undressed me, Christopher Robin got in the way again. I wanted to get up and stride out of the flat, as impressively as I had strode out of the chartroom after the boy Waterman had called me with a catch in his voice; but she held me down. While she was undoing my tie I wanted to say, "Don't be so bloody noble about helping the poor sailors to forget their fears; be a tart and have done with it," but as this was too complicated to say, I said, "I'm drunk." My voice sounded so sad and sincere, that I looked up with tears in my eyes.

I saw her moving over me, shapelessly, as if I was looking at her through a glass of water. She didn't say anything; she undressed me quietly and expertly, like a trained nurse. I thought of the cure for all ailments: to bed with the nurse; I thought of God, and hoped He would have mercy upon us. When I felt I was naked I expected that now she would tuck me under, but I felt her putting things on me again. I looked up, couldn't focus my eyes, but vaguely discerned an expanse of green and white stripes, like an awning, and assumed they were pyjamas. I wanted to say, "Whose are these? De Jong's? Barger's? Dop's?" but it was too complicated. I said "Drunk," felt I had left out something, couldn't remember what, and said, "Sorry." Then something was pulled away from underneath me, and covered me with a gush of wind. I said, "Blankets."

After that there was a silence, in which I heard a slow rattling noise. I couldn't make out what it was until she began to speak, then I realized that it had been the dialing of a telephone. I heard her say that if a call came I was at the flat and not at the hotel. I thought she had a lot of pluck.

After that I just lay there without thinking, waiting for her to get into the bed. She took a long time; I heard rumbling noises and the sound of cupboards being opened and shut, and they went on for so long that I suddenly thought: she is moving out. I tried to call her, but didn't get further than a shapeless moan. She was by my side instantly, she couldn't have been far away for the moan had been a faint one. I tried to say, "Don't go away," but couldn't. I made some noises which must have been more intelligible than they sounded to me, for I heard her say, "Don't worry, I won't go away." Then I heard the click of the switch and the red glow of my eyelids went dark.

In the darkness thin lines of light crossed from horizon to

68

horizon, like tracer bullets; some exploded into specks that floated down to the sea, like flares. I wanted to call her, for I was afraid; but I was too tired, I fell asleep.

၏

When I woke up the next morning I heard a girl's voice humming, and the soft tinkle of small things on a hard surface. The girl's voice hummed a tune I had never heard; I realized that I was lying in Dop's bed and that Stella was washing up in the kitchen.

I listened to the tune and wanted to ask her what it was called, for I liked it. I never did ask her, for I fell asleep again while I was listening. I heard it many times later over the radio, bellowed by throaty contraltos or arranged for brass band. It was called "Ye Banks and Braes."

When I woke up for the second time she was standing beside me in her blue dressing gown, her hair long and shiny. She had a cup in her hand.

"Would you like a cup of coffee?" she asked.

I said, "Yes," and sat up. The moment I did so it felt as if I had left my head behind on the pillow, and I clutched it.

She said, "Here, take this. It will make you feel better."

I said, "Thanks," took the cup from her and drank a few sips. It tasted good.

"Is it sweet enough?"

I nodded and drank some more with my eyes closed, enjoying it. Then I looked up at her.

So far I had only seen her by artificial light, except the morning I came in to tell her that Dop was dead; but that didn't count, she had not been herself then. By daylight she looked more beautiful than ever. I searched her eyes for uncleanliness or corruption, but they were of virginal clarity. Perhaps our ideas of sin were as old-fashioned as our ideas of courage.

"You haven't been sitting up in the kitchen all night?" I asked.

"No," she said, "I put up the camp bed."

I nodded, as if I knew the camp bed, and went on sipping the coffee. I thought that I ought to feel embarrassed now, but I realized that it takes two for that. She wasn't embarrassed at all,

69

she had been humming in the kitchen as if the man asleep in the bedroom had been living with her for years. Perhaps he had.

I remembered thinking this the night before, when I had been about to open the door with my key. It was curious that an obviously drunken thought should come back in the clearness of the morning and still make sense. Perhaps it was she who was sending out that thought, perhaps it had been she all the time. Perhaps she had heard me climb the stairs and lean against the doorpost, hiccuping; perhaps she had sat at the table, listening, waiting for what she knew was coming, and thinking the thought so strongly that it had penetrated the door and my alcoholic fog until it reached some center of awareness inside me.

As I sat sipping the coffee I realized that I was more quiet and clearheaded than I had been for a long time; when the name came back to me it seemed harmless. "Hasenfratz." I smiled as I pictured him: a red-faced German bully, scolding recruits. I remembered the angry mother's gestures with which someone had called back the boy who had gone on fumbling with the cover of the gun when our pom-pom started firing; I was sure now that it was Hasenfratz.

The quiet amusement with which I could recall that picture made me think of Van Dam, when he sat expounding his philosophy on war in his shirt sleeves. I felt for the first time as if I almost agreed with him, as if to remain sane under all this was more important than to be able to shoot back. I felt as if I was approaching some essential truth, which would enable me to see this war and all that happened in it in relation to the evolution of mankind. I thought of the First World War, and how the conquerors had been smitten with the diseases of the vanquished. I wondered whether this would happen again, whether the ideals and the mottoes that had sounded so sincere under the occupation had been just the symptoms of an epidemic of lunacy, a moral blindness that obscured our view of the truth. If that was so, then the conquerors after this war would be smitten by the same diseases they were now fighting. If we were the conquerors, we would turn fascist, chauvinist, anti-Semitic and aggressive, and be unable to do anything about it. In that case Van Dam was right; then the future of mankind would indeed be in the hands of the few who had somehow managed to remain sane, like him.

She took the empty cup out of my hands and said, "I'll run a bath for you; you take it while I make some breakfast."

She went into the bathroom and turned on the taps; then she crossed the room again on her way to the kitchen, humming. I felt so good that it made me wary; I started looking for the snake in the grass.

It didn't take me long to find it. I was sitting in that bed a happy man, because I was no longer alone. All that my superior thoughts of a moment ago amounted to was that she had given me a false feeling of security.

૭৵৩

I was having my bath when the telephone rang. Stella answered it; I heard her say, "Hold the line, please," she sounded very secretarial. Then she opened the door of the bathroom and said, "You had better come out, it is Commander Wadlow." I said I had never heard of him. "The British liaison officer," she said.

I gave myself a hasty rub with the towel and put on a dressing gown and a pair of slippers I found in the corner. I remembered, as I went out of the bathroom, how I had seen Dop come out of it with the same things on. When I picked up the receiver lying on the night table and said, "Yes?" the bland voice of the British officer answered, "Oh hello, old man, I wonder whether you would be good enough to pop in sometime this morning. I should like to talk to you on the subject we were discussing yesterday. Do you think you can manage that?"

I said, "You mean about Hasenfratz?"

"That's right," he said, "I think we may have found a sort of intermediary solution, if you see what I mean." I didn't, but I said I would be round in about half an hour's time. He said, "Splendid," with the enthusiasm the British display only about completely trivial things, and hung up. When I turned round I saw Stella standing in the doorway. She had been listening and looked at me with eyes that made me feel proud and important. She was worried.

"Anything serious?" she asked.

71

I said, "No, no; just a routine thing," and thought how very British I sounded. I wondered whether this was going to be a new character: Captain Forthright, the African explorer. I decided to avoid it if I could; but I felt the need of some sort of character to hide behind, for by now I had become embarrassed all right.

I went into the kitchen and had breakfast. During breakfast I told her about Hasenfratz and his artillery school; after I had finished and saw her looking at me I realized that the way I had told it was so offhanded as to become silly. She knew instantly that this was the thing I had made all the fuss about last night.

"Does anybody else know about this?" she asked, and when I said, "No," she said, "I wouldn't tell them if I were you."

If I had known her well enough to be myself with her when sober, I would have asked her why not; but Captain Forthright answered blandly, "Of course. Could I have some more coffee, please?" I just checked myself from adding "old girl."

For some reason the atmosphere during breakfast got rather strained toward the end. I heard myself talking more and more blandly, until my upper lip seemed to have stretched to twice its length; and there was nothing I could do about it. Either I sat there as Captain Forthright having breakfast with Lady Cynthia in the Manor, or I had to get out. It was a relief when I had finished, could sneak out to dress, and beat it.

When I arrived in the office I found the British officer in the company of a gigantic pilot of the Fleet Air Arm, and we started to talk about Hasenfratz. The pilot was so large that I found it difficult to look at more than one thing at a time; my eyes wandered from the fruit salad on the expanse of his chest to his Buddha-like ear lobes, and from there to his straw-colored eyebrows and his enormous red nose. He was very hearty and talked as if he was addressing a barracks; his vast fat hands lay on the desk on top of each other like two sleeping piglets. It was amazing that a man could produce such a volume of sound and yet sit quite still.

The British officer said that he had told Harcourt about this Hasenfratz business and that Harcourt, who was the C.O. of our section of Coastal Command, thought he might wangle it so that one of his planes would nip out one day and plonk that floating kindergarten on the head; the more so as Hasenfratz now seemed to have started giving torpedo instructions as well. Because we all agreed that we had better keep this thing more or less to ourselves, he thought the best way to go about it was for me to give the signal when I came across Hasenfratz next time; so we had better agree on a code to be signaled to Headquarters by my Sparks the moment I spotted the U-boat on my next operation.

We agreed on a code; the big pilot said that he would be on the spot within the hour, if it wasn't too far out. I asked him what kind of treatment he thought he would give Hasenfratz, and he boomed, "Oh, I'll plaster him with D.C.s until I see his oil float up; so you had better make yourself scarce once we get going." I said I'd do my best to run away as fast as I could, but would he please remember that my top speed was sixteen, and that a tugboat was a fragile kind of vessel. He laughed, showing a pink cave full of healthy white teeth, and one of the piglets woke up and jumped on my shoulder as he said, "Don't worry, old man, we won't let off the crackers underneath your tail." I thanked him and left.

Once outside, I wondered what to do. Van Dam wasn't home yet, and as it was a nice morning I decided to go for a walk. I had a look at Memorial Hill and was amazed to find lovers in the straggling grass at this hour, rolling about underneath the notice "Carpet beating strictly forbidden." I walked the streets for a while, not really noticing where I was going, for I was thinking of Stella all the time. The feeling of security she had given me that morning might have been false, but it persisted. She had somehow stimulated the instinctive feeling that nothing would happen to me; I began to wonder why the discovery about Hasenfratz should have driven me to such extremes of abject fear last night. I knew the feeling was instinctive, and common to every sailor, soldier and airman fighting this war; and as things happened to thousands of them every day the feeling was obviously nonsense. Even so I felt as safe as if it was peace; the skirmish between OTWA and Hasenfratz was a battle of wits, and that morning I felt sure I could outwit him. I was even slightly disappointed at the idea that he would be plastered with

73

D.C.s so soon; with Stella to come home to I felt sure I would have got him singlehanded in the end.

I passed a sudden bit of color on my way through the gray ruins; it was a flower shop with a tiny window in a large square of asbestos. The window was crammed with tight bunches of flowers and looked like a picture on a wall. I went inside and bought a pot with a little tree in it, from which bell-like red flowers dangled. The old woman asked whether I'd like it wrapped up; I thought I had better, because I would look silly walking about with that thing in my arm.

As she was wrapping it up in a newspaper, I asked myself why I thought it would be silly; and I saw myself coming down the street, a tugboat Captain carrying a pot with a little flowering tree. Only when I imagined what others would think seeing this, did I realize that I was in love.

∾

When I gave her the little tree she was very sweet. She said, "Oh, thank you, it's lovely!" but she didn't kiss me. She took the pot to the sink and watered the little tree, then she put it on the window sill with a plate underneath it and turned it round until the side that carried the most flowers faced the room.

While she was doing this she asked how my discussion at Headquarters had got on. I told her what Wadlow had arranged; she listened with her back to me. When she turned round she didn't seem to be pleased about it. "What are you going to do during the hour before the plane gets there?" she asked, and I said, "Same as I did before: keep him busy and dodge him."

"It seems an awfully long time," she said, and I answered that an hour went quickly if you were being shot at, and that on previous occasions I must have dodged them for longer than that. But while I was saying this I wondered if it was true. I had never checked the time; now I came to think of it, it might not have been as much as that. She saw me thinking about it and my face must have expressed a certain doubt, even though I was busy being Captain Forthright again. "Don't worry," she said, "you'll be all right."

I said, "You've said that to me once before."

74

"Well?" she asked. "I was right that time, wasn't I?"

I said, "Yes, I suppose so," which was a silly answer, but at the same time I was wondering whether she really knew, or whether it was just part of her routine. "Suppose I was not going to be all right one day?" I asked. "Would you know that as well?"

She said, "Yes," quite casually, as if I had asked her whether the milkman had been. I watched her, while she was opening a fresh tin of coffee and got down the percolator from the shelf over the sink, and my feeling of security waned for the first time since that morning. "How do you know?" I asked. "Are you psychic?"

"No," she said, still with her back to me, "I don't think so, I just know these things occasionally. Lots of people have it in my part of the world."

Captain Forthright said, "Must be jolly uncomfortable some-times," and the feeling in the back of my knees returned, that had become such a familiar sensation during the past weeks that I had forgotten it meant something. She didn't reply to that one, but filled the percolator with water and lit the little spirit-stove underneath it.

"Did you know about the others?" I asked.

She turned round and faced me, her eyes were so full of that curious gentleness that I knew what would happen before it did. She kissed me. Her mouth was very soft.

I didn't put my arms around her, for it was not that kind of kiss, and I couldn't forget Dop. I had watched her kiss him in what must have been exactly the same way, for the feeling in the back of my knees vanished. I didn't realize that until later, after she had turned away again and gone on making the coffee. I had been right, that time I saw her kiss Dop when he was incoherent with fear and I had thought that her kiss cured him. I didn't care any longer whether she had foreseen the death of the others, for suddenly I was sure again that it wouldn't hap-pen to me. It just wouldn't, I knew it. The certainty was so abso-lute, that it couldn't be the old instinctive feeling of all men in war; this time it was different, as if I had felt during one second the fullness of the future, the happiness of peace. Perhaps I was psychic too.

75

I didn't think of kissing her myself, until she turned round again to get something out of a cupboard on the other side of the kitchen. When she turned our eyes met, and she wavered a second, as if she expected me to.

But I didn't; I let her pass close to me and go to the cupboard without moving, without looking round after she had gone. For when I had seen her eyes again I had suddenly felt shy.

I knew at that moment that I was going to make a fool of myself over her. I still knew that she was just a tart, who took anyone that was coming in this key game of death; but at the same time I knew that very soon I would be explaining the others away until I would be convinced that she had waited for me all her life, and I for her. I remembered someone had said to me once that in every love affair there came a moment when you could still say "stop" for the last time; if you let that moment pass you were done for and had to see the thing through to its bitter end. I knew this was that moment, and I let it pass. I knew what I was letting myself in for and how it would end; yet I let it pass.

If I had kissed her it would all have been different. I would have found the woman I had longed for after every trip: any woman. I would have crushed the shyness of love that withheld me.

But I didn't, for her secret was that she made me feel I knew how it would end: in tears and misery and jealousy and bitter hatred and all the other tortures in hell, but not with my death. If I had still lived in the terrible urgency of fear, which had made me long to grab any woman before it was too late, I would have grabbed her; she had taken that away from me, she had made me certain that we had all the time in the world.

I was safe.

Chapter IV

THAT NIGHT SHE PUT UP THE CAMP BED AGAIN IN THE KITCHEN, AND I watched her doing it. I sat smoking a pipe in Dop's dressing gown, my stockinged feet on the kitchen table. I enjoyed watching her, she looked lovelier every hour.

76

During dinner I had discovered things about her face that I had not noticed before. While we were talking about whether it would be nice to have a radio and about a kind of chair they had in the Hebrides that closed you in entirely and was lined with sheepskin, I looked at her forehead, her eyebrows, her nose, her mouth, and wondered which it was that made her so beautiful. When I had first seen her I had thought her nose was too upturned and her mouth a bit too sensual; now I saw that I had been wrong. She had the kind of nose that I had only seen on English girls: the partition between the nostrils was lower than the nostrils themselves, and so delicately sculptured that it looked very vulnerable and sensitive; it gave her face a hidden nervousness that in contrast with the serenity of her eyes amounted to beauty. Her mouth was not really sensual at all when I looked at it that night, watching it while she talked. I realized that what I had taken for animal passion was human compassion, that she was not at all inverted in herself, but desperately concerned about other people. It seemed incongruous that she should live such a shut-off life; I remembered what the postman had said, and Dop telling me that she didn't like to go out and hardly ever left the flat. I had just taken it for granted at the time; now I wondered why she should be a recluse, it wasn't her nature at all. I was about to ask her, when I remembered what Goatskin had said. She must be aware of what people thought about her, and didn't like to face them for that reason.

After she had finished making the camp bed we had a cup of chocolate and talked some more. We were very snug in that kitchen, a tiny cube of light and warmth and cosiness floating in the great empty silence of a world at rest. She talked about her island; how the sheep grazing on the little aerodrome near her village scattered when a plane landed; there were people living in hamlets on the storm side who still thought that stars were specks of light shining through holes pierced in the sky. She told me that when she was a little girl she had heard a story about two lovers separated by the sea, who wrote secret letters to each other and put them in a little watertight box, with some charms and little presents, and then floated them across to one another with the tide. She had been so impressed by that story that she had written, "I love you," on a piece of ruled paper, put it in a tin,

77

sealed the lid with candle wax and let it float away to the mainland, secretly, one early morning when the tide went out, hoping that someone on the distant shore would find it and reply.

When she said that I remembered the poem on the wall, and looked for some hidden significance in her story. But I couldn't find any, just a story about a little girl on an island; that seemed to be all there was to it.

While I finished my chocolate she went to the bathroom; when she came back she was wearing a nightgown. I suppose I should have felt a manly desire when she passed me; but although it was quite an ordinary nightgown it made her look very young and innocent, like a girl in boarding school going to bed. Perhaps it was her hair that made her look so young; she had plaited it into two braids and pinned them on top of her head. I saw for the first time how small and delicate her ears were, and how graceful her neck. She saw me looking at her and smiled; somehow that smile turned her into a child.

I didn't fall into the trap of giving her a fatherly kiss, and I thought that was a proof that I had all my wits about me. I felt warm and gay and contented when I switched off the light for her, opened the kitchen window and went into the bedroom. When I finally had got into bed I felt even better: warmer, gayer, more contented. I suppose I was just happy.

෴

When the telephone rang, the luminous hands of the little alarm on the night table pointed at five to two. I let the telephone ring three times, and had already stretched out my hand to pick up the receiver when I heard the door squeak and felt the draught of someone passing close to me.

Our hands met on the telephone as it rang for the fourth time; she took my hand away and I felt something soft and warm touch the back of it. She had kissed it.

The telephone rang for the fifth time, then she answered it. She said, "Hello, yes?" and I heard a small mechanical voice quacking in the instrument. I couldn't understand what it said, but I knew. She listened to its quacking for a few seconds, then I heard

78

her say, "All right, he'll be there in a minute." The bell of the telephone tinkled as the receiver was put back on the hook.

I asked the darkness, "Anything up?"

Her voice answered, "Yes, darling."

It was the first time she called me that; it was nice to hear, but at the same time it gave me a ghostly feeling, as if she didn't quite know whom she was addressing. As if in the darkness Dop and I and the others were one.

I wanted to get up, when I felt her cold hands on my face and then her kiss. I put my arms around her; as my hands touched her back I thought how thin the nightdress was, until I realized that she was not wearing it. I sank back on the pillow with her in my arms; her hands still clasping my face, her mouth on mine.

When the telephone rang again, twenty minutes later, I groped for it and knocked over the little clock. It fell on the carpet with a thud; the shock released the alarm and it started ringing shrilly with the telephone. It rang through the angry quacking of the old Captain's voice, asking what the hell was going on. When I said that I was just on my way out, he quacked, "Tell that to your grandmother! You're all the same, once you get into that bloody flat! Cut the cuddling, and beat it over here! There are people drowning, screaming for help!" Then he slammed down the receiver. The ringing of the alarm had slowed down; when I picked it up it fell silent.

I groped my way along the wall to the kitchen door and switched the lights on. She was lying on her back, her head on one side, her eyes closed. She might have been asleep, if her breathing hadn't come so quickly. I stood for a moment looking at her from a great peace. She was beautiful the way she lay there; but her face was almost tragic with the agony of love.

As I stood looking at her a new thought rose in me: I had to come back for her sake. To lie there like that, and again have the man she loved torn away from her by screaming bells and squeaking voices was more than she could bear. It was not I any longer, who had to be assured that I would be back, it was she. I went back to the bed and bent over her and kissed her cheek, and said, "Don't worry, I'll be all right." She did not react, but I knew that she had heard me. I covered her up, then I dressed. When I

79

looked round at her from the doorway for the last time, she was still lying as I had left her: her head on one side, her eyes closed, her plaits like frayed silk ropes on the pillow. I switched off the light and went.

The great peace from which I had stood looking at her went with me; I moved within it all the way along the dark boulevard to the pier. I thought of what the old Captain had said, how we were all the same once we got into that flat, and it did not make any difference in my feelings toward her. I knew now that she was not a tart, but I knew also that I would never be able to explain to anybody why not. We shared a secret with the dead that no one could ever hope to fathom.

As I turned the corner to the pier a motorcycle came roaring through the night, and swerved on squealing tires, missing me by a hand's width. It stopped at the end of the pier; I saw the door of the office open and in its faint light a man in a duffle coat get out of a side car. He was so large, once he got to his feet, that the only one I could think of that size was Harcourt.

When I entered the office I saw I was right. I was glad he had arrived just ahead of me, for the old red-faced Captain looked as if he had been sitting there, piling up steam for half an hour, waiting to blow my top off. Harcourt's enormous presence shut him up.

Wadlow was there also, and with the two of them I had a look at the chart. The duck was an Englishman, with a torpedo hole on starboard in number two hold, sinking rapidly in square 539, which was nice and close. Harcourt said that he would zip back to base the moment I left, and fly the kite himself; everything had been lined up over there and he was ready to take off at a moment's notice. The weather was perfect, visibility clear, wind three, no cloud, temperature minus five. I could see it was, for our breaths steamed in the lamplight as we stood bent over the chart, talking.

Harcourt was worried that the duck might sink before I got to it; he couldn't wait to see Hasenfratz break up in boiling milk. He seemed to have a personal feeling toward the man; perhaps it was just his name that irritated him, for he went on saying it until it sounded as if he was putting a charm over him. After a while I

80

expected him to take a little leather doll from his pocket and start sticking pins in it.

Wadlow seemed emotionally affected in the opposite way. He had been hunting the mysterious U-boat for so long in the maze of the reports of our operations that he had come to like the man, now he was no longer Commandant X, but a nice little human character called Hasenfratz. When we had agreed on our operation and were about to go, Wadlow said in a dreamy voice, "Pity we can't work it so that we could lay hands on the chap alive. There are a few points I'd like to see cleared up."

Harcourt scowled. "Ask the Skipper here to fish for him," he said; "then you can have his head stuffed with glass eyes and hang it on your wall with a brass plate saying Hasenfratz." He put the hood of his duffel coat over his cap, which suddenly made him look like a highwayman disguised as a monk. "Hasenfratz!" he said, for the last time; before he had brought out a rabbit's paw and crossed himself with it, he turned away and was gone. I heard his motorcycle spring to life the moment he shut the door; it took off when I followed him into the night, and streaked down the pier, blue flames spurting from its exhaust. Harcourt struck me as being a bit too enthusiastic to last. I wondered what would happen if I should not come across Hasenfratz this time, nor the next, nor the one after. Nobody could hate a name for that long.

The first thing I asked the bosun when I got on board was whether the pom-pom had been fixed. He said it hadn't; he had passed the order on to his opposite number when the second crew took over; when they had come home again and handed over his colleague had told him that Captain Van Dam had canceled the order. Captain Van Dam didn't believe in the pom-pom.

As I went to the chartroom I reflected that this was carrying the blessings of humanism a bit too far, and I decided not to accept it. It was a decision I could never have made the night before; I knew now that it was not fear that made me take it, it was just common sense. If I met Hasenfratz I was expected to keep him busy for an hour, a prospect that wasn't pleasing under any circumstances; without a pom-pom to keep him at bay if he edged in too close it was suicide.

I went back to the office and said, "Sorry, but I can't leave."

81

The old Captain's mouth fell open; Wadlow, who was studying the chart all by himself, asked, "Why not?" in a quiet tone, that from an Englishman spelled death. I said, "On my last operation my pom-pom got stuck; I left the order for it to be put right, but Van Dam canceled it. I don't want to be a spoilsport, but I've got to let our friend play with me for an hour, and I'm not risking a good ship and a good crew by throwing myself at him without any gun at all."

The old Captain said, "Well, I must say!" Wadlow eyed me for a second as if I was a fish gone bad. Then he asked, "Can your C.E. fix it himself, or do you want me to ring the Section?" I said, "I'll tell him to have a go at it again, but he said before that he couldn't. So you had better ring the Section." Wadlow said, "All right," as if it was a famous last word, and started telephoning.

It took the Section an hour and a half to fix the gun. One of the recoils had got stuck and most of the time went in trying to find an antiquarian familiar with the model. When he finally arrived he looked as if he had been dug up from an old pensioners' home: a gnomelike old Corporal with gnarled hands and two fingers missing. He said, "Arr" five times, while looking at the gun by the thin light of a blacked-out torch, his eyes close to the metal, as if he was trying to read a pocket edition of the Bible without spectacles. After that it took him seven minutes to do the job. When I finally sailed, I sailed under a cloud.

Alone on the bridge, in the wind and the darkness, I wondered whether I would feel guilty if I should find the duck sunk and its lifeboats gunned, within the one hour and a half before my arrival. I decided I would have, if my insistence on having that gun fixed had been caused by fear. Now I was sure it wasn't I didn't see where I was to blame; and I knew that Wadlow, despite the way he had looked at me, thought I was right. It took an Englishman to see my point; I knew that Van Dam and the others, if they came to hear of it, would consider me a coward. It was Stella's final victory; she had given me the courage to let myself be called a coward.

I may have been sure on the bridge; I don't think if it had worked out that way I would have remained sure. But when we got to square 539, six hours later, the duck was still afloat and no

82

U-boat in sight. We made fast and towed her home through a sunny cold day; the horizon was so clear that they could have seen us crawling along for miles around. But no one bothered us; it was hard to believe that there was a war on at all.

When I took the Captain of the duck on board outside the harbor, he told me that a U-boat had circled around him until we had come into sight, then it had dived and vanished.

Perhaps not only girls from the Hebrides were psychic; perhaps old German artillery instructors had a sixth sense too. It was a thought that didn't make me happy.

∽

When I came home and opened the door with my key I found the kitchen empty. The door to the bedroom stood ajar. I called, "Hey, where are you?" and Stella came in, in her blue dressing gown and with the white ribbon in her hair. She put her arms around my neck and kissed me; I asked her, "Did you sleep well?" and she nodded and kissed me again with a hunger that choked me. She asked what the trip had been like, and I answered, "Oh, all right. An Englishman with a list over starboard; no sign of Hasenfratz." She said, "I'm so happy you're back," and I kissed her again and ruffled her hair. We were very much in love.

While she cooked the meal I had a wash. I tried to sing the tune I had overheard her humming when I woke up that first morning, long ago. I called to her, "Darling! How does it go?" She called back, "What, darling?" and I hummed the first bar.

When she started to sing it, loudly, so that I would hear, I went silently into the kitchen; as she finished I stood behind her without her knowing it. She called, "Now you sing it yourself!" and I started to hum it, softly.

She swung around as if she had been stung. When I saw her face, my cheeks contracted; never had I seen such horror in human eyes. We stood for a second facing each other, very close, motionless. Then she gave a sound, a moan so terrible and desperate, that I already was holding out my arms to put around her when she fell with her head on my shoulder, sobbing.

I tried to comfort her, by stroking her hair and saying soft soothing things, while I took her gently to a chair. She slumped down on it, flung out her arms on the table, and her head bumped down so hard that I heard it hit. She howled; never in my life had I heard anyone cry like that. I was frightened, I didn't know what to do with her, I got a glass of water and tried to make her drink it, but she wouldn't. She lay there, her head on the table, her arms with the red boy's hands flung out, howling.

All I could do was to sit down beside her, put my arm around her shoulder and stroke her hair, a helpless gesture of protection. I didn't understand why my starting to hum behind her should have upset her so much. She must have been all worked up; she must have nursed the others through ever-returning crises of fear and hysteria without a chance of letting herself go. Then her sobs turned into a name. "David!" she cried. "Oh God, David, David."

I felt such compassion and understanding and love for her that it didn't make any difference. I stopped stroking her hair; I just sat with my arm round her and waited for her pain to pass. During those moments I had a strange feeling, as if we were not alone.

∽

After she had calmed down I put her to bed. She let me take her to the bedroom without caring where she was going. Her eyes were closed and her face was wet. I almost had to carry her; she collapsed on the bed. I took off her slippers and covered her with the eiderdown. I pulled up a chair and sat by her side until she fell asleep, exhausted.

Once she slept I dressed again; when I came back in the kitchen I smelt something burning and turned off the gas under the little pan with soup that had boiled dry. I wanted to go, but caught sight of the table on my way out. I went back to the sink, took the rag and wiped the table, then I went out.

I went out without a purpose; I thought I'd just take a stroll on Memorial Hill to give her time to recover. As I turned the corner I noticed a little locksmith's shop, between the tattooist's and the florist's where I had bought the little tree. I had seen the shop before, but now I noticed for the first time what was hanging in its square little window. Bunches of keys.

I don't know why I decided at that moment to have the duplicate of my key made. Perhaps it was just because I had promised Dop I would, and this was the first time I passed the shop with time on my hands.

The interior of the shop was very dark; as I entered it I saw only an old man's face and hands in the square beam of sunlight slanting through the little window in the shutter of asbestos. He had steel-rimmed spectacles on the tip of his nose, and was fumbling with something small and shiny gripped in a vice. He reminded me of the old corporal who had mended our gun.

I asked him how long it would take to have a duplicate of a key made. He answered that it depended on what sort of key it was. I said, "Oh, just an ordinary latchkey," and handed it to him. He grunted as he turned it round in the beam of sunlight, looking at it; then he frowned, shoved his spectacles on the bridge of his nose, muttered something, put his spectacles back on the tip of his nose, and peered at me, his eyes narrowed in the sunlight. "What the dickens do you boys do with those keys?" he asked. "This is the fourth one!"

I said, "Oh, we just lose them."

He asked, "Then why don't you have half a dozen made at a time? It would come much cheaper."

I said, "We've never thought of that, and I only want one, thank you."

He shrugged his shoulders, said, "Suit yourself. Money seems to be no object in this war"; then he pulled out a drawer in the darkness, rummaged in it, took the little glittering thing out of the vice, and put a key in its stead. After he had started filing, he asked, "What kind of place is it you boys live in? A boarding house?" I said no, it was a private house. He filed some more, filling the little room with shrieks; then he asked, "What happened to that young airman, the first one? I haven't seen him for a long time."

I said, "Oh, he's been transferred."

He asked, "Where?"

I didn't answer, but just smiled. He looked up, pushed his spectacles down, peered at me again with narrowed eyes, then he said, "Ah, I forgot. You're not supposed to divulge any troop movements."

85

I said, "That's right."

His file shrieked again for a minute or so, then he said, "You're not supposed to do a lot of things nowadays. It's quite a job to keep them all sorted."

I said, "That's right."

After that he didn't say any more. He finished his filing; my ears rang when he stopped. "Here you are," he said, sounding faraway; "that will be a florin." When I didn't seem to understand, he said, "Two shillings."

I paid him, and put the two keys in my pocket. When I left he called after me, "Good luck, sailor; and don't lose it this time!" I said I'd do my best.

I had known I was the fourth, before he told me. It didn't come as a shock to me; it wouldn't have come as a shock if I had found out that I was the twelfth or the fifteenth. I knew now that whatever our names might be, to her we were all one man, called Captain David de Jong, K.L.M.

I wasn't jealous of him, nor of any of the others, for I knew that I was going to be the last. One day she and I would wake up together, and it would be peace, and we would realize that it had all been a nightmare. I was so sure that I would survive the war that I didn't think of giving the duplicate of my key to anyone. I would just keep it, a token of friendship toward the dead.

∽

When I came home she was still asleep on the bed, exactly as I had left her. I was hungry and so I spread some buns with Marmite and made myself a cup of tea.

The sun was setting, the shadow of the little tree lay across the floor and the table like dark foliage. I put on my slippers and my dressing gown after I had eaten; I was quiet in order not to disturb her. The neighbors' radio banged a symphony against the wall; in the flat below people were laughing and talking. I sat with my feet on the table, my chair tilted back, smoking my pipe, and drank three cups of tea. I felt tired for the first time since I had been woken up by the telephone, and realized that was forty hours ago. I didn't think I needed any pills to sleep, I felt relaxed and quiet.

I sat there thinking how good it would be if I could take her away with me to some faraway island, and sit by a log fire in a chair lined with sheepskin, with snow falling silently outside. I thought of the other girls I had known and with whom I had imagined I was in love; I knew now that it had not been love. As I sat there, thinking, while the shadow of the little tree slowly grew up the door opposite the window, I again had that strange feeling of not being alone. It was not a ghostly feeling; it was like what I had felt when I lay listening in the darkness to the wheezing and snoring of the sleeping boys round me during my first night in Westport, but much stronger. As if the distant shore had drawn very close while I sat there, with my feet on the table.

Perhaps the shore was not distant at all, in the sense of time and place. Perhaps it was right here: the table, at which all four of us had sat in turn, happy and at peace in the security of our love. I hadn't any wish or desire left, but for the one dream of taking her to that island, far away. And that was not a wish, but just an expression of my happiness and peace. If the distant shore was here, then I had reached a point of no return. I knew that I would never be afraid again and that death would hold no horror for me any more, for I no longer believed in it.

When I got up it was almost dark, I undressed in the dusk. When I touched her, Stella sighed and stirred; I did not want to wake her up but I couldn't take off her dressing gown while she was lying down. I tried to lift her off the bed, and she half woke up. She stood on her feet drowsily and asked, "What's the time?" with a sleepy voice. I said, "It's late, time to sleep," and opened the bed. Then I helped her take off her dressing gown and put it on the chair, supporting her with one hand. As we got into bed she said, "I must do my hair," but I said, "Ssh, never mind, sleep."

When she lay in my arms, her head on my shoulder, she mumbled, "So happy you're back," as if she was dreaming. Then she fell asleep, her hand cold on my chest.

I took it in mine to warm it, and floated away into that peace.

87

It felt as if we were floating away together toward our island, enclosed in a little box, carried out by the tide of time.

სა

When the telephone rang it was morning. Wintry sunlight fell into the room through the gap between the curtains. The moment it rang she gripped me so tightly in her sleep that I had difficulty in reaching it. As I picked up the receiver I saw that the time was 8:30 A.M., and wondered what could be the matter. Even if Van Dam had sailed instantly after we came in, he could not possibly be back yet; perhaps he was ill and they wanted me to take over.

When she heard me say, "Hello, yes?" she gripped me even tighter and began to tremble. I said, "Take it easy, darling, take it easy," and I heard Wadlow's voice in the instrument asking, "I beg your pardon?"

I said, "Sorry, I was talking to someone else. What's up?"

He said, "I rang you because I thought you might be interested to know that the United States of America have entered the war."

I said, "No kidding, on which side?"

"That is in very poor taste," he said, primly. "The Americans have done more . . ."

"All right," I said. "Sorry, I have only just woken up. How did it happen?"

He told me that Japanese aircraft had bombed the naval base of Pearl Harbor out of the blue, and done a lot of damage. I said, "Good Lord!" stroking Stella's hair, and whispered, "It's all right, darling, it's good news."

Wadlow said, "Isn't it. I suppose you realize this means that you will get your guns now."

I said that would be wonderful, and how long did he think it would take until we got them. He said he didn't know; but without divulging any military secrets he thought he could tell me that the first all-American convoy would be sailing the Western Approaches pretty soon. I was just beginning to wake up then, and, as always first thing in the morning, a brilliant thought occurred to me. I said, "Never mind about the convoy; how long

88

do you think it will take them before they start shipping troops over here?"

He answered, "I haven't the foggiest idea, old boy. Why?"

I said, "Because I can tell you here and now that we won't get our guns until then."

He asked, "What on earth makes you think that?"

I said, "Oh, just intuition. I'm psychic."

He asked, "I beg your pardon?"

I said, "Never mind. Congratulations, anyhow, and thanks for ringing me," and I hung up.

When I turned round, Stella lay looking at me as if she was three years old. The fact that the telephone had rung with a message that was cheerful seemed to have taken twenty years off her age. I said, "Congratulate me. America has entered the war."

She said, "Oh," looking in my eyes for the snag.

I said, "Wadlow thinks that means that we'll be fitted out with guns now, instead of vacuum cleaners."

She still looked at me intently, as if she was undecided what I was thinking. "Don't you think so, yourself?" she asked.

I said, "Of course, it is wonderful news. Before the day is over we'll all be bristling with four inchers. If you look out of your window tonight, and you see a steaming wake flash past, that will be Hasenfratz going for a holiday. Now let's have come more sleep."

I closed my eyes and began to sink slowly back into a warm drowsiness. Her voice said, "You don't really believe it. You're just trying to be funny." I said, "Go to sleep, don't nag." She sighed on my shoulder. "And don't breathe down my neck," I said.

She was silent for a while, and I was nearly asleep when I heard her say, "You're the sweetest man I've ever known." That threatened to wake me up, but I decided to take it as it came. "You're an angel," I said. "Now shut up." She began kissing my ear, and I shouted, "Shut up!" with the ringing voice of Captain Ironsides. She lay very still after that, so still that it threatened to wake me up again. I said, "For God's sake, breathe." Then she began to giggle.

I realized that I might as well give up the idea of sleep. I

89

turned round and faced her, but I didn't open my eyes. I felt her face very close to mine; her hair tickled my nose. I opened my eyes wide and saw hers very near, staring at me like an owl. I said, "If you don't go to sleep I'll put up the camp bed. I've got work to do. I'm tired.'

She kissed me.

෧෪

It must have been about ten when I fell asleep again; when she woke me up with morning coffee it was three o'clock in the afternoon. The sunlight had gone; as she drew the curtains I saw a gray wintry sky. I had a feeling of holiday and knew something nice had happened, but I couldn't remember what. As she sat down on the bed with her knees drawn up, after she had given me my cup, I asked her, "Something nice has happened while I was asleep. What was it?"

She raised her eyebrows, looking innocent.

I said, "I know, America has entered the war."

Her face changed. "That means bigger convoys, doesn't it?"

"Yes."

"Do you think they have got the stuff to protect them?"

"No. Not at this stage."

She looked at me for a while. "I thought that was it. Why didn't you say so this morning, if that was the truth?"

I said, "Give me some more coffee," and held out my cup; but she didn't take it.

"You were very sweet to me yesterday," she said, "when I got silly."

I said, "Sweet? I didn't do a thing."

"Yes you did. You put me to bed. And you didn't ask questions."

I hesitated for a moment whether I should let her go on. I knew that she was about to tell me things I didn't particularly want to know, and she might regret it later. I said, "I think it's silly to ask questions if you know the answers."

"Do you?" she asked.

I said, "Yes," and held out my cup again.

90

She bent forward and kissed me, then she took it, and went into the kitchen.

I leaned back and stretched and yawned. When I finally managed to close my mouth and open my eyes again, I found myself looking at the portrait on the wardrobe. He seemed a nice boy, if not very intelligent, but perhaps it was unfair to hold him responsible for his smile. I myself had had some pretty grim pictures taken in my time. As I lay looking at the picture I heard her voice say, "That's not my brother."

I had not heard her come in, and I felt a faint echo of what she must have felt when I started humming behind her back. I didn't turn round; I said, "I never thought he was."

"Why not? Did someone tell you?"

"No, I was told he was your brother. But I didn't believe it."

"He is from our island. He's called Alan, and he is fighting in the desert. I write him a letter every week."

I wondered what she wrote, but I let it pass. "Does he reply?" I asked; but she wasn't listening.

"I write to him about the family and the people we know," she said, "and I make him remember little things we used to do together when we were children. We were neighbors."

I looked at him and his smile and what he had written on his collar: "I'll walk beside you." I thought of him, a boy from the Hebrides, slinking through the desert with a Tommy gun, taking a whispered communion from a cracked cup before stalking all the demons out of the Egyptian Book of the Dead. I knew I would never be able to do that; deserts had frightened me ever since I was a child. One week of his warfare would turn me into a raving lunatic. Next time I got into a state, I had better take a look at that picture and realize how lucky I was to have nothing to worry about but Hasenfratz. "All right," I said, "that's all I want to know." I turned round and reached out for the cup of coffee she carried.

"I'd like to tell you some more," she said, but I looked at her with authority and said, "You heard me."

She smiled, uncertainly. I realized that she was dying to tell me everything. Perhaps that was what she needed: to tell it all

91

and get rid of it. But I didn't think I could stand that yet; I was not jealous and I didn't think I ever would be, but I wasn't sure.

"You tell me some other day," I said. "We've got all the time in the world."

Her smile grew until her whole face was radiant. "We have," she said.

Chapter V

HASENFRATZ STAYED AWAY. SINCE THAT MORNING WHEN THE ENGLISH Captain had seen him dive as soon as we appeared on the horizon, he had not been spotted again. The ducks that were torpedoed might have been hit by him, but for over a fortnight he never surfaced near one of us. I was strafed once by a plane, but it caused no casualties because we all saw it coming and had plenty of time to run for shelter. It riddled a pail full of soup Cook had put outside to cool off; the ship reeked of peas and pig's trotters for hours afterward and Cook didn't calm down until we got home. Apart from that incident we might as well have been sailing in peacetime. We didn't even have sinkers any more; it looked as if the Germans just fired four or five torpedoes at each convoy, regardless, and scurried away before the wreckage came down from the sky. Goatskin, who had succeeded Dop in command of the *Vlieland,* thought it was because the Americans had entered the war and Jerry must be busy elsewhere. Van Dam shrugged his shoulders and said that it didn't mean a thing, for madness came in waves.

The first time I sailed, after Harcourt and Wadlow and I had made our little plan, Harcourt had come streaking down on a motorcycle. The second time he just rang up to find out what square the duck was in. The third time Wadlow had to ring him, and hold the line for almost a quarter of an hour until he was hunted down. The fourth time I asked, "I suppose our plan still holds good, in case I should come across Hasenfratz?" Wadlow answered, "Of course, old boy, of course." I said, "In that case, hadn't we better get hold of Harcourt and tell him to stand by?"

92

Wadlow answered, "Don't worry, old boy, I'll do that the moment you have left." The fact that America had entered the war had an exhilarating effect on the British, they behaved as if victory was as good as won.

Perhaps it was, but I doubted whether Hasenfratz had been as easily convinced. Perhaps I knew the German mentality better because of my months under the occupation; I couldn't help feeling that our friend's absence from our course was to be taken as a warning rather than as a reassurance. But all I could do on my part was to keep my eyes open and our pom-pom well oiled; on every trip I made the bosun practice and shoot off a few rounds. We tried to find out where the bullets struck the water, but we never did. It was so eerie, that I had to convince myself by weighing them in my hand that what we put into the thing were indeed bullets and not duds; the bosun ventured that they might be striking behind the horizon. Wherever they were striking, it was a long way away.

My Chief, whose professional pride had been injured by the fact that a dotard with eight fingers had done in seven minutes what he hadn't been able to do in twenty hours, was fascinated and maddened by the gun. He filed away at it for hours, trying to make it dip deep enough to shoot level, but he didn't succeed. He broke a file and two hack saws on the thing, threw them on the deck, and started kicking it as the bosun had done. I began to suspect that we had been singled out unwittingly as the bearers of one of those ghost guns with a life of its own that I had heard talked about in the harbor pubs by sailors who had served in the last war. I got so above myself with self-assurance that I even thought I would regret it if the thing was finally replaced by a gun that let itself be pointed instead of taking its own aim. I knew that I was getting dangerously lighthearted, but I couldn't help it. I was just dreaming all the time, humming, smiling; when Hasenfratz came back I had forgotten how dangerous he was.

It happened on a cold, sunny morning, when we were on our way to a rudderless Dane in square 353. I stood on the bridge, looking at a faint feathery cloud high up in the empty blue sky. When I looked down again I was dizzy with gazing into nothing and dreaming about Stella and breathing the crisp, cold air. I

93

saw something move in the sea on our port side about a hundred yards away from us; it looked like a stick being dragged very fast through the water. I was so far away from the war that, instead of recognizing it instantly, I gazed at it for over a second before I woke up; when I did I was so frightened that it took me another second before I could shout, "Periscope on port!" whistle, "all hands," and ring the alarm on the engine-room telegraph. What had frightened me was not the periscope itself, but the fact that it had taken me so long to react to it.

The U-boat surfaced almost immediately afterward, so close that I heard the water gushing from its nostrils as it rose. First I was sure it was Hasenfratz, then I looked at the emerging gun traveling by itself and thought it was someone else, for it looked much bigger than the one Hasenfratz carried. A minute later I recognized the conning tower and the rest of the ship; it was Hasenfratz all right.

While the bosun and his gunners rushed at our pom-pom, I saw the lid of the tower flap open, the mannikins tumble out; when they uncovered the gun I understood why Hasenfratz had been away for so long. The thing they started to wheel round at us was a monster; he had been fitted out with a gun twice the size.

I cannot say I was afraid, I was too busy thinking of a way out. But the feeling in the back of my knees came back. I felt it when I ran to the starboard side, as Hasenfratz swung round behind us. I yelled, "Hard starboard hard!" at the man at the wheel, and "Fire!" at the bosun; we turned at full speed, spraying bullets at the sky with a sound as if we were drilling macadam.

Hasenfratz got us on the side. There was a report, so loud that it shook the air around us; then a sound as if a colossal bomb came soaring down; I fell headlong on the bridge and thought: this is it. There followed a breathless silence, in which Stella quivered in a white emptiness, slowly stretching out her arms toward me, then another explosion, far away, so thick that I felt the sound rather than heard it. Before I had got back on my feet I heard people cheering.

As I looked over the railing I saw the bosun and the two gunners dancing on the fo'c'sle, slapping each other's shoulders, point-

94

ing overboard. I thought they had gone mad, then I looked over-board myself.

The U-boat was lying so close to us that I could discern the features of the Germans clearly. They were all sitting on their behinds round the gun, looking very stupid. A fat officer stood screaming at them, halfway out of the conning tower like the old woman who lived in a shoe. The gun itself looked strangely elongated, and pointed at the sky.

I shouted at the wheel, "Port!" as we were heading straight at them; we nearly skinned their nose as we swerved past. Even to me, who knew nothing whatever about guns, it was obvious what had happened to Hasenfratz's new monster: its recoil had stuck. What the madmen on my fo'c'sle were dancing and screaming about was that our recoil had got stuck too.

For a few seconds I was still aware of the danger we had escaped by the skin of our teeth; then the mood of the ship got me, too. I laughed until the tears ran down my face; I had to support myself at the rail in order not to sink on my knees laughing; when the befuddled Germans had scrambled to their feet and started filing back into the conning tower at the shrieked commands of the fat officer, one of them kicked the gun and limped the rest of the way. That just finished me; and not only me, it finished everybody. I even saw the last of the Germans double up with laughter, and then I did a crazy thing: I waved. I felt it was crazy even while I did it; but the German waved back.

It was a curious moment. In one flash of superhuman sanity I saw us finish our war then and there. I saw myself pull alongside Hasenfratz, lean over the rail, and say, "Now look here, chum, why don't we call it a day? This is just silly." Then the German who had waved was snatched down into the conning tower, the lid slammed shut, and the U-boat dived, blowing big bubbles.

We didn't see Hasenfratz again for the rest of the way. We picked up the duck and towed her home and put back into port underneath a black cloudless sky ablaze with stars, sparkling bluishly like diamonds. I tried, all the way home, to recapture the alertness I had felt during the few minutes between the moment I recognized the periscope and the moment the cheering started;

but I couldn't. I just went on thinking of the German who had waved back, and the silliness of men shooting at each other; and then I realized what Stella had done to me.

When I was a boy on my first voyage I bought in Port Said one of those things one buys only on one's first voyage: a boudoir edition of Omar Khayyám's poems in English, bound in red leather, with a little lock and a key on it to keep it private. I remembered one of the poems that night; not its actual words, but what they said: That love is like a fountain, it shoots up toward one person and rains down on all mankind. It seemed rather romantic in connection with Stella and me, yet it gave the best description of what had happened that I could think of. I loved her so much that I felt a great sympathy for everybody round me; even for old Hasenfratz, who had been made to look so silly by his splendid new gun.

It was a wonderful feeling, and yet I knew it was somehow dangerous, but I could not think why.

❧

When I told Wadlow about Hasenfratz's new gun he wasn't so interested as I had thought he would be. Hasenfratz was his baby, and several times during the past fortnight he had been worrying in an almost motherly fashion about what could have happened to him; but he took the news of his return absent-mindedly.

I told him about the recoils that had got stuck, and he thought that was a very funny story; when I said that but for that funny story I would not have come back, he patted me on the back and said, "Come, come, old boy; no need to get gloomy. It's a lot more difficult for inexperienced pupils to hit a target as small as you are with a heavy gun than it is with a light one." I told him that he was talking nonsense, and that it was all right with me if he had lost interest, but I would thank him to keep his bedside manner for his private patients. It wasn't a particularly good joke, but he thought it was awfully funny; he haw-hawed and said, "I must remember to tell that one to Harcourt."

I said I'd prefer him to remind Harcourt of our combined operation. I even went so far as to say that I wouldn't sail next time unless Harcourt was on the spot and we had plotted my course together.

Then Wadlow got angry. It was an Englishman's anger, so it sounded charming. "I somehow don't think that you've got quite the right approach to this business," he said. "The Harcourt setup was a thing I organized off my own bat. I have no authority whatever from Headquarters to bring in Coastal Command, and Harcourt agreed to do it only because we happen to know each other personally. I don't think it's quite the ticket that you should use this more or less private arrangement as the basis for an ultimatum."

I stood for a moment in doubt, then I shrugged my shoulders, and said, "All right, Wadlow; have it your own way," and turned to go. He saw me to the door, assuring me that of course our plan still stood, and that if Harcourt wasn't out on operation he would certainly come and do the job. He had agreed to do it and once he agreed to something he would stick to it; I needn't ever worry that he would not play the game.

Before he shut the door he held out his hand, and for a second I thought he meant to warn me that one of the buttons of my coat was coming off, as we had never shaken hands before. "Chin up, old boy," he said, "and no hard feelings." His hand was small and dry.

As I walked along the pier in the starlight I tried to think about Hasenfratz, for I knew that if I wanted to outwit him now I would have to think fast. But I couldn't be bothered, for I was on my way to Stella. Between now and the next time I should have to sail I would spend at least twenty-four hours with her, and our hours were longer than any hours I had ever lived through. I had often shaken the little clock on the night table, thinking it had stopped, for it had seemed impossible that we should have gone through so much talk and love and happy silence in so short a time. In those hours we had come to know each other as if we had lived together for years. Last time I left I had been looking in the bathroom for the comb, while she was busy in the kitchen cooking the breakfast. I had muttered to myself, "Where is the damn thing?" and she had called, "On the medicine cupboard, darling!" That was indeed where it was, and I combed my hair without giving it a second thought.

Only on the bridge, hours later, when I came across the incident again while remembering the things we had done together this time, did I realize how odd this was, for I had never mentioned the comb. It was a thing one would only expect from an old married couple, and we had known each other for sixteen days. Of those sixteen days I had spent ten at sea and forty-six hours asleep in bed; so all we had really known each other for was ninety-eight hours. It seemed a convincing proof that our idea of time was nonsense.

When I entered the flat I had a big surprise, for Stella was in the kitchen. The table was laid for two and decorated with holly; on a big plate in the center was a cake. When I asked, "What's this?" she put her arms around my neck, said, "Happy Christmas," and kissed me.

I had completely forgotten it was Christmas; I had forgotten that such a thing as Christmas existed. I was very sorry, for I should have thought of it and bought her a present.

She gave me no time to say so; she took me by the hand and led me into the bedroom. A faint light shone through the door, when I stood in the doorway and looked over her shoulder I saw it was candlelight. On the night table stood a little Christmas tree with candles on it and silver balls and little glass birds with colored tails, on top of it was a star. She took me to the tree; underneath it I saw, between the clock and the telephone, a little parcel wrapped in Christmas paper tied with gold thread. I felt miserable because I hadn't got her a present, but I didn't want to spoil this moment for her by saying so for she was watching my face with anxious, expectant eyes. I asked, "Is that for me?" and she nodded with a smile that made me feel worse. I picked up the little parcel and tried to untie the gold thread. It took me some time, for it was knotted very tightly. While I was doing this she sat on the edge of the bed, watching me, and I smiled at her, feeling awful. When I had finally unwrapped the parcel I found a small wooden box.

98

It was the tiniest box I had ever seen, very nicely carved. I said, "How wonderful," turning it round in my fingers, wondering what on earth I could use it for; it was too small even for a collar stud. Then I opened it, because she still sat looking at me with that heartbreaking expectancy. There must be something inside.

I found a tiny piece of paper, folded neatly. I tried to shake it out on my hand, but it stuck in the box. I tried to prize it out with the nail of my little finger; then I fumbled in the pockets of my greatcoat for a match. I had to sharpen the match by breaking it before I could get it out. When I unfolded it I found it was a tiny strip of ruled notepaper. On it was written "I love you."

I looked at her with surprise, for during all the time we had lived together she had not once said those words to me, and never before had she looked at me like that. I felt embarrassed and at the same time very happy and proud. I didn't know what to say to her; so I said, "I have got nothing for you. I forgot it was Christmas."

She said, "Will you marry me?"

I sat quite still after that. If Dop hadn't whispered to me in the office the night before he was killed, asking me to be his best man, it would have been a wonderful moment; now it seemed as if a U-boat surfaced right behind her. I looked her in the eyes without moving a muscle in my face; during a few seconds I stared at the terrible truth that I was nothing but a link in a chain, that we were both caught in a nightmare of love and death and destruction. De Jong must have been killed after they had agreed to get married, so was Barger, so was Dop.

But when I thought, "So will I," I woke up from that nightmare. Her eyes were so sincere, so gentle, that it just couldn't be true. She meant it, she loved me because of what I was, not just because I had closed the ranks. Even if I had started as just another man with a key, she had given me the little box with its secret message; I was the unknown lover on the distant shore who had found it and replied. I was not just a link in a chain, the other three had led up to me. The other three might have been killed, I wouldn't be, never. I was safe, I was immortal; this time we would make it, it would be I who would break the spell.

I took her hand in mine. It was very cold. I looked at her eyes, tragic with love; her lips, parted in agonizing suspense.

I said, "Yes, Stella."

෴

From that moment on I was walking on clouds. We took the little Christmas tree into the kitchen and put it on the table and switched off the light. While she was heating up the first course at the stove I sat looking at the candles and the little glass birds with a feeling as if I was dreaming. When she put a plate of soup in front of me, I woke up and wanted to start eating; I looked up when she laughed.

"Do you know how you are sitting there?" she asked.

I realized I must be sitting there like an idiot, so I laughed too, and said, "Sorry, I . . ." I forgot what I was going to say, for she looked so beautiful in the candlelight that all I could do was just gaze at her, like a dog.

She said, "Darling, wake up," and stretched out her hand. I thought she wanted me to kiss it, but she took something off my head. It was my cap. I still had my greatcoat on as well. I got up to take it off, knocked the chair over, bent to pick it up and nearly knocked over the Christmas tree. She grabbed it just in time, and I felt a lumbering oaf, for I had spilled soup on the table cloth that she had brought out specially for the occasion.

But all this happened below the clouds, whatever I did and whatever I said: I sat looking at her all the time. I wasn't even thinking any coherent thoughts, and it got worse as the evening went on. The dinner wasn't a success, for when she wanted to bring out the fish dish she had specially prepared for the occasion it was quite raw as she had forgotten to turn the oven on. She nearly cried when she discovered this, but I was secretly delighted for it proved, I thought, that she had been walking on clouds too.

The cake hadn't come off very well either, the top of the outer part was edible, but the center was uncooked and the bottom soggy. She was terribly disappointed, and I tried to laugh it off by saying, "If you had asked me after this meal I would have said no." For some reason this made it worse; perhaps no woman

100

has a sense of humor when it comes to her cooking. Her eyes brimmed over, a fat tear ran down her nose and hung for a moment at the tip, flashing in the candlelight before she wiped it off with the back of her hand. I took her on my lap and said, "Darling, don't be silly, what do I care about the meal? We're going to be married! Even if you had cooked the best dinner I'd ever had, I wouldn't have noticed it."

She felt better after that; she blew her nose in my handkerchief with a very manly sound and sniffed some more and smiled again, and said, "I'm sorry, I know it's silly, but I was so sure it would be all right; they are the two things I do best." I said nonsense, she was a wonderful cook, no girl could be expected to have her mind on her work while she was summing up the courage to propose to a man. That made her laugh, and although I was glad that she was getting over her disappointment, I felt a bit hurt for I had fancied myself as being rather hard to get. "Did you ever consider the possibility of me saying no?" I asked. She said, "Oh, yes, I was terribly nervous," but she obviously meant it as a joke. I didn't think it all that funny and I told her so; but she had only to kiss me to make me lose all sense of dignity and proportion. She could have made me balance an umbrella on my nose that night.

She virtually did: she made me sing the descant to "Come All Ye Faithful" and "Noël, Noël" while we were washing up, after we had some buns with Marmite to replace the fish and the cake. I knew I had not much of a voice except early in the morning, but I barked the descant like a trained seal until the neighbors put a stop to it by hammering on the wall.

When the table was cleared and everything stored away, she suddenly cried, "Oh, no!" I asked her what was the matter; she answered miserably that she had known all through the meal that she had forgotten something, and now only remembered what it was: the wine.

I said, "Well, it's never too late for that. Let's have it now." After protesting for a bit, saying that wine didn't taste nice unless you had it with food, she brought out a bottle; and I started looking through the drawers for a corkscrew to open it with. There was none, and because she looked as if this was the last straw,

101

I said, "I know!" as if I had a brilliant idea, and tried to push the cork inside the bottle with the handle of a wooden spoon. She cried, "Don't! You'll break it!" but I said, "Don't be silly, I've done this hundreds of times," and managed to ram the thing in by using all my strength. As I did so I was hit in the face by a spurt of wine; when I got up and had wiped my eyes, my shirt looked as if it was covered with blood from the waist up. I was ready to laugh it off, but the sight of me made her burst into tears, quite beyond proportion.

This time it took me a lot longer to get her out of it; when at last I had succeeded we were so tired and the whole thing had fallen so flat that there seemed to be little else left to do but to go to bed. The candles had burned down to blue flickering flames; I switched the light on and put them out.

It didn't seem to be one of our lucky nights, for the moment we were in bed, and I took her in my arms, the air raid sirens sounded. It was the first time I had heard them in Westport, but I knew there had been alerts while I was at sea. We got up, but decided not go down to the shelter until we were sure there was going to be a raid. We opened the curtains and stood looking at the sky for a while; she shivered and I took her inside my dressing gown. There were only a few stars to be seen, the town was very silent. When the first guns started booming behind the horizon I thought: if the star of Bethlehem should rise over us tonight, it would be shot at by ack-ack. I didn't say it, for I wasn't sure how she would take it. We heard planes approaching and decided to go down.

So far I had never seen any of the other tenants living in the house. When we entered the air-raid shelter in the cellar, I was amazed to see how many there were. I didn't count them, but there must have been well over fifty people there, sitting on benches along the wall in dressing gowns and overcoats. Among them was a Rear Admiral in greatcoat and long drawers, with carpet slippers on. I wondered whether I was supposed to do something about him, for I too was wearing my greatcoat over my pyjamas; but he never looked my way. He sat staring gloomily at a cat with a bell round its neck, that had caught a mouse and was playing with it.

102

We sat down in a corner, on an upturned bath among the bicycles, and waited. Nobody spoke; a baby at the other end of the cellar cried with high screeches, like a sea gull. The ack-ack opened up all round us and we felt the trembling of distant bombs exploding; by then everybody was staring at the cat, who was having a lot of fun with the mouse and stayed in the center all the time, as if she was giving a little floor show. The mouse must have been quite dead by then, but she went on tossing it in the air and batting it with her paw until the Admiral got up, picked it up by the tail and took it to the old janitor who was sitting in the corner. The old janitor was the only one I knew by sight; I had seen him once or twice, going through ritual movements with a broom in the hall or on the stairs, and Stella had told me that he did her shopping for her. He got up when he saw the Admiral approaching and stood at attention; when he took over the mouse he said, "Thank you, sir," and vanished into the coal cellar. By then the ack-ack had died down and there were no more bombs. We heard the sound of engines roaring past; they must be the fire brigade, so the raid was probably over.

It was a long time before the all-clear sounded. We all sat waiting for it, listening to the noises outside. It was a pity that the Admiral had taken the mouse away, for now we had nothing else to look at but one another, and I became aware that people avoided looking at us. It made me feel embarrassed and worried, for I was sure that Stella must be conscious of it too. It certainly wasn't one of her lucky nights, poor kid.

When the all-clear finally sounded everybody got up and started trooping out. As we were sitting near the door, we managed to get up the stairs ahead of everybody. We looked out of the window on the top landing and saw a few fires in the town, but the black mass of the Grand Hotel was still standing, and in the harbor itself there was no sign of anything going on. I considered for a moment ringing up the office to find out if everything was all right, but I thought: the hell with it, if they want me for anything they can ring me.

Perhaps I would have rung them if Stella had not looked so ill. She was very pale as we entered the flat; when we got to the bedroom she fell on the bed, exhausted. I switched off the light in the

103

kitchen and opened the window; then I helped her take off her raincoat and her dressing gown; when I got into bed she seemed to be already asleep. I felt very sorry for her, for everything seemed to have gone wrong that night; yet I was so happy that I almost felt ashamed of it. I was sure that we were going to have a nice life.

∽

An hour later I was woken up by Stella; she whispered, "Darling, there's someone at the door."

I listened, heard a banging noise in the kitchen, and wondered who it could be. Perhaps it was the warden and we were showing a light. I put on my dressing gown and my slippers; as I groped my way to the front door I decided that it couldn't be the warden, for every light in the house was switched off.

It was my Chief Engineer. He said, "Sorry, Skipper, but I'm afraid you'll have to come out. Van Dam is missing."

I said, "What? With the ship?"

"No, no," he said, "just he, himself. And as an S.O.S. came in just now, they sent me over to call you."

I heard Stella come in from the bedroom and turned round. "It's my C.E.," I said. "Do you mind if he comes in? There's something the matter with Van Dam."

She said, "Of course." I switched on the light and let him in. He made an awkward little bow when he saw her, and saluted. "Sorry, ma'am," he said, "but we couldn't get hold of him on the phone; your line must have got out of order during the raid."

I asked him what had happened; he said that the Savage Club had received a direct hit while Van Dam was inside, singing.

"Singing?" I asked, for in connection with Van Dam it sounded grotesque.

"Yes," he said, "didn't you know? He was a member of a male quartet, with a clergyman and two R.A.F. officers. We poked fun at him all last week, for he was rehearsing "Sound the Alarm" in his room; you could hear him bellowing all over the hotel. To-night was the night of the concert."

I asked him whether they had found his body, but the Chief said they hadn't. The whole place was in such a mess that they

104

hadn't been able to sort it out yet. But he certainly had been inside, for he had left word with Headquarters that if anything came up before midnight, he would be at the Savage Club.

"Well," I said, "in that case I had better go." I hadn't got around to disliking the idea yet, for the news about Van Dam had affected me more than I would have thought. I suddenly realized that I had been fond of the man.

"O.K.," said the Chief. "I don't want to hurry you, but you had better come as quick as you can, for when I left the office the duck was screaming her head off."

I said I'd be there in five minutes; he saluted, bowed to Stella again, tried to go to get out while doing so, and backed into the doorpost. He said, "Sorry," gave a sheepish little laugh and scurried out. He didn't seem to be at ease with girls in dressing gowns.

While he was there, I hadn't looked at Stella; as I turned round to go to the bedroom and get dressed I saw her, and understood why the Chief had been so embarrassed. She was sitting at the table, her dressing gown open, her eyes staring into nothing, her face as white as a sheet. I patted her on the shoulder and said, "Brace up, darling; I know it's bad luck, but there can't be much left that can go wrong tonight." She woke up out of her blank stare as if she had been far away, smiled, and said, "Yes . . ." She obviously hadn't been listening to me.

I said, "Come on, darling, get up and get me another shirt. I said I would be there in five minutes." She said, "Yes, yes," smiling, but she didn't sound as if she was all there yet. I said, "Did you hear what I asked you?" She answered, "Yes, shirt; I'll get it." I wanted to kiss her and make a fuss of her, because she looked so miserable, but there was no time.

I dressed in a hurry. She got me a clean shirt; I didn't pay much attention to her while I was dressing. When I stood in the kitchen with my cap and greatcoat on, I was surprised to see that she was fully dressed. "What's all this?" I asked.

"I'll see you to the ship," she said.

It was a nice thought, but I didn't like it. If I went there alone I could run, and I didn't want her to go back to the flat all by herself at dead of night, there were always a lot of drunken characters about in the boulevard at this hour. But as there wasn't

105

time to explain all this to her, I decided not to top off the evening by refusing to take her. I said, "O.K., let's go," and we went.

We didn't say a word all the way. The boulevard was very crowded, and I liked the idea of her going back by herself less and less. It looked as if after the air raid all the drunks of Westport had crawled into the open; there were so many of them that I couldn't have run even if I had been by myself. She clung to my arm with both hands as we walked; when we got to the bottom of the pier and I said, "Well, darling, let's say good night here," she wouldn't let go of me. She said, "Please, please," in a way that broke my heart but I was firm about it. I didn't want to go up the pier trailing her, and I didn't want her to work her way down again by herself. I said, "No, Stella, I'm not going to take you any farther. Let's kiss good night here and you go home, there's a good girl. I'll be back before you know I've gone."

She must have realized that I couldn't be talked out of it, for she gave in. She looked dead tired. I took her in my arms and kissed her. Her lips were cold and unresponsive. I heard drunks whistling at us, close by; I gave her a furtive hug and hurried away.

I didn't look round, for I knew she would be standing where I had left her, looking after me until I had got out of sight. I felt very sorry for her, for obviously even this last thing of the day had fallen flat, but I was still walking on clouds. I was going to marry her as soon as I came back. I was the happiest man in the world.

When I opened the door of the office, the first thing I noticed was that everyone there was silent, sitting as if they were listening to music. One of the loud-speakers on the wall was twittering frantically; even though my knowledge of Morse was poor I heard it was an S.O.S., followed by what sounded like the markings of a position. I asked, "Who's that?" and the wireless operator answered, "That's your baby."

I said, "Don't be silly," and looked at Wadlow, sitting behind his desk. "Do you mean that this bird has been squeaking all the time?"

Wadlow looked up, shiftily. "I'm afraid so," he said, "the chap obviously forgot to open envelope D."

106

I said, "Can't be. I've never come across anybody yet who didn't rip open that envelope the minute he gets hit. Doesn't he realize that he is concentrating every U-boat in the region on himself?"

"I wouldn't know," said Wadlow; "you had better go and ask him yourself."

"Don't you think it might have been a good idea if someone had told him?" I asked, in an attempt to be British about it that didn't quite come off, and I pointed at the radio desk. "What else have you got all those blokes lined up for?"

"Take it easy, chum," said the W.O. "We can't do a thing. He has messed up his receiver."

At that moment Goatskin came in, with a wiry little Captain who looked like a jockey. He saw us and noticed there was something wrong; then he too became conscious of the frantic twittering going on all the time. His knowledge of Morse was obviously better than mine, for he listened for a few seconds, then looked at me, and said, "That's nice. Yours?"

"Not yet," I said. "They're still trying to sell it to me."

Wadlow asked what the dickens I meant by that; I told him that I would be damned if I'd sail into what by now must be a concentration of U-boats and a couple of planes thrown in, with a crew that was dead tired, and a gun that couldn't shoot, just because Van Dam had got it into his head to sing "Sound the Alarm" at a concert. I said that I was anybody's dream of a sucker, but that for once I was not going to play the game. I said to Wadlow, "I won't sound the alarm this time; you bloody well put your little manicuring set away and go yourself. I'm sick of being a hero; other people may rejoice in the thought of getting themselves gutted by gunfire for the sake of a donkey who won't even open an envelope and read what is inside, I don't."

"What is it?" asked Goatskin, and Wadlow answered, "Tanker on fire in Square 539. American."

"That's the first one, isn't it?" asked Goatskin.

"Yes," said Wadlow. "The first American we've got; I don't know about the other stations."

I said, "I don't care whether it's an American or a Hottentot, I—"

The W.O. called, "Ssh"; and we listened. "They say they are drawing gunfire now," he said. "So whether you go or not that's probably the end of baby."

"Isn't it Van Dam's watch?" asked Goatskin.

"Yes," said Wadlow, "but he got killed in the air raid about an hour ago."

"Oh," said Goatskin, then he looked at me. Since Dop's death we had got on rather well, but this was the same look he had given me twice before. I got angry with him because he made me realize that, sensible as my attitude might be, it had some points against it. I said, "O.K., I'll take her, but, by God, it's the last time. As soon as I come back I'll start kicking up such a stink over this gun business that they'll either come across with them, or lock me up in the asylum. Where is Harcourt?"

Wadlow said, "Where do you think, with this air raid on?"

I said, "O.K., I get it. All the air cover I'll get on this operation will be the angels."

Then the wiry old Captain piped up. So far he had stood quietly in the corner on his bowlegs, his hands behind his back, waiting for his turn; now he said, "Could we get the form business over, gentlemen, please? I don't want to interrupt anything, but I have to get on, you see."

"O.K., Captain," said Goatskin, "sit down, please." The jockey sat down in the empty chair on the other side of the desk, put his cap upside down on it and took off his gloves, which he put inside.

I asked, "Don't tell me old Foghorn was a member of the male quartet too?" for I hadn't registered until then that our red-faced shore Captain wasn't there.

"No," said Wadlow, "he's probably eating a goose somewhere, he's on twenty-four hours' Christmas leave."

We bent over the chart and started plotting my course. The loud-speaker went on twittering all the time, and while we were talking I thought that the W.O. was probably right. This baby couldn't last much longer.

∾

I was wrong. All during the way to square 539 my Sparks came to the bridge at regular intervals to report that the duck was still

108

squeaking. Toward daybreak he came to say that they were being slowly grilled, the ship was burning in a big way and they were under constant gunfire which they tried to hold off with everything they had got.

I said, "Jesus Christ! Don't tell me that fool has been firing back all the time?"

Sparks said, "Sounds like it."

"That's wonderful," I said. "By the time we arrive he'll probably have used up all his ammunition. Do you know anything about American captains? Can't they read?"

Sparks said, "Doesn't sound like it." He was a great talker, that boy.

I said, "O.K., go back and listen some more."

After he had gone I resumed my pacing up and down, worried. I wasn't afraid, for I was sure that we would get through somehow; but it seemed a tricky setup. The only way to tackle it was to follow Van Dam's advise and aim three squares higher, pass the duck for about a square or two, and then sneak up on her from the rear, ready to do some backing business the moment a U-boat spotted us. But even while I planned this I doubted whether it would work. Unless the Unterseebootwaffe Western Approaches was celebrating Christmas in the mess, all the available U-boats must have concentrated on the screaming American by now, and the way the Luftwaffe had chased us out of bed at midnight didn't seem to indicate that they were aglow with the Christmas spirit.

I didn't think about Stella much, but she was at the back of everything I did and thought. If she hadn't asked me to marry her, I would have been creeping up and down that bridge holding on to the rail, instead of running at hiking speed the way I was doing. I held the little box in my pocket and felt safe. I was so certain that I would get through somehow that I could see the whole thing from an objective point of view, almost as if it didn't concern me. It was this objectiveness that had enabled me to say the things I said in the office, if I had been afraid I would have kept my mouth shut so tightly that I should have had trouble to put my pipe in.

I realized that I ought to have felt tired, for I hadn't slept for forty hours, except for the short shut-eye between the all-clear

109

and the moment my Chief started banging the front door; but I felt very vigorous and awake. I kept the boy Waterman walking by my side for miles, nattering at him like a woman for sheer vigor and awakeness. In the end he nearly dropped dead, and I wanted to send him down to his bunk for a snooze before the business started, when we heard a sound in the distance. A sound of heavy gunfire, like faraway thunder.

We listened to it for a while, then the boy Waterman said, "God, this is awful."

I had not noticed before that he was afraid, I had been too busy nattering; now I realized that during all the miles we had tramped side by side he had barely said a word. I said, "I wouldn't worry; we'll be all right."

He gave a little snigger in the darkness, touching in its failing bravery. "I don't quite see how we can be," he said, in a polite little voice, and he added, "frankly."

I said, "It's very simple: the moment I see that it would be suicide to get near that madman, I'll just turn round and go home."

He said, "Oh," in an undecided way, as if he was telling himself that he ought to believe it and couldn't.

I didn't believe it myself.

∽

When we got near the duck I saw it was pointless to try any evading tactics. From whatever angle we approached her, we would be seen as clearly as if it was daylight.

She was burning like a wildfire and listing heavily; we couldn't distinguish her clearly, for she was hidden in red clouds which must be steam. Behind the clouds yellow flames flickered, and although the gunfire thundered on without pause we saw no flashes, so she must be firing over the other side.

I decided to close in, for I assumed that she must be firing at something, and whatever it was, she lay between us and it. I warned the engine room that we were in for it, and whistled all hands. The boy Waterman said, "Well, good luck, Skipper," bravely. Now I could see his face in the sunrise of the distant fire he looked preposterously young; perhaps because he had just had a haircut, his ears looked twice the size.

110

I had no idea how to tackle the duck, whether to make fast afore or astern, for she was so hidden by steam and smoke that I couldn't even see which side was facing us. There was no wind; the smoke rose perpendicularly into the sky. If there had been wind I could have approached her under her own screen.

But the approach was not the most difficult part of the job. Even if I forgot about the U-boats and tackled this as if it was peacetime, I didn't quite see what we could do to save her. The fire seemed to be out of control; the moment we started towing the speed would fan the fire. I had to find out which end of the ship was least damaged and had most people on it; I would have to tow her from that end. The people marooned on the other would have to be written off, unless we made them jump and picked them up before we started to travel.

I was working all this out in my mind when I heard the boy Waterman say, "Periscope on starboard, sir." He said it quietly; only the fact that he called me "sir" betrayed how he felt. He pointed and I looked; I saw the periscope silhouetted clearly in the red path the flames made on the water. I dashed toward the engine-room telegraph, put my hand on the handle, but didn't ring it, for I realized there was nothing I could do. Either I must start backing away or carry on, steering clear of it. I pulled the handle on "Slow" and stared at the periscope. It was an unpleasant idea that the periscope must be staring at us too.

We proceeded slowly, and I never took my eyes off it. It seemed to be lying quite still, and it made no attempt at surfacing. One thing was certain: no U-boat would ever waste a torpedo on a tug; so long as it didn't surface to use its gun, we could breathe. As I stood staring at it, wondering why it didn't surface, I noticed something. It moved in an odd way. It could never move like that if it had a whole U-boat underneath it to keep it steady; it moved up and down, like a buoy.

I said to the boy Waterman, "Three starboard three," and he called the order through to the wheel. We swung slowly toward the periscope.

"You—you're heading for it?" he asked, politely.

I said, "Yes. It's not a periscope."

It took him some time to realize that I was right, then he asked, "What do you think it is? A mine?"

"Either that or a decoy."

"Decoy?"

"Yes," I said. "I think I begin to see it all now."

I didn't quite yet, but I was sure I was on to something. If the periscope was a decoy, it must have been sown for some purpose. The only purpose could be to create the impression that there were several U-boats around instead of only one. And the only reason why they should want to create that impression was that a periscope seen from a burning wreck would draw gunfire. If the thing we were now approaching was indeed a decoy, then the American must have been gunning his ammunition away at nothing.

We skimmed the thing so closely that there was no doubt left. It was a decoy all right, and a clumsily made one at that. I considered fishing it, but decided not to; they might have put a booby trap inside just for the hell of it. I saw it turn round in our wake after we passed, and pulled the telegraph on "Full ahead."

While we approached the duck the boy Waterman scanned the sea with his binoculars for other decoys; I just stared at the fire ahead, thinking. The more I thought of it, the more sure I became that I was right: only Hasenfratz could have sown the things. It was a typical lone wolf's ruse: only someone sent out inadequately armed on suicide expeditions would think of a thing like that.

Then I saw it all: Hasenfratz had been detailed to finish off the lame ducks left behind by the convoys just as we had been detailed to pick them up: all by himself, with a gun that was inferior to those the merchant ships carried. He must have felt as much at the wrong end of a shooting gallery as we did, and he had gone on protesting for months, writing petitions for a better gun, just as we had. The difference between us was that he had got his new gun first, but even so it evidently was not strong enough to compete with the artillery he was ordered to meet, so he had hit upon the idea of making the ducks bleed themselves white on a couple of decoys. The moment their guns fell silent he would move in for the kill; this American was what he must have been waiting for, for a long time: a fool, who would let himself be tricked into firing.

I knew now that it could not have been Hasenfratz who had torpedoed the ducks we lost the week before: they must have been bagged by some of his big brothers who still had a cigar to spend on their way home. All he had got to survive with was a bunch of untrained recruits, an inferior gun, and his wits. He and we were in exactly the same boat; if we hadn't been at war we might have been friends.

And then, suddenly, a preposterous thought came to me. I knew it was preposterous the moment I thought it, but I stood there considering it for a long time, for it seemed to explain the last mystery that remained. I had found explanations for everything, except for one undeniable fact: if Hasenfratz had really wanted to, he could have sunk all of us on our first operation. Van Dam had thought that his own cunning maneuvering had saved him; Dop had thought it was his ruse of making a tugboat sail; but I had always known in my heart that their explanations were nonsense. I had dodged Hasenfratz's gun often enough by now to realize that his shooting was exceptionally bad, even for an instructor; no one could tell me any longer that our ruse of backing away from him would not have been spotted by him the first time it happened. A man clever enough to think of using decoys to exhaust the enemy's ammunition could never have fallen for the clumsy device that both Van Dam and I had tried to sell to him at least twenty times. Hasenfratz had decided to let us go scot free.

It was a preposterous thought, and yet it must be true. Daamen and Frankendaal had not been sunk by gunfire. God knew what had happened to them, perhaps they had struck a mine or been bombed by a plane, but they had not been sunk by Hasenfratz.

But as I started circling round the duck to find out what was going on, I realized that this was going to be a situation in which neither Hasenfratz nor I had ever been before. Even if all I thought about him was right, I didn't see how we could get out of this in a friendly way. If I started towing the duck Hasenfratz had to move, whether he liked it or not; if only that silly Amer-

113

ican had read his instructions from envelope D, this situation would never have occurred.

I put myself in Hasenfratz's place. I assumed that I was the Captain of a U-boat, who just didn't like sinking defenseless tugboats, and had decided to do some gun practicing on them, taking care not to do any damage, and then to let them go. If I was Hasenfratz I would stand there worrying, while scanning the sea through my periscope, how the devil we could get out of this situation, just as I was doing on my bridge. Then I knew. Hasenfratz would let me make fast and start towing; when the duck's guns fell silent he would sink her, for that was his job. But he would let me go.

As we rounded the duck's stern we saw the flashes of her gun-fire. I ordered, "Hard starboard hard." The boy Waterman repeated the order to the wheel; then he asked, "Are we making fast?"

I answered, "Yes. Stand by with the line gun." He passed on the order to the bosun on the aftdeck. I made our siren howl: one long blast, which according to envelope D ought to make the duck hold her fire. Frantic people started waving on her poop, but her guns thundered on, crazily. I let the siren howl again; the boy Waterman said, quietly, "That ought to waken the dead."

I knew it would, but I knew also that it wouldn't make any difference to Hasenfratz. He had seen us long ago, and probably said to his second in command, "It's the *Zeeland* tonight." Perhaps he even knew my name as well as I knew his, and had foreseen my coming before I was there, for he must have worked out the schedule of our watches by now.

Then I remembered that this was Van Dam's watch and that he was dead. I was sure that Hasenfratz would be sorry if he heard that the stolid little Dutchman he knew so well had been killed in an air raid while singing at a Christmas concert. If we had had radio contact I would have told him; I thought of flashing the news to him with our Aldis lamp from the bridge, as soon as we caught sight of each other. I wondered where he was.

Wherever he was, he was well within the spray of my fountain
114

of love that night. But for Stella I should have known what would happen.

∽

We didn't see him until after we had made fast and started towing the duck. We towed for quite a way, while she went on firing; then her guns fell silent.

In the silence we heard the roaring of the fire behind us; it was louder than the roaring of our safety valve. It seemed incredible that men could have survived in that hell. Then the boy Waterman said, "There he is."

He surfaced over starboard, about three hundred yards away. I saw the conning tower open and the mannikins come out. I knew he would open fire on the duck, but I decided to play the game. I whistled "lifebelts on," and told the engine room through the blower that we were in for action. I saw the gun being uncovered and felt very sorry for the men on the duck. They had done everything they shouldn't have and so they deserved what they had coming to them, but all the same they had put up one hell of a fight. With a fire like that going on, I myself would have abandoned ship hours before, and taken to the boats before they were burned in the davits. Their very tenacity was foolish; it seemed a pity that they wouldn't live to read the long list of the things they had done wrong. Then I was blown clean off my feet and flung down the length of the bridge, while the world seemed to explode around me.

When I got to my feet again I still didn't believe it; then the second shell came and struck our funnel with a sickening sound of screaming iron. Hasenfratz wasn't aiming at the duck, he was aiming at us.

That was the moment I woke up. In one merciless flash of lightning I saw that the paradise I had lived in for the last weeks was a fool's. I didn't think this, I just knew it, all at once, within one split second, as if I had fallen into icy water. The shock made me act: it wasn't a reflex; it was a short circuit between my instinct for survival and my intelligence. I screamed, "Hard port hard!" ripped the whistle out of the blower, blew, and shouted, "Shut off the safety valve and come on deck in your

115

lifebelts! We're abandoning ship!" The ship swung around sharply; the third shell struck our mast. I whistled the bosun on the aftdeck, and shouted, "Stand by with the hatchets, ready to cut!" The boy Waterman lay on his knees behind the railing, moaning. I asked, "Are you wounded?" When he shook his head I kicked him, and shouted, "Hurry aft! When I call 'cut,' jump!" He scurried away, more terrified by my kick than by the shells. The fifth shell came whining at us and missed; I saw something move on the foredeck, whistled, and shouted, "All hands aft! Hurry!" Then I ran to the wheelhouse, pushed away the man at the wheel, said, "Stay outside and pass on the word when I shout 'cut'; after that, scram." The sixth shell came whining at us and struck something on starboard. The windows of the wheelhouse were blown in. After the racket had died down there was a silence, and I realized that our safety valve had been shut off. The ship started to tremble as the number of revolutions mounted. Within ten minutes the boilers might explode; we lay straining at the leash of our hawser with all our horses lashed into frenzy. Another shell passed very close and missed us. Then I saw Hasenfratz swing into view.

He was very near, his starboard side turned toward us. I righted the wheel and shouted, "Cut!" I heard the sailor outside pass on the command as a scream. I saw a flash spurt from Hasenfratz's gun, heard the whine of a shell soaring at us; then the ship seemed to jump. I was thrown backward against the wall and thought we had received another hit, but we hadn't. We were racing straight at Hasenfratz, at top speed.

I got hold of the wheel again and saw the mannikins scurry away from the gun and scramble into the tower. I thought, "Jesus Christ, the fool!" for I knew he couldn't make it. He ought to have sprinted ahead the moment he realized what I was up to; he had no time for diving, he must have no idea of the speed of my ship. When I felt that she would hold her course I left the wheel and ran outside. I felt in my pocket for Stella's little box. I closed my hand around it just before we struck.

We struck with a blow that sounded like an explosion. I was flung against the rail. What was left of funnel and mast came crashing down; I heard a rumbling noise below and knew it was

116

the boilers torn off their foundations. I knew the ship would blow up; I climbed over the rail and jumped.

When I struck the water I knew this was it. I seemed to go down a long way and had no breath. I felt a scorching heat, realized it was cold, and knew that even if the ship did not blow up and I floated clear of the sinking wrecks I could not survive, but would freeze to death.

I opened my hand and let the little box float away. My last thought was: I love you.

I died in peace.

Chapter VI

I WOKE UP IN A TUGBOAT'S CHARTROOM. IT TOOK ME A LONG TIME before I realized where I was. First I noticed that I was naked and that people were rubbing me; then I recognized Goatskin. I felt as if only one half of me was there, the other half was dead. I wanted to touch the side of my face that was dead, but Goatskin kept my hand away. I heard his voice, far away, "Leave that alone, we'll see to it in a minute."

I tried to speak, but it was difficult with one half of my face dead. I spoke out of the corner of my mouth. I said, "What . . ."

He said, "Take it easy, you're all right. You've only been in the water for ten minutes."

I wanted to ask him what the hell he was doing here; but all I could say was, "You?"

He said, "I was right behind you all the time. I couldn't let you tackle this setup alone, so I followed you."

I said, "Boys."

"All but three," he said. "Two stokers and your bosun. He looked at me the way Dop had looked at me sometimes. "Would you like anything? Some more brandy, cigarette?"

I said, "Duck?"

"Doing fine," he said. "I took over after your little show. We'll have her home and dry within three hours."

Then I remembered when Dop had looked at me like that.

117

It was just after we had met again. He had grabbed my shoulders, held me at arm's length, and said, "Fancy seeing you here! God, this is wonderful." There was another time he had looked like that, but I couldn't remember.

Goatskin lit a cigarette and held it out to me. "Here," he said. "Can you hold it yourself?"

I put out my hand, which didn't seem to belong to me. I took the cigarette and put it in the live corner of my mouth. I drew in the smoke and felt dizzy. I heard Goatskin say, "Hold it, boys; that'll do. Get a blanket." Then I heard steps and Goatskin's voice again, "And take these bottles to be refilled. Tell cook to make them good and hot." I heard a door open and a gush of sea and wind; then the door shut. I opened my eyes.

Goatskin sat looking at me. "I must say I take my hat off to you," he said. "I don't think I could have done it."

I wondered what he was talking about; then I remembered Hasenfratz. "Sunk?" I asked.

"Both of you," he said. "But his had all the birds inside. We looked for survivors as a matter of manners, but not one. He locked himself in his coffin good and proper."

I felt suddenly sick, and held out my cigarette, my eyes closed. He took it out of my hand; I closed my eyes tighter and for a moment I was nothing but sickness. Then I remembered the other time Dop had looked at me like that: just before he sailed for the last time, when he had whispered to me in the office, "We're going to be married!" Then I remembered Stella.

I had known it, the moment I realized that Hasenfratz wasn't aiming at the duck but at us, and that I would have to kill him to save my life. The moment had been so short that it hadn't done any harm; when I opened my hand to let the little box float away I still felt so close to her that I drowned in happiness. Now the harm happened, slowly. As I lay there on my back, my eyes closed, my body still numb, my thoughts were very clear. I felt no emotion, I just thought, with a cold logic.

Stella had foreseen what would happen; when we kissed she had known it was for the last time. It looked now as if she had been wrong for once, but she hadn't. Even though I was still alive, she had lost me forever; she could never love me any more

118

now I had joined the murderers. As I thought that, I saw Van Dam, his uniform torn, his face covered with blood, staring at me with his pale blue eyes, and it seemed as if I heard him say, "So they got you at last." I tried to chase him away; Goatskin's voice said, "Easy, easy," and I felt his hand on my shoulder. I heard the door opening and a mumbling of voices, then something hot was put under my feet and in my dead side, and something soft and warm was spread on top of me. I remembered how she had covered me with a blanket, and I felt a hollow despair. I was alone again, and would always be, from now on. It wasn't our common fear which had made her love us all as if we were one, it was our innocence. The blood she had seen on me when I pushed the cork into the bottle of wine, and that had made her scream with horror, hadn't been mine.

I wished Goatskin had never fished me. I wished I had never been forced to do what I had done. I wished the bloody American had had the sense to open envelope D. That last wish stuck. My thoughts from that moment onward concentrated on that wish. As I woke up more and more I hated the American with a growing hatred. It was he who had done all this to me. He had made me sail right into Hasenfratz's arms. He had made me scuttle my ship that had served me so faithfully. He had made me kill my bosun, one of the best men who ever sailed, and two stokers who had trusted me blindly. He had yelped with his wireless, squandered his ammunition, bungled the fire on his ship, and now he was being towed home to safety, a victorious hero. My hatred for him grew to such an extent that in the end I realized that I would not be able to face him. When I pictured him, strutting into the office, grinning, I felt like jumping at him and wringing his neck.

I was groggy as I got up, as if I had taken too many sleeping pills. I felt no pain, but I wasn't sure whether I should have if I hadn't been feeling so doped. I felt a dull ache, every time I thought of Stella; I avoided thinking of her, but it was difficult. The only thing stronger than she was my hatred for the American.

I was very calm and composed; I got up, moved about, put on some dry clothes Goatskin gave me; but all the time I was think-

119

ing how I would put my hands round the American's neck and tighten my grip and bang his head on the floor. I still knew, secretly, that it was all a reaction, that I was shell-shocked and couldn't be held responsible for what I thought and felt, but that secret knowledge vanished when I saw my face in the mirror. The right hand side was blue and swollen and covered with blood. I had turned into a monster. I could never let Stella see me like this. I had the face of a murderer.

I mumbled, "Christ! How did that happen?"

Goatskin, who seemed to be around all the time, said, "I don't know, it looks like flying glass to me. Don't you remember your windows being blown in, or something?"

I remembered. The sixth shell. It had blown in the windows of the wheelhouse. I didn't remember feeling anything at the time. I said, "The bastard."

Goatskin said, "Well, he's dead now."

I had meant the American.

∽

I got him on the pier, and it was his own fault. When he was brought on board by the British Navy launch I took care to be out of the chartroom before he came in. I went to see the survivors of my crew in the fo'c'sle and in the messroom. All had more or less recovered from lying in the icy water, only the boy Waterman looked bad; he had waited too long before he jumped and been dragged down by the sinking ships, deeper than was good for him. I asked him why the devil he hadn't jumped the moment the hawser was cut, as he had been ordered to do; he answered with a sick little voice, "I was waiting for you, Skipper." Instead of being moved I hated him for it, and said, "So if you kick the bucket it's my fault. Thank you very much."

On my way between the fo'c'sle and the messroom I glanced at the duck being taken over by the channel tugs. She was still burning, but the fire had been pushed back to her midships. I couldn't see what she looked like because it was three o'clock in the morning and pitch dark, but in the glow of what was left of the fire I saw that the superstructure on her poop was a shambles. Her funnel hung over the ruins of her bridge; underneath the bridge was a large ragged hole which looked like a shell wound.

When we moored I stopped Goatskin on his way to the bridge, and asked him to keep the American busy in the chartroom for a couple of minutes while I nipped across to the office to make my report. The moment he came in with the American I would leave. He asked, "Why, for God's sake?" I answered, "I just don't want to set eyes on the bastard, that's all," and hurried away.

The moment our stern touched the quay I jumped. When I came into the office I found Wadlow sitting behind his desk. He looked tired and his eyes were pale, as if he had a hangover. He said, "Well, that was a neat little job you did there." When I asked him how he knew, he answered that the duck had been giving a running commentary of the whole operation over her wireless.

I clenched my teeth, and said, "That's the reason why I'm not going to make a full report until you've put that bugger through the routine. If you don't mind I'll make myself scarce while he is here."

Wadlow said, "Why on earth . . ." but he didn't finish the sentence; the door banged open and in stumbled a giant in a dirty torn uniform, his captain's stripes dangling from his sleeve. It was impossible to make out his age, for his face was covered with soot and he had no eyebrows left; he brought with him a sickening stench of petrol. Goatskin was behind him, and looked as if he had been trying to hold him back. The giant roared, "Where is he? Where is the Goddam son-of-a-gun! I wanta thank him for saving my life!" His voice boomed like a hooter, he sounded shell-shocked too.

The sight of him made me see red. I knew that if I didn't get out fast, there would be accidents. I tried to slip past him toward the door, but he grabbed hold of my sleeve. "Are you the Captain?" he hollered. "Are you the Captain of that Goddam tug?" I snarled, "Let go of me, you big . . ." and tried to tear myself loose, but he swung out his other arm and put a black swollen paw under my nose palm upward. It was covered with

121

dirty open blisters. "Put it there, bud!" he bellowed. "Put it there, you Goddam son-of-bitch! Let me thank you for saving my life!" I got sick with rage at seeing that paw and hearing that voice, I shouted, "Let go, you moron!" and kicked his shin with all my might.

He gave an animal squeal of pain and surprise. His big mouth fell open until he looked like a child, struck in the face by its favorite playmate; but the kick had made him let go of me, and I ran out into the night. I ran in pitch darkness toward the distant dusk of the blacked out lanterns of the esplanade. I couldn't see a hand in front of my face, but I ran on, recklessly, because I heard a voice bellow behind me, "Hey, wait a minute! Hey, come here!" and galloping steps overtook me, as if I was being hunted by an elephant. I heard his breathing pump behind me, then I tripped over something and fell. He tripped over me, and crashed on the pier like a tree.

I lay there for a moment, dazed by the impact, then I was turned on my back and nearly suffocated by a stench of petrol. One of his paws held me down while the other groped for my hand; I struggled but he got hold of my fist and wrung it, shouting, "You Goddam fool! I want to thank you for saving my life!" I screamed, "Get off, you bastard! Get off!" kicking his enormous body with my knees, trying to get away; but he shouted, "I'll thank you if I've got to break your skull! Thank you! Thank you, you Goddam . . ." Then I heard him bark, and he was pulled off me.

I heard sounds of a violent struggle, as if many men were trying to rope a bull. Then the thin beam of a blacked-out torch shone in my face and a hand touched my shoulder. I wanted to fight again, although I felt very weak; then I heard a quiet Cockney voice say, "I'm sorry, sir; but you'd better come quietly."

I gave in and the hand pulled me to my feet. I felt very dizzy; he put his arm round my shoulders to steady me, and asked, "Are you hurt, sir?"

I said, "No; but for God's sake, keep that lunatic away."

He said, "Yes, sir. Very good, sir. Now would you be kind enough to come back to your headquarters with me, sir; a mere

122

formality, but I'm afraid I'll have to ask you to come quietly, sir." I said, "All right, all right; only don't let me set eyes on that maniac again or I'll wring his bloody neck."

He said, "Don't worry, sir, everything will be all right, sir. Take it easy, sir," and we started walking.

We seemed to walk for hours. I saw a faintly lighted doorway in the distance and knew we were going back to the office; it was incredible that I should have run all that distance in so short a time. My face hurt as we walked; I didn't feel any hatred any more, I felt nothing but the pain. The dead side seemed very cold; when I touched it with my hand it was wet. I decided that it must be blood, and the moment I thought so the pain seemed to get much worse, but when I entered the office I forgot it, for the hatred sprang up in me again.

The American was sitting in old Foghorn's chair; he looked horrible. His clothes, that had been torn before, were now ripped to rags. His chest was bare, and among the hair hung a silver dog tag on a chain. The moment he saw me he put out his hand, and tried to struggle to his feet; but Wadlow, who was standing behind him, held him down in his chair. He slumped back like a big doped animal; his eyes filmed over and he muttered, "What's the matter with you folks? All I want is just to shake hands."

Wadlow said, "All right, old chap, all right; we'll get round to that in a minute." He sounded maddeningly British. "Now may I ask what was the cause of this scuffle, please? I'm afraid that I'll have to get at least some notion of it, if you want me to keep you out of the care of the good sergeant here." With that he nodded at the M.P., who was standing uncomfortably at ease between us.

"A mere formality, sir," said the M.P., "you'll understand that."

I felt suddenly cold and very tired. I looked at the clock over the radio desk, and tried to work out how long I hadn't slept, but I gave up when I got to sixty-eight hours. "I'll tell you what was the cause," I said. "He made me kill thirty-three people, and scuttle the best ship I ever had, and . . ." I wanted to add, "And lose the only woman I have ever loved in my life," but I noticed

123

them staring at me in time, so I said, "And hurt me," instead. It sounded very plaintive and feeble, and I began to hate the American again for having made me say such a childish thing. But the hatred was listless and weary; it sank back into tiredness again. I started going through the list of all the things the big clumsy fool had done wrong, but before I had even got to his gunning of decoys until his ammunition had been exhausted, Goatskin said, "He never opened envelope D, because his chartroom was shot away in the first attack. So he couldn't help that."

I said, "He could have used his ears," knowing it was silly while I said it, for I remembered clearly how the W.O. had told me that the duck's receiver wasn't working before I set out. Goatskin told me so, and there was a lot more talk by everybody that I didn't listen to. I sat looking at the American, slumped in his chair; and after a while he began looking at me too. He was young to be a captain of a tanker, he couldn't be much older than I was. He looked at me with sad, hurt eyes and I began to feel sorry for him. Then Wadlow said, "All right, now shake hands, you two. What the whole thing amounts to is that both of you are just dog tired after doing a splendid job; so now shake hands and go to bed."

I got up after a moment's hesitation, because somebody nudged me into it. It must have been Goatskin, who was standing behind me all the time. I went toward the American with a feeling as if I was walking on thin ice, and held out my hand. He lifted his paw with difficulty, as if it weighed a ton, and grabbed mine. We shook hands, and his eyes brimmed over. "Let me show you the people who'll never forget what you did to-night," he said; then he pulled out a wallet from the ruins of his coat and took two snapshots out of it. They had got stuck face to face, probably with the heat. He tried to pull them apart, and when he had done so all he had got to show was two mutilated pictures with a raw white patch in the center, where he had torn the film off. I saw a little naked leg on one, probably a baby's; then he let the things fall out of his hands, said, "Goddam this war. Goddam it," and leaned with his elbows on the desk, his face in his hands.

124

I suddenly had a feeling of a great difference in age between us, as I realized that his war was only three weeks old.

တ

When we stood in the darkness again, Goatskin said, "O.K., now let me take you to the flat. I have given you your keys and things, haven't I?"

It was the moment that I had known would come all the time, but I had managed to keep my thoughts away from it. Perhaps I had started the fight with the American only to postpone this moment. Now I couldn't evade it any longer. I felt tired and sick; I seemed to move in a cold feelingless clarity. I didn't feel any pain any more, nor hatred. I just knew I should never set eyes on her again.

I said, "No, I'm not going back to the flat. I want you to go there and tell her that I won't come back any more."

Goatskin said, "Don't be silly. You're just . . ."

I said, "Never mind about me. I want you to go to the flat now, and tell her that I won't come back any more. I don't even think that you'll need tell her anything. The moment she sees you after you've opened that door, she'll know."

"Jesus Christ!" said Goatskin. "You're mad."

I said, "I'll give you the key," and started fumbling in my pockets.

"But where are you going to sleep?" he asked. "You can't go back to the hotel, your bunk has been taken by someone else."

"I'll take Waterman's bunk," I said, "or Van Dam's. There'll be plenty of room tonight."

"You're crazy," said Goatskin. "And you ought to see a doctor, you may have glass splinters in your face."

I said, "Never mind my face. Here is the key, and do as I told you."

He sighed when I caught his hand and put the key in it. "O.K.," he said, "now let me take you to the hotel. You won't be able to stand on your feet much longer."

I said, "Oh, I feel fine," but I knew he was right.

When we got to the hotel I said, "All right, now you run along and do as I told you." But he said, "No, let me take you to my bunk first. When I come back I'll take any other that may be going, but I want to see you put up first. I'll take you to a doctor first thing in the morning."

I said, "All right," and he helped me through the swing doors. When we entered the hall the old porter rose from his grave behind the counter with the glass with his dentures on it. Goatskin led me to the stairs without taking any notice of him; the old man called, "Hey, hey, where are you going? That gentleman doesn't live in the hotel!"

Goatskin said, "I'm taking him to my bunk. He's wounded."

"That's got nothing to do with me," the old man said, "we are full up, we've got no room for any new ones."

"He isn't a new one," said Goatskin, "he was living here up to three weeks ago."

The old man peered at me, but no look of recognition changed his face. "Don't try to pull that one on me," he said. "People have tried that one before, but they've always been sorry after. Show me his billeting papers."

Goatskin got angry. "Oh, shut up!" he said. "Can't you see he's nearly dropping? His papers must still be in your files. I'll sort them out for you when I come down."

The porter went on calling after us as Goatskin took me up the stairs. He called that he would tell Miss Headland, that we would be sorry for using bad language at him, that he had served in this hotel for forty years but never known such brutes and foul-mouthed bastards as this lot. He was still shouting when we got to the first floor; the last I heard was, "Bloody foreigners."

Goatskin's room was exactly like the one I had slept in before. It had three tiers of three berths each, a cracked wash basin in the corner, a chair heaped with clothes in the center, and drawings on the walls and the ceiling. In every bunk but one lay a sleeper, wheezing and snoring. Goatskin shook one of them by the shoulder, and said, "I've got someone here who is wounded and needs sleep. If the boys start quacking, tell them to shut up. I'll be back later with a doctor." The sleeper grunted. "My second engineer," said Goatskin, "he's all right; if anybody starts making a racket, call him. His name is Henk."

126

He wanted to help me undress, but I said, "I can manage. Now do as I told you."

He looked at me for a second, the way he had looked at the bottom of the pier after Dop's death. He asked, "Are you sure that's the way you want it?"

I said, "Yes."

Then he said, "I can't blame you," and turned away.

He shut the door behind him, and left me staring at it. I had not remembered it before: he hated Stella's guts. I had seen how he would look at her when she came out of the bedroom with her chalk white face and her bright red mouth. He would not tell her that I was still alive, though dead tired and half mad after killing thirty-three people and sinking two ships. He would tell her nothing, he would just look at her with his cold blue eyes and see her suffer without blinking. He wouldn't believe she cared two hoots whether I was dead or alive, he would eat his beans on toast and sip his coffee and if he felt like it go to bed with her this very night and take her as he would take a tart.

The moment I realized what he was up to I knew I had to stop him at any cost; never mind if it meant that I should have to tell her myself that I would never come back any more, I could not let him do this to her. It wasn't her fault that all of us had been killed one after the other; she had been good to us, she had loved us, truly and sincerely, even if we were all the same man to her; she was a sad, dazed creature from a faraway island with nobody in the whole world to care about her, except a ghost in the desert and me.

The moment I realized what I had done I went after him. I ran down the corridor, stumbled down the stairs, but by the time I got back to the hall I was so dizzy that I had to sit down. I groped my way to one of the chairs and lowered myself into it, cautiously; when I leaned back, I felt very sick. I wanted to get up again, instantly, and run to Stella, but I couldn't. The hall seemed to contract and to expand round me; I saw the counter and the glass with the dentures swim in a faint, eerie light, as if they were reflected in rippling water. The porter's reflection rose from behind the counter and he had something in his hand. "Want a drink, Captain?" he asked. "Canteen price." I remem-

127

bered how I had been sitting here the night before I went to the flat, how I had to get drunk first before I could summon the courage to face her. I had a ghostly feeling, as if this was the same night and I should have to go through it all again, knowing what would happen. Perhaps the whole thing was a nightmare, perhaps I had never got up after finishing that bottle of hooch, but been sitting here all the time, drunk, dreaming.

I knew it wasn't true, and yet I couldn't convince myself that it wasn't. The dead side of my face was throbbing. I daren't move for fear of vomiting. I was drunker with exhaustion than I had been with hooch that other night. But the thought of what Goatskin would do to her if I didn't prevent him horrified me so that I staggered back to my feet and began to grope my way to the swing doors.

When I lurched out into the night the cold air gave me a short illusion of waking up and feeling strong enough to make it. I steered my way from lantern to lantern, stumbling over lumps of masonry and nearly falling several times. But I managed to remain on my feet, for I knew that if I should fall I would not be able to get up again unless someone helped me and there seemed to be nobody about. A distant hooter boomed in the harbor, and somewhere far away a steam winch was hammering, they were the only sounds of human life in the night.

I had to wait at a lamppost to regain my breath and my strength; my eyes blurred, it seemed as if it was snowing. I lifted up my face to feel if it was true, but it wasn't, my face stayed hot and dry. I staggered on drunkenly; I couldn't think any more, it seemed as if I had forgotten all the words, the only word I could remember was her name. I started whispering, "Stella, Stella, Stella," and that helped me to get to the entrance of Seaview. When I reached the hall, I leaned against the wall, and looked up the first flight of stairs. I could never manage all those flights; the first one alone looked quite impossible, and there were ten of them. Then I took the duplicate key from my pocket, for that gave me the illusion that I was nearly there, and started to climb the stairs.

I don't know how long it took me to get to the top floor. I started to whisper her name again half way up; without that I would not have made it. When at last I pulled myself up at the doorpost I hesitated and listened, but I heard nothing except my own breath. Then I stuck the key in the lock, turned it, and pushed the door open, holding on to the post with my other hand.

I saw Goatskin sitting at the table, a plate in front of him. I saw her, a white death mask with a clown's mouth painted on it, turn round in front of the stove, a plate in her hand. She stared at me for a second with such horror in her eyes that I knew all was lost. Then she dropped the plate and screamed.

It was the most terrible scream I ever heard a living being give; then she seemed to crumple up in front of my eyes. Her face sagged and wrinkled, in one second's time she aged twenty years and turned into an ugly, middle-aged prostitute. Then she crashed into a chair and fell headlong across the table, screaming, "Go away! Go away!"

I turned round and fled. I fell down the stairs, stumbled out of the house, ran into the narrow street round the corner, fleeing from what I had seen happen before my eyes, from what I had done to her. By sending Goatskin and then coming back, I had turned her into a whore; for she had never seen two of us together.

∽

I ended up on Memorial Hill. I wandered among the ruins of the benches in the straggling grass and wanted to sit down several times, but I heard lovers giggling and whispering around me. I climbed to the top, leaned on the parapet, and saw dawn breaking over the notice "Carpet Beating Strictly Forbidden." I was beyond being tired or ill; it was as if my body lay on the map of Africa in front of the door with the inverted "2," and the thing that wandered among the lovers and stood looking at the daybreak was my ghost.

It was quite light when Goatskin found me. I had seen the silhouette of another lonely walker wandering on the hill as the daylight grew, but I had avoided him. When he found me I understood that it had been Goatskin.

He asked, "Where have you been?" and when I answered,

"Here," he said, "But I've been here myself for hours, looking for you all the time!" I asked, "What's happened to her?" and he answered, "How should I know? I followed you the moment you ran away. Jesus Christ! Do you think I could stay there after the scream she gave when she saw you? I've never heard anything so terrifying in my life."

The moment I realized that he had left her alone, I started running back to the flat. I don't know how I managed it, I just didn't feel my body any more. I started to run because I suddenly had a horrible vision. I knew she had committed suicide.

Goatskin tried to hold me back at first, running by my side, pulling at my arms to stop me, shouting, "Jesus Christ! Where are you going?" He gave up in the end, and ran with me all the way, panting, muttering, "Jesus Christ!" and "Doctor; I must get a doctor!" It was the first time I had seen him lose his self-control; he ran beside me like a terrified boy.

When we got to the house I jumped up the stairs two steps at a time. We passed the old janitor on one of the landings, a broom in his hands. I pushed him out of my way; he stumbled against the wall, calling, "Captain! Captain!" after me.

The door of the flat stood open. The kitchen was empty, the light still burning, Goatskin's plate still on the table, the mess of the plate she had dropped on the floor.

The bedroom was empty too; the bed hadn't been slept in, the wardrobe stood open, the portrait on top of it was gone.

She wasn't in the bathroom either; when I opened the medicine cupboard I saw that her things had gone.

Then I heard voices in the kitchen, and Goatskin came in, saying, "She has gone to the station. The old man says she asked him to get her a taxi half an hour ago, he carried her bags."

I ran out of the flat and started down the stairs again. Goatskin followed me, shouting, "For Christ's sake! Where are you going this time?"

I didn't answer, I ran out of the house with him at my heels. We ran all the way to the station. When we got there, I barged into the transport office and asked if they had written out a ticket for a girl with blue eyes and long fair hair. The transport

130

officer said, "What do you think we are doing here? Writing out tickets for blondes?"

Goatskin started to explain that I was mad, that I had been wounded in action, that I had rammed a U-boat, had been fished unconscious out of the sea, that I hadn't slept for eighty hours, that my girl had run away; before he had finished going through the list, I was out of the office, running toward the civilian ticket windows.

Only one of them was open, and there was a queue in front of it. I pushed the first man aside; he started protesting, but he shut up when he saw my face. So did the man behind the window. I asked him if he had sold a ticket to a girl with blue eyes and long fair hair; she might have gone back to the Hebrides. He looked at me as if I frightened him, and said, "I sold a ticket to Glasgow to a young lady who asked for one for the Hebrides; I told her I couldn't give her one direct."

I asked, "What time? What platform?" He answered, "The seven-fifteen, platform five."

Goatskin had caught up with me again, and started pulling my sleeve, shouting something, but I didn't listen. I broke away and ran toward platform five. A train stood waiting at the dead end, its big red taillight still burning. The platform was full of steam and the shadows of people; over the steam floated a clock, it was ten past seven.

I was stopped at the barrier by a ticket collector and an M.P. The ticket collector was ready to let me through, but the M.P. was not. He wanted to see my pass. Goatskin caught up with me; he had the transport officer with him. Both of them started talking; I leaned on the barrier, exhausted, the station reeled round me. In that sickening whirl I heard Goatskin's voice. It said, "What in God's name do you want to see her for? Don't you think she's had enough?"

I said, "I want to see if she's all right."

"Jesus Christ!" said Goatskin, with such rage in his voice that I realized he too was cracking up. "You know now that she's all right! She's bought a ticket, she's going home! If you show your crazy mug once more, she'll go to pieces all over again! I know she's a tart; but have a heart, will you!"

131

I said, "I want to see if she's all right."

Then I heard a voice say, "I'll go and look for you. I'll go through the train, find her, and see how she is. You men look after the Captain in the meantime, he's folding up."

I felt hands grip me under the arms and put me back on my feet. I hadn't noticed that I had started sagging. I opened my eyes and saw the transport officer go through the gate. I heard Goatskin say, "Blue eyes, long hair, blonde, you can't miss her." A porter said, "I know where the lady is, sir. Third class, car number five; I carried her luggage." I saw the transport officer walk away with the porter, and called, "See what she is doing! See if she is all right!" Then they vanished among the shadows in the steam.

I hung over the barrier, supported by the hands under my arms. They seemed to stay away for a long time; I knew something had happened. I felt very weary, very weak, and stared at the red taillight in the steam. It looked like a sun rising, a round red disc in the clouds. I concentrated on that light, for I didn't want to think of what I knew had happened. She was dead, soon I would see them coming out of the steam, carrying a stretcher. I heard voices behind me; one of the hands under my arms was taken away, someone put his arm round my shoulder; I looked up and saw it was Goatskin.

Then the transport officer came back, alone. I wanted him to tell me, instantly, but he passed through the gate first. The ticket collector saluted and he saluted back. Then he came toward me, and the other man who had supported me took his hand away and stepped back. The transport officer took his place and put his hand on my shoulder. He had a little mustache and green eyes. He said, "I have seen her and she's perfectly all right. She's sitting in a corner seat, asleep, with a writing pad on her lap. She must have dozed off after having started her letter. She looked tired, but all right."

I asked, "Letter?" and he said, "Yes. I even took the trouble to take a close look at it. It said: 'Dear Alan, No special news this week.' That was how far she got. Now are you satisfied?"

I said, "Yes."

They wanted to take me away then, but I said I'd like to see

132

the train leave. People talked round me, and I heard the word "Ambulance." Then a whistle sounded and the train left. I saw its red taillight draw away, and vanish in the steam. Then I broke down; the last I heard was Goatskin's voice, saying, "Don't worry, you'll be all right."

The boy Waterman died that night.

Part II PEACE

Chapter VII

WHEN I CAME OUT OF HOSPITAL, SOME TWO MONTHS LATER, THINGS had changed. The Americans had entered the war good and proper, and after their first conyoys made bad crossings they started to deal with the U-boats good and proper. By the time I came back to it, OTWA had become a nice, regular service in which people took baths, cleaned their nails, and went on leave with little suitcases.

I had a hard time picking up, but Goatskin was a help. On his visits to the hospital he looked flashier every fortnight and he turned out to be quite a conversationalist; his talk was mainly about London and how his feet never touched the ground from the moment he came out of Paddington Station until he staggered back into it. He grew a little mustache, collected photographs with "Love and Kisses" written on the back with lipstick, and locks of hair that he pasted in a diary. He said I'd be a different man once he had shown me round the town and introduced me to some of his correspondents. But when I came out, I had hardly adjusted my eyes to the sunlight before I was called to H.Q. and commissioned to the Arctic with the *Vlieland*; we were to sail as a rescue ship with the convoys to Murmansk. I told them there must be a mistake, for the *Vlieland* was commanded by Goatskin. There was no mistake, they said; his had been a temporary promotion, he would sail with me as my mate.

If it had happened to me, I would have been rather relieved; but I knew he would not take it that way. He liked being a captain. At first I thought I'd let him get the news from H.Q. but he would realize I had known all along and not dared to tell him.

So I told him myself in the end, over a glass of Coca-Cola in the Social Center. The loud-speakers blared, the short-skirted girls were flung about by jitterbugging Americans, who made the place unsafe to sit in as they kicked like kangaroos. Goatskin was happy, his captain's stripes made him look at the girls with confidence, almost boredom. Then I told him.

He never looked away from the girls, but he remained silent for a long time. Then he said, "Well, that's how it is, I guess."

I said, "I'm sorry."

"To have me as your mate?"

"No."

"That's all right then. When do we sail?"

"Tomorrow at sunrise. Destination Greenock."

"That's what I have against this war," he said, "the Goddam waste of it." Then he hailed a waitress, and we had another bottle of Coca-Cola.

When we sailed the next morning he was wearing his goatskin again, and he had shaved off his little mustache. We would have to grow beards in the Arctic, he said, and he liked the hair to grow evenly all over.

After a day or two it was difficult to believe that things had ever been different, Westport seemed far away. I liked sailing with him better than with the boy Waterman; he was a good mate, quiet, competent, and as brave as they come. We had a hard time with the convoys, but so had a lot of people. Once or twice I thought I'd crack up; so did he, I suppose. The war was ugly up there, the cold made things worse. I often thought of Van Dam and his epidemic of madness. We were lunatics, murdering one another on the brink of nothing, the edge of the world. We only mentioned Stella once, by mistake.

In March, '44, we were directed to London, for orders. This was surprising, as we hadn't been anywhere near London all during the war. Everybody said that this was going to be the Invasion. The Invasion had been in the air for years, and become a matter of faith, like personal survival after death. Either you believed in the invasion, or you didn't; it depended on your religious nature. The Russians, for instance, didn't believe in it,

138

and the people who escaped from occupied Europe did. We neither did nor didn't; we were intellectuals.

It was Goatskin who suggested that we should take up chess. We had to take up something, after we had been lying in Shadwell Basin for a fortnight and it began to dawn on us that we might be lying there for a very long time indeed. The fortnight had been exciting; all the ocean-going tugboats we knew were concentrated in Shadwell Basin, there was a prison ship that gave cocktail parties, and in the West India Dock Road was a Ceylonese restaurant called "The Light of Asia," where curried chicken cost two shillings.

The Light of Asia had become the daily meeting place for the tugboat captains. We were nine in all, five old ones and four young ones, all that was left of our fleet of thirty-two ocean-going tugboats when the war started. Of those thirty-two, six ships had had old captains, the rest youngsters. It was alarming to realize, four years later, that five of the six old captains were still alive and that the sixth had been killed in an air raid ashore. We looked for an explanation of this; we tried to define the magical reason for the survival of the old captains. The reason must be magical, for all five of them were extraordinarily stupid. They were superstitious, bald and fat, with very short sleeves and thick hairy pulses. Their conversation in The Light of Asia was bewildering to hear. "Jews," one of them would say, "dangerous people, Jews. Jewesses are all right, but Jews . . ." Negroes were dangerous too. Old Captain Bakker of the *Texel* told how he had an affair with a Negro woman in Central Africa, who had so terrified him with her size and the blackness of her eyes, that he had nightmares of her for years after. "Perhaps my age had something to do with it," he concluded. "I was thirteen."

The old captains fitted snugly into the atmosphere of The Light of Asia; we did not. We felt ill at ease with the proprietor, a fierce little Ceylonese who was violently anti-British and had the German radio blaring all day as a demonstration. It took us some time to find out that he obviously didn't speak any German himself, for he was tuned in on the German broadcast of the B.B.C. The old captains felt perfectly at home; we had to take up something to defend ourselves. Goatskin thought of chess.

139

He bought a chessboard and a box of chessmen and we settled down one night in the messroom with the game between us. He shook the pawns in his hands; I chose a fist, and opened the game with white. It was the beginning of a long slow disease, that ended in murderous lunacy. I had never been very good at games because I didn't really care whether I won or not. In Shadwell Basin, during those long nights of March, April, and May, '44, I began to care terribly. I don't know what got into us, but to win a game of chess became a matter of life and death; as we played an average of fifteen games a day we became very tense. I had sailed with Goatskin for almost a year and we had become friends, but in Shadwell Basin we became enemies again. Every time he won a game I felt like breaking his skull; every time I won he looked at me with murder in his eyes. While we had still been friends I had hardly been conscious of his presence; the moment we took up chess I could never forget that he was there. Wherever I went, on ship or ashore, I felt irksome, looking around to see where he was, and he was nearly always there, as he had been for the last year, only I had never noticed it. On my way to The Light of Asia, hearing steps behind me, I would look round, say through clenched teeth, "Can't you go somewhere else?" and he would answer, "Since when do you own this street?" We would march on toward The Light of Asia, our jaws set, our fists in our pockets, to say at the door, "After you," and, "No, no, after you," and when he went in first I felt like kicking him down the stairs. In the cellar we would find the five old captains, the curried chicken, the anti-British Ceylonese and the German news of the B.B.C. We would sit down at the billiard table, which during the daytime was covered with an oilcloth and served as a communal dining table. The old captains would look at us with their fishlike stare and say at random, "Don't you ever have your tonsils out, for if you drink gin later it may give you heart failure." Goatskin would sit down at the far corner of the table and smile at me and I could taste the hatred on my lips as I licked them. I suppose it was the reaction to the Northeast Passage.

The night before D-day, Goatskin and I played seven games of chess. It worked against the fear we felt; by the end of the seventh game I didn't care any more whether I lived or died, if only I could wring that bastard's neck. Then, at midnight, the news came that there would be no D-day. Operations were postponed because of the gales. It was a pity, because now we got afraid. The second night even our games of chess didn't work. When we finally sailed, we felt awful; I don't think any of us had ever been more afraid in his life. We were ordered to tow the Mulberry harbors to the beaches of Normandy, and we were sure that none of the sections would ever get there.

It turned out to be a walkover. The Germans hardly put up any resistance at all. The sea was more dangerous than they were, for there was a strong wind blowing. The war seemed to be in the bag.

The invasion of the South of France, a few months later, was different. It was much less spectacular, but there the Germans took a heavy toll. It was very hot, the sea was oily, and most of us were suffering from sunburn because we had stripped to the waist, and realized too late how fierce the sun was. We had gone in with the idea that it would be a walkover once more, but when we saw the Liberty ships go down around us one after the other, under the hellishly accurate artillery fire from the mountains, we got panicky. We had been lying in the mothballs for too long. Those months in Shadwell Basin and the peaceful ferrying of lighters and barges across the Channel after D-day, with not an enemy plane or a U-boat in sight, had made us slide back into peacetime. The war wasn't in the bag at all.

Around three o'clock in the afternoon our ship got a direct hit that blew out the engine room, took half of the bridge away and left us a wreck without a funnel, full of howling wounded. Goatskin and the cook were the only ones who came off without a scratch. I got shrapnel in both legs, and screamed like a rabbit. It wasn't so much the pain that made me scream, as the fear that my legs would have to be amputated. We got assistance, were put on stretchers, put on board a landing craft, and taken ashore. Goatskin stayed with us all the time. The Chief Engineer was badly wounded, so was Sparks; the second engineer was dead. Of the crew, only the new bosun and two sailors were left. They went with us in the ambulance to a small hospital among the palm trees.

141

We were put down, all our stretchers in a row, in an empty room with pink walls, waiting for a doctor. Goatskin had taken the emergency kit with him when we left the ship, and he was messing around with bandages and splints when a girl came in. She was about twenty, had dark hair and dark eyes. She had a nurse's dress on that didn't fit the hips and a cap that had slid off her head and now dangled on her back. We were so sick and frightened and hot that we didn't react to the girl at all. We were just waiting for someone to help us and tell us we would be all right. She had a thermometer in her hand and looked at us very bravely. We must have been quite a sight.

"Do you speak English?" she asked, with a very British accent. Goatskin answered for us, "Yes." We just moaned. "I've come to take your temperatures," she said. Then she went over to the bosun, who was lying in the corner next to me, and said, "Take this in your mouth, please." The bosun obeyed without opening his eyes. He went on moaning with the thing in his mouth.

Goatskin handed her the thermometer from our emergency kit. "This any use to you?" he asked. She said, "Oh, thank you," took the thermometer, and came toward me. "Open your mouth please," she said.

I answered, "Certainly not," for the Dutch take their temperatures in a different way from the English. I had taken many temperatures myself with the thing, whenever a member of my crew imagined he had something the matter with him, so I knew where it had been.

"But you must," she said. "The doctor told me to take your temperatures and he may be here any minute. Please do as I tell you."

I said, "I'm very sorry, but I won't. And that's final."

She began to get flustered; it was obvious that it was her first day as a nurse, and the blood and the wounded began to get her down. I saw her eyes fill with tears and she suppressed a trembling of her lips before she said, "Please, please, open your mouth, for *me* . . ."

I said to Goatskin, "Explain to the young lady why I can't," but he answered, "No, thank you, you tell her yourself."

The moaning had stopped around me. Despite their pain the

142

others were listening. She looked at me with pleading eyes. Then there were steps in the corridor and she looked nervously over her shoulder. "There's the doctor," she said. "Please help me, please take it in your mouth; please—it means so much to me."

I don't know what it was, in her face or in her eyes, but I thought, "If I am going to have my legs cut off, this can't do me much harm." So I took the thing in my mouth. And then the others began to laugh. They were suffering like hell, and terrified and feverish, but the sight of me with that thermometer in my mouth just made them bellow with laughter. When the doctor came in, he looked with his eyebrows raised at the six wounded men on stretchers, splitting their sides. Then he looked at the nurse and said, "Well, Miss Simmons, is this your work?" She stammered, "No, sir, yes, sir," and fled, stumbling over the threshold.

Miss Simmons made my day. She and the information the doctor gave me that he would not have to cut my legs off. There was nothing the matter with them, only a few bits of shrapnel in the bone. We were all very cheered by him. He seemed supremely confident that none of us had anything the matter with him worse than a cold in the nose. One of the sailors died at daybreak.

The next day they operated on my leg. When I woke up, feeling very sick, a girl was standing by my bedside in a state of great emotion. "I'm so awfully sorry," she said. "What can I do to make good? I'm sure you'll never forgive me." A horrible thought reeled through my mind: she was the operating nurse who had cut something off by mistake.

She was Miss Simmons. Somebody had put her wise to the way in which the Dutch took their temperatures. I tried to soothe her but my speech was not very intelligible. Seen on waking up from an ether sleep, she looked very pretty. A vision of beauty and girlish purity. Waking up all the time, I wondered why I hadn't recognized her straight away. Then I realized it was her cap. She wore it on her head today; it made her look like a member of the Dagenham Girl Pipers' Band. She had serious, soft eyes. She seemed to be worried about something. I asked her

143

what it was, and she started to tell me; I must have fallen asleep again, for when I woke up once more she was gone. In her place stood Goatskin, grinning from ear to ear. When he saw me open my eyes, he showed me something: a chessboard. I must have made a noise, for suddenly the room was full of nurses and orderlies and he was taken out backward. I fell asleep for the third time.

When I woke up again, and this time definitely, it was morning. I saw the same room with the pink walls but now there were beds in it. In the one next to me, Sparks was sitting up. His arms were bandaged across his chest in an oriental praying position and he was having his teeth brushed by Miss Simmons. In the bed furthest away, the huge bulk of the Chief lay covered with a sheet. For an awful moment I thought he had died overnight; then I heard his deep rumbling voice give commentaries on Miss Simmons, taking advantage of the fact that Sparks couldn't answer with that brush in his mouth. He was talking in Dutch and I told him to shut up. Miss Simmons was still wearing her Dagenham Girl Pipers' cap, but it was sitting on her forehead now. It seemed to go through phases, like the moon.

After she had finished with Sparks, she came to me. She had a brand-new toothbrush in her hand and a tube of Dr. Pierre's dental cream. When she told me to open my mouth I grinned at her and she began to tell me again how sorry she was. She had a very pretty blush and dimples in her cheeks; I wanted to ask her some questions but she put the brush in my mouth and started scrubbing away like a bosun. She was doing a very thorough job on my gums when the doctor appeared in the doorway and cried, "Miss Simmons! What in the name of Trinity are you doing?" Her cap, by then, was sitting on her eyebrows. The doctor looked exasperated when he pointed out to her that there was no need to brush the teeth of patients who could use their hands. Or had she assumed by any chance that I was in the habit of brushing my teeth with my feet? I felt sorry for the poor girl when she hurried out, leaving me with a mouth full of soapsuds and taking the glass with her. The doctor said, "If any of you gentlemen have the intention of marrying her, please be quick about it." The

144

Chief answered with a colossal, lewd laugh. Whatever was the matter with him, he would live.

Goatskin came back that afternoon, looking shifty. The doctor was around, feeling pulses; while he was there Goatskin told us that the ship had remained afloat and been towed into the harbor but probably would never sail again; he himself was hanging around, waiting for orders. The moment the doctor had turned his back he put his hand in his inside pocket, like a man selling dirty postcards, and brought out a miniature game of chess. I remembered vaguely that he had been thrown out the day before, and, like a sportsman, I had a game with him. I liked it because I won; he went on looking over his shoulder to see whether anyone was coming in. During the second game, Miss Simmons surprised us, her cap on the back of her head once more, carrying a tray with four glasses of milk. Goatskin covered the game with his hand but she had seen it. She was very stern about it, but only to him, not to me. He knew the doctor had forbidden him to excite the wounded, he ought to be ashamed of himself. He tried to look dignified as he put the game back in his pocket. I felt pleased, I had the better of him at last. A week later he was called away, back to London. I didn't set eyes on him again until a year later.

During that year peace had come and I had started to walk again. First on crutches, then with a stick, aided by Miss Simmons. We shuffled around on the clean gravel among the palm trees and sat on a bench looking at the Mediterranean. She told me that she had been in the South of France all during the war and that nobody had ever found out that she was English and so she had remained free. She had joined the Resistance and taken a secret training as a nurse; on the day of the Invasion she had volunteered and we had been her first patients. Before us she had rehearsed with farmers of the Resistance, who had held themselves limp to imitate wounded. She was a nice girl, very English, and I liked her a great deal. Sitting on the bench, playing with the gravel with my stick, listening to her talking, I had my first taste of peace.

It was the only taste, for once I got on my way home to Holland with Sparks, the Chief and the bosun, we soon found out

145

that there was something the matter with the peace. Nothing very serious yet, only nobody seemed quite to believe in it. We went home via Paris and Brussels. The last bit was done in a truck. We said good-by in Amsterdam, and promised to look each other up within a week's time. None of us did.

I found my job with the harbor police in Amsterdam was taken and I was glad of it. I applied for a vacancy on a tugboat but there were very few ships left; all I got offered was a trip to the Dutch East Indies as a mate. I took it and sailed with old Captain Bakker on the *Texel*.

I hadn't seen Captain Bakker again since Shadwell Basin and he didn't remember seeing me. When he asked me for my record and I said, "We lunched together for three months in The Light of Asia," his face changed and he answered, "Oh, were you one of those?" That was all.

The trip was a lesson to me in many ways. I found out, to start with, that if you have once commanded a ship you cannot sail as a second again. Perhaps I also found out the magical reason for the survival of the old captains: they took it easy. Nothing excited old Bakker or got him out of his slow, fishlike train of thought. He spent most of his time in his bunk, half sitting up, playing patience on his thighs with a very small set of cards. At first I thought this meant that he would leave the command of the ship virtually to me, but nothing of the kind. His bunk was right underneath the bridge and every half hour or so he would bellow, "Mate!" through his porthole. I would rush down the bridge steps, break my neck on the threshold of the chartroom, open the communicating door and ask, panting, "Yes, sir?" He would turn over a couple more cards on his thighs, without looking up, and say, "Nothing." I would go back to the bridge, my hands twitching.

It took me a week to realize that he yelled, "Mate!" as soon as he heard my steps stop pacing overhead. I don't know what he thought, perhaps that I had gone to sleep or something. In his eyes, an officer of the watch ought to keep walking the bridge all the time, which was steep for a man who never moved a foot. He took his watches sitting in a deck chair, playing patience on his thighs, outside if there was no wind, in the wheelhouse if there

146

was. I hardly ever saw him stand up. On entering the harbor, he would sit on the helmsman's stool brought out of the wheelhouse, his eyes just over the spray shield, his fat, hairy hand on the handle of the engine-room telegraph. If there was no pilot to bring us in, he'd use the maneuver to frighten the pants off me by heading straight for a rock or a lighthouse, motionless on his stool, until my heart pounded in my ears because it seemed humanly impossible that he should not run the ship aground. The first time this happened I got very nervous, glancing at him all the time, and I was about to make a jump for the engine-room telegraph when he pulled it back and muttered, "Hard port." I yelled the order through to the wheelhouse as if I was sizzling at a stake. He looked up at me with such sleepy disdain in his fish eyes that I blushed to the roots of my hair.

The next time, I didn't play. I just stood stolidly looking over the spray shield with my hands behind my back and didn't shoot him a single glance. Only when perdition seemed inevitable I shut my eyes, and swallowed my saliva. Then he muttered, "Three starboard, three," and I sang the order through with a strained voice that ended in a yodel.

The third time, I was hardened to his treatment. I kept my eyes wide open, stared death in the face without batting an eyelid, and when he pulled the engine-room telegraph on "full astern" in the last split second, I went quietly on breathing, like a cow. This seemed to disturb him, for he looked up and asked, "What?" I answered, "Nothing, sir." It set him frowning, and I am proud to say that during the rest of the trip, although he did his damnedest, he never rattled me again.

He handled his ship as an invalid his wheel chair, that much must be said of him. He could moor her between two ten-thousand-ton merchantmen with only a hand's breath to spare fore and aft, and he would do so without getting up and without ever raising his voice above a conversational tone. I admired him, but during the three months I sailed with him we never spoke about anything personal at all. Only when we were approaching Ymuiden harbor on our way home, with the pier lights ahead, he asked, "What are you going to do with your life?" I was so

147

taken aback by this sudden interest in my person, that I answered, "Nothing." He nodded and said, "I thought so." That was all.

⧉

Back in Amsterdam I found myself in a quandary. During my watches in the course of my trip with Captain Bakker I had been thinking. I hadn't done so for a long time, not since I lost Stella. I had settled down to an unthinking life, saying to myself: first let's get this war over, then think.

During my trip with Bakker I took up thinking again. They weren't constructive thoughts; I found out that there was very little positive left in me. The only certainty I could discover was negative: I would never have anything to do with war again. For immediately after this one had been over, the preparations for a new one seemed to have started. People got very excited about the Russians, and there was a lot of indignant talk on platforms and in the papers. I didn't know how my shipmates thought about it, for I hadn't seen them again since the evening we said good-by in the lorry that took us to Amsterdam; but I for one had had my war.

At first, this certainty was rather quiet and vague; it became more aggressive as I saw more of the papers, in Suez, Port Said, Colombo, Billiton, and then Colombo, Port Said, and Suez again. Things seemed to be moving fast. Some German in some meeting had delivered a wonderful speech against the Russians which had been heartily applauded by everybody present, and after the applause he had said, "I have to inform you that the speech I just read has been delivered by Doctor Goebbels three years ago." The paper in which I read that took it as a joke. I thought of the dead, of the second engineer for instance, whose widow I hadn't been to see yet. She would not be very receptive to the joke.

I decided that not only would I have nothing to do with the next war if it came, I would even steer clear of anything that looked like a preparation for it. The tin dredger that old Bakker and I had towed to the Dutch East Indies was part of those preparations. On further reflection practically anything that tugboats towed was part of the preparations. Well, I wouldn't have any of it. I would sooner loaf with a monkey on my shoulder and earn

148

my living with a barrel organ than be connected, however sideways, with World War III. I suppose I wasn't the only one, but I felt that I was. I felt lonely, as if in that lorry I had said good-by to more than just my crew.

So in Amsterdam I handed in my card and announced that I was going to take a holiday. I had decided to make a trip to the past; I wanted to look them up, and see how they felt. The first one I wanted to see was Goatskin, but nobody knew where he was. He had not taken a job with the Company again after V-J Day, and he had no relatives who could tell me his address. So I moved on to the next one—Sparks. I inquired in the office of Radio Holland, and found out that he was in Paris. The one after that was the Chief. He was in Holland all right; he had bought a little bicycle repair shop somewhere in the New Province—the land that had been reclaimed from the Zuider Zee.

I got there by means of a number of buses, ferries and finally an ex-Army lorry that took passengers along the mud tracks that one day would be roads. When I got out in the village square all I saw was a couple of shacks, the village existed only on paper. One of the shacks was a communal restaurant; the other the Governor's office. Behind them were a number of chicken coops, I was directed toward one of them. I began to like the New Province as I walked along the muddy street. It was the newest part of our planet, there was something creative in the atmosphere. After the ruins of bombed-out Europe, it was nice to see something constructive being born.

When I knocked on the door of No. 16, somebody bellowed. As I opened the door, a little bell tinkled. The Chief roared like a lion when he saw me against the light; the little building quivered as he stamped toward me, threw his arms around my neck, and knocked the breath out of me. He asked me, after he had finished mauling me, "What are you doing here?" I said that I was on my way to the North and had thought this a nice occasion to look him up. "Wonderful!" he said. "You're staying the night, aren't you? I'm just about to go out for choir practice. Come with me." I looked at him agape. All I'd ever heard him sing was "Roll me over in the clover," with a voice as if someone was trying it out on a steam whistle. "Choir?" I asked. "Yes," he said. "I am with the basses. We are rehearsing 'The Messiah.'" I fell silent after that for I remembered Van Dam.

He put on a clean shirt and boots, put his head in the wash basin, combed his hair with the part in the middle, and cleaned his nails with a pen knife, all for "The Messiah." He talked about his little shop, that was very promising but would only get into its full stride once there were roads for people to ride bicycles on; now he was mainly doing repair work on excavators and tractors and the like.

The rehearsal was held in the communal restaurant. There, by the light of two oil lamps, about thirty people were gathered of whom twenty-three were men; once the singing started it became clear that of those twenty-three men twenty were basses. The conductor was an agitated little schoolmaster with spectacles and oddly incongruous mud boots. He asked would the ladies and gentlemen please open their books on page forty-three. "I know that my Redeemer liveth." There was a lot of throat scraping and paper rustling, then the little man raised his baton and a silence fell. The wind had risen outside and moaned through the window cracks. The shack croaked faintly, like a windjammer at sea. The little man struck a tuning fork, sang, "Ah-h!" and the women took up the note. They sallied heroically at the dark mass of waiting basses, but were smothered at once. The basses roared like seals, it was a massacre.

I was sitting alone in the far corner of the empty restaurant and watching the Chief. He was putting all he had into his singing, and could be heard above the rest. I wondered what had come over him; something was changed. I realized what it was when they came to the solo phrase "I know that my Redeemer liveth," for then he looked at the thin soprano singing it, as if she was singing it to him. She was a nondescript creature, with a voice like a parrot, but he glowed with coyness and admiration.

After the Redeemer had been slaughtered five times, and the little man with the glasses had announced that He would rise again next Saturday at the same place, same hour, the Chief came toward me, leading the little soprano by the hand. "This is Miss de Roos," he said. "She would like to meet you." Miss de Roos offered a small, dry hand and fluted, "How do you do, Captain?

Benny has told me so much about you," but she looked at me as if she had pins in her mouth. The Chief beamed all over. He offered a round of grenadine and asked whether I'd like a slice of New Province cake with it, it was very good. I had a look at the New Province cake and said I didn't think I would just now, thank you, which was unfortunate, for the Chief continued, "Oh, but you must try it! It's Miss de Roos who makes it." I hurried to make good my mistake, but it was too late. Miss de Roos sat looking at me from that moment onward as if I was a destitute relative.

We took her home after the grenadine. We had to offer her an arm each, for the wind was blowing in its sevens by then and she looked as if she might take off if we didn't keep her down. The Chief went on shouting when we had got outside, but Miss de Roos didn't utter another sound. We dragged her to chicken coop No. 13 where the Chief opened the door for her. She was blown inside the moment we let go of her, and squealed, "Good night!" from the darkness. Then the Chief put his arm round my shoulder and pressed me against him, a thing he hadn't dared do to Miss de Roos. "God!" he said, "it's wonderful to see you." I wished I could believe him.

We went back to No. 16 and he made a cup of tea on a little oil stove that gave a nice homey smell. The wind rattled the windows and smashed against the little house in gusts, like the surf. The Chief sat opposite me at the crude table, beaming in the lamplight, and whatever he talked about, it all led up to Miss de Roos. His whole view on things, past and future, was colored by his love. I couldn't talk to him about the things that bothered me because for him they didn't exist. Nothing existed but Miss de Roos and the wonderful life they would have together. I was jealous.

I didn't sleep much that night. First I thought the building was going to come down, as the wind grew to a gale; then the Chief started snoring. He was one of those alarming snorers, who suddenly break off with a bark and stay for minutes without breathing. I felt very lonely that night.

At six in the morning he brought my heart to my throat by sud-

151

denly bursting into song: "I know that my Redeemer liveth!" I looked out of my bunk and saw him standing at the oil stove in long woolen underwear, frying eggs. When he turned round, he beamed and said, "Hello, did you sleep well?" in a tone that made me wait for the word "darling." I said I had slept quite well, thank you. I was getting a bit sick of acting as a substitute for Miss de Roos.

He was miles away; he had even got over the war, because if there had been no war they would never have met. I hurried through breakfast, on the pretext that I had to catch the early lorry toward the north. He took me to it, and when the vehicle started wobbling down the mud track, he stood waving at me for quite a while. She had a good man there.

In the lorry, I became jealous again. Perhaps the sole explanation for my pessimism and my grim principle never to co-operate with any preparation for a new war was that I was lonely. If only I were in love with somebody, peace might really start for me. But I wasn't; and while I had my insides shaken on the mud track through the New Province, I realized that I didn't particularly want to be in love either. There had only been one girl in my life who amounted to anything at all, and after the morning I saw her train pull out of Westport station, I hadn't wanted to be in love again, because I still was. While convalescing in the South, sitting on that bench, playing with the gravel with my stick, I had thought of falling in love with Miss Simmons, for she was certainly as nice a girl as I had ever met. I had even tried to fall in love with her by imagining how nice it would be, the two of us married, with a little house in the country, dogs, chickens, the neighbors to tea, and once a week in our little car to the pictures. But it hadn't worked. One reason was, perhaps, that Miss Simmons was not in love with me. I had tried to hold her hand, sitting on the bench, on the pretext that I had a sudden pain in my leg. But she had not fallen for it. She had said, "Don't be silly, Captain. You go and play some ping-pong with the Colonel." That had put me off. She was supremely sensible, but I didn't like the idea of being sent to play ping-pong with the Colonel, who used the game to express his feelings toward mankind. Yet, if the memory of Stella had not haunted me so, I think I could really have loved Miss Simmons. For in her presence it was impossible to dramatize myself. I had told her long stories of my childhood and the sea and the war, I had even told her about the U-boat we had rammed and how I couldn't get over the thought of the thirty people who had gone down with it. She wouldn't have anything of that; when I started musing about being murderer, she again said, "Don't be silly, Captain," this time in a very grown-up way.

Well, she was probably back in England now, being wooed by a squire with leather on his elbows, and his behind to the fire. He had a good woman there.

༄

On the northern border of the New Province, I got out of the lorry and took a train to a little town in the northwest of Friesland where, so I had been told, Cook had opened a restaurant, called "The Secret of the Seven Seas." I had never liked Cook, although he was the only one with whom I had sailed from the very beginning, when I first arrived in Westport. The name "The Secret of the Seven Seas" sounded just like him. He had been too feminine to my taste, but a very good cook. We had all been proud of him; his reputation stood high in the fleet.

The little town, when I got out of the station, was utterly depressing. I almost smelled the dust of the archives and the baize of the billiard tables. It rained; thick drops dripped from the trees and clattered on the corrugated iron roof of the empty bandstand in the station square. I found the restaurant at once, because it was the only building in the row of gray brick houses that was painted bright yellow. On the windows two mermaids were painted, holding a menu. Outside hung an anchor with a little lantern attached to it.

As I came in, it seemed as if, by an act of magic, I was back in the messroom of my ship. The interior of The Secret of the Seven Seas had nothing to do with this. It was just a restaurant, rather dark, with cane chairs and red and white checkered cloths on the tables. It was the smell that did it. All during the war, our messroom had smelled exactly like this.

153

There wasn't a client in the place. After a few moments, a door in the back was opened and Cook minced in. When he recognized me he gave a little squeal, and cried, "Captain! Is it you? In the flesh?"

I said it was me in the flesh, and he pumped my arm with both hands. A pimply youth emerged from the shadows with an apron and Cook warbled, "Charles, look who's here! This is the Captain I told you so much about! Sit down, Captain. What will you have? A little apéritif? Luncheon starts in half an hour."

I took the little apéritif, while Cook and his boy hovered around me, talking. The boy first brought a bottle of Cinzano, but Cook snapped, "No, silly, bring the Geneva!" Cook had a little glass with me, glancing nervously at the door, waiting for his first customers. He had quite a nice table d'hôte, he said, with the notary, the chief constable and the headmaster of the Reform School as regular clients, and ever such an interesting crowd of birds of passage. He had got very refined in that year; his hands were washed at last and he wore a ring with a blue stone. He said he was doing very well indeed; a little restaurant like his had been the very thing needed in this charming town.

The first client soon arrived, an irritated little man with a high rubber collar, looking like a surgical contraption for a broken neck. Cook cooed, "Oh, Mr. Notary, how *do* you do?" and went to meet him. The spotty boy hissed a nasty word through his teeth and minced back into the kitchen. I was introduced to Mr. Notary, who couldn't have been less interested, and after that to the chief constable and the headmaster of the Reform School. As I sat watching them, while they were waiting for their meal to be served, I again had a curious sensation of witchery. The three notables, who had come in like personifications of provincial town life, seemed to change in front of my eyes into ship's officers waiting for the first table. They looked like the Chief, Sparks and me, seen in a dream. They sat in the same way, they called the same words to the kitchen, and when Cook came out with the first dish he looked exactly as he had always looked coming down the messroom stairs, angry, but smiling. I got a little dish all my own, and after the first bite the spell was complete. This was exactly the kind of food he had been cooking all through the war. What-

154

ever the ingredients were, it had always had the same, rather rancid taste. It tasted of him.

While I sat eating, I realized for the first time that his grub was awful. I had never realized it during the war; we had told ourselves so often how extraordinarily lucky we were to have such a wonderful cook, that we had hypnotized one another into thinking that what we were eating tasted good. That morning it tasted terrible, and I realized it always had. I wondered why we had been so convinced that he was a wonderful cook; there must have been some truth in it somewhere, for one just can't keep up that self-suggestion for nearly four years. I remembered the trips we had made, the attacks of the U-boats on the Western Approaches, the constant bombing and the frightful cold of the Northeast Passage; and then I discovered why he had, indeed, been a wonderful cook. He had always cooked something, whatever the circumstances. Never had we gone without a meal at the regular hours. During the war he had been a genius; but it hadn't been the way he cooked things. It had been the fact that he had cooked them at all.

While thinking this, I had a feeling I had never had before: a sudden sympathy for him, a contact with him as a human being. He gave me a new sensation that emerged from nothing in particular, but that disturbed me profoundly. For the first time since the guns had stopped firing I felt a nostalgia for the war. I found myself thinking of us, thirteen men on board that small ship, as of something wonderful that was lost. It was a shocking thought.

An hour or so later, after the notables had left and we drank our coffee at my table, I realized that it had been Cook who sent out that thought. While we sat stirring in our cups, talking about the days gone by, with the spotty boy singing in a falsetto while washing the dishes in the kitchen, I discovered that, despite his city manners, he was homesick for the sea. "It's a lovely business," he said. "I've really got a future here. Are you going to sail again?"

I knew that if I said, "Yes" and added, "I'll miss you on board my ship," he would answer, "Oh, I might be able to break away for a trip." I looked at him for a moment in silence and then I answered, "No, I don't think I'll sail again."

He said, "Oh," and he said it in such a pathetic way that I felt

155

more sympathy for him than before. I got up, put out my hand, and said, "Well, Cook, so long."

He remained seated and took my hand. His blue ring gleamed in the rainy light. "So long, Captain," he said. "God bless."

I crossed the square with the bandstand on which the trees still dripped with heavy drops. I sat on the chilly platform of the station for three quarters of an hour, waiting for the train. While sitting there, looking at the rain, the rails and the posters, I thought of going back to that horrible little restaurant, opening the door, and calling, "Cook!" as I had called so often before, when he was late bringing in the grub. And then, when he emerged from the dark kitchen with his smell, I would say, "Come on, let's see if we can find a ship." But those were just the thoughts one has while waiting for a train, on an empty platform. Others imagine they save beautiful women off sinking windjammers, or discover the cure for cancer, or sell the Queen a car. I bought a newspaper to take my mind off it, and read about the tension between the Occupying Powers in Germany.

∽

I went back to Amsterdam, counted my money, and took a third-class ticket to Paris to look up Sparks. He was the last one I could go to apart from the bosun who was at sea, and Goatskin who was lost.

I had wired him from Amsterdam and he met me at the Gare du Nord. He looked different in his civilian clothes: they seemed to bring out the righteousness in his character. He had always been a very calm man, but now his calmness seemed to have acquired a slight edge of disdain.

As we sat sipping coffee on a terrace, opposite the station, he told me that he was the representative of a factory of wireless sets, and building quite a career for himself. But the bit of information that would interest me most, he thought, was that he was engaged to a very nice girl of a very respectable family. French, but not flighty. A really solid piece of work.

We had a meal with the solid piece of work. She was a big-eyed girl, who listened with her mouth open. I soon found out that she probably did so to let the thoughts escape that entered

156

her head through her ears. Sparks was very proud of her; he watched me all through the meal and I nodded several times at him to indicate that he had indeed got something there. She worked in the Galeries Lafayette and told a long story about her floor manager in a very rapid French, full of oh-la-la's. Sparks got quite excited about her story; his eyes lit up and he patted her hand the way I had seen the Chief do sometimes to the dynamo, after he had repaired it and it was ticking over beautifully once more.

We took her home in a taxi. I sat next to the driver and caught an occasional glimpse of them in the little mirror, wrestling on the back seat. After that we walked home to Sparks's boardinghouse, where I would sleep on the couch in his room to save money.

Once I had settled on the couch, and he in his bed, and the lights were out, we talked for the first time the way we had done on board ship. For the first time since peace had started, I spoke aloud the thoughts that bothered me. He listened attentively in the darkness, and when I had finished he said, "I know what's the matter with you, Skipper: you need a girl. You can't settle down to a normal life, after the years we have had, all by yourself. You don't know what meeting Françoise has meant to me; only when I met her was my war really over. I thought you were getting on very nicely with little Simmons a year ago. Haven't you seen her again?"

I said I hadn't, and he started selling her to me. She was just the girl I needed, he said. Sensible, well-educated, sense of humor, healthy. As I lay listening to him, she sounded like a prize cow. I told him so and he rose on his elbows in the darkness and got schoolmastery. "I begin to think you are one of those who cling to their pessimism and make it their one thing in life," he said. "It's all very well to say that the world stinks and that there is another war coming and that you'll be damned if you will have anything to do with it, but are you sure that you aren't secretly longing for it? That you aren't just saying those things because in your heart of hearts you would like to be back in Westport, or in Murmansk, or off the French coast even?"

He took me aback, for I hadn't told him about that part of my thoughts yet. I asked what he thought I should do and he was

157

very definite about it. "First," he said, "for the next day or so, as long as you are staying here, we'll have to find you some company. I think I know somebody—a friend of a friend of Françoise's —a Scottish girl who is spending her holidays in Paris; she comes from the Orkneys, I think. Very nice, big blonde, refined. Her father is something in the Food Office. You play around with her a bit and get a taste back for life. Then you board the London train and go to see little Simmons, and if you still like her as much as you did, you ask her father for her hand."

The hand business spoiled it a bit, but I still thought his advice was sensible. I said, "All right, let's have a look at your big blonde. Good night," and I tried to go to sleep. But I couldn't, for his mentioning the Orkneys had set me thinking of Stella. I thought of Stella for a while, asking myself for at least the hundredth time why I hadn't gone to the Hebrides immediately after the war was over. Well, there were many reasons for it. I hoped the big blonde would be a bit like her.

She was, but on a large scale. She was almost a head taller than I, had long golden hair that hung down on a couple of heavy-weight shoulders, and big blue bedroom eyes. But she was re-fined all right. She told us, over a meal in Montmartre, about the wonderful tea they served at Marshall & Snelgrove's. Sparks looked at me inquiringly, and I nodded approvingly whenever she wasn't looking, which was not often. The one thing that rather attracted me to her were her hands. They were boyish, like Stella's had been, and looked as if they had done a lot of washing up. Perhaps the Marshal & Snelgrove line was just for the holidays.

We took them home in a taxi and she and I sat on the *strapontins* holding hands, looking straight ahead while Sparks and his girl were champing away behind us. When she got out we agreed that we would meet at half-past eleven the next morning under the needle on the Concorde.

When I saw her in daylight she looked a lot nicer. She wore a sensible tweed dress, with a brass bonzo to hold her scarf together, and her smile was very nice and sunny. She called me "skipper," as she had heard Sparks do, and I liked that somehow. The night before, in the dark, I had asked Sparks's advice, as he knew the town a lot better than I did. "Tomorrow, you go to Versailles," he had said. "Show her the waterworks, and the Little Trianon, and play around in the woods a bit. Don't start sparking on all plugs yet, she is a refined girl. Come home in the evening and I'll give you the program for the day after."

I had decided to follow his instructions to the letter. He was a sensible man with a head on his shoulders, and all during the war he had been the image of correctness. So I took her to Versailles, showed her the waterworks and a thing I suppose was the Little Trianon, anyhow they sold tea in it. She didn't mention Marshall & Snelgrove while we were sitting there, watching the sparrows pick crumbs of our cake off the edge of the table. It was a sunny autumn day and there was a nutty smell in the air. The town seemed far away. We didn't say much, we just sat watching the sparrows and I stroked her hand with a feeling of genuine sympathy. She talked a bit about her island and said that most people didn't know that Scapa Flow was pronounced Skeepy Floo.

I was relieved to find out that she was really a nice girl, but it was a pity that she made me think of Stella all the time. After the tea we went into the woods hand in hand and listened to the nightingales and stepped in puddles. We got to one puddle where I had to carry her, and I did so, recklessly, forgetting that the doctor had forbidden me to carry heavy loads. I got her across all right, but it was a bit of a docker's job, without romance. I had a pain in my right leg for the rest of the way, and her bonzo had scratched my nose. At the Metro station we agreed to meet again in the same place, the next morning.

Sparks's instructions that night were businesslike and to the point. "Tomorrow," he said, "you go to the Isle d'Amour, in the Marne. I'll tell you how to get there. It's a very romantic spot full of high reeds and cozy nooks. You are ferried across by an old longshoreman and with three steps you are in the jungle. There you let nature take its course."

I followed his instructions to the dot. We went to the Isle d'Amour, ferried across by an old *batelier*, got into the jungle with three steps, sat down on the soft grass in a little nest of reeds and kissed each other, rather shyly for people of our age. I think we both had the feeling that we were obeying a program that we

159

hadn't made up ourselves; perhaps she had received instructions from Françoise. Anyhow we kissed, and her mouth was soft and warm, and I thought she was very sweet, and then I felt a sudden itch on my ankle and had to scratch whether I liked it or not. We kissed some more and then I had an itch at the back of my knee. As I scratched, I saw out of the corner of my eye that she was scratching too. After a short time we were both scratching ourselves secretly up to the waist. Then she screamed and said, "Look!" and pointed at her ankle. I looked, asked, "What?" and she said, "Fleas!"

She was right. Sparks's little paradise must have been the spawning ground for all the fleas of Paris. We ran back to the jetty and I hollered for the old *batelier*; we went on scratching all the way home. I tried to laugh it off but she didn't think it funny, Marshall & Snelgrove got in the way again.

When I told Sparks that night what had happened, he was very sorry and supposed it must have been the time of the year, for Françoise and he had spent wonderful hours there. But nothing was lost, only a different course of action had to be taken. I was going to meet her again the next afternoon, and he gave me the address of a discreet little hotel somewhere near Gare Montparnasse, where I could get a room for a couple of hours and be quiet and undisturbed in congenial surroundings. Paris was a wonderful city, people never made any fuss about love; all I need do was go to the little hotel, ask for a room, pay, they would give me the number and when I came back with her I could walk straight up without seeing anybody. I should tell her that I had found a little place of my own, with a wonderful view over the roofs of Paris, and would she like to see it, and then show her up there and let nature take its course.

I was a bit worried when I made my preparations according to his instructions, but probably I was fussing too much. He and Françoise had spent wonderful hours there. The hotel was a bit shady and the woman behind the desk looked rather frightening, with the beginnings of a beard and an enormous bust, caught in a net. When I asked her whether by any chance she had a room for a day, she answered, "No, only for a couple of hours. Have you got Madame with you?" I said I hadn't, but that I would come back later and could I pay now. She shrugged her shoulders and said, "If you like." When I gave her the money, she put it in a tin that bore the label "Durant's Baby Powder." I was even more worried when I came out than I had been when I went in, but I decided not to be silly and see it through. After all, one thing about Sparks was undeniable: he was very correct. He and his Françoise would never have gone to a place that wasn't.

She was very gay when I met her at the appointed hour, but somehow a bit strained. Perhaps she too had her apprehensions. I told her about the little place of my own with the view over the roofs of Paris, and she was delighted to come and see it. When we entered the hotel, the old woman was not behind her desk. This was a relief. I took her up the stairs, peering unobtrusively at the room numbers; I had been given number fourteen on the third floor, all I need do was push the door and it would open. I found number fourteen in the end, pushed, and the door did indeed open. I let her go in first, and she stifled a scream.

When I entered after her, I got a shock too. The room was full of mirrors and the walls were covered with murals that left no doubt as to the nature of the establishment. There was no view over the roofs of Paris. She sat down on the bed, sobbing, and I felt sorry for her, but at the same time I had to suppress a hysterical laughter. She sobbed, "Oh, this is hell, hell! Take me out of here!" I tried to soothe her by saying that it wasn't hell at all but just a mistake, and that I was very sorry but that I had never set eyes on the place before, or I wouldn't have taken her here. But she refused to be got out of it, she went all Marshall & Snelgrove again and that was a pity, because I had a feeling that if we had just lain down on that bed and smoked a cigarette and been ourselves we could have talked about something real at last, about the war and what the hell were we to do with our lives. But she didn't feel that way at all; she sobbed that she felt "like one of those awful Parisian women." I had to take her back to the street. I wanted to see her home, but she bolted like a rabbit the moment she sniffed fresh air. I thought of running after her, but didn't.

I wrote her a note on a terrace somewhere, thanking her for the nice time and hoping that we would meet once more. I also wrote to Sparks, saying that I had to leave unexpectedly. I left the notes in his room, collected my stuff and went to the Gare du Nord where I took a ticket to London.

∽

In the blue underwater light of a dimmed-out compartment between Paris and Calais I made the decision. I wouldn't go and see Miss Simmons, there was no point. I had only loved one girl in my life and I still loved her and it was no use trying to shape my future until I had seen her again.

Once I had made that decision the very color of my life seemed to change. I suddenly got hope again and vitality, and the will to do something constructive. I couldn't understand why I hadn't done this long ago. I remembered all the reasons why I hadn't, and I found they were all nonsense because I was sure now that she still loved me too.

I didn't sleep at all that night. I just sat there, dreaming, wide awake, chain smoking, seeing visions of the future. The house, the children, the table, the lamp; the wind in the chimney, the bosun knocking on the door, calling "Captain, S.O.S.!" Why hadn't I thought of it before? That was the one thing I could do with a tugboat that had nothing to do with the preparations for war: the rescue service, to sail to the assistance of ships in distress. It would be the same work we had done in Westport, and I would come back to her after each trip, the way I had done then. What a wonderful life it would be, the only kind of life I was born to, and no other woman would ever understand it the way she would. In London, I bought a ticket to her island. It cost a fortune but it was cheap at the price. I could have stood the whole town a drink, I felt so wonderful. I was sure, in an almost psychic way, that everything would be all right and that we were going to have a wonderful life together.

It took me three days to get to her island. At each station I made up my mind to send her a wire and decided at the last moment not to. I would just go to the door and knock, and when

162

she opened I would say, "Hello, Stella." I missed the last boat and stayed on the mainland for the night in a drafty little hotel, smelling of peat fires.

I arrived on the island by midday the next day. I found her house and knocked and an old woman opened. When I asked whether her daughter was in, her daughter Stella, she said, "But didn't you know? She married a Polish Air Force Officer and is living in Warsaw." I said, "Oh, I'm sorry," and went back to the jetty, just in time to catch the same boat back. The whole thing had lasted less than three minutes.

On that ferry, I spent a nasty hour. I felt completely empty and at a loss. I didn't know where to go. The idea of joining the rescue service had just been a boyish dream. There was no vacancy for captains. Even though eighty per cent of the young ones had been killed, there were still too many of us about, for the old ones were immortal. They had a magic secret, that we would never know.

The sensible thing to do would have been to go back to London, but somehow I couldn't face that idea. I wanted to do something in Scotland just to make myself believe that I had gone there for another reason than just to hear an old woman say, "But didn't you know?" In the station on the other side I saw a poster announcing Highland Games in Pitlochry. I went to Pitlochry, took a room in a hotel that was called "Le Moulin Rouge," and watched giants in kilts throw telegraph poles at each other. They were wildly applauded by the most foreign crowd I ever got lost in, and there came a lucid moment in which I asked myself, quite calmly, what the hell I was doing here. I went back to the hotel, sat down in the hall, picked up a magazine and saw that it was the *International Shipping Information*. It was extraordinary to find it here, but at second thought no more extraordinary than finding a hotel called Le Moulin Rouge in Pitlochry. I leafed through it, smelling nostalgically the distant sea, and then suddenly my heart shot in my throat. I saw the name of my ship.

"Wreck Dutch Tugboat Vlieland, towed to Antwerp Firma Klaassen & Cy, for demolition."

163

I went to the desk to say that I would leave that night, and could they get me a ticket to Antwerp.

∽

I got to Antwerp a few days later, in the evening. The enormous harbor had always depressed me; that evening it was more depressing than ever. There was a smoky fog hanging over the Scheldt and the town, that occasionally turned into a drizzle. The neon lights of *Dancings* and *Cinemas* flashing on and off in the streets made the skyline look as if the town was burning after an air raid.

It took me several hours before I had located the demolition wharf of the firm Klaassen & Cy. It would have been more sensible to wait until the morning, but this wasn't a sensible expedition anyhow. The wharf was in a far corner of the harbor, called The Church Yard. It wasn't the only one, I found out. There were scores of demolition wharfs, side by side. It was a corner without lights, only some sparsely sown street lamps and an occasional glimmer of candlelight behind the windows of a watchman's hut. The taxi I had taken put me down at the end of the quay; the driver said that his springs couldn't stand the rest of the way. The quay was paved with enormous cobble stones that seemed to have been laid down in waves. Muddy puddles reflected the street lamps.

Klaassen & Cy was at the very end. Behind the gate was a little watchman's hut, and behind the hut the tall masts of a windjammer. I tried to open the gate but found it shut. I called through the bars and my voice echoed back to me from three directions. The drizzle mingled on my forehead with the sweat. After I had stood there calling for quite a while a door in the watchman's hut was opened and an old man came shuffling out with a lantern, muttering. "What do you want?" he called, halfway to the gate.

I said that I would like to visit the wreck of the tugboat *Vlieland*. It made him angry. He said he'd be damned if he'd let any more people on tonight. The sale was tomorrow, and if I wanted to have a look at the inventory, I could come in the morning like everybody else. I said I hadn't come for the sale, just to have a look at the ship; that I had been her captain during the

164

war and had come all the way from Scotland to see her once more before she was broken up. "Tell that to your grandmother!" he shouted. "What do you people take me for? The village idiot? One who pulls that story on me is enough, isn't it? I may be old, but I'm not half-witted yet. Get the hell out of here before I throw a bolt at you." I had no idea what he was talking about and I spoke to him quietly and kindly through the bars, like a doctor.

It took me a quarter of an hour and a hundred Belgian francs. He opened the padlock on the gate with a key he selected from a big rusty bunch, by the light of his lantern. He went on muttering all the time. After the gate had creaked open on rusty hinges, and I had squeezed myself through the gap, he said, "Come to my office before you go out, and I'll search you." I said, "All right, granddad. Where's the ship?" "Alongside the windjammer," he answered. "And if you break your neck on her deck, I'll be delighted." After that nice Christian thought, he retired to his hut, a mole with a lantern.

His wish nearly came true. The windjammer's deck was strewn with rubbish and I had to proceed cautiously, striking matches all the time. When I finally got to her starboard side and looked down over the rail, I saw my ship, and my eyes shot full of tears. I was a little amazed at this for I didn't feel any particular emotion. Perhaps the tears were just a conditioned reflex. She looked very small down there and quite dead. I wouldn't have recognized her if I hadn't known it was she, for I had never seen her after the shelling. When I was carried off for the last time I had been too ill to look. Her funnel was gone, her bridge was a shambles, her radio hut an open grave. That's where the shell had struck and penetrated to the engine room. I found a pilot's ladder hanging down the flank of the windjammer and I lowered myself on board. As I walked cautiously aft, I saw a light shining from the messroom.

It gave me quite a shock. I hadn't seen it from above. I thought it must be another watchman; but when I went down the messroom stairs, the man who sat at the table and looked up gave me another shock. It was Goatskin, very thin and sunburned, in a sailor's outfit. Blue jersey, blue coat, and peaked cap without emblem. "Hello, Skipper," he said. I asked him where he came

165

from, and he said that he had read the news of her demolition in a paper in the South of France. I said, "Well, well," and sat down opposite him.

I had sat down like this so many times that it wasn't as strange a situation to me as I suppose it should have been. It seemed somehow quite normal. The only differences were that the electric light wasn't working, that the table was very dirty and that there was no emblem on his cap. I looked at the oil lantern, wanted to ask him where he had got it from, but recognized it before. It was the bosun's. He must have found it in the foc's'le. "Well, well," I said. "And what have you been doing with yourself?"

"Oh, all sorts of things," he answered. "Just now I've got a job in Marseilles."

"As what?"

"As a diver." He smiled, a bit thinly. "There's quite some money in it. We dive down to the decks of the Liberty ships that were sunk during the Invasion, take off the wheels of the jeeps that are still lashed on the decks. The air in the tires makes them float, we collect them, and sell the tires on the black market."

I said, "Well, well. How long have you been doing that for?"

"About three months," he answered. "We've skimmed the easy ones off by now. The next lot is lying too deep for just mask diving. We'll have to get at them with a scaphander or with bottles."

I said, "I see."

He went on for a while about his diving, and I looked at him. He hadn't changed much except for his sunburn, yet there was a difference. I couldn't quite place the difference at first. Last time I had seen him, he had been a quiet, competent boy who didn't worry much about life and the future. He had just been a good sailor and proud of it. Now, he looked much older, and a bit bitter and worried. Perhaps he looked just the way I did, for he returned my stare and smiled his new thin smile and said, "Well, what have you been doing with yourself?"

I said, "Oh, I made one trip as a mate with old Bakker to the East Indies, and after that I loafed a bit and traveled around. I have just come from Scotland."

"So," he said. "What were you doing there?"

166

When I answered, "I went to look at the Highland Games," he stared, and said, "I see."

There was a silence after that, which became a bit oppressive because he went on looking at me with his blue eyes that seemed a lot bluer now his face was so tanned. Then he opened the drawer in the messroom table, said, "Hey, look what's here!" and took out a chessboard. We looked at each other with a wry smile, yet enjoying it, and he said, casually, "What about a game?"

"Are the chessmen there?" I asked.

He rumbled in a drawer and brought out a pocketknife. It was the second engineer's. I remembered he had been looking for it as far back as Gibraltar. I wanted to say something about it, but I let it pass. "Yes," he said, "here they are. Shall we?"

I hesitated, then I said, "In a minute. Let's look around the ship first."

"I wouldn't if I were you," he said. "You won't like it. Let's have a game and then go and have a drink somewhere. I don't think there's any point in tearing the live skin off your body just for the fun of it."

I said, "All right. Let's play."

He put up the game, took two pawns in his hands, shook them, and held out his fists. I chose one, and opened the game with white.

We played cautiously and with concentration. I was good, but he was better. At the beginning of the game, I felt all mellow and sad inside. The friendship I felt for him was as strong as any emotion I had ever known toward another human being, but as the game went on and it became obvious that he was going to win, my feelings began to change. When there were only half a dozen men left on the board and he had me cornered, I was back in Shadwell Basin with the same sour taste in my mouth and the same itchy feeling in my hands. It was silly, but there was nothing I could do about it.

He sat pondering for a long time before he made his last move. Yet it was very simple, any fool could see it two miles off. If he put my king in check with his castle there was only one place I could go to, and after that it would be his. I sat staring at the board with my arms folded, my jaw set, thinking how lovely it

167

would be to beat the hell out of him at last. Then he looked up with his new smile and said, "All right, Skipper, I give up." I stared at him in amazement, but there was something in the way he looked at me that made me say, "O.K. What about that drink?"

He picked up the lantern and we went out, leaving the game unfinished on the table. There was something gratifying in it, something symbolical, only I had no idea what the symbol stood for. We climbed back on the deck of the windjammer and there he said, "Let's have a look at her. Shall we?" We groped our way through the jungle of rusty iron and old ropes toward her poop, climbed down the stairs to her officer's quarters, and opened a door on which an enameled plate said "Messroom." She must have been a rich ship in her days; everything was made of teak and solid brass, and the benches of her messroom were covered with real leather. But she was as empty as a shell on the beach. We opened a cupboard and found nothing in it. Only the shelves, covered with newspaper. He lifted the lantern and looked at a newspaper on a shelf and said, "Look at this." It was a newspaper called *Les Annales* of September 15, 1918. It showed a drawing of a fat soldier, kissing a coy, plump girl's hand. The girl was in a factory uniform. Underneath it, it read: "*La Tourneuse d'Obus*— to her murdered little hands he owes his victory." It was extraordinary how comical the drawing looked.

We looked around her quarters a bit more; in her captain's cabin, we found a photograph of her crew, screwed onto the wall in a teak frame. Her officers looked very young; the captain, who sat proudly in the center, couldn't have been more than twenty-five. I said how young they looked, and he said that all crews of the last windjammers had been youngsters. They had been good sailors, he said. The only pity was that they were no good for any other job, once their ships were laid up, when they were about thirty. I asked him, as he seemed to be informed on the subject, what had happened to them, and he answered with a shrug of his shoulders, "God knows."

When we crossed the yard with our lantern, the old watchman came out of his hut, barking like a dog. He wanted to know where we had got that lantern from. When Goatskin said that he

168

had found it on board our ship, the old man ripped it out of his hand and said, "Don't you know there's a sale tomorrow? That everything has been listed? If that lamp is missing, I'll have to pay it out of my own pocket. What else have you got?" We answered, "Nothing," but he wouldn't believe us. He searched our pockets with the light of the lantern swinging beams in the fog like a lighthouse, and our shadows tumbling to and fro. Goatskin gave him a bank note, which he looked at in the light of the lantern before he put it in his pocket. I saw it was a thousand francs. He certainly must have been making money down South.

We had our drink in a tavern on the quay side. An automatic piano jingled German tunes and a couple of lascars were playing billiards in flat clouds of low-hanging cigar smoke, which the light of the lamps over the table cut into cones. He said that any time I wanted a job, all I had to do was to go to Marseilles, Hotel Atlantic, and ask for Maurice. I said I'd think of it and he didn't go on about it. All he said was, "I would, if I were you. There aren't many jobs around for the like of us. I should know, for I've tried them all." Then he finished his beer and said, "Well, I'll have to be off. I've got a girl waiting." I asked him, politely, who she was and he answered with his thin little smile, "Her name is Thalassa." He was already standing, about to go, when he asked, "Did you see her up there in Scotland?"

I said, "No, she's married. She is living in Warsaw."

He patted my shoulder, said, "Skipper," and went away.

❧

The next morning, when I woke up, I had a very clear picture of the future. I didn't know where I got it from, perhaps I had dreamed it that night. I counted my money; I had to count it several times and do some Chinese calculations before I concluded that I could just make it.

She had given me her address before I left, asking me to write her how I was doing, some time in the future. I never had. Probably she didn't live there any longer. I took the risk: "The Rectory, Woodcliffe, near Oxford" it said, so I went to Oxford. I made the trip in a curious, sleep-walking way. I didn't think about anything; I had a feeling that all thoughts should be postponed until I could speak them aloud in her presence and hear the inevitable answer, "Don't be silly, Captain." I still pictured her in her nurse's dress, straining at the hips, with her Dagenham Girl Pipers' cap around her neck, or on her forehead.

I telephoned her from Oxford station, and only after we had agreed that she'd meet me at the five o'clock bus did it occur to me how extraordinary it was that she should have been there at all. She hadn't sounded surprised on the telephone, and she didn't look surprised when she saw me get out of the bus. She looked different in civilian clothes, younger and a lot prettier than before. She wore a little red pirate's bonnet with a tassel that was perfectly ridiculous. I couldn't help grinning when I saw her, I was glad I had come. She shook me warmly by the hand, said, "How jolly nice of you to come. Have you had tea?" Then we walked briskly up the hill toward a little village of Cotswold-stone houses, with a fat church tower rising above the roofs. "There are some very nice Elizabethan houses here," she said, "that one for instance." She gestured with her head and that sent the tassel flying. As I climbed the steep streets with her I noticed that I was limping, out of habit.

I expected her father to be the rector, but he wasn't. He was a thin man in breeches, who met us in the doorway on his way to let the dog out. "Oh, there you are," he said. "I've been hearing a lot about you. See you in a minute. Have some tea." Gray hairs were growing out of his nose and his ears, and he had bushy eyebrows; the rest of his head was bald. I liked him.

The inside of the rectory was so dark that I didn't see the Elizabethan chest she pointed out to me, but hurt my shin on it, on my way to the dining room. The house seemed to consist entirely of vaults. The dining vault was furnished with heavy Portuguese chairs, a French polished table and a black shiny square in a gilt frame over the mantelpiece, of which she said, "My grandfather." We sat down in a Portuguese chair each and made conversation across the table; the reflection of the lamp in the French polish dazzled me. I started to tell her about my trip with old Captain Bakker; then the words stuck in my throat on

170

hearing what sounded like a streetcar rattling and clanging down the passage.

It was a trolley with tea things, pushed by an old maid who looked exactly like her father with skirts on. "No more butter," said the maid, "and I hope he's brought sugar with him."

"Don't be gloomy, Suzy," said Miss Simmons. "Just leave the trolley, I'll put the things out." The maid shot a steely glance at me, exhaled through her whiskers and clattered off. I realized that her iron-heeled slippers had made part of the noise.

When I looked at Miss Simmons after the door had been slammed shut, she smiled, and I felt very glad I had come. I smiled back at her, and went on telling her about my trip, while she poured out the tea and cut the cake with the tassel dangling in front of her nose. A quarter of an hour later her father came back with the dog and he had some tea too, which he drank noisily during his report on meeting the vicar in the street and arranging a jumble sale for the benefit of the Mothers' Union. I wondered whether she had a mother, and if so where she was.

I met her that night after dinner, after smoking a cigar with her father in the dining room. The first announcement I got of her presence was the plural he used when he said, "Shall we join the ladies?" On entering the sitting vault, I saw an old woman, propped up on a sofa, with a couple of pillows in her back. She looked sweet and gentle and welcomed me with a smile, saying, "So, you are the Flying Dutchman."

It was she who destroyed my hopes, for during the preceding hours I had made up my mind to ask Miss Simmons if she would marry me. It was a bit quick, but I had come to the conclusion that I had been a fool not to have asked her in the South of France; no man could wish himself a better wife. But her mother put a stop to all this. I took her thin hand and pressed it gently. I inquired, politely, but with genuine interest, whether she was seriously ill, and she answered with a radiant smile, "Oh, no, I've got cancer. Isn't it stupid of me?"

That reply put a stop to my lonely man's dreams concerning Miss Simmons. Never before had I felt more alien to the English than at that moment. If I had a cold in the nose, the whole ship had to know it; Cook had to ply me with hot grogs, Goatskin had

171

to come in at least every half hour to inquire how I felt, and I could be heard moaning down in the engine room. I suppose it was unmanly, but that happened to be the way in which I liked my illnesses. If I married Miss Simmons, after the reply the mother gave me, I would have to break a leg and say, "Oh, nothing at all; only my right stilt seems to be a little shorter than the other." Well, I wasn't going to. Not only I couldn't, but I didn't want to, for somehow I felt one couldn't take cancer lightly and treat the war seriously. It was all in the day's work. Miss Simmons' formula, "Don't be silly, Captain," that I had so much longed for, suddenly took on an awesome aspect. From that dazzling height of human sublimation anything I would ever feel or do would be silly.

All the same, she was a charming old lady, with a great sense of humor and an exquisite tact. The way she got the two of us out into the garden was so subtle, that when I found myself hand in hand with Miss Simmons, strolling among the ilexes in the scented darkness, I couldn't for the life of me remember how I'd got there. This should have been the night of the great confession, but as it was I felt obliged to make light of my own problems. Compared with what the old lady was going through, they were chicken feed. I told her about seeing the wreck of my ship again, the game of chess with Goatskin, and she thought it a funny story. I did myself. I laughed with a hawing sound in the darkness, and frightened an owl which, in its turn, frightened me. What a pity, I thought when we strolled back to the house treading on molehills, that I hadn't spoken to her before.

Of course the real reason of this last minute retirement was that I didn't love her. If I had, her mother could have said, "Oh, nothing serious: I'm dead, you know. Isn't it killing?" and it wouldn't have made the slightest difference. She was a very sweet girl and I was sure that we would have been happy together, once we had eased out the national differences; but there was nothing I could do about it: I didn't love her. As for the passion she evoked in me, I might as well have been strolling in that scented summer garden with my aunt.

When we came back to the living vault, her mother was reading *The Farmers' Weekly* and her father was asleep in an arm-

172

chair, with his head back and his knees wider apart than seemed humanly possible. The gloomy maid on hoofs made us a cup of chocolate and we drank it silently while her father snored away like a fog signal. He woke up when the cups were put together, opened his eyes wide, and said, "No, no, my darling, I'm listening." Then he noticed us two and said, "Oh, sorry, I must have dozed off. Did I?" Miss Simmons answered, "Only for a minute, Daddy," and kissed his forehead. I wished to God at that moment that I loved her. She was a wonderful girl. As it was, I spent a night of nightmares between damp sheets underneath a heavy eiderdown in a four-poster that creaked even when I remained quite still.

In the morning the maid came in with a cup of tea without sugar. I had a little conversation with her about the Government; never had I heard such bloodthirsty talk in my life. We had breakfast in the dining vault; her father wore a corduroy dressing gown and carpet slippers and growled at *The Times*. She went on looking at me all through breakfast with a smile that didn't tally with her eyes, as if there was something that worried her. After she had taken me to the bus stop and we stood waiting in a queue of women with shopping bags, she asked, as the bus horn sounded round the bend, "Are you sure there isn't something you'd like to ask me?"

I looked at her and said, "No, June."

She smiled so widely that it almost became a grin and said, "That's a pity, isn't it?"

I said, "Yes."

I waved back at her from the back window of the bus as it drove away, and I didn't feel happy.

Chapter VIII

I HAD EXPECTED THE HOTEL ATLANTIC IN MARSEILLES TO BE A sinister, shady place, but I had been influenced by the French films. It was a smart establishment with a dancing annex, looking out over the old harbor. It seemed hardly the place to go and ask for Maurice, but as his instructions had been precise, I advanced

173

on the hall porter who looked like a rear admiral, and asked whether Maurice was in. No, he said, he was out on an expedition and wouldn't be home until the day after tomorrow at the earliest. This came as a shock to me, I had so counted on his being there that I had fifty-three francs left in my pocket. I said, "Thank you, I'll be back," and walked out as nonchalantly as I could.

It had never happened to me to find myself in a foreign port without a penny in my pocket, and I was at a loss what to do. There were very few things one could buy for fifty-three francs and, like a fool, I spent them on a glass of *vin rosé* on the terrace of a bistro next door, that looked cheap but wasn't. It was very hot and I was wearing my northern clothes which were all I had. While sipping what was likely to be my last food for a couple of days, I did some thinking. The best plan seemed to be to move as little as possible, so as not to stimulate the appetite, and to find a cozy corner somewhere near the old harbor where I could spend the night.

There weren't many cozy corners to be seen at first glance. The quay was the busiest I had ever known. Old cars and rattling lorries jostled each other in what seemed to be a giant game of Dodgems, and ships and yachts lay so tightly moored side by side with their poops to the quay that I couldn't see the water. I paid for my *vin rosé*, crossed the street leisurely, trying to look rich and carefree, and was knocked down at once by a blow like from a diving board. When I crawled to my knees, after a moment of stupefaction, I saw a fat man get out of a very old car, the back door of which was hanging open. It must have been the door that got me. He was profuse in his apologies, of which I didn't understand a word, and I did a Mrs. Simmons on him by saying, "Oh, it doesn't matter in the least, only my vertebral column broken." He was quick to see his chance, laughed heartily, slapped me on the back, which set me cringing, and drove off with his rattletrap, his back door still open, waiting for the next customer.

I sat down on a bollard with my head in my hands, arrived at the all-time low in my life. The pain in my back robbed me of my sense of humor. I thought of my mother and what she would

174

have thought if she had seen me sitting here: a bum without a penny in his pocket hovering on the brink of anonymity. All the despair, the lack of self-confidence, and the loneliness I had bottled up inside me took possession of me; I sat there, my head in my hands, thinking about suicide. Then I looked up, startled by the sound of a spitfire diving at me. I saw a nun in fluttering gowns streak past on a motor bicycle at eighty miles an hour. She separated a man from a barrel he was rolling across the street, and he stood screaming atheist slogans after her while the barrel quietly wobbled on toward the water, to be stopped by the back of an angler who had managed to worm a fishing rod between two ships. The angler and the barrel man started a row, during which the angler whisked his fishing rod up; the hook caught the shirt of a sailor who was painting a lifebuoy on the poop of one of the ships. This started the angler and the sailor off, who in his turn got involved with another sailor who was hit by the paintbrush as he gesticulated. At that point the row vanished out of my field of vision, but I felt sure that it would ripple all over the Vieux Port and the town of Marseilles until it would stop at the sea.

The nun cured me. It was impossible to see this kind of thing happen in front of my eyes and take myself seriously. After all it was only a matter of three days; if I couldn't get through those in some way or another I wasn't worth my salt. I flung my jacket over my shoulder, got up, and vanished in the crowd.

∽

I led a bum's life for three days, and I discovered to my amazement that it was a delightful existence. I was at complete liberty to do whatever I pleased; I had never suspected that to be rid of money was a liberation. Up till now I had been worrying all the time, counting and recounting my money; I had lain awake at night seeing the darkness of poverty approaching. Now I discovered that poverty wasn't a darkness at all but a sunlit day, the end of all worries and responsibilities. My fellow loafers on the waterfront were charming people, generous and full of fascinating stories. I sat for hours baking in the sun, my cap on my eyebrows, listening to their fairy tales, that sounded as if they

175

came straight out of the *Arabian Nights.* It was an enormous relief, after having spent my entire life in the shackles of Nordic
understatement, to be among people who made no secret of
their feelings. If a man hurt his toe he yelled the place down,
and whenever I came across a crowd around two cars and two
screaming drivers, it was always a difference of opinion as to who
had crashed into the other with the right of priority. Every
person in this town lived in a little universe entirely his own;
they were all suns in search of planets. That was perhaps the
reason why they made friends so easily.

The first day I had been worrying about food. It turned out to
be very easy. If I wanted a meal all I had to do was to go to the
gangway of a tramp steamer that didn't look too rich, and holler,
"Hey, chum! Anything left for a white man?" I was never refused; the generosity of the sailors regardless of their nationality
was astonishing. I suppose they had all been beach-combers themselves in the past and were aware of the fact that they might be
once more. As to my sleeping accommodation I had been worrying
needlessly too. I had forgotten that Marseilles in the summer is
so hot that even the richest people sleep in the open, uncomfortably, in deck chairs on their balconies. I slept underneath a
wheelbarrow next door to a police station, on an armful of straw
I had pinched off a barge. I woke up every time a singing
drunkard was dragged in, or screaming tart; I smoked cigarettes
with the constables on duty who sat on kitchen chairs on the
pavement, listened to their stories and their jokes, said, "Well,
I think I'll turn in again," and crawled back underneath my
wheelbarrow. They woke me up in the morning with a cup of
coffee; it was a curious town.

When I went back to the Hotel Atlantic at noon on the third
day, the hall porter told me that Maurice would come in any
minute now. I sat down in a chair in the hall, and waited. I had
been wondering during the past week or so who Maurice would
be, never suspecting him to be Goatskin himself. He entered
the swing doors of the lobby at three o'clock on the dot, dressed
in a smart pin-striped suit, wearing a panama hat, and twirling a
bamboo cane. He was followed by two tough-looking boys in
shorts and a couple of girls on very high heels, who seemed to

176

run in order not to fall on their faces. They were of the brassy blonde type, with a corkscrew curl glued to each forehead. The moment he saw me, Goatskin stopped twirling his cane, cried, "Skipper!" made a dash for me, pulled me out of my chair, threw his arms round my neck, and kissed me on both cheeks. At first I thought that he had become very Mediterranean, but as he kissed me I smelled that he was drunk. The twirling of the cane must have been a gyrostatic device to help him keep upright. After he had embraced me, he shut his eyes, said, "God, I'm tired," and slumped down in my chair with his legs outstretched. He was wearing blue socks with a purple hue that were red on the inside, and suede shoes. He looked young and pathetic, with dark blue rings under his eyes beneath his sunburn. One of the tough boys asked me, gruffly, "Do you know him?" while the other led the giggling blondes to the bar with his arms round their waists. Goatskin answered for me, without opening his eyes, "He's the man I've been waiting for. Buy him a room with a bath and a drink. Make a note of the number." The tough boy said, "O.K." and took me to the desk.

I was given a room with a bath, overlooking the old harbor. A waiter brought up a bottle of whisky and a glass, and went out again without a word. Neither the bath nor the whisky were any good to me as I hadn't got soap or a corkscrew. The room was very luxurious, but a bit depressing, perhaps because there were so many mirrors. Wherever I looked, I saw myself, and I certainly needed a shave. I sat down on the window sill, looking at the old port and the busy quay side, and felt homesick for the world down there that I had come to like so much. I thought of sneaking out of the room, back to the street; I was sure I would find a job somewhere and even if I didn't, lots of people seemed to live quite comfortably without. I got bored, alone in that room, waiting for Goatskin to sleep his alcohol off, or for one of the tough boys to come up to tell me what I was supposed to do. On a little bureau was an inkwell, a pen, and a stack of postcards with a picture of the hotel on them. I thought of someone I could send a postcard to. The only ones I knew were Miss Simmons and the Chief. I didn't feel like sending a postcard to Sparks. I wrote to the Chief first, saying that I was having a wonderful time and

177

asking how "The Messiah" was getting on. I hoped Miss de Roos was feeling well and begged to be remembered to her. When I reread it, it was rather a formal postcard, but I decided to send it anyhow. To Miss Simmons I wrote thanking her for the nice week end; I told her the weather was fine and that I hoped it was the same in England. I sat thinking for a long time, chewing the pen, of something else to write. In the end I added, "I hope to write to you more extensively later. Yours very sincerely, The Flying Dutchman."

I had just finished the postcard when there was a knock on the door and a Chinese girl came in. I was sure she had mistaken my door for somebody else's, and was about to say, "That's quite all right," when she said, "Maurice has sent me."

I said, "Oh, I see. Well?"

She looked at me, a bit amazed, and answered, "Well, here I am."

I again said, "I see," rather embarrassed, because God only knew what the drunk had been up to. She sat down on one of the gilt chairs, at a loss it seemed, tapping on her kneecap with delicate fingers. Then she asked, "Wouldn't you like a bath?" I said I would, but that I hadn't got any soap. That seemed to cheer her up; it gave her something to do. She went to the telephone and ordered a cake of soap—"No, no, not lavender, verbena"—and a big bottle of Eau de Cologne. Then she went into the bathroom and I heard her turn on the taps.

The whole thing had taken me by surprise, and I felt self-conscious about the postcards on the bureau, as if Miss Simmons and the Chief were sitting there, watching me. The urge to get back into the street became stronger. Then there was a knock on the door again and the same silent waiter came in with a cake of soap and a bottle on a silver tray. The Chinese girl emerged from the bathroom and started scolding him because he hadn't brought a corkscrew. He turned silently on his heels and marched out again. After he had gone, she said, "All right, your bath is ready." I said, "Thank you," stood a moment in the middle of the floor, looking silly, and then sauntered into the bathroom. I tried to lock the door from the inside but found that this was not provided for. So I stripped like the wind, plunged into the tub, and

178

started frantically to work up a lather before she should come in, which I was sure she would.

She did, a couple of minutes later. She came in with a cork-screw and a bottle. She pulled the cork out, then went to the washstand, took a glass and filled it. I hadn't realized that it was the whisky bottle she had brought in. She took it to me in the bath and said, "There you are." I hesitated a second, then I filled the rest of the glass with water from the tap, said, "Cheers," and drank it with an air of unconcern. It didn't quite come off, for my first gulp went down the wrong hole and I sat there choking, while she patted my back, soothingly, as to a child. After that I gave up being disconcerted. I said, "Look, I don't know who you are or what the hell you're doing here, but would you mind just sitting outside and look at the view while I have a wash? There's a good girl."

She looked so astonished that she almost convinced me that I had committed a social offense. "Don't you want me to scrub your back for you?" she asked.

I looked at her, the bathroom, the cake of verbena soap, and the bottle of whisky on the washstand and I said, "All right, I don't see why not." I put the glass down at the head of the bath, turned round and said, "Go ahead." Looking at the glass while she gently scrubbed my back, I expected it at any moment to turn into the dial of an alarm clock. Never before had I realized that the platitude "I felt as if I was dreaming" had so much accuracy in it. I had been transplanted in one swoop from a bum's existence into that of Harun El Rashid. Goatskin certainly had things worked out here.

After she had finished with my back, she offered to scrub my front, but that was where I drew the line. I said, "Thank you, I'll see to that myself." She said, "As you like," handed me the brush and the soap, sat down on the stool in the corner, and started filing her nails. Although she seemed entirely uninhibited I got up with my back to her and washed my front in an uncomfortable position. I soon lost my balance and crashed down in the bath with an oath, sending water flying up to the ceiling. That got her out all right. She vanished into the bedroom but left the door open. I finished my washing in at least a moderate privacy.

When I got out of the bath, I found that the towel was a dressing gown and I put it on. I looked at myself in one of the mirrors and woke up. Here I was, Sinbad the Sailor in a Roman outfit, and so far I had behaved like a teetotaler in a wine cellar. Good old Goatskin had prepared a feast for me from the bottom of his generous heart and his wallet; he had given me a rich man's paradise complete with Eau de Cologne and a bathing beauty; if I went on like this, throwing up my hands and saying, Get thee behind me, it was high time I went to see a doctor.

I entered the bedroom full of bad intentions. I was sure that I would find her in the bed or, at least, in the preliminary stages. It came as a surprise when I saw her sitting on the window sill, fully dressed, still filing her nails. I went toward her, put a hand on her shoulder like an uncle, looked at the view, and sighed, "Beautiful." Then I bent over and kissed her on the crown of her head. It was a bit smelly. She looked up, gave me a sweet smile, and continued filing her nails. When I kissed her again, this time like a cousin, she darted away and said, "Come! To bed." I said, "O.K.," strode toward the bed, slipped out of my gown, put my chest out and pulled my stomach in, walked round the bed once to impress her with my torso, and lay down.

The moment I lay down I felt dizzy. It was a long time since I had a bed under me. I looked up when I felt something on my forehead and saw it was her hand. She stood by my bedside like a nurse, and said, "Ssh—sleep."

I said, "Sleep? Are you mad? It's four o'clock."

"Oh," she said, "everybody here sleeps in the afternoon. We never eat before ten at night."

"That may be," I said, "but I won't." Then I put my arm round her and gave her a solid kiss. I might as well have kissed the back of my own hand for all the response I got. She calmly took my arm away and said, "Sorry. That's not included."

It made me angry, for in that case the way I was lying there was perfectly ridiculous. "You could have told me," I said. "I'm sorry if I frightened you, but if a girl puts me in a bath, scrubs my back for me, and offers to do the front too, it puts ideas into my head."

180

She looked at me with dim amazement. "Maurice told me to go and see if you had everything you wanted," she said.

"All right," I said, "in that case I tell him you have bungled it." I was furious, and felt like taking her across my knee. I shut my eyes tight and the moment I did so I felt dizzy again.

She put her hand on my forehead once more. I tried to stay furious but I couldn't. I found that I was very tired; it must have been the whisky. Her hand stroking my forehead was soothing.

I said, slowly, "Two postcards. On the desk. Post them."

"Ssh," she whispered, "sleep."

I did.

∽

When I woke up, it was dark. I saw her silhouetted against a deep blue sky, sitting on the window sill. I got up, put the bath-robe around my shoulders and joined her on the window sill.

She smiled at me and said, "You certainly slept well."

"Did I?"

"Maurice came in and wanted to talk to you. You didn't answer. You didn't even wake up when he shook you by the shoulder."

I said, "Fancy that."

"Would you like a glass of whisky?" she asked.

"You people seem to have a whisky complex," I said.

She shrugged her shoulders. "It's Maurice. He never drinks anything else, so he never wants anyone to drink something else either."

"That's curious," I said. "When I knew him, he detested the stuff. I wonder what gave him this passion for it."

She shrugged her shoulders again with a little laugh that wasn't gay. "I suppose he likes it because it's expensive," she said.

We sat looking for a while at the illuminated terraces, the yellow lamp-lit window squares in the dark row of houses across the harbor, and the sweep of the lighthouse beam, scything the slender shadows of the masts. We sat a yard apart, but I felt close to her. For the first time there was something real about her, something human.

"You sailed with him, didn't you?" she asked suddenly.

"Yes."

181

"What was he like during the war?"

"A very good sailor, and a good friend."

"How long is it since you saw him last?"

"About a month ago."

"Here, in the South of France?"

"No, in Antwerp."

"What was he doing there?"

"We went to see the wreck of our ship, before it was broken up."

"Oh," she said. And then, after a silence, "So that's where he went."

It sounded mysterious, but I let it pass, waiting for her to tell me some more.

She didn't. She sat looking at the masts and the stars; accordion-music came from a distance in waves with the wind. It was growing darker. I could hardly distinguish her face and her arms any more, as if she was slowly vanishing out of the white shell of her dress. Then she asked, "Has he always been such a liar?"

It took me aback. I didn't answer straight away; I looked back in the past, but I couldn't remember a single instance in which he had lied, to my knowledge. He had always been a rather tense, dry sort of chap, not at all the imaginative type. "No," I said, "I don't think so. Is he now?"

She laughed again, without gaiety. "He's very sweet," she said. "But he doesn't know the difference between reality and his imagination any more. You were his captain, weren't you?"

"Yes, once. But he is a captain himself."

"He talked a lot about you, nights, after dinner, when he was a bit drunk. He said you were a pirate; one of the toughest men he had ever known, and that you took women like other people took a cigarette."

I said, "Well, well," and felt like laughing. But I didn't, because at second thought I rather liked that picture of myself. The fact that she had told me this as a proof of what a liar he was didn't please me altogether; I must have given her the impression of one of Snow White's dwarfs. As it was dark, the rich blue darkness of the South, and as I was still trailing the last wisps

182

of the dream of Sinbad the Sailor, I asked, "What makes you think that it isn't the truth?"

She didn't answer. She must have looked at me in the darkness, for suddenly she bent forward, and kissed me. Then she got up and I saw her ghost vanish in the blackness of the bedroom.

I knew I was behaving like a boy, but I couldn't help asking, "Honestly, what makes you think that there isn't some truth in that?"

Her voice answered from the darkness, "I saw you asleep."

For some reason that irritated me. I said, "All right, put the light on. Let's have something to eat."

She put the light on and I saw her again as she really was: a thin Chinese girl, with a tired face and straight hair. She seemed a quite different person from the one that had talked to me in the darkness.

I was dressing when the door was opened without a knock. It was Goatskin, in his pin-striped suit but without his cane and his hat. He looked like a provincial boy on Sunday. "All right," he said to the Chinese girl, "scram."

I wanted to say something pompous, like: "The lady is my guest now," but I let it pass. For one thing, she was out of the room too soon, she flitted out like a cat. Goatskin kicked the door shut behind her, pulled out a long, chromium cigarette case, snapped it open, and held it out to me. I said, "No, thanks"; he stuck one in his mouth and struck a match on the sole of his shoe. As it was crepe, it didn't work; so he struck it on the table, making a scratch on the polish. I watched his performance, curiously. He looked as if he was acting a gangster in an amateur show. Perhaps I would have fallen for it if I hadn't known him so long and so well. To me he was just Goatskin putting on an act. Perhaps he put it on a bit thick for my benefit.

"Well," he said. "So there you are. I told you you would come." I couldn't remember him telling me, but I let it pass. "Is she to your liking?" he asked.

There were various answers to this; I stood a moment in doubt which line to take. Then the memory of him when I was lying on the couch in his chartroom got the upper hand. I said, "Are you sure you want me here?"

He looked at me, amazed at first, then suspicious. "Why?"

"Because I'm not going to take that act from you," I said. "I don't mind if you want the rest of the world to believe that you're a baby Al Capone; to me you're just my mate with a hat on and pansy socks. And the hell with Maurice."

At first I thought he was going to be nasty. Then he suddenly deflated, fell down on the bed, stretched his arms over his head, and said, "Jesus, what a life." I smelled another act coming on; this time the lonely ring leader, a victim of circumstances. But I wasn't sure yet, so I decided to let him swim on for a bit. "Suppose you tell me something about that life," I said, "and stop throwing Chinese girls at me and filling my bath with whisky. What are you doing here, apart from throwing your weight around?"

"I told you," he said. "Tires, and cut the captain business because here it's me who is the boss."

I said, "Get the idea out of your head that everybody is acting a role. I'm asking you a straight question. If you prefer to make rings around me, tell me so and I'll be off."

"All right," he said. "Keep your shirt on." He had got a lot weaker in the meantime. I wondered why. In Antwerp he had still seemed his old tough self. Perhaps he was better off the stage.

I tried my best to get him off the stage. It took about half an hour of bootlegger's wisecracks before, at last, he sat up on the bed, forgetting his pin-striped suit and the gaudy bedroom. For the first time, sincerity flickered in his eyes. "All right," he said. "I'll give you the full case history. After I left you in that hospital, I went to Holland. Only the South had been liberated by then. I got a ride on a lorry from Brussels to Antwerp. There were Dutch girls in the lorry, who worked in Headquarters in Brussels and were on their way home for the holidays, because it was Christmas. One of them got out in Antwerp to buy something—a present for her mother. You'll ask what this has to do with me; I'm getting to it. She came back after a few minutes, radiant, with a leather handbag. She was a very nice girl. The kind of girl I had been dreaming about all during the war, while laying the United Nations. 'I had a lovely stroke of luck,' she said. 'The old woman charged me five hundred francs for this thing and although

184

it was much too dear, I decided to take it. I gave her a thousand franc note, and what do you think she did? She gave me two thousand in return.' All the other girls in that lorry laughed their heads off. And I looked at them and felt—Jesus, I don't know how I felt. Only it was that girl that started me off."

"On what?" I asked.

"On the road that led to—here," he said. "It was only the beginning, perhaps I got mixed up with the wrong crowd. When I came to Holland all the girls were like that. They had no sense of honesty, of decency. As far as they are concerned, we lost the war. Well, after that, I began to look around for signs of rot, and I found plenty, let me tell you. When the North was liberated, I thought things would be different there. The people had suffered a lot. There had been famine and what they call heroism. But when I walked through the Vondel Park in Amsterdam, a few days after the Liberation, I broke my neck over copulating couples at every three steps: the Canadians had arrived. And then those boys of the Resistance—I didn't like the sight of them either. I may be mistaken, but I had the feeling that most of them were profiteers, who had joined at the last minute. The real ones had been shot or beaten to death in concentration camps. I know that all this doesn't seem to add up to anything, and I can't very well talk about it. It's the first time I'm telling anybody and it doesn't sound convincing, now I hear it. It must have been the outcome of all sorts of little things, things I can't remember now. But the general effect was to give me the feeling that Dop had died, and Waterman and Van Dam and the rest, for nothing, for a mystification. That I'd been living in a fool's paradise all during the war, thinking that I was defending something which was true and real and worth dying for, to leave it to the children, even if they weren't your own. Oh well . . ." He fell back on the bed and stretched his arms over his head again. "I suppose it was just one man's fate—what happened to me. Perhaps the same would have happened if I'd found our country full of angels, playing harps. Perhaps all I'm doing and have been doing for the last year is just trying to find a justification for my going to hell. Because I suppose that's what this is." He made a vague gesture round the room. "Hell."

I felt he was getting onto the stage once more, and I tried to drag him off again by saying, "A very pleasant hell, if you ask me. I wouldn't take yourself too seriously, you know. It clouds the issue."

"All right," he said. "I'll give it to you straight, without commentary. I tried at first to do a decent job, but for many reasons I couldn't stick it anywhere. For one thing people just didn't want to see the facts as they were; they talked and thought in preposterous platitudes about liberty and the Queen and national honor and those filthy Germans, and at the same time they all voted for the annexation of a bit of German territory along the border —'Straightening out the frontier,' they called it. Nobody seemed to remember that what got us into trouble in the first place was Mr. Hitler wanting to straighten out some frontiers too. And then they all read the papers, and yet they didn't see the headlines I saw. "Market Declines as Peace Scare Widens," for instance. They didn't see the advertisement of a big steel factory, saying, "What does your country sell to Bethlehem?" Perhaps I was already on my road to here and unconsciously looking for justifications. But I made a collection of those headlines and articles and advertisements and speeches, I became quite a collector. In the end those things stopped making me feel indignant or miserable. On the contrary, they delighted me. I felt a sort of collector's joy every time I found a new beauty to stick in my album. So I was one of the few people, I think, who saw this next war coming even before the last one was quite over. And when I was offered a lucrative job by a casual friend whom I met in a bar in Brussels, I took it because I didn't feel under the moral obligation to be a nice, clean, honest citizen any more."

"What kind of job was that?" I asked.

"Smuggling," he said. "Cognac and spirits and other stuff to England. It was quite a foolproof scheme. We had two identical tank landing craft, both called *Crazy Lady*. The name was painted on their sterns in exactly the same lettering. One of them was lying in a harbor in the South of England with a crew of jolly young camping people; the other in a harbor in Normandy with another crew, including me as the skipper. We played around with those craft for about a month, chugging in and out

186

of our harbors, staying within the three-mile limit, until the customs came to know us quite well and started waving at us from their launches when we came in from a trip, without bothering to search us any more. After that, the operations started. The *Crazy Lady* from the South of England and we, from Normandy, sailed for the open at exactly the same hour. But this time we were loaded with stuff. We met our partners that night halfway across the Channel. And there we changed crews. So the *Crazy Lady* from the South of England, at whom the customs waved the next morning, was really the *Crazy Lady* from Normandy. We kept that up for almost half a year."

"Whose idea was that?" I asked.

He laughed. "Not mine. I'm not a brain, just a sucker. In all these games, there are brains and suckers. The brains sit somewhere quite safe, in London or Paris or Brussels, smoking cigars and taking their ladies out, just like during the war."

"Were you found out in the end?"

"I wasn't," he said. "I left in time, when I thought they were getting too confident of themselves. They were caught a month later. After that I came here. The tire racket seemed quite a wholesome job compared to the smuggling. Easy money too. And I liked the crowd. You will too, once you get to know them. No, what happened to me here was different. The sea got me."

I thought he was play acting again. But he wasn't. He sat up on the bed once more, put his arms round his knees, and looked at me with eyes that were completely sincere. He was old Goatskin again, the boy with whom I shared so many memories neither of us had ever spoken about. "When I dived for the first time," he said, "something happened to me. I can't describe to you what. I can only compare it to something: to dive for the first time with a mask and to see the world under water is like making love to a woman for the first time in your life. It is a shock, a birth, being torn loose from everything you have known before. Once you get underneath the mirror of the sea, you are cut off from everything, even your own personality. You're like the first man on the moon, completely alone, and you change into something, I don't know, a superhuman being, with a tremendous feeling of power. A hunter in a jungle where no man has ever

187

been. I suppose you don't believe me. You think I'm exaggerating. Well, wait till you get there yourself. Perhaps it won't work on you the way it did on me, but then you'll be an exception. When you meet my crowd, Pierre and Bernard and Jacques and the little Russian, you'll meet four people who live in a dream as long as they are ashore, who don't care a damn about what they do above the water or what people do to them. They begin to live only when they've got their masks on and their frogman's feet, and their tubes in their mouths. You'll see."

I waited for him to go on but he fell silent. He looked at his hands. I looked too and noticed for the first time how wrinkled they were. The skin seemed loose, as if he had just got out of a bath. "And this spiv's setup," I asked, "how does that fit in?"

He looked at me, not understanding at first. Then he said, "Oh, this you mean," including the room, the rumpled bed, the socks, the whisky. "This is just a way of killing time ashore. We are all a bit frightened, you know, of the spell the sea has thrown over us. And that's why we try to make our life above the water as attractive a possible. I, for one, like a lot of girls and good food and drinks and a lot of loose money. I like to throw parties and swagger around a bit, because once I am back among other human beings, back from my prehistoric jungle, there is one thing I want to forget: the war. The rottenness of men. The exploitation of sentiments that were decent and noble once. The lies, the speeches, the steel of Bethlehem, the concentration camps in our own country. Because, now, I have a feeling that I would go on like this for ever, living the life of a male mermaid, loving the girls, loving my friends, feeling one with the whole of humanity, gay and carefree and hopeful. But there is one thing that might mess all that up, and that's the new war they are preparing. I want to forget that. To forget it like hell."

I said, "Suppose you did something about it. Opened your mouth, for instance, instead of getting blind drunk or hiding with the fish."

He shrugged his shoulders and looked at me with a smile that made me feel slightly ill at ease, for it was a smile of indulgence. "Good old Skipper," he said. "Let's go and eat."

I took my jacket over my arm and went to the door. He got up

188

from the bed and followed me; one of his trouser legs stuck half-way up his calf. When I was about to open the door, he put his hand on my shoulder and said, "I'm glad you came. I like you a lot, after all."

I said, "Straighten your trousers," and we went down the carpeted stairs to the lobby, where the hall porter saluted when he saw us, and the blondes came tottering out of the bar, cackling like chickens. "Where are we going?" they cried.

"To Ginette's," he said. "Call the crowd."

～

We had dinner in a very nice restaurant, full of jolly people, in candlelight, at a long table heaped with food, on which the bottles were changed all the time and a little cat gingerly trod its way across the remains of bouillabaisse and empty oyster shells. I was introduced to over a dozen people and called "Skipper"; their names escaped me. At first I felt rather out of it, but the Chinese girl appeared after a while and sat down by my side and started telling me which ones out of the crowd I should remember. There were the two boys with whom Maurice had come in when I was waiting for him in the hotel lobby, the tall one was Bernard and the fat one Jacques. They were deep-sea hunters and very nice; both had been in the Resistance. The small fat man with the child's face, sitting between the blondes at the other end of the table, was Pjotr, who acted as a cook on board, but all he ever cooked was the fish he caught himself. He was an underwater hunter too, he worked with a mask and a harpoon gun. The rest were just charming people having a free meal. She hadn't the faintest idea who they were.

We drank a lot of *vin rosé* and all of us got very gay. Goatskin sat, flushed, between two candles at the head of the table, holding the hand of a gorgeous creature who was quite bored, for he told long stories in what he obviously thought was excellent French. I listened to him with amazement; he told about his adventures during the war and practically every word he uttered was a lie with an accent. I looked at the Chinese girl by my side, and wondered what had happened to make such a liar out of this boy, whom I had always known as a wonderful guy.

189

After the meal we went to a "dancing." On our way there, Goatskin and the three boys that had been pointed out to me took me in their midst, and Goatskin told me incoherently what I was supposed to do on board their ship. I wouldn't have to dive, I could try if I liked but it wasn't necessary because it wasn't a diver they wanted. The schooner with which they sailed didn't belong to them, but to a Captain, who was very old and nearly blind and a very bad sailor. What they really wanted me for was to keep an eye on the navigation, and replace the Captain as much as possible without hurting his feelings. I said I'd do my best, but that it seemed a tricky proposition. The captains I had sailed with so far wouldn't let themselves be replaced; not even Captain Goatskin of the old *Vlieland.*

The dancing was in a cellar bursting with the most hellish noise I had ever heard musical instruments make. There was a snarling trumpet that pierced the eardrums and a percussion battery that gave me palpitations by the sheer volume of its thunder. The dancing that was going on in the couple of square yards among the tables was of the postwar kind. Men in zoot suits tugged with girls with horse tails on their heads and flung them over their shoulders; I thought I couldn't stand much of this.

But after a while the injections of sound jabbed into me had a vitalizing effect; also there was a lot of whisky going. I got so above myself that I ventured to dance with the Chinese girl, but the space between the tables was too small for me. First I cleared the floor by swirling round like a dervish, then I knocked over a table full of glasses. I had a great success with this and sat down amidst generous applause. Goatskin had tears streaming down his face, and I heard him say, "You haven't seen anything yet, wait till he gets going properly." I was too drunk to mind by then. He was a wonderful guy, he could lie as much as he liked.

When at last I got back to the hotel, the room behaved as if there were a heavy swell going. I fell on the bed as into the sea, and fell asleep like a sinking plate.

I woke up in a pink morning. By my bedside stood the Chinese girl with a cup of coffee and a croissant. When she saw me open my eyes she dipped the croissant in the coffee and held it out to me, which was rather messy but made me feel luxurious and oriental. "Good morning," I said, and tried to manage the croissant. I found I had to eat it like a chicken drinking. I wanted to sip my coffee, when I suddenly remembered with alarm that we had been supposed to sail this morning at five o'clock. When I said this she smiled and said, "My friend, you are in the South of France now. If people say here that they'll sail at five o'clock in the morning, you'll be lucky if everybody is on board by midnight." I thought how sweet she would be, and how I would like her, if only her eyes weren't so black. I couldn't see anything at all in them, just two black discs the size of a farthing. I liked her ears, though; they were very delicate despite their size. "Tell me something about yourself," I said. "Where do you fit in?"

She smiled and looked at me for a while before she answered. I got a bit uneasy under that look; it was as if she was searching my eyes through dark glasses. "I was a student," she said. "And when the Liberation came, I was very enthusiastic. I thought that, after the war, there would be no more racial prejudices and a new unity of men. When I found out that I was wrong, I decided to have a good time."

I said, "I see," instead of the other things I felt like saying. "Do you sail with us?" I asked.

"No," she said.

"Well," I said, "I suppose I had better get up and have a look at that ship. Or doesn't it exist after all?"

"Oh, yes," she said. "It exists all right. And it's quite a sight. You'll see."

She was right. When I had finally located the ship in a far corner of the bombed-out harbor, I stood looking at it, musing, for quite a while. She was called *Euridice*, had the body of a barge and the rigging of a two-masted schooner. Her sails were lying on the beams like heaps of laundry, hastily ripped off the line, her deck was littered with a multitude of things in wild confusion: diving masks, frogmen's feet, bathing trunks, deck chairs, harpoon guns, respirators, rubber dingies, a motor bicycle, folding tables and two wine barrels. The center piece of this sailor's nightmare was an old upright piano, lashed to the back of the midships, where I supposed the galley was.

191

She looked quite deserted and was moored in a way that made me think her crew had fled in a panic. She lay, with her stern to the quay, at anchor. She was attached to the quay by a solitary mooring rope, the size of a flag line.

I went on board, trod my way cautiously through the litter on her deck, opened the lid of the piano, to find out if it was true. It was. I advanced slowly toward her foredeck and ended up at the anchor winch. There I saw that they had paid out the full chain, so any time there might be a breeze that wasn't right on, she'd break her flag line and start sailing.

As I stood contemplating this, I heard a sound behind me: snoring. It came from the wheelhouse, which was midships. I looked through the dirty window, saw two bunks, one above the other against the back wall. From the top bunk dangled a thin, white leg. The interior of the wheelhouse, as far as I could see it, was worse than her deck. Every square inch of horizontal space was covered with objects; on the walls hung yet another rash of diving masks, respiration tubes, dirty towels, long underwear and a hunting horn.

I felt like giving up and thumbing a lift on the road toward the North as fast as I could. But when I strolled back to the hotel in the very hot sunlight, I felt a laziness overcome me, a sleepy desire to get into the shadow, and an indifference toward life and all its problems that was new to me. After all, I had nowhere to go to, nobody was waiting for me anywhere on this earth, so who the hell was I to feel a moral indignation at the presence of an upright piano on the deck of a seagoing ship? I found the Chinese girl, sitting on the terrace in front of the hotel, in the company of Pjotr and the tall Bernard. They were having a Pernod and so I had a Pernod too. It did its work quickly and pleasantly. After one glass I began to like the idea of the piano. After the second I asked myself why nobody had ever thought of it before. It would make no end of difference to seafaring life if one could sit down at odd moments to tinkle: "Tiptoe through the Tulips with Me." And then a revolutionary thought dawned on me, as I was sitting there enjoying the taste of aniseed and feeling an agreeable morning mist rise in my brain. For three thousand years people had taken the art of navigation

192

much too seriously. All of us, young, ambitious sailors, dreaming of being master mariners, were the victims of several hundred generations of impostors. I didn't think of giving up any more. I couldn't wait for the moment when I would see the helmsman leave the wheel to play the piano.

After my second glass, as I began to grin in anticipation of our first cruise, I had the impression that the Chinese girl was watching me. I couldn't make sure, for she was indeed wearing dark glasses now. I looked at her eyeless skull and said, "By the way, sweetheart, what's your name? Thalassa?"

She smiled without gaiety. "No," she said, "Nicole. What did you say the other was?"

I said, "Never mind," and raised my glass. "Here's luck."

She looked at me, expressionless, while I drank.

⁓

We sailed at eleven o'clock that evening. It was a very hot night, full of stars and harmonica music, and the drunks could be heard yodeling blocks away. The drunks weren't our crew; they were all brand sober and very agitated. I didn't quite grasp the number of them, because there were many people about and I wasn't sure who was intended to sail with us. I sat on a bollard, in a corner, and listened with amazement to the rows.

The whole ship seemed to be full of rows. Everybody was screaming at somebody else, and every few minutes or so there was the same furious exclamation that rose above the rest: "All right, in that case we can't sail!" At first I tried to follow the arguments, but I discovered that this exclamation was traditional, and did not really mean what it said. For, while everybody was screaming that we couldn't sail, some absent-minded shadows on the fo'c'sle were weighing anchor. Then came the moment which I had seen coming for the last ten minutes, when the strain of the anchor chain being pulled taut became too much for the flag line on the poop, so it snapped and the ship started sailing.

There were wild cries of "Stop, stop!" and "I have got to go ashore!" and "Hey, who is that at the anchor winch?" A crowd of dark silhouettes gathered on the poop, gesticulating, throwing ropes at the beachcombers ashore, that fell far short and splashed

193

into the water. Somebody yelled, "Full speed astern!" which was a wish rather than a command, for the engine wasn't running. The chorus on the back started chanting "Full speed astern!" until somebody realized that the engine hadn't been started yet. That brought forth another chorus: "Captain!"

The crowd surged from the poop to the midships where they gathered round the wheelhouse. Two silhouettes opened the door, from the inside came shouts and curses, and after a few moments a white ghost was dragged out, struggling: an old man in pyjamas. Before he was forced down the hatch to the engine room, he too yelled the war cry, "In that case we can't sail!" Then he vanished. The ship, in the meantime, was slowly drifting out and started swinging round. There were sounds of blows and a clanking of iron from the engine room, then a loud explosion, and blue smoke poured from the hatch through the lamplight. The lamp had been brought by somebody from somewhere and put on the piano. After the explosion the engine started running, full astern. But as the ship's stern was not pointing at the quay any longer, the crowd started shouting, "Ahead, ahead!" The ghost in pyjamas emerged from the engine room hatch, put his hand over his eyes, looked around and asked, "Where is the shore?"

At that moment I began to giggle, one of those nervous giggles that are so difficult to get out of. I sat in the darkness, giggling helplessly, while the crowd argued on the deck and the ship made the full tour of the compass until, for some reason, it ended up with its stern toward the quay once more. I was just getting over my giggles, when suddenly, above the general noise, I heard a flapping sound and saw the little fat Russian advance on me in bathing trunks and with frogman's feet on. I expected him to sit down and start playing the piano, but he touched my shoulder, said, "Sorry, old man, would you mind shifting? I want that rope." I got up, laughing again; the little fat man took the rope between his teeth and dived overboard with a splash. Then he swam to the shore, while about seven people were paying out the rope after him, climbed the quay, and handed it to the beachcombers, who fastened it to a mooring ring. There were more shouts of "full speed astern!" until somebody remembered that the anchor

194

chain had been shortened. Then some people rushed toward the winch and the chain thundered out again.

A quarter of an hour later we were back where we had been an hour before. Half of the crowd filed ashore as soon as the gangplank was put down, and the little fat man with the frogman's feet flapped back on board. Somebody hollered, "Let go!" and the beachcombers were loosening the rope, when somebody else cried, "Maurice! Maurice isn't back yet!" So the chorus chanted, "Maurice!" and, "Make fast!" then, at last, peace descended.

I was delighted to see the little man with the frogman's feet roll a wine barrel toward the piano, sit down on top of it, open the piano's lid and start playing a *berceuse* by Chopin. Somebody asked me from the darkness, "Well, Skipper? Happy?"

I said, "Yes." I had never said it more sincerely.

∾

Goatskin was brought on board several hours later, dead drunk, carried on a stretcher by two gay people and followed by the staggering blondes. When I saw the small cortege approaching it chilled me; as a boy, in South Shields, I had seen a drowned sailor carried on board and the picture of his boots with his dead feet inside was still very clear, I had forgotten his face. When I say them carry Goatskin on board I thought he was dead.

I was the only one who felt a moment's alarm, the others took the spectacle as a matter of course. He was gently lowered down the steep ladder to the fo'c'sle, where we all had our bunks, and laid out on the couch after the usual heap of dirty clothes, bathing trunks, shoes, and empty bottles had been swept onto the floor. Once he lay there the ship left.

I didn't go on deck, but I knew what happened by the noises. I wasn't worried, yet I felt ill at ease, sitting by Goatskin's side, listening to his sick breathing, that seemed louder than the rattle of the anchor winch, the frantic shouts and curses outside. I looked at his face in the yellow light of the oil lamp, and again the memory of that night I woke up on the couch in his chartroom came back to me. He must have sat looking at me the way I sat looking at him now, and he must have felt the same.

He woke up after a quarter of an hour or so, opened his eyes, and looked at me with a drunken dazedness.

"Cigarette?" I asked.

The words took a long time reaching him, then he nodded, with difficulty. I lit one and stuck it in his mouth. He puffed at it, then it fell from his lips onto his collar. I took it away.

He wanted to say something, I couldn't make out what. Then he put out his hand; only after he had groped for a while I realized he was groping for mine. It was a strange moment; I suddenly thought of Dop and Barger and the boy Waterman and the poem on the wall in room 77 in the Grand Hotel. It was the first time I realized that all of our old friends were now on that distant shore; he and I were the only ones left this side.

Then the others came down and Pjotr opened a bottle of Pernod. We had many Pernods, so many that I don't quite remember when we went to bed. I remember lying on my back at a given moment under a very low ceiling, hearing the creaking of the rigging, the slow swish of waves, and an old man's voice singing in the distance *"Le joli printemps des roses."* It struck me, because I realized in a slow, serious way that there were no roses in the spring. But then I remembered that I was in the South of France, where everything was different, and I fell asleep with a lovely glow of happiness and peace and love for everybody, alive or dead, for there wasn't any real difference, the only difference was time.

Chapter IX

THE FOLLOWING NIGHT, TOWARD SUNSET, WE ARRIVED AT A LITTLE island off the coast. I remembered it from the Invasion; that hot day in August, '44,, seemed far away. The island looked innocent now. It hadn't been then. I remembered the armada of ships, the flashes of gunfire from the mountains, the explosions, the fires, the frantic birds, the thousands of dead fish coming to the surface after each explosion. Now it was beautiful and still; the sea was like a mirror, gently rocking and distorting the reflection of the

196

island. I stood looking at it, leaning on the rail at the foremost spot of the ship. Then I heard the sound of flapping steps behind me and saw the four boys come out of the fo'c'sle with their frogman's feet on, their masks on their heads, their respiration tubes and their harpoon guns in their hands. "We'll see whether we can get some dinner," Bernard said. "Would you like to join us?" I said I'd rather wait and see; I'd never swum with a mask and a respirator.

That morning I had got a first notion of what terrific swimmers they were. Contrary to all the rules imbued in me since my childhood, they had all had a swim immediately after breakfast and no one had gone down with a cramp. As the ship had been making no speed at all, they had splashed around lustily and I had watched them as if I were standing on the beach. Then the Captain had come out of the wheelhouse in his pyjamas, vanished down the hatch to the engine room, and started explosions. As the engine started running full speed, the bathers yelled from the sea. Luckily I heard them. The Captain, arising with the smoke from the inside of the ship, became furious when I said there were four people in the sea, being left behind. He said that if he stopped the engine now, it would take another hour to start it up again for the fuel pump would be drowned. I said that he had to make up his mind as to whom he preferred to be drowned; he muttered, "All right. Next trip I retire. I'm sick of this," but he went down the engine hatch again and stopped the thing with a reverberating explosion. It had taken the bathers about twenty minutes to catch up with us; but when they finally climbed on board, they hadn't seemed to be tired in the least.

That evening I understood why. After they had put their masks in front of their faces and stuck their tubes in their mouths, they went down the pilot's ladder and swam round the ship several times before striking out toward the island. It was a curious sight, for just the four tubes stuck out above the water, and they could be heard breathing for many yards away. They all breathed in a different way: Bernard with slow deep sighs, Jacques with short puffs; Goatskin and Pjotr breathed like whales, with a little spout of water spurting from their tubes at every exhalation, and were

197

the first to be off, at terrific speed. As it was near sunset, the sea got slightly hazy and they vanished soon from sight.

The moment they were off, everybody on board ship went to sleep. I remained alone on the deck, waiting for them, until it became dark. That was three hours later, and they still hadn't come home. I began to get worried and called the captain. He half woke up when I shook him and said that the swimmers had been away for over three hours and that it was getting dark. "Don't worry," he mumbled. "They never come back within four hours," and turned over on his other side.

"But it's getting dark," I said. "They may not be able to find us."

"Put out a light," he mumbled, "if you're nervous. Now let me sleep."

I lit the lantern on the piano and sat waiting for them, like an anxious mother, peering overboard at every splash I heard. I heard many splashes as the night got darker, and discovered that they were fish jumping at the light. In the end I got so bored and worried that I sat down at the piano, opened the lid, and stared at the yellow teeth of the keyboard, thinking that if a fairy came to say that I could make a wish and it would be granted, I'd wish to play the piano like Rachmaninoff. As it was, I tried out, "Ye Banks and Braes," with one finger. I remembered Stella, humming it in our little flat, that morning, long ago. I lit a cigarette, leaned back with my feet on the piano, and thought about Stella, but she seemed far away. Not only because she was married now and living in Warsaw, of all places, but because I could no longer take myself and her and our love and the war quite as seriously as I'd been doing. It was difficult to take anything seriously in these surroundings, not even the fact that four people had probably just drowned. If it pleased them to get drowned they were at perfect liberty to do so; everybody was at perfect liberty to do whatever he pleased in this world of the Mediterranean. I felt at peace, sitting there, smoking, looking at the first stars and the hazy silhouette of the grim little island, wreathed in memories. I felt that nobody could hurt me very much, because they couldn't get in touch with me any more. I remembered how on the quays of Marseilles everybody had seemed to live in a little universe all his own. The same thing was happening to me; it was rather

198

a pleasant state. I felt entirely rid of all responsibility, even toward my own life. Then they came home.

The first I heard was a soft, puffing sound, rapidly approaching, as of a little engine. It was Pjotr's staccato breathing. He climbed the pilot's ladder, with the sound of a sea lion emerging from the water. His feet flapped on the deck like flippers. From his belt dangled three loops of steel wire, full of fish, still alive, twitching their tails and gaping. Their gold eyes glittered in the lamplight. "I saw liches," he said, "as big as a man. Over there, in that wreck. Golly, if we had only had the boat! Maurice and Bernard got one of them, but I don't think they managed to tow it over here. And I saw a lovely ray, as big as an eagle. Tomorrow morning you come, with the boat. Follow us. Ray with butter. Wonderful!" He flapped toward the galley, loosening his belt with the fish. "Didn't you get cold?" I asked. "Of course," he said, "I'm frozen. Let's have a drink."

I went to get a drink from the fo'c'sle; when I came back the others had arrived. They were standing in the lamplight, on the poop, their masks on their heads, all of them with huge bunches of twitching fish dangling from their belts. Goatskin looked quite different from the way I'd ever seen him; his blue eyes were lighter than ever and his face thin and beaky, his wet hair matted on his forehead. He looked almost mad. "I'm sure there are jeeps in the holds of that wreck," he said. "And even if there aren't, I'm going to have a look tomorrow."

"With luck, you might find a nice nest of conger eels," Pjotr said. "The holds are shut. They like the dark."

"But how could they have got in?" I asked, "if the holds are shut?"

They laughed and Bernard said, "Why do you think that ship sank? Through lack of breath? There must be a hole in its side the size of a house. Let's have a drink."

They had their drinks by lantern light, with towels round their shoulders. The fish they had caught made little flapping noises on the deck and glistened in the darkness. They glistened like fish themselves. When I sat looking at them and saw them laugh in the lantern light, I thought how voracious their teeth looked and how cruelly excited were their eyes. I felt as if I were having a

199

drink with beings from another world. The kind, gay people of the days before seemed to have shed their magic cloaks that made them look like human beings; now they looked like deep-sea monsters. I was very romantic that night.

Pjotr cooked the fish. It smelled delicious when I passed the galley, but three quarters of their catch lay still twitching on the deck. When I asked Bernard what they were going to do with those, he said, "Oh, I don't know, throw them away." As I had never been a hunter, I thought it was rather gruesome, this happy passion for slaughter for slaughter's sake. When the fish was served, I didn't enjoy it the way I had thought I would. The soft flapping noises in the corner spoiled my appetite. I knew I was being sentimental but I was living in my own universe now and could be as sentimental as I damn well pleased.

After the meal, when they had put on jerseys and trousers, we sat on the aft deck of the idly drifting ship and talked about hunting and fish and the deep sea. I asked them what was the attraction of killing animals under water, just for the sake of killing? I found out that they all were as tenderhearted as spinsters so long as it concerned nice woolly things ashore, like bunnies and foxes and the defenseless grouse. But under water it was different, they said. Fish were different from other animals. They didn't have the same sensations of pain and fear, they were cold-blooded and they didn't scream. Rays, for instance, were evil monsters; once I'd seen a ray advance on me, slowly flapping its wings like an evil bird, I'd feel how different fish were from other animals. I was very interested in their arguments, and I thought of the German officer I had talked to at the beginning of the war who had said practically the same things about Jews, compared to other people.

Pjotr got quite lyrical in his descriptions of underwater hunting. He said it was vital, beautiful, ferocious, a world that had remained unchanged for millions of years, where man entered like a terror that fell from the sky. I asked what was the attraction of feeling like a terror that fell from the sky; he looked at me in amazement and said, "Why, it's beautiful!" In the past, in pubs and Nissen bars in the outposts of the war, I had often tried to trick bomber pilots into that very same confession, but they had never fallen into the trap, however drunk they were. It was odd that an innocent Russian boy, on the deck of an idly floating ship under the diamond sky of the Mediterranean, should speak for them at last. It gave me, somehow, a grim satisfaction.

Goatskin looked at me with the thin smile I remembered from our meeting on board the wreck of our ship. "That's right, Skipper," he said. "Feel fine and righteous while there's still time. For this is your last chance, you know. Tomorrow we'll throw you in the water with a mask on and you'll have your first look at what you have been sailing on top of all your life. You've been crawling on the skin of a monster ever since you were little. Tomorrow you'll see the X-ray. Have you ever been in one of those modern shoe shops in England, where you try on a new pair and they put your foot in a little box and you look through a slot and you see the bones of your feet wriggling inside, and then a nice girl asks you, 'You see how it fits, sir?' That's nothing, Skipper, compared to what you'll see tomorrow. It will frighten the pants off you."

"Don't be ridiculous," said Pjotr. "It's the most wonderful sight you have ever seen. He doesn't know what beauty is until he has seen a wonderful light rock with sea urchins and sea stars, and thousands of little fish that come toward him and peer in his mask. It's the most beautiful thing in the world."

"I'm not going to show him the sea urchins and the little fish," Goatskin said. "I'm going to show him the wreck."

I asked, "Why? Is this a special treatment?"

He smiled again and looked at me with his cruel blue eyes. I didn't like him then. "Yes," he said. "I want you to remember a U-boat with a captain called Hasenfratz. When you see the wreck tomorrow, remember that somewhere off the coast of England, he is lying just like that, among the sea urchins and the little fish. He, and your first ship."

I said, "That's a pretty nasty thing to say. Why?"

He looked at me, still smiling, and answered, "Because you are too damned snooty. You think that you are the only one with beautiful thoughts and refined sentiments. You think little Pjotr is a bloodthirsty animal of prey, because he harpoons rays and fights with congers. It'll do you good to remember that when it

201

comes to killing fish, you out of the lot of us have killed the biggest one."

I looked at him, trying to see in his eyes whether that was the truth or whether there was something else. But I could see nothing in them. He looked at me without expression, like the sea.

∞

The next morning at sunrise I followed them down the pilot's ladder with frogman's feet on, a respirator in my hand, and a mask on my head. The longboat had been lowered; in it sat Goatskin, with a diving apparatus on his back. It consisted of two bottles of compressed air and two rubber tubes that came together in a mouthpiece. He also had a mask on his head, and a belt with lead weights round his waist and a knife with a cork handle stuck in the belt. It was the so-called Cousteau apparatus, a French invention with which it was possible to dive down to a hundred meters without being bothered by a diving suit with its ropes and tubes. He was going to investigate the holds of the wreck.

While we were still rowing to the spot he looked like a boy with bottles on his back and a mask on his head; the moment Pjotr said, "Here we are," after looking through the mask he held in the water, Goatskin put his mask in front of his face, the mouthpiece underneath his lips, and became entirely inhuman, an evil robot with a dagger in his hands. As he breathed, the apparatus gave a soft, whistling sound in the nape of his neck. When he gently lowered himself over the edge of the boat and sunk below the surface, bursts of bubbles rose on the spot where he had vanished.

"All right," said Pjotr. "Now you have a look. Take your mask off." I obeyed. "Now, spit in it. That's right. Now rub the saliva over the surface of the glass. Good. Now rinse it with sea water." I obeyed. "That's right. Now put it in front of your face. No, no, your nose inside. Blow through your nose." I blew and the air escaped from the mask with an unpleasant sound. "Now suck. No, no, through your nose." I breathed in through my nose and the mask flattened itself against my face. "All right, that fits. Now stick the tube underneath the strap of your mask on the left side

202

of your head. No, no, in front of your ear. That's it. Now take the mouthpiece in your mouth." The mouthpiece was a surgical look-ing rubber flange, with a hole in the middle to let the air from the tube through and two little warts that fitted behind my teeth. I took the thing in my mouth, put my lips over it and clenched my teeth over the warts. As I breathed through the mouth, the tube made a hollow, hornlike sound. It felt uncomfortable.

"All right," said Pjotr. "Go ahead. Float face downward. Don't dive yet. Just look and breathe slowly, regularly. Don't get into a panic and pull your mouthpiece out, or you'll get into trouble. If you want to dive, fold yourself double, your hands touching your feet, and you'll go down like a stone. Don't go too deep at first. If you get a pain in your ears, come back. And don't forget to blow the water out of your tube first thing when you come back to the surface. You'll find there'll be a good tumblerful of water in there. Blow and it will spurt out. Then breathe again. All right?"

I said, "All right," but could not form the word with the tube in my mouth.

"Are your frogman's feet comfortable?" he asked.

They weren't, for I had put them on much too soon and sat in the sun with them. Now they pinched my feet. I said, "Yes."

"All right," he said. "Off you go."

I lowered myself slowly over the edge of the boat. The water was very warm. When I first put my face in the water, breathing crampily through the tube, my heart nearly stopped, for I saw a giant orange hand gesture in front of me. It was my own. I let go of the boat, tried to breathe regularly with my eyes closed, lying face downward in the water. When I felt that I would float, I opened my eyes.

The sight I saw made me forget whether I breathed or not. I saw, in a curious blue light, a fantastic landscape of hills and rocks, overgrown with curious dreamlike shrubs and long waving grass. I saw hundreds of little fish, hovering like birds, and lower down, on the grass that stretched out from horizon to horizon like a prairie, big dark animals, like cows seen from above, that seemed to be quietly grazing. It was a world of absolute silence; I heard nothing but a faint crackling noise in my ears, like fire heard from a distance. Then, suddenly, there was a sound, a sharp, metallic clank, that seemed to come from very close by, on my left hand side. I paddled with my feet, and swerved round much faster than I had foreseen. Then I saw it.

Below me, half submerged in a blue ground mist in which the prairie vanished, lay a ship. It seemed enormous. It was lying half on its side, and looked real and new as if it had sunk only a couple of days ago. I saw its funnel, its masts, its bridge. Everything looked quite normal, though quite deserted. What gave it the sinister spell of a nightmare was that its boats were floating upside down above their davits.

I was staring at the ship, not feeling anything but a blank amazement, when suddenly I noticed something moving. Along the foremast a small orange creature descended slowly, not like a bird, nor like a thing sinking, it was a movement unlike any I had ever seen. A slow spurt of silver bubbles came from its neck in regular bursts, rose all the way to the surface like a little flight of soap bubbles, glittering in the sun, until they vanished in the golden mist of the sky. The creature moved its feet slowly, the frogman's fins had come to an eerie, undulating life, as if they were a part of the living body.

I saw him gently descend on the bridge and open the door to the wheelhouse. At that moment there seemed to be a soundless explosion. In one split second, thousands of little silver fish burst from the windows and the door, in a blinding, scattering flash. Then I saw the orange creature go blue, as he vanished through the shadow into the inside. The little bursts of bubbles went on floating playfully upwards through the open door, although I couldn't see him any more. I heard again the curious clanking noise that seemed very near; and suddenly the bubbles stopped. Nothing rose from the door any more, and I lay staring at it, my heart pounding. Then, a dark streak changing into white, something shot out of the door, a huge bat, flapping its wings, twisting and turning in the air. The bubbles burst from the doorway again, the creature shot out, changed from blue to orange, and chased the bat at an astonishing speed.

The bat was a ray, one of the biggest I had ever seen. It winged toward the surface, twisting and turning, and I saw something

204

like thin, brown smoke trail behind it. It spurted from a spot in the white of its belly, where a thick handle stuck out. It was Goatskin's knife. Then, suddenly, as the ray came closer, and I already had begun paddling backward in fright, a second creature shot down toward it. It was Pjotri; a long blue harpoon gun, stretched out along his right arm, glistened on his shoulder. The ray didn't see him coming. He shot straight down at it, the gun pointing. At a yard he pressed the trigger. I heard the loud clank of the report, saw the arrow flash out and pierce the ray.

The ray struggled with colossal force. It winged downward, trailing him by the line of his harpoon. Then he released the gun, and rose back to the surface.

The orange creature went after the ray, swooping and turning, and grabbed the gun. There followed a struggle that was horrible to watch. The orange creature and the huge, dark bat seemed to sink toward the blue, in a struggling embrace. Then I saw them rise again, struggling, straight toward me. I turned round to flee, lifted my head out of the water to see where the boat was, and instantly I suffocated, my mouth full of sea water. I got into a panic, pulled the mouthpiece out, and gasped for air. I had the horrible feeling that I was drowning, the moment I wasn't breathing through the tube any more. I felt as if I were sinking. I managed to reach the boat, kicking with my frogman's feet that suddenly seemed to suck me down, hoisted myself over the edge and tumbled inside, hurting my knees. I was very cold.

Pjotr was the first whose hands I saw, grabbing the edge. He pulled himself up, spouted water through his tube, swung a fat leg over the edge and pulled off his mask. "Have you seen that?" he asked, breathlessly. "I had to let him go, for I was bursting. God, what a beauty! Ray and butter tonight, old boy!" He slapped my naked shoulder with such force that it hurt. Then I heard the sound of bubbles, and a hand grabbed the edge. Then another hand appeared, waving, holding the gun that seemed to be twitching and pulling. Pjotr bent over the side and got hold of it. "Pull!" he called to me. "Quick, or he'll get stung!" I grabbed hold of the gun with him and felt a terrific force, pulling at it in wild jerks. The sound of bubbles went round the boat to the other side.

205

Then the boat heeled sharply as Goatskin heaved himself in, with his heavy diving apparatus.

It took a quarter of an hour before the ray was finally pulled into the boat. When it fell on the floor between the benches, flapping its wings wildly, it looked much smaller than it had seemed in the water. On its back a little tail stuck out, quivering. It ended in a point as sharp as a needle. "Don't touch it!" Pjotr said, panting. "If you are stung, you'll get blood poisoning." Then he pulled a knife out of his belt and jabbed the head of the ray several times. With the last jab, he nailed the head to the floor.

I sat looking at the black, slimy animal in horror. For it breathed; its fleshy wings lay quivering on the floor. Despite the knife through its body, the knife through its head, and the harpoon that had pierced it, it went on breathing and twitching its wings, that slapped in the blood.

Pjotr rowed back to the ship. The ray went on breathing all the time. It still breathed after it had been hoisted on board with a hook and pinned to the deck in front of the galley. It went on breathing all through the day. Every time I passed it, I thought it looked dead, but it wasn't. Its little eyes, on stalks on its square head, remained open and staring, and its wings quivered all the time. I asked, after three hours of this torture, why he didn't kill it. He answered, "Are you mad? We won't eat it until tonight, and the moment it's dead it goes bad in the sun."

Bernard and Jacques came back, loaded with fish. It would have been enough for a crew of twenty. The fish were thrown on their steel wire loops by the side of the twitching ray; but they didn't last as long. That night there were delicious smells from the kitchen again and fragrant blue smoke rose from the open door toward the stars. There was an hors d'oeuvre of small fish, braised, and then delicious ray in butter. They all had a gorgeous time; the *vin rosé* in the glasses gleamed like rubies in the lantern light. When Jacques asked why I wasn't eating I said I wasn't hungry.

After the meal was over the old sailor made coffee, and Bernard sang Spanish songs that sounded very fierce and nostalgic in the moonlight. The crew, a little group of dark shadows on the

206

lower deck, murmured "Olé, olé" after every phrase of the songs. The dead fish glistened, coldly, behind the piano.

∾

The next day Goatskin went down to the wreck again with his diving apparatus and started looking for tires in the holds. His bottles had been recharged with compressed air, by means of a little engine on the deck, that I hadn't discovered so far because it was carefully wrapped up in a tarpaulin. It was the only thing on board that got some care, for on it depended their existence. If the little engine should get out of order, they would have to go to Nice or Cannes to have their bottles recharged. Every charge lasted for about twenty minutes per bottle, at a depth down to twenty meters. If they went down lower they used more air.

I watched Goatskin dive again through my mask. The sight of the wreck gave me that curious dreamlike sensation once more, that was unlike anything I had ever felt; my mind seemed to be undecided yet how to react to that vision: with horror or delight. I thought of Hasenfratz this time, and pictured our two ships lying on the sandy soil of the Western Approaches. It wasn't the ship that gave me a feeling of coldness, it was the thought of those inside. The two stokers: white skeletons in the dusk of the engine room, between the still, dead pistons and the little iron staircase, through which little fish would be swimming, catching the faint light from above. As I was looking down at the wreck and saw the little orange creature slowly descend toward its deck, I suddenly thought of the fairy tale about the man left alone in an empty house with the key to one room that he was forbidden to open. He opened it and saw a vision of delight and wonder that ended in some nightmarish horror, from which only a miracle of love would rescue him. I felt as if I hadn't quite opened that door yet, but was peeping through the keyhole. As I saw the little orange creature, with the small swarms of silver bubbles slowly rising from its neck, tear the tarpaulin covering the holds and open up the hatch, my heart started pounding again and I had a sudden feeling of deep insecurity. The miracle of love spun idly around in my thoughts, and brought forth two faces, hazily. They were faint and helpless and faraway: Nicole and June Simmons. I knew that if I were ever to penetrate into that world of silence, I would need someone as strong as Stella to hold the slowly unwinding life line that I would trail into the darkness. Odd, fairy-tale thoughts; the orange creature had opened two hatches now and vanished in the black, square hole as in a grave.

No fish came bursting from the darkness this time; only the bubbles rose, playfully, in little silver bursts to the golden mist of the surface. Everything was peaceful; little fish hung watching, motionlessly, in the still water. My breath made a soft, hollow sound in the tube at every exhalation; there still was the crackling sound as of a distant fire in my ears. Then, suddenly, one of the hatches was pushed upward by a colossal blow from below and a dark thing shot up from the darkness. Only as it rose into the sunlight, swirling, I saw it was a wheel. The bubbles went on rising from the hatch, irregularly by now; the wheels floated upward in a steady succession. I counted ten, before the little orange creature came floating out of the grave again and slowly swam toward the midships. As he entered the wheelhouse once more, there was again the explosion of thousands of silver fish, scattering from the windows. After that nothing happened. The bubbles went on rising now from the door, then from a window; then the orange creature appeared again, swam past the funnel and the upturned boats and descended in front of the radio hut. He seemed to have difficulty opening the door; he succeeded only by pulling with all his strength, with his feet against the wall, and he fell over backward when it opened. He made a slow, graceful somersault, trailing a stream of silver bubbles; then he swam back to the door and vanished inside. The bubbles went on rising from the doorway; something gray came sneaking out of the door, at the top, and rose slowly to the surface, turning. It was a tropical helmet. The bubbles stopped. I knew this meant something. The orange creature was holding its breath. Then it shot out of the doorway, feet first, fighting something, in a cloud. It was a dark cloud, almost black; I saw snakelike arms and something that looked like a bald skull. Then there was another sudden cloud, in which the orange creature vanished, struggling;

208

then I saw a whole set of entrails sink down from the cloud; silver guts gleamed in the sunlight, between the upturned boats, curling, as if still alive. I lifted my head and got my mouth full of sea water again as I breathed; this time I blew it out and I swam back to the boat as quick as I could. Bernard was floating alongside it, one hand on the edge, looking down.

I touched his shoulder and he looked up. I took the mouthpiece out and asked, "What is that? What's happening?"

He took out his mouthpiece as well, said, "He's caught an octopus," and wanted to put it back again.

"But what were those entrails?" I asked. "Whose were they?"

He laughed and answered, "The animal's, what did you think? He turned its bag inside out." Then he stuck the mouthpiece back and went on looking.

Goatskin surfaced shortly afterward. On his left shoulder sat the horrible bald skull. Its tentacles groped round his neck, his arms, and his chest. He took his mouthpiece out and shouted, "Cut it off! Its sucking like hell! Isn't it a beauty?" Bernard started carving away at the thing with his knife. As he pulled it off Goatskin's shoulder it made a sucking sound, and I saw that the tentacles around his arms, although cut off, went on twisting and groping. It took quite some time to get them all off.

"Are you going down again?" Bernard asked.

"No," said Goatskin. "I've only got about ten minutes' air left. It isn't worth the trouble. Take off my bottles, will you?"

Bernard, while unstrapping the harness, asked, "Didn't you come up a bit quick from that hold? How deep were you?"

"Oh," said Goatskin, "only twenty meters or so. Perhaps twenty-five. Nothing to worry about."

But Bernard wasn't satisfied. After he had helped him into the boat, he said, "You're too damned reckless. You were at thirty-five at least. If you get the illness it will be your own fault."

Goatskin said, "Ah, shut up," and pointed at the octopus, slithering in the boat with the bilge water. "There's a nice dinner," he said. "Ever eaten that, Skipper?"

I said, "No."

He laughed. "Getting used to it?" he asked. "Tomorrow you

209

go down with the Cousteau. This floating on the surface is nothing."

I said I didn't think I'd care to go down here, I'd rather try it out somewhere neutral. He chuckled. "Hasenfratz, eh? Yes, my boy, your sins come back to you." I wanted to say something, but let it pass.

That night we had lovely cooked octopus with tomato sauce. I was getting rather hungry but I stuck to the small fry Pjotr and Jacques had brought home. We drank lots of wine again and this time there was community singing around the piano, mostly scabrous French sea chanteys that sounded very nostalgic. Goatskin and I sang Dutch children's songs, the only ones we both knew. "A little cart drove down a sandy road" and "Two mice in a cornfield, peep, peep, peep." Pjotr played the *berceuse* by Chopin again and "Teddybear's Wedding March."

Goatskin got drunk; when we finally went to the fo'c'sle to sleep, he said, "Skipper, come here a moment." I was about to go down the ladder and asked, "What?" He beckoned me toward the stacks of wheels piled up out front. "I want to talk to you," he said. "God, I'm dizzy."

He sat down on the deck and I leaned against the tires. The night was very still, the reflection of the stars quivered on the sea. "I'm probably a fool to tell you," he said thickly, "but do you know why I said those things about that U-boat? About Hasenfratz? Do you? You don't."

I said, "I don't."

"Well," he said. "I'll tell you. Because I like you. Because I'm loyal. Do you hear? Loyal." He shook his finger at me, drunkenly.

I remembered him as he had been: a quiet figure in a goatskin coat on the bridge, a friend. I hated him for letting himself be changed into this. I said, "Don't be a fool. Stop play acting."

He looked up and sniggered. "So I'm play acting, eh?" he said. "So you are still little skipper God Almighty? Composed and unrattled, and so snooty that I could knock your teeth out."

I said, "Go ahead. It will be a pleasure."

He sat looking at me from below. I couldn't see his eyes but I could imagine what they were like. Then he said, "It may come

210

to that, you know. One day I may grab you by that self-satisfied throat of yours and bang your snooty skull on the deck."

"You're talking nonsense," I said, and went toward the hatch. "Go to sleep."

He wheedled after me, "Don't you want to hear the secret, little Hasenfratz?"

I don't know what made me do it; perhaps the fact that I kicked against the bucket on my way to the hatch. I took it to the rail, threw it in the sea, heaved it up full of water and threw it in his face.

He remained quite still. The water could be heard dripping off his body on to the deck. Then he said, "Would you believe that that did me a lot of good? Thank you, old boy." And he got to his feet. His fist caught me unawares, it hit me on the jaw. I felt a blind rage spring up inside me, and I shut my eyes. I said, "You'd better go down now, before I break your neck." Then he hit me again.

It was Pjotr who pulled us apart. I had been whacking into him, cursing, possessed by a dark brutality that was utterly frightening. I hadn't known Pjotr was that strong; he held my arms pinned on my back like a vice. "Come, come," he said. "That's not the way we like things on board here." I felt suddenly very silly, and very much alone. I said, "I'm sorry." Goatskin got shakily to his feet. "All right, Pjotr," he said. "It was my fault. I asked for it." Bernard's head came out of the hatch. "What's going on?" he asked. "Nothing," said Pjotr. "The Dutchmen have beaten each other up." Bernard asked, "Why?"

"Because of the Chinese whore," said Goatskin.

That made me see red again. I shook Pjotr off and grabbed his neck and said, "If you say that again, I'll kill you." It sounded very adolescent. The whole thing became preposterous and embarrassing.

He said, "O.K. I'm sorry. I'm drunk."

"Let's all go down and talk it over," said Pjotr, "and have a drink."

We went down; I didn't want to talk anything over, but I didn't mind the drink. The others were very interested. They seemed to think it quite normal that two lifelong friends should beat the sparks off each other because of a girl neither of them cared about. When I lay on my bunk, my jaw hurt and I had a headache. My hands clenched to fists all the time, automatically, like the octopus' tentacles after they had been cut off. I asked myself why we had done this; whether it was indeed because of the Chinese girl. He had sent her to me in the first place, so he could not be very interested, and I didn't feel any tenderness toward her, nor desire. Remembering her gave me a feeling of distant comradeship, as if we had a lot in common but wouldn't ever be able to express it, because we were worlds apart. I was nearly asleep when suddenly a head appeared by my side. It was Pjotr.

"Something to eat?" he whispered.

I said, "God, no," and turned away.

Before I fell asleep I remembered that I should take nothing seriously, least of all myself. It was quite a relief, that thought, and I fell asleep smiling, thinking of the Chief, Miss de Roos, and New Province cake.

Chapter X

I FOUND I COULDN'T TAKE A FIGHT LIKE A BIT OF HORSEPLAY ANY more; I took it as a proof that I was growing up. I had hated the fight with Goatskin when it happened, hated the anger and the brutality it had released in me. Somewhere inside me was an aggressive animal, whose existence I had only felt once before: during my fight with the American after I had sunk Hasenfratz.

The fight with Goatskin had an odd effect. It made me see the crew and the ship in another light. I didn't think they were so funny any more. Their daily slaughter revolted me; their constant drinking became a bore, and the piano got on my nerves. The crew, whom at first I had thought so picturesque and French, became a pain in the neck; the dear old Captain in his pyjamas wasn't funny any more either. I found out that he was asleep most of the time because he drank himself to a standstill; as the boys refused to give him alcohol, he had to buy it himself and

212

to that end he sold, this trip, the ship's bell, in an island called Port Cros. Before my fight with Goatskin I would have thought it amusing; now I couldn't help thinking what would happen if we should find ourselves in a fog. The only solution seemed to be to line up the crew along the rail and make them shout "Boo" every two seconds, for there wasn't a foghorn either. There weren't a lot of things. There was no sextant, no chronometer, no log, no logbook, no parallel rules, no table of logarithms, the charts were of 1916 and the nautical instructions of 1920, the bilge pump didn't work and the compasses in the wheelhouse and on the poop disagreed seven degrees. As I was supposed to occupy myself with the navigation, I made a list of things that were missing and showed it to Goatskin. He was airy about it and said we should buy those things in Marseilles. Bernard asked, "With what?" There was no answer.

Yet all this didn't depress me, nor give me the wish to be off. I had been diving again every day; I called "diving" floating on the surface and looking down at the world under the sea. I had actually dived a couple of times down to about three meters, but choked. It had been more a matter of pride than of interest, for I saw things much better from above. The underwater world was fascinating, and looking at it had a soothing effect. It seemed to take the edge off everything that happened elsewhere. When I floated above the dream landscape, with the blue mist in the valleys, the dark fish grazing on the plains, the banks of flowers, the deserts of sand with sea urchins and dark, sausagelike things —I didn't know whether they were plants or animals—I felt far away from it all.

We crawled on along the coast and I saw different landscapes of breath-taking beauty, lit by slanting sunbeams that fell through the water, and in which dust seemed to be dancing, as in a cathedral. Slowly the world below seemed to open up for me, I saw more every day. I began to know the fish, of which only the smallest and silliest paid any attention to me; I saw columns of yellow and black striped ones parade and knew that the solitary one in front was the leader, for if he came to an obstacle he turned smartly round and the others followed his command in a single, hundred-fold movement, like Prussians. I began to

213

know the rays, dark, melancholy bats of the depth, that were entirely inoffensive, and seemed to be looking for something lost, absent-mindedly. I began to know the *mérous*, monsters to look at, but who never did anybody any harm. I began to know the little octopi, who seemed to be the most intelligent down there, and who changed colors like a chameleon according to their background as soon they spotted me and wanted to hide themselves. The better I came to know that world, the less dream-like it seemed; the dream seemed to shift toward the other world: the ship. Occasionally, at night, when they were drinking and playing games in the fo'c'sle I watched them with a feeling as if this was a dream, and not that million-year-old world we were floating on. I knew I was indulging in a kind of dope, like opium; I couldn't say that I hadn't been warned in advance. But it seemed a harmless dope.

What struck me most about the underwater world was its harmlessness. The only things terrible under the sea were either man-made or man himself. Off the island of Port Cros, when floating over what seemed to be a magic summer garden, full of golden little fish and blue and pink flowers, I saw something white, swam toward it and saw it was a newspaper with a head-line about the Civil War in Greece. Another time I came across a twisted horror of steel girders and torn aluminum sheets, a weird animal with its back broken and twisted wings: the wreck of a plane. Inside its cockpit a little dome of plexiglass, I saw something white that was, even before I had recognized it, terrifying. It was a skeleton with a leather cap on its skull. But these things were exceptions, strange phenomena that stuck out from the landscape like things utterly alien. Occasionally, as I lay contemplating the silent life below and its graceful gentleness, an orange monster would soar down on a fish grazing, or an octopus playing with colors, and there would be the sharp clank of a gun's spring and the harpoon would pierce the flesh and an agonizing struggle would start as the terrified animal was dragged up toward its death, trailing the thin smoke of blood. I hated the hunters in those moments, and began to understand why I had fought with Goatskin that night. It hadn't been be-cause of the Chinese girl, nor anything else to do with the world

214

of men. It had been because of the ray and the octopus and the bunches of gaping fish, glistening in the dark behind the piano. I was offered daily to try out the diving apparatus and go for a walk on the bottom of the sea. But I didn't feel like it yet; so far I hadn't seen anything down below that had given me the wish to change my bird's life for that of a pedestrian.

We pottered around the small islands for a week or so, without finding anything that justified the expedition economically. Goatskin searched three more wrecks, none of which I saw at close quarters because they were lying too deep. The sea was light as the day down to twenty meters; there the blue started, followed by the purple at fifty meters; and at eighty meters it was dark. The wrecks were lying in the purple; all I saw, of one of them, were two mastheads, sticking out of the blue. Of the others I saw nothing.

I watched him diving, though. The little, orange creature descended slowly, like an autumn leaf falling, into the mist, trailing a line to which at every five meters a rag had been attached. When he went down deeper than thirty meters he had to come up slowly, to avoid the diver's illness: *le mal de caisson*. Bernard explained it to me at great length, full of medical and chemical terms. As far as I understood it the nitrogen in the air, which commonly wasn't absorbed by the blood of the human being but passed out of the lungs again as it came in, became absorbed by the blood if the body was exposed to a heavy pressure. If the pressure was lifted too quickly, the nitrogen turned into gas in the blood, and the result was that the blood vessels became full of little gas bubbles. If those bubbles reached the heart or the brain the consequences could be madness, paralysis, stroke, or blindness. So a diver, once he went down into the purple, had to take his time rising to the surface again. At every five meters of his ascent, he had to hover for periods that varied in length with the depths, so as to adapt his body to the diminishing pressure and give the nitrogen a chance to get worked out of his blood without having turned into gas.

It was an eerie sight to see Goatskin rise out of the mist. He would stop at the next rag, his hand to the line, and hover like a hawk, his frogman's feet slowly flapping. The underwater world became as still and deserted as a rabbit warren with a hawk hovering over it, only the smallest fish would stay to watch. The moment he vanished in the sky, after a couple more periods of hovering at a higher level, life would come back. The melancholy ray would wing out of the dusk again; the *mérou* would run busily along, like an ugly old woman continuing her shopping, the gentle calves would start grazing again on the grassy slope of the hill that rose from the mist, and the octopi would continue their elflike dance and play with colors when they saw me. The fact that the animals reappeared the moment the orange creature was gone gave me a certain satisfaction, for it seemed to prove that they weren't afraid of me. They seemed to have understood that I wasn't a bird of prey, hovering over them to kill, but just a fat, pink bird of contemplation.

Toward the end of the trip, the atmosphere on board became gloomy. There were long conversations about money. All they had to show for their catch were ten tires, much the worse for having been submerged in salt water for so long, for the canvas inside had rotted. Bernard had no more money, all they had to rely on now was Goatskin's luck at roulette. He was very confident about this, for he had a system. He explained the system, but I didn't understand it; all I understood was that he had to spend days at the Casino before it worked.

We went to Cannes, and had quite a time entering the port. There weren't nearly as many yachts moored at the quay as there had been before the war, but we managed to bang into practically all of them. After the fourth collision Goatskin dragged the old Captain to the rail and wanted to drown him. Even taking into account the Mediterranean passion for exaggeration, it seemed a strong measure. Pjotr and Jacques prevented it; the old bosun started dropping the anchor while everybody's back was turned. During the altercation a boy with a red cyclist's cap sat at the wheel, knitting.

In the end we were moored by the harbor master's launch; he wanted to see the Captain's papers and got a drink instead, which seemed to satisfy him. When, finally, the gangplank was out Goatskin said, flustered, "Honestly, Skipper, next time you must take over command. This is ridiculous." He was wearing his

216

pin-striped suit again and his purple socks. His hat and his cane had remained behind in Marseilles.

For two days running he stayed away from noon till midnight, and labored in the Casino. But this time his system didn't work. When he came back, dejected, at one o'clock in the morning of the fourth day, he had on him exactly the same amount of money with which he had left three days ago. They had got wise to his system, he said, those crooks had fiddled with the roulette table. Every time he had put a bet on the red, black had come up. There was nothing to do but to leave for Marseilles; to carry on under these circumstances would be folly.

That night we left, and I took command of the maneuver. I had expected it to be an ugly moment when I told the old Captain that I would take her out; I put it as tactfully as I could, in a little speech I had been rehearsing. I said I would so love to do some maneuvering once more, after all these years, and would he please let me and watch me closely and tell me honestly if I did something wrong. It wasn't at all necessary; the moment he understood that he could go back to bed, he did.

I came to the harrowing conclusion that what we had taken to be the Captain's incompetence was in reality the character of the ship. She was mad. If I put the rudder to port, with her engine running ahead, she started traveling astern; and when I put it to starboard there came an explosion like a detonating mine from the engine room, followed by a pall of black smoke, and the engine stopped. I tried to make it run again, but didn't succeed. In the meantime we had kissed three yachts moored at the quay; when I came back on deck, black in the face with tears running down my cheeks from the stinging smoke, Goatskin watched me coldly, but didn't say a word.

There was a slight breeze blowing from the shore, so I decided to sail her out. This was a fatal decision, for once the sails had been set, after a lot of slapstick comedy, the ship would only travel sideways. We were approaching a new cluster of yachts at an alarming speed, when I got an inspiration. If she wanted to travel sideways she should be allowed to do so, in the direction in which I wanted her to travel stern first. After all, who said that ships shouldn't travel sideways? Just another silly tradition,

217

kept up to make navigation an esoteric trade. So I steered point blank at the yachts, on which shivering little crowds in pyjamas and dressing gowns stood screaming in panic, and we drifted out to sea like a crab. In the open, as I went into the wheelhouse to look at the chart, wiping the sweat off my brow, a toothless voice said from the upper bunk, "Very good, young man. You haven't forgotten a thing. Next time don't ask me, I'll be happy to let you handle her." I said, "Thank you, sir," and he said, "You're welcome."

The idea was that we should go to Marseilles, but the ship wanted to go to Saint Tropez. I tried everything to stop her from drifting there, but in the end I had to give up. Like the old captain, I found myself forced to think up an excuse for her, like a mother for an idiot child. I said that reasons of navigation made it necessary for us to go to Saint Tropez: we had a rope in our propeller. It was a stupid excuse, I hadn't had time to think of a better one and I realized too late that this was probably the one ship on earth where a rope in the propeller was the easiest thing to remedy. Pjotr jumped into the sea at once with his mask on, dived under her poop and came back with the message that there was no rope. I said, lamely, "Fancy. The tide must have washed it out," forgetting that the Mediterranean was the only sea on earth where there was no tide. In the end I gave up finding an excuse. I just said, "We'll go to Saint Tropez, and that's final." They didn't argue, but from that moment onward I lived under a cloud.

Our entry into the harbor of Saint Tropez was something that would have delighted a connoisseur of medieval harlequinade. We entered the port backward. When our stern rammed the quay, the deck was full of silent figures, sitting with their heads in their hands. The harbor master came on board and the first thing he said was, "Good Lord, that was a lovely piece of sea-manship. How did you manage, captain? Ships have been swing-ing on their anchors in this damn port for nine centuries; you hadn't got your engine running, had you?" At first I thought it was heavy irony, but when I looked at his innocent dark eyes I realized, with a feeling of nausea, that he was sincere. I looked round, like a man waking up from a nightmare, and realized that

218

Saint Tropez was indeed a hell of a port to get into for any normal ship. I hadn't noticed it before, I had been too occupied with the fit of epileptics our *Euridice* had got into between the pier heads. Saint Tropez obviously was the place she wanted to go to, and I began to wonder whether she could ever be made to leave it again.

As we had no money left worth speaking of, the days of whisky and Grand Hotels were over. We stayed on board. Only Goatskin took a room in a boardinghouse, because it was necessary for the plans he had made for our future. It was very simple, he said; the tire racket was obviously no good any more and so he had had to think of something else. Well, he had found it. This place was full of tired businessmen on holiday, who wanted fresh air, healthy food and relaxation. They wouldn't find those sitting on the terraces of bistros, sipping Pernods, and ogling the girls, so we would organize a cruise for them, show them lovely underwater sights, teach them to hunt, eat glorious seafood, listen to jolly yarns on the poop at night and sing chanteys at the piano. That was the reason why he had come to Saint Tropez. I thought we had come to Saint Tropez because of circumstances beyond our control, but I let it pass, as it lifted the cloud a bit under which I had been living.

I must say, to his credit, that he worked his ropes fast. He tore into the ruminating herd of tired businessmen like a lassoing cowboy. By nightfall of the first day he had caught three; at the end of the week sixteen. It was fascinating to watch the catch mounting nightly, but when we passed half a dozen I began to get worried. Everybody had become so excited over the game, that they seemed to forget about having to put all these people up. They couldn't be shoved into the fo'c'sle in layers, like loaves into an oven. Once Goatskin had reached the number of sixteen, which seemed to have something to do with his gambling system and hence appeared to satisfy him, he started making his preparations for the cruise. The businessmen had all paid in advance, which seemed unbusinesslike but said a great deal for his power of persuasion. So we were rich once more, and the first preparation he made was to telephone to Marseilles for his cane, his hat, the blondes, and the Chinese girl.

She arrived at a critical moment, carrying the cane and the hat. We were sitting in the fo'c'sle, trying to work out the geometrical problem of putting sixteen businessmen up, when she appeared at the top of the ladder, said, "Hello, boys," and came down, her slender legs moving into the lamplight. Goatskin asked boorishly, "Are you alone?" and she answered, "Yes, the others could not come." He muttered something, turned his back on her, and continued tackling the geometrical problem.

She asked, "Where do you want your cane and hat?"

He answered, without looking, "On my bunk. Now boys, how far have we got? Two in the double bunk, seven in the singles, five on the floor, and if we take the door out of that cupboard, that would mean one more. It leaves us with. . . ." While he counted on his fingers, she smiled at me and put out her hand. I shook it secretly and whispered, "Drink?" She nodded, and we sneaked out.

Goatskin cried, "Fifteen! Where the hell are we going to put the odd one?"

I didn't hear the answer, for we were out.

∞

We had a Pastis on one of the terraces facing the harbor, underneath a blue parasol that made her look green. I hoped she would take off her sunglasses in the shade, but she didn't.

After I had ordered our drinks, she said, "I've got some mail for you," opened her bag, and took two letters out.

I had no idea whom they could be from, until I saw that they were addressed to Hotel Atlantic in Marseilles and remembered the postcards. I said, "Thank you" and put them in my pocket. I felt so excited that my mind was not on the conversation for a while. She asked what the trip had been like and I began to tell her, but I gave up because the adjectives failed me.

"Have you dived?" she asked.

I said I had.

"Liked it?"

"I like to look. I don't think I'll ever be a hunter."

"You didn't go down with the Cousteau yet?"

"No, but I've had my first spell of the deep, if that's what you are trying to find out."

"I am not trying to find out anything," she said, smiling. "I'm just making conversation."

I realized that I had been thinking about her a good deal. I wished she would take those glasses off. "I had a fight with Maurice," I said.

"So?" She took it very calmly. "What about?"

"About you."

"How did it happen?"

"We were drunk," I said. And then, to change the subject; "Would you mind taking your glasses off? I'd like to see you."

She said "Sorry" and took them off. It didn't make much difference; I had forgotten about that. "Are you going to sail with us next time?" I asked.

"No," she said, "I've got a hotel room booked. I'll stay here and wait for your return. What's this new plan Maurice has?"

I told her about the businessmen and tried to be witty about it, but it petered out. It was difficult to take up contact with her again, probably my imagination had been at work at sea and I had started shaping her into somebody different. We sat watching the passers-by for a while; they were dressed in miniature shorts and the women wore a ribbon around the chest. They showed burns in various grades and glistened with oil in the sunlight.

"You might like to call on me tonight," she said, getting up. "The hotel is called 'Majestic.' Thanks for the drink."

I said, "You're welcome," and watched her as she walked away. She looked slim and dressed among the nudists. The moment she had turned the corner, I took the letters from my pocket.

I opened the one from the Chief first. He wrote with ill-spelled exuberation about the joy he had experienced upon getting my postcard, and then went on about Miss de Roos. He gave me a description of her qualities as a housewife, cook, comrade, and soprano and said that she had accepted him as her future husband. They were going to be married as soon as the temporary church was finished, which would be a month from now, God willing. As either of their little houses was too small for a couple, they were thinking of taking one of them apart and joining it to the other. They hadn't decided yet which one. Yours sincerely.

June Simmons had written four pages. The size of her letter alarmed me a bit; my postcard had sprung entirely from boredom and hardly merited such an extensive reply. Her letter was amusing and very English; she wrote about nothing at all, except at the very end. "I have been thinking about you a lot. There is something that worries me, but probably I'm imagining things. Take care of yourself and don't get depressed. You have got friends. Yours ever."

I ordered another Pastis and sat thoughtless in the sun with my eyes closed, like a cat. Then Goatskin descended on me, full of pep. "I've got it!" he cried. "Hammocks!"

I failed him.

જીસ

I went to see her that night. I had decided not to, but then I had thought of her, alone in that hotel room. I didn't want to get involved, but there was no harm in being kind.

I shaved first. While I was doing so Goatskin and the boys were putting up hammocks in the fo'c'sle. It had a depressing effect on me, I imagined the businessmen inside them, swinging. When Goatskin saw me leave he asked where I was going and I said I was going for a walk. As I mounted the ladder, he called after me, "Give the bitch my love!"

She looked pretty and composed in a thin, pink dressing gown. The room was frightful, with a cracked ceiling, roses on the wallpaper, and a dark grease stain above the head of the bed; but it had a nice view on the masts and the night sky.

She asked if I would like a drink and when I said I wouldn't she put out the light and sat down on the window sill, trying to recapture Marseilles. It didn't work; in Marseilles there had been a comradeship between us, now there was nothing. I gave her Goatskin's message, verbally; only after I had said it I realized that there had been no need to.

She took it very calmly. "I don't know why," she said after

222

a while, "but there must be something in me that makes men want to hurt me."

She was right. I hadn't deliberately wanted to hurt her, but I had. I sat looking at her silhouette, wanting to feel something, some warmth, some contact. "All right," I said, suddenly tired. "I don't care a damn what that lunatic is obsessed by. Let's go to bed."

She obeyed at once, without saying a word. I remembered how promptly she had obeyed all my wishes in Marseilles, and it irritated me. I said, "I'm sorry, I didn't want to order you about. I'll sit and smoke a cigarette for a minute."

I sat in the window and lit a cigarette. It tasted foul; after a few puffs I shot it into the darkness, got up and went toward her, a dark patch on the white bed. I sat down, found her hand, felt a sudden tenderness toward her, and said, "I've been thinking about you a lot." Then I remembered that June Simmons had written the same words to me, and it was over.

"Well?" she asked, as I remained silent.

Just to say something nice, I said, "I love you, Nicole"; and then she threw her arms round my neck and hid her head on my shoulder, sobbing. She gave me quite a shock, I didn't like this. But I put my arms around her and stroked her hair and said, "come, come," and "don't" and "sweetheart." She recovered, said, "I'm sorry," and lay down again. I lay down with her, feeling uncomfortable.

"Aren't you frightfully hot?" she asked.

I said, "No."

We lay rigidly in silence, listening to the babbling of the little waves against the ships in the harbor and somebody whistling "Trees." I wished I were at sea at sunrise; I would put on my mask and my frogman's feet and go to have a look at the world under water, which was very pretty early in the morning. The sunlight didn't quite penetrate the waves yet; the landscape was covered by a golden mist. Then, as the sun rose, slanting beams of light would start quivering in the mist, and catch the flicker of silver fish, with long shadows. Still later the hills would emerge, the white rocks, the plains of seaweed with the dark

223

animals lazily grazing, and there wouldn't be a danger nor an enemy in sight, and I'd feel far away and happy.

When I woke up it was a hot morning and she was brushing her teeth. I opened my eyes and looked at her. She had a lovely figure. I shut my eyes again; then I heard a soft stroking sound that brought a memory: Stella brushing her hair in the silent bedroom while I sat waiting in the kitchen with the message of Dop's death. I opened my eyes and saw her start plucking her eyebrows, her face very close to the mirror. I thought how odd it was, this complete intimacy between us, without us having made love. If she hadn't been Chinese, she could have been my sister.

She saw me look at her in the mirror and smiled and asked, "Slept well?"

I said, "Fine."

"Are you going to sail today, do you think?"

"I don't know."

"I wonder what will happen to those businessmen."

"What worries me is what will happen to us, once we are in the open and they find out."

There was a silence, and then she said, "I know he's awful, but I can't help feeling sorry for him."

I said, "H'm."

"Was he a good captain during the war?"

"You have put me that question once before, and the answer was yes."

She went on plucking her eyebrows and I lay looking at her and then the door was opened without a knock and Goatskin came in. He looked at her, then at me, said, "Sorry," and went out again, slamming the door.

"Well," I said. "That's that."

She didn't say anything. She sat down on the window sill, her back to the quay, the tweezers in her hand. Her face didn't express anything, but the way she sat there did. I said, "Would you remember that you are naked? It might attract a crowd."

She said, "Sorry," came to the bed and sat down.

I asked, "You are in love with him, aren't you?"

224

"No," she said. "I've never been in love with anybody. All I have ever felt was pity."

"That's grim," I said. "I'm not sure I feel flattered."

"With you it's different," she said. "With you I feel that we have a lot in common, but . . ."

"But that we are worlds apart," I completed, smiling.

"That's it," she said.

I shut my eyes. I didn't want to get involved. All I wanted was to get back to sea. Yet I wanted to talk to her about the war, and our life, and the newspaper between the sea urchins, and the wreck of the plane, and the hopelessness of it all, and the beauty of the slanting sunbeams in the water. But it was all too blurred, too much a feeling, not thoughts. I said, "I love you, Nicole."

"I know," she said. "I love you too."

I knew it was not true, but that she had felt the same thing, wanting to talk about the war and the students and the hope and the disillusion and the whisky and the blondes and us all going to hell. I wanted to kiss her, but I didn't. I didn't want to get involved. I asked, "What about breakfast?"

She said, "All right. On the terrace?"

I said, "Let's."

She dressed and we went down and had breakfast on the terrace.

Chapter XI

THE CRUISE WITH THE BUSINESSMEN WAS A FAILURE, AS EVERYBODY had known it would be. Yet it was extraordinary how much they took, before they stopped being amused.

The moment they got on board they became very hearty and jocular, started calling each other "tu" and loved their hammocks and the confusion of shoes and shirts in the fo'c'sle. They loved everything, even the poisonous smoke that poured through the partition as soon as the engine started running; they were determined to recapture their boyhood and be scouts again; the fo'c'sle looked like a messy tent. The blankets were greasy with sun oil, they hit their heads on the deck every time they sat up, they twisted their ankles on the ladder and kicked each other in the stomach coming down, but it was all part of a wonderful memory, of youth revived.

Pjotr did it. The idea had been to show them lovely underwater landscapes and open up for them the beauty of the sea. None of them had bathed with a mask yet and they were all looking forward to it tremendously. Pjotr, who was to cook for the lot, got very worried about the fish. There had been too much hunting going on along the coast, the fish had hidden in some stark, terrifying precipices where the rocky coast sank perpendicularly into the blue and where the sun hardly ever penetrated. So, for their first swim, he flung them into the water at this spot. The first view they got of the beauty of the underwater world was a vision of a dark hell. It was a psychological mistake, that might have been remedied if Pjotr, Bernard, and Jacques hadn't left them to their fate and shot off like sharks to hunt the dinner. And they had taken the longboat with them.

I watched the floating businessmen through the captain's binoculars from the deck of the ship. They stayed together at first; then some of them splashed toward the shore and hoisted themselves on a rock, hurting their legs, their behinds full of sea urchins' needles. They stood there, shivering, flailing their arms, and hollered, "Ahoy!" at the vanishing longboat. The braver ones remained in the water, spread out above the precipice, staring down, fascinated by the horror of it. I saw one of them, who was floating quite by himself, swim slowly round; then another one overtook him, touched his foot and they both nearly drowned, one from fright, the other from laughter. They reached the shore with difficulty and climbed a rock on the other side.

There were still three left in the water when Pjotr's voice hollered from the distance, "A shark! A shark!" It was not a warning of danger, just a call to Jacques and Bernard to join him with their guns to harpoon the prize; but the remaining businessmen swam to the shore in panic. I could see the blood on their knees after they had scrambled up the rock, much too fast. I thought of attracting Pjotr's attention but, like a coward, I wanted to postpone Judgment Day as long as I could.

226

When the marooned bathers were finally collected, it was nearly night. Pjotr and the others had caught the shark and it was lying in the boat; at least, I couldn't think of any other reason why the businessmen did not want to enter it. Pjotr didn't throw the shark's corpse back into the sea, which would have been the reasonable thing to do, for he couldn't cook it. But the fool was so proud of his catch that he couldn't let go of it, and rowed back all the way to the ship to have it hauled on board first, before he went back to collect the businessmen. It was a very small shark, still gaping, although he had broken its back. It hung upside down from one of the davits, dripping blood.

When the businessmen came back on board it was obvious that the thing was over. They were scouts no longer. They clamored angrily for iodine and adhesive tape and drinks and a hot meal; we only had drinks, and they finished the lot during a powwow in the fo'c'sle. After half an hour two of them came on deck, called for Goatskin, and told him that they wanted to return to port at once. He passed the order on to me, angrily. He repeated, "At once," and said that there was no point in continuing the cruise with a lot of unsporting, spoiled, foul-mouthed night-club characters. There was no room at sea for those; let them go back to their smoky joints and pinch bottoms. "At once, do you hear?" This conversation took place in the wheelhouse. The old Captain chuckled in his bunk.

I did what I could, but it took us three days. In the end they went ashore in La Ciotat, which seemed to be the ship's port of preference this time. La Ciotat wasn't a holiday resort, it was an industrial town with shipyards and factories and looked like Grimstadt in Norway. After the businessmen had left, without saying good-by, we watched them being taken ashore in the long-boat, for I hadn't managed to get to the quay. We lay anchored in the middle of the harbor.

Pjotr and the old bosun rowed, and Pjotr lost his oar. It took them a quarter of an hour to paddle back to the spot where the oar drifted. The businessmen sat in solid rows on the benches, their suitcases and their brand new kit bags on their knees. It was all rather sad, for they had been so happy in the beginning that I had hoped against reason that it would end well.

Goatskin went to Cannes from La Ciotat and stayed away for

three days. He came back very excited; when he stood hollering on the shore for the longboat, we all thought he had broken the bank. He had lost every penny he had on him, but he had something else: a job for us. A very nice old antiquarian had chartered the ship to go to Greece, and he wanted us to dive for some antiques that were submerged off one of the little islands. He would come on board himself in Saint Tropez, with perhaps one or two guests, and we would leave at once because the whole thing had to be over in eight weeks' time.

The others were delighted, but the word "Greece" made me gloomy. I was sure the ship didn't dream of going to Greece. I was getting superstitious about her; I didn't mention the word "Greece" in our conversations, out of some half-witted fear that she might prick up her ears and make up her mind. Yet I had come to like her; like the old Captain I felt that I could do a lot with patience and kindness and a poker face. When I told the old Captain that we were going to Greece, he said, "Oh, that's all right. She has been there." For some reason this relieved me.

The antiquarian had paid some money in advance; but not to Goatskin. He had written out a cheque to a shop in Sainte Maxime for a second Cousteau apparatus. "We'll have to do a lot of diving," Goatskin said. "You'd better start to get used to the thing, for I think it will be us two who'll have to bring up the loot. If I let Pjotr or the others do it, they'll be off the moment they see a fish and forget all about the antiques." I said I was willing to try.

I tried that same afternoon, in the harbor of La Ciotat. Goatskin put the bottles on my back and adjusted the straps; the thing seemed to weigh a ton. He put the mouthpiece in my mouth and I breathed the compressed air. It tasted stale and gassy. The mouthpiece was much bigger than the one on my respirator, and I felt slightly sick after having had it in my mouth for a minute. "You're too fat," Goatskin said, "for my ballast belt. We'll have to add some lead. Four kilos in all, I think." He added two blocks of lead to the belt that I had seen him wear; when he put it round my waist my knees nearly gave in.

"Surely, this is too much?" I asked. "I'll go down like a stone."

But he said, "Nonsense. You'll find when you are in the water that you have no weight at all. Now listen carefully. This is very

228

easy, but there are a few simple rules. First: you must breathe as little as possible, for the air is precious. If you take it in gulps, the bottles will be finished much too soon. Inhale not to the full, but half, wait three seconds, then exhale. You'll find that after a while you'll do that automatically. Then: don't splash around on the surface but dive; fold yourself double, hands to your toes, and down you go. When you feel a pain in your ears, rise again for about one meter and swallow your saliva. You'll find that it relieves the pressure. Fold double again and go down to the next stage, which is about five meters deeper, where you'll feel a pain again in your ears. Do the same thing: rise one meter, swallow your saliva until the pain stops, go down five meters more. As you go deeper, you'll meet fish that aren't afraid of you because they never have seen a man at their depth. They are curious, and they'll come for you, to look. Don't get panicky; they won't do you any harm, and don't forget that under water they look twice their size. You won't meet anything interesting down here, in this harbor, perhaps a liche or two. They are very big and look alarming but they are harmless. If you want to chase them away for some reason, flap your feet. In case you should meet a shark, which is practically impossible, but you never know: take your knife and tap on your bottles. It'll go away. If it comes back, it'll come very close because they are myopic and anything white attracts them. Then just prick it gently with your knife and it'll go away. Don't stab, just give a little push, like this," and he prodded my side with his finger. "Got it?"

I said, "Yes." My mouth was very dry.

"One more thing," he said. "These bottles have a little spare tank. The opener is on the left-hand side, at the bottom, just on your hip. If your air gives out, open it and you'll have ten minutes left." Then he asked the bosun to sound the harbor. It was twenty-five meters. "In that case, don't quite go to the bottom," he said. "Stay at twenty meters."

"But how do I know that I am at twenty meters?" I asked.

"That's very simple," he answered. "You get a pain in your ears and have to make a ceiling the way I told you every five meters. So if you do that three times, you'll be between fifteen and twenty meters. In you go."

I put on my mask, but I had forgotten to spit in it. It filmed over. I took it off and spat. "Bring a potato," Goatskin said to Pjotr. "This spitting business is not enough." Pjotr brought a potato, Goatskin cut it in half and rubbed the inside of my mask with it. "You'd better rinse it under the tap," he said. "Then you needn't do it in the harbor."

I wanted to go to the galley, but found I had to walk bent forward because of the heavy load on my back. My feet seemed to have swollen under the weight. My frogman's feet hurt badly. "Don't bother," said Goatskin. "I'll do it for you."

He took my mask to the galley and rinsed it. After I had put it on and inhaled through the nose to see whether it was well closed, he said, "One more thing. When you go lower down, you may find that your mask gets pressed against your nose and hurts. Breathe out through your nose, and you'll be all right again. That's all."

Before I went down the pilot's ladder, I looked at the water. It wasn't very clean. I said, like a child at the dentist's, "Don't you think we'd better wait a bit?"

"Wait?" he asked. "What for?"

"Well, the water seems rather dirty."

"Don't be silly. Hurry up."

I climbed down the pilot's ladder. I had to use all the strength in my hands, for the load pulled me backward. I couldn't look down because of it. When my foot first touched water, it felt cold.

"Hey!" Goatskin called from above. "What about putting your mouthpiece in?"

I said, "Sorry," feeling very nervous, and let go with one hand to put the mouthpiece in. The ladder swung round; I hit the side of the ship with a bang and hurt myself. I was shaken now. The bottles on my back had shifted. I called up to him, "They've shifted!"

He called back, "What?"

"The bottles!"

He called, "Go down, you fool, or I'll cut the ladder!"

I said, "O.K., O.K." and put the mouthpiece in my mouth. It seemed bigger than before, and hurt on the inside of my lip underneath my nose. The air hissed through the tubes with a me-

230

chanical noise. I descended a few more steps, swallowing. Then one more step and my foot groped in vain. There were no more steps. This was it. I tried to hover on the last step with my knee, thinking of some excuse for climbing back on board that wouldn't sound too silly. Then Goatskin cried, "Hey!" and shook the ladder. I lost my balance and fell into the water backward.

I went down a couple of meters, breathing like a stag, and I was terrified out of my wits when I heard the sound of a double horn, like a Paris fire engine: "tee-ta, tee-ta," very loud. It was a nightmare: drowning in what seemed to be liquid mud, chased by a fire engine. I got back to the surface so short of breath that I had only one urge: to take my mouthpiece out. I heard Goatskin's voice, shouting, "If you take it out, you'll drown! Lie flat on your face! Breathe!"

It seemed to be the last voice in the universe. I surrendered myself to it, trying to master my panic. Turn on your face—I did. Breathe—I breathed, in long, greedy gulps. I couldn't remember what else he had called, but I remembered him saying "breathe slowly, not full, three seconds." I tried, and it worked. I calmed down a bit. At every exhalation there was a loud bubbling noise in my neck. I didn't hear the horn any more.

Then I looked, for the first time consciously. The water was very dirty, a dull green. I saw nothing at all; my vision was limited to about two meters. At first I thought I'd be damned if I'd dive into that; I thought of the sharks I had to prod gently with my knife, and groped for it on my back. Doing so made me turn over and slide down, head first, toward the depth. I heard the horn again: tee-ta, tee-ta, at every breath. Then I thought what a fool I was making of myself. There was no place safer than La Ciotat harbor. Yet I daren't dive into that ugly green, like a blind man groping. I needed something to hold onto, something solid and reliable in this fog. I thought of the anchor chain. I lifted my head out of the water, with bubbles spluttering from my neck, saw that I was very near it, and swam. I saw it emerge from the fog at close quarters, took hold of it with one hand, breathed quietly, shut my eyes and folded double.

I had to let go of the anchor chain to dive, for it made me turn round again. I tried once more, feeling grim and indifferent. If I

231

had to drown, all right. I shut my eyes again, bent double, groping for my feet, and slid down into the silence. The horn sounded its two notes loudly in my ears; they began to hurt, and I heard the crackling of fire again, louder than ever. I opened my eyes, saw nothing at all, only the green fog, pushed myself upward and swallowed my saliva.

The crackling of fire died down. I felt the bottles float on my back. I didn't weigh anything; even the square lead weights on my belt seemed to float, for they didn't hurt me any more. I looked round for the anchor chain, but couldn't find it. The horn sounded softer now, as if it was further away. I bent double again and slid down deeper, the bottles moving on my back. I heard again the crackling in my ears, mounting, and the pain started. Ten meters. The height of a house. I swallowed my saliva, not only to relieve the pressure on my ears. I swallowed it several times. I hovered for a while, my arms spread out in the fog, looking for the anchor chain. It was nowhere. Then I bent double again, feeling cold and disinterested, and I slid down once more. I was just thinking that I was not doing badly, that I might get used to this after a couple of times and be a little orange creature myself, descending into the silent summer garden like a falling leaf, when, suddenly, I saw something. An enormous crab, with two horns, very close by. My heart pounded, I thought I'd die. Then I recognized it. It was an old bicycle. It made me laugh. The horn sounded in my ears in rapid succession. Then I felt something soft and slimy on my leg, pulled it in like a flash, and realized it must have been mud. I rose a couple of meters, back in the fog again, seeing nothing. And then a huge, silent shadow slid past. A fish. It looked enormous, and was about to vanish in the fog when I saw it flip its tail sharply, and turn round to approach me from the back.

Then I got into a panic. I jerked myself upright and pushed with my legs. I hit the bicycle with my right foot. It must have been the bicycle, for it was sharp and stung me. I shot up toward the surface, holding my breath.

My ears hurt again and the crackling of fire rose to the sound of splintering wood. I swallowed several times, but I had no saliva left. Something stung in my eyes and my vision became blurred.

232

I realized that water had got into my mask. I gasped for breath, inhaled through the nose, sucked up the water and choked.

Then my head rose above the water. I saw the anchor chain, very close to, grabbed it, pulled myself up, ripped off my mask, pulled out the mouthpiece, and shouted, with my last breath, "Help!"

He was there, right overhead. His voice sounded calm, I hadn't heard it like this since the war. "Don't worry," he said. "You're all right. Hang on for a bit. I'll put the boat out."

I shut my eyes and felt sick. My mouth tasted acid and sickly. His voice said, quietly, overhead, "Don't worry, it's always like that the first time. You did very well. I didn't think you would go down that deep. Good old Skipper, well done."

I heard the splashing of oars and voices and then I felt the coolness of the shadow of the boat. "Take off his bottles," he said, in French. I hadn't realized that he had been talking Dutch to me. "Take his mask," he said. "It's about to fall off." They helped me out of my harness and then his voice said, "All right, Skipper, get into the boat. You're home and dry now."

I climbed into the boat, shivering, suddenly cold. The world seemed a very light place to come back to; it dazzled me. I still had the sickly taste in my mouth of locked-up air and rubber.

When I climbed the pilot's ladder again, he came towards me and patted my shoulder. "Sorry to have thrown you into this soup," he said, "but you've had the worst now. You'll see, next time it's wonderful."

I tried to laugh and said, "I wonder. I don't think I'm any good at this."

"Don't be silly," he said. "You're a born diver." Then he lit a cigarette and gave it to me. The war had come very close.

He patted my shoulder again and left his hand there. "Sorry about the other things," he said. "We'll be all right now. Now, you're one of us." Then he turned round and went to the fo'c'sle.

ᑯᖎ

That night, on a marble table of a bistro, I wrote a letter to June Simmons. When I started it I didn't know why I had suddenly felt the need to write to her; I discovered it only when I

233

wrote. I told her about the diving and Goatskin, and when I arrived at where he had said, "Now you're one of us," I stopped. It was this remark that had set me writing. I ordered another drink and continued the letter. "You said that there was something that worried you. I should like to know what it is. I am taking care of myself and am not getting depressed at all. I know I have got friends. Yours ever."

As I sat there, watching the crowd of workmen and their girls stroll along the quay, laughing and kissing, I thought it was nonsense to think of Goatskin and Pjotr and the others as belonging to another world of which, from now on, I would be part. It was very tempting to consider my first dive with the Cousteau as a sort of baptism, but one could go too far in being romantic.

I thought it would be a good idea to take a stroll myself, and I walked along the quay and the shipyards. It was hard to believe that this was the South of France. It looked more like Brest or Le Havre. A thin fog came from the harbor, and the street lamps made cones in it through which lovers and cats slid silently.

There was a stale smell of welding in the cul-de-sac where I ended up; behind the wooden hoarding I heard the bubbling sound of vats of carbide. I turned round and walked back to the harbor. Now my eyes were accustomed to the darkness I saw sleeping bums at the bottom of the hoarding.

On the quay I called for the longboat. It was Goatskin who came to fetch me. When he stepped ashore he said, "Let's have one more drink," so we went back to the bistro. It was odd the way he had changed since that afternoon. We were sitting in the bistro like we had so often sat in the Social Center.

It was he who started talking about Nicole. He said she was a nice girl, but that occasionally he felt like kicking her up the stairs. Perhaps because she was so damn even tempered. Had I noticed that?

I said I had, but that it didn't bother me.

He lit a cigarette. "Well, you wait. If you tell her that you have dived, you're in for it. She's got a thing about diving, some oriental twist in her mind, I suppose. Hasn't she told you yet that the dividing line between life and death is the mirror of the sea, and that what we are doing is penetrating in the realm of death?"

234

I said she hadn't and he laughed, stubbing out the cigarette he had just lit. "Well, you'll get it, don't worry," he said. "It's her favorite topic. And there is something else I should tell you."

I asked, "What?" because he didn't go on.

"I know it's none of my business," he said, "but just as a matter of interest: have you been to bed with her yet?" Before I could answer he continued, "Well, whether you have or haven't, you'll see that from now on, that's finished. She won't let you touch her anymore once you've started going down with the Cousteau, until the day you give it up." He snorted. "The cheek of it! Girls—you never know what they'll think of next."

I wanted to ask him several things, but I sat there silently, thinking of Stella. She had loved us all, so long as we had been innocent and defenseless. The moment we had killed our first enemy it had been all over. "Yes," I said, "women are odd. I don't think we'll ever know what motivates them. Maybe she has got something there."

"Of course," he said. "But what's the use?"

I didn't quite get what he meant, but I left it at that. While we finished our drinks we talked about the trip to Greece and wondered what the old antiquarian expected us to bring up for him. I asked what he was like.

"Oh, a charmer," Goatskin said.

He was his new self again.

❧

The charmer arrived within the hour of our arrival in Saint Tropez. He was called Mr. Astanasia, and for once Goatskin had been right. He was indeed a charming old man. He looked delicate and cultured, had steely gray hair and dark eyes, and his smile was very winning. We all liked him at first sight.

He had a crook with him on crutches, who looked so much like a musical-comedy pirate that the one thing lacking was a screaming parrot on his shoulder. He was introduced by Mr. Astanasia as a Greek sea captain; his name was very Greek and nobody quite got it. He was tentatively called Captain Perpendiculous, and as he didn't seem to find anything wrong with that we must have been pretty close.

235

Captain Perpendiculous was obviously looking for trouble. He whispered in Mr. Astanasia's ear all the time while they made the tour of the ship, guided by Goatskin. He was obviously telling him the truth about the ship, but Mr. Astanasia wasn't in the least impressed. He loved the ship, was delighted to see the old Captain in the wheelhouse, peering out of his bunk like a suspicious cat; he muttered "charming" all the time. We all felt greatly heartened and Pjotr said, "There goes a wonderful man." Mr. Astanasia was delighted also with the little cabin he got underneath the piano; Captain Perpediculous was not as pleased with his, although it was exactly the same only on the starboard side. He said it was a death trap and that the mattress stank and asked whether engine fumes ever penetrated into it. Goatskin said, "No, no," on the sound principle that once we had got him at sea he wouldn't be able to get off.

The only one who wasn't delighted with Mr. Astanasia was the old Captain. He called me with a conspiratory "Psst!" as I passed the wheelhouse on my way to the fo'c'sle. He asked whether the little man with the gray hair was going to sail with us. I said he was.

"Is he the one who's paying for the trip?"

"Yes."

"In that case," said the Captain, "we can't sail."

I asked him why not, but he just went on doggedly repeating the classic phrase. At first I thought he had one of his usual tempers, but later on I heard the sounds of a colossal row in the wheelhouse. When I came back on deck I saw Goatskin, beside himself, in a curious position, half bent over the chart table, as if he was kneeding dough. He was busy strangling the Captain. As I came in the old man was on the edge of a fit; he screamed that the ship was his, that he would have us taken off by the police and put in jail; that this was France, the country of justice, where no bloody foreigner could go too far. We could stand on our heads, or plate him with gold, if that man was sailing with us, we must find another ship! That was final, final! I was afraid it was indeed, because at that moment he clutched his chest, rumpling his pyjamas, and sat down in the lower bunk gasping for breath. It was the worst row we had had so far; but I still wasn't acclimatized to the South of France entirely yet. An hour later it seemed as if nothing had happened; only the old Captain had gone ashore with a handsome bank note in his pocket to take a rest in a hotel while we were away. His nerves were overstrained and he had agreed that as I had been sailing the ship for several weeks now, I knew her well enough and if anything happened to her the insurance would pay. I asked Goatskin where he had got the banknote from; he said that Mr. Astanasia had advanced it when he heard of the trouble.

Mr. Astanasia came to see me when I was shifting my bed sheets and my clothes from the fo'c'sle to the wheelhouse. He said that he was very pleased to know that I would command the ship and that if he was in my way at all at any given moment I shouldn't hesitate to say so. Captain Perpendiculous swung into view behind him on his crutches, shot me a Long John Silver glance, and whispered something in his ear; Mr. Astanasia laughed and said, "Nonsense, Captain." I didn't know what Captain Perpendiculous had said, but judging from the look he gave me his remark must have expressed a doubt as to my abilities.

We would leave as soon as the new Cousteau apparatus had been delivered. After I had finished clearing out the wheelhouse I started looking among the charts for the Greek Archipelago. It wasn't there. I told Goatskin, and said that if we hadn't got those charts we couldn't sail. Only after the words had left my mouth I realized that I had taken over the classic phrase. Goatskin sighed and said, through clenched teeth, "One of these days I'm going to settle everybody." He must have gone to tell Mr. Astanasia about it, for a few minutes later the old gentleman appeared in the wheelhouse with a roll of paper under his arm. "I forgot to tell you, Captain," he said, "that I've got a complete set of charts with me."

I said, "Thank you, sir. Could we have a look at the route now or would you prefer to do that later?"

He laughed and said, patting me on the shoulder, "We'll have plenty of time for that, Captain, on our way to Corsica. Your first point of reference is Cap Corse."

That sounded fair enough. I began to like the old man. He was at least sensible, and seemed to take a lot of things in his stride.

While waiting for the new Cousteau we had a drink on a terrace, Goatskin and I. He was quite his new self again. He babbled on without interruption about how splendid things were and how rich we would be in four weeks' time. As we were sitting there, a quiet girl's voice said, "Hello. Mind if I sit down with you?" It was Nicole, very pretty, in a black dress with a plunging neckline and with her sun glasses on. Goatskin didn't answer, just made a vague gesture at a chair.

She asked what the trip with the businessmen had been like, and I began to tell her, but Goatskin interrupted by saying, "Oh, for God's sake, shut up! We've had that now. No, this time we've got something much better." And he went on telling her about the wonderful Mr. Astanasia and the Greek treasure. He hadn't finished singing the praises of Mr. Astanasia yet, when the old gentleman passed our table, spotted us, and came toward us, smiling. I introduced him to Nicole whom I called "Miss Nicole" because that was all I knew. He was very charming and old-world to her and ordered expensive drinks for all of us. Nicole sat looking at him through her dark glasses, smiling.

Mr. Astanasia was really an exquisitely mannered man, for he finished his drink quickly and left us before a silence had fallen in the conversation. He said he was going to do some last minute shopping, and we saw him disappear in a *parfumerie,* which bore a notice saying "Have yourself perfumed before you leave."

Then Nicole put her staggering suggestion to us. She said, calmly, "What if I went with you this time?"

We both looked at her with our mouths open; before we answered she went on, saying that although the old gentleman was very charming, he shouldn't be left to the cares of Pjotr and the old bosun as far as his food and the cleaning of his cabin was concerned. If we wanted him to remain charming it would be a good idea if we took somebody on board to look after these little things. Well, she was willing to come if we thought she might be any use.

Goatskin had recovered from his amazement by then and become boorish once more. He shrugged his shoulders and said, nodding at me, "Ask him. Not only is he the Captain, but you're

238

his moll now." I swallowed a lot of things; then I said that I would be delighted. She said, "Thank you, Skipper."

After that there was a long silence which got strained to breaking point; then, luckily, a little van stopped at the gangway of our ship. "Ah," said Goatskin, jumping up. "That must be the new Cousteau! Excuse me," and he ran across the quay to welcome his new toy.

"Another diving set?" she asked.

I said, "Yes."

"Whom for?"

"Me."

"Are you going to work as a diver?"

"Yes."

"I see." We were silent for a while; then she got up. "Well, I suppose I had better pack my things now. Are we leaving soon?"

"In about twenty minutes."

"All right," she said, "I'll be there," and she went away.

As I crossed the quay to go to the ship I saw Captain Perpendiculous swing along, causing quite a sensation among the population. He looked like a sandwich man in a fancy costume, looking for his board with the advertisement of Jamaica Rum. As I mounted the gangway I saw him enter the perfumer's. They certainly had a handful coming.

∽

Goatskin put her in the lower bunk in the wheelhouse.

I was on the poop taking the watch, after we had left the harbor on our way to Corsica, so I didn't see her go in there. I found her in the bunk when I entered the wheelhouse after he had taken over.

I asked, "What are you doing here?" stupidly, and she said, "This is the bed I've been given."

I felt like going back to the poop and having it out with him, once and for all; but I thought of Mr. Astanasia underneath, with his portholes open, and decided to let the lunatic get away with it once more. What made me see red was the deliberate callousness of it toward her. She must be a strong girl indeed to lie there, smiling, understanding it all and letting it pass. I

239

asked, "Wouldn't you rather have a cabin? Here there will be people in and out all the time."

"Oh, no," she said. "I'm quite happy. If we leave the doors open it will be nice and fresh at night and I may not get seasick."

As it was going to be my watch again in four hours' time I wanted to get some sleep, so I just said, "As you like. Good night," and she said, "Good night, Skipper. Thank you."

"For what?" I asked, halfway up the ladder to my bunk.

"You know," she said. "Good night."

I wasn't sure I did know, but I shrugged my shoulders and climbed into my bunk.

Although I had changed the sheets and aired the mattress, it still smelled of the old captain. At the head of the bunk there was a little bookshelf, with an edge to it to prevent the books from falling out with the rolling of the ship. It looked empty, but when I put down my pack of cigarettes on it I noticed there was one book left, lying flat. It was a cheap edition of Negro spirituals, very battered and torn. I looked through it. One of the songs was marked with a heavy penciled cross and two exclamation marks. It ran:

> Sometimes I feel like a motherless child
> Sometimes I feel like a motherless child
> Sometimes I feel like a motherless child
> Far away from ho-o-ome
> Far away from home.

I looked at the flyleaf and saw it belonged to the old Captain. I put it back on the shelf, blew out the light, and went to sleep.

Chapter XII

THE TRIP TO CAP CORSE WENT WELL. I HAD LOOKED FORWARD WITH apprehension to the moment when we would lose the land, for not only were the compasses suspect, but no Mediterranean helmsman could be made to stick to his course. The old bosun and the boy with the red cyclist's cap would greet each other at the changing of the watch like long lost friends after years

240

of separation, embrace one another, kiss on both cheeks, and ask what their health was like, to arrive at the mentioning of the course only after at least five minutes, during which the wheel spun to and fro at every wave. Once the next man had taken the wheel he began to sing or, in case of the boy, to knit. Every time I checked the course we were at least five degrees out.

The second night I got sick of this, and I told the old bosun what I thought of his steering without mincing my words. An airplane was coming over low at that moment, and it drowned my little speech with the drone of its engine. "But, *mon commandant*, what are you worrying about?" the old bosun asked, sincerely amazed. "We are on the right course. There goes the plane to Corsica." After that I gave up.

The other one who worried about the course was Captain Perpendiculous; but then, he was worrying about everything. We never exchanged a word, he didn't seem to be talkative. He just appeared on the poop at irregular times and glowered at the compass, the sails, and the dozing helmsman. To see him emerge from the hatch was an eerie sight. First he threw his crutches onto the deck from below, then he mounted the stairs on his knees, collected his crutches, put them up, and hoisted himself to his one foot. The only proof of his experience as a sailor was that the moment he got on board he had taken the rubber caps off the butts of his crutches and driven a nail into each of them to prevent them from slipping. Within twenty-four hours the poop deck was already getting pockmarked with holes.

We saw the snow on the mountains of Corsica in the sky a full day before we arrived. At first I thought they were thin white clouds. I had no idea at what point we were going to hit the island, so when toward sunset a mistral started I got worried, it was blowing right on the beam. I had never come across the mistral before. It rose within five minutes from zero to seven, and after half an hour it was a gale. I had all sails taken in except the jib, and never had I known *Euridice* to run faster. I insisted on steering north-northeast when the mistral hit us, although this made the ship roll like a barrel, I didn't want to run smack into Corsica. The old bosun shrugged his shoulders and sighed. At nightfall, when the lighthouses began to wink on the horizon, I saw to my astonishment that we had been heading straight for Cap Corse, without knowing it. So I brought the ship back on her course and we lunged heavily toward the flashing light. As Goatskin took over my watch and I went to the wheelhouse I found Nicole lying dead still in her bunk with her eyes closed, moaning softly. I asked, "Seasick?" and she nodded without opening her eyes. I said, "You'd better get up and come out on deck with me for a minute. It'll make you feel better." She tried to get up but was too weak. I wrapped her in a blanket, carried her out, and put her down on a wine barrel in the shelter of the wheelhouse. I sat down beside her, my arm around her shoulders, and she leaned against me, breathing heavily. I stroked her arm, the way Goatskin had done when I lay on the bridge wounded after the shelling of our ship. It had been very comforting, and it seemed to work on her too. After a while she relaxed a bit and her breathing became normal. "Better?" I asked. I felt her nod. We sat there for at least an hour, and I had dozed off when a torch shone in our faces. I blinked and asked, "Who's that?" The torch flicked out, and a shadow said, "Sorry." It was Goatskin.

I carried her back to the wheelhouse, put her down on her bunk, and covered her with a blanket. She wasn't feeling all right yet, for when I wanted to stand up and climb in my bunk she held on to my hand, squeezing it hard. I sat down on the edge of her bunk, her hand in mine, waiting until she would go to sleep.

I went to sleep first; when I woke up because the old bosun called, "*Commandant!* Cap Corse on the green!" I was lying on her bunk with my head on her shoulder.

The gale had freshened. When I came out on the deck I was nearly blown off my feet. As I reached the poop I saw Captain Perpendiculous stand behind the helmsman in the compass light, his crutches spread out, looking like a spider. Goatskin was there too, trying to light a pipe. I said, "I think we'd better take shelter behind the peninsula, don't you think so?" He answered, "Can't you make love if the ship's rolling?" I said: "All right, if you want it that way," called the bosun and told him we'd round the cape and try to enter the port of Macinaggio. He said we

242

drew too much water for that, but we could anchor in the roads. He knew the corner, there was quite a nice little bay there.

When we dropped anchor off Macinaggio we were alone, and I was worried that it wasn't such a healthy corner after all. But within a matter of hours three other ships lay anchored with us, and by noon the next day our number had grown to nine. It was funny to think that these old Mediterranean salts had followed our example, trusting our appearance. We looked indeed very experienced; we had covered the piano with a tarpaulin when the gale started.

∽

We lay anchored off Macinaggio for two days, waiting for the mistral to blow itself out. Goatskin suggested that I should try out the Cousteau once more.

I knew instantly why he suggested this, because he was watching Nicole while he said it. She was wearing her dark glasses and didn't react. She looked as if she wasn't listening.

As I was putting on the diving set Mr. Astanasia was very interested. He had never seen this before, he said, and while Goatskin was adjusting the straps of my harness he put intelligent questions about the thing. What seemed to interest him most was how deep we could go with it, and how long the bottles lasted. The answer seemed to satisfy him. I wasn't surprised, for Goatskin said that he could go down to a hundred and twenty meters at least and that the bottles lasted an hour and a half. As a matter of fact they lasted about an hour, and the record depth for the Cousteau, so Pjotr had told me, was a hundred and twenty-four meters; but when the diver came back to the surface he was dead.

The whole crew stood watching me as I went down the pilot's ladder. On the poop I saw the pirate, trying to look disinterested but watching like a hawk. Nicole was the only one who wasn't there. As I put my foot in the water it was very cold, much colder than it had been in La Ciotat. The mistral had cooled it off. This time I dived straight away, for the water was so crystal clear that I could see everything: our anchor buried in the seaweed, the yellow plate Pjotr had broken the day before and

243

thrown overboard, the little fish flitting over a beautiful, white rocky bottom. I couldn't see any big fish from above, the mistral must have chased them away. As I slid down deeper I heard the two-toned horn again and the crackling in my ears. When the pain started I rose for a meter, swallowed, and dived deeper. I knew we were lying at fifteen meters, and the rocky soil looked very clean and inviting, so after having made a ceiling once more I went down to the bottom and stood up.

It was the most curious sensation I had ever had. I hadn't thought that the difference between floating and standing upright on the bottom of the sea was so striking. I had difficulty in remaining upright, for there was a slow ground swell that lifted me off the ground and gently put me down again. I tried to walk, but the moment I advanced, my feet were lifted off the ground and I came back to a horizontal position once more. It was my frogman's feet that did it, and after a short hesitation I took them off, feeling reckless. It did indeed make a difference. Once I had them in my hands I could walk. It wasn't normal walking, it was a slow, graceful dancing, like an athlete jumping on a slow motion film. It gave me an extraordinary sensation of joy and power; I touched the weeds with my hands and felt they were real. This was, at last, the heart of the dream; for in my dreams, ever since childhood, whenever I had stretched out my hand toward something, first a little cake and later a girl, I had woken up the moment before my fingers touched. The underwater world had looked like that from above; when I lay floating on the surface and looked down at the landscape with its waving shrubs, its flowers and its grassy plains, it had looked as if it would vanish at the touch of my big orange hand.

Now I was there, and touched it. I let go of the piece of seaweed, and as it floated away I caught it again, and I felt such a joy that I jumped like a child and rose five meters in the air. It wasn't water any longer; it was air. The clumsy mouthpiece, the sound of the horn, the staleness of the air I breathed, they all vanished the moment I stood upright with that bit of seaweed in my hand. The garden was mine.

I danced through the garden until I suddenly felt I was choking. I realized that my bottles had run out and opened the spare tank on my back. I had ten minutes left and I looked up to see where the ship was.

I saw it float above me, among the others, very small, like a model. I saw its propeller, and its rudder and the anchor chain going down. Now I had opened my spare tank it was high time I went back. I was about to rise when I saw a little flower of an extraordinary transparent blue in a little nest of seaweed. I danced toward it, and it was so beautiful that I couldn't resist the temptation to take it with me. I bent down, my feet rose in the air and I picked it, hovering like a humming bird. Then I rose back to the surface.

As I climbed the pilot's ladder I saw them all standing there, looking down at me, the orange creature coming back from the depth with a little flower in his hand. Goatskin asked, "Where the hell are your frogman's feet?" He gave me a shock, I had forgotten about them. They must be lying somewhere below in the garden. I thought of going back, but I remembered my air was finished so I climbed the rest of the ladder and was helped over the rail by many hands. I took the mouthpiece out and said, "I've left them below. I'll go and get them later."

Mr. Astanasia patted me on the shoulder as I was taking off my mask. "My hearty respect, Captain," he said. "What a wonderful diver you are. Could you have stayed down there longer?" I said, "No, sorry." Goatskin got angry and said, "Nonsense! He had at least three quarters of an hour left." When I told him that I had to open my spare tank he looked at me furiously and said, "In the first place your bottles weren't full; second, you're a bloody amateur. I watched your bubbles. You breathe much too fast." I said, "Give me a chance will you?" and went into the wheelhouse to look for a towel.

Nicole was sitting on her bunk, doing nothing. When I came in, she looked up. I said, "I've got something for you," and gave her the little flower. She said, "Oh, thank you. That's very nice of you," and looked at it, a bit startled, I thought. When I saw it in her hand I couldn't believe my eyes. The little flower that had looked so beautiful below was now a limp, leathery thing without any color at all, just a slimy piece of muck.

I said, "I'm so sorry, it looked ravishing below."

245

She put her arms round my neck, kissed me and said, "I'm sure it did, darling."

I was very disappointed, but her kiss made it good.

༃

Mr. Astanasia told us our destination, at last, on the evening of the day we sailed from Macinaggio. He came to the poop in a white dressing gown, the sleeves rolled up to the elbows, looking like a Roman senator, carrying a lantern. He had his roll of charts with him and asked the bosun to call Goatskin, who had just gone down to sleep. After Goatskin had joined us he unrolled one of his charts and pointed at a little island in the farthest southwest of the Cyclades. "This is where we are going," he said. "Just here, at my finger, are the ruins of a Greek temple, submerged three thousand years ago after a landslide. I want you two to dive for it and have a look at what's inside. Probably nothing, but I thought it would be amusing to find out."

"How deep is it?" Goatskin asked.

"That's the point: I don't know. I got my information from the Greek gentleman who is with me, and who had a little sponge fishing business with a couple of divers. His fisherman found a wreck on one of their expeditions: an old three-master that was shipwrecked there about eighty years ago. They wanted to search the wreck, but it was lying too deep for them. They could see it quite clearly though; it seemed to rest on a curious scaffolding of white pillars. The news spread in the bistros ashore and got to some official, who passed it on to the Historical Institute in Athens, and there somebody came to the conclusion that the white scaffolding must be the ruins of a temple of Pallas Athene which they knew had been submerged three thousand years ago, only nobody knew exactly where. All this happened during the war. They kept the news a secret, for fear that the Germans would organize an expedition and pilfer the temple. They were about to organize an expedition after the war themselves, when their civil war started."

"Did they tell you about this?" Goatskin asked, boyishly.

Mr. Astanasia smiled in the lantern light. "No," he said; and then, after a silence in which Goatskin looked foolish, he added,

246

"And I'd appreciate it if you young gentlemen could be as discreet as possible when you go down with your diving apparatus. I think that the best solution is that you go down on the side that is turned away from the shore. Although at the moment they have other things to do, there may be people looking at us through binoculars. Let's keep this little expedition private."

After that he asked me how long I thought it would take us to get there, and we discussed the route, and had a glass of wine together. He offered us one of his long, fragrant cigarettes, and was very charming and aristocratic.

When I told Nicole about the temple, she sat thinking for a while and then she asked, "Did he mention what he expected to find in there?"

I said he hadn't mentioned it, but that I remembered that some famous statue which was now in the Louvre had been found under water. She said it was called "The Victory of Samothrace." "Well," I said, "I suppose he hopes for yet another Victory." And then I remembered the newspaper in the cupboard on the dead windjammer in Antwerp, the picture of the soldier kissing the fat girl's hand. "To her murdered little hands, he owes his Victory." I realized for the first time what I had found under the sea. It was peace.

∽

When we reached our Treasure Island, one starry night, the whole thing became too romantic for words, for Long John Silver came into action. He threw his crutches onto the deck from below, climbed the stairs on his knees, crawled over the threshold, and spread out a piece of paper on the deck. We knelt around him; Mr. Astanasia put down the lantern and we saw on the paper a crude, handmade map: the map of an island. It was scribbled full of Greek, which made it look even more picturesque; off the southeast coast was a rock, and at that rock was drawn a cross. He put a finger the size of a banana on the cross and said, "There." No actor in Hollywood could have said it better.

We were all very impressed and excited; this was what we had been reading about with glowing ears very long ago, when somebody had angrily said, "If you don't put that book down at once and go to bed, I'll take it away for good."

After we had got over our boyhood we started investigating the depths on the official chart. The soundings were from five to seven hundred meters within half a mile off the coast; so, unless the temple was sitting on a plateau with a precipice going down right in front of it, there either was no temple or we would need a bathyscope. We tried to get out of Captain Perpendiculous what exactly he had seen, and he gave a long flowery description of which the first six words were French and the rest Greek. Mr. Astanasia translated it for us; the upshot seemed to be that he had seen the wreck very clearly and that the white pillars had loomed in the blue. If that was true the temple must be at thirty or forty meters at the utmost, which was nothing. Anyhow, we would soon know. Goatskin and I would go down together first thing in the morning.

The next morning, when we stood ready with our bottles on in the wheelhouse, where we had put ourselves so as not to be seen from the shore, Mr. Astanasia came to wish us luck and said that in case a warship or a patrol from the shore hailed us we should say we were hunting. Goatskin said that it had all been arranged; Pjotr, Bernard, and Jacques would get into the water first with their respirators and their guns, to make the whole thing look natural. Captain Perpendiculous came swinging to the door and said something excitedly in Greek. Mr. Astanasia remained calm and aristocratic, but he took out a cigarette, which he forgot to light. "He says we're there," he said, "so perhaps you two might care to go down and have a look."

I called to the bosun to stop the engine, for we had approached the rock under power as there was no wind. The Greek coast showed blue and hazy in the distance; the little island seemed to be entirely uninhabited. There wasn't even a lighthouse on it, and no ships were in sight. Goatskin explained to Mr. Astanasia that Pjotr and the others would go first to see whether we were overhead, it would be a pity if we wasted our air on searching. If the Greek Captain had indeed seen it from the surface, then the boys would too.

Pjotr, Jacques, and Bernard went down the ladder and splashed

248

into the water. They had hardly been in it three minutes when Bernard cried, "Here!" at about fifty yards distance from the ship. "All right," said Goatskin. "Let's go, Skipper. Good luck." Before he put in his mouthpiece he added, "Let's stay close together this time; if anything should happen that we don't want to happen, tap on your bottles. I'll do the same," I said, "O.K.," and we went down.

He got in first. When I followed him I felt the water was much warmer than it had been off the French coast. When I looked down, before I dived, I saw a sight so breath-taking that I lay floating on the surface blowing spluttering bubbles from my neck for minutes on end.

The rock near which we had descended was stark and bare above the water, but as soon as it vanished under the sea it turned into a mountain slope full of flowers of such unearthly colors that I stared at them in amazement and wonder. They were all shades of blue and pink and silver, and yellow and turquoise green; among them flitted millions of little fish of dazzling colors themselves, like butterflies. The flowered slope went down almost perpendicularly into the blue, but ahead of me I saw something dark jut out of it. I swam slowly toward it, after I had gone down my first five meters, and I saw the stern of a ship emerge from the blue. The first thing I recognized was a broken steering wheel, overgrown with weeds. Then, as I swam further, I recognized stumps of masts and the dark holes of holds. She must have been lying there for a very long time, for she was entirely overgrown; garlands of flowers hung down her sides and vanished in the blue.

I saw Goatskin pass underneath me and swim over her deck. When he reached the other side he stopped. He stayed motionless for about a minute. Then he suddenly turned round, looked, and I saw him pull his knife and tap on the bottles; it sounded as if he was just by my side. I went down five meters deeper, made my ceiling and swam toward him, crossing the wreck at about three meters above her deck.

On the other side the water was green and full of quivering, slanting beams of sunlight. At first I couldn't make out what it was, then I recognized a rectangular pattern, like the foundation of a house, but it was all overgrown with weeds and there were thousands of fish of all sizes who obscured the view.

I saw Goatskin go down, and I followed him. I made one more ceiling, and then another, and then yet another. I was now at thirty meters, in the green dusk of the depth. Then I touched ground and stood upright.

Again I had the curious sensation of a complete change, the moment I stood on my feet. I stood in what seemed to be the courtyard of a ruin. Huge pillars were lying among the weeds, broken in round discs. Only where the wreck was some of them stood upright. The wreck was resting on what must have been a roof three thousand years ago. She was silhouetted darkly against the blue and the silver of the sea, and sunlight slanted through the pillars. We stood looking at it, motionless, and saw the shadow of fish pass behind the pillars like birds against the deep blue of an evening sky. It was so fantastic and beautiful and unreal that we took a long time before we started dancing from pillar to pillar with long slow steps, looking. I had forgotten about Goatskin and he about me; yet we stayed close to one another instinctively, like geese.

We were sitting side by side on one of the sections of a fallen pillar in the courtyard when I saw it: a long dark silhouette, which slid silently past behind the standing pillars.

I had never seen one that size. It looked enormous, the triangular fin on its back stood out like a sail. I put out my hand and touched Goatskin's arm. It was the first time I touched a living body under water, it felt very cold.

We saw the shark pass from gap to gap, until it vanished in the blue behind the wreck's curved stem. From the stem a bowsprit hung down, broken; there were still ropes attached to it, garlands of weeds. Then we saw a round dark shape come toward us.

It was the shark again, heading for us. I didn't feel afraid, but I couldn't let go of Goatskin's arm. He had to shake me off to pull his knife. I pulled mine too, but I didn't intend to use it. I was very calm and not afraid of the shark attacking me; I was afraid of Goatskin attacking the shark.

It came gliding toward us silently, then it swerved and passed

250

at five yards distance in front of us. I saw its white belly with three little fish hanging from it, sucked to its skin. I saw its small myopic eyes and its huge blue body beautifully shaped, and its tail, that moved gently but gave the impression of colossal strength. I turned round, following it with my eyes, and tried to see us as seen by him: two little orange creatures, sitting side by side on a pillar covered with seaweed, silver bubbles rising from their necks, that floated upward in little twin clusters, glistening in the sun. I would come and have a closer look if I was a shark; I would be much too amazed to think about eating straight away. I wouldn't believe my eyes; the shark did nothing that wasn't natural.

It made a circle around us, and then another much closer; and then Goatskin rose to his feet and waved his arms, but he didn't make any impression. He only made us more interesting to look at, two thin orange tentacles, waving, with something glistening in one. I got to my feet too, slipped on the seaweed and made a slow somersault backward. For a second I lost my sense of direction, then I saw Goatskin rise, and the long blue shape slide past below him, and then the shark rose perpendicularly too, and I saw it and Goatskin side by side for a moment, which gave me a feeling of nausea, for it was twice as tall as he.

Goatskin rose about five meters higher, became horizontal again, and hovered. I thought I had seen enough; as I rose past him I pointed upward, indicating that I was going to the surface. I looked up at the silver mist of the sky as I rose, then suddenly something gripped my right leg. I choked with fright, lost control of my breath, for one terrible moment I knew I was drowning. Then I looked down and saw it was Goatskin who had gripped me. He tugged at my leg angrily, and tapped his forehead. Then I remembered: we had been at thirty meters. If I went to the surface without hovering first at an intermediate level I would go blind, or paralyzed, or mad, or get a stroke. So I hovered, shaking, looking for the shark.

I had lost it from sight and thought it had gone away, but then the huge blue thing slid past again, turning. Goatskin's frogman's feet moved slowly by the side of my head; he had put himself like this so that we would be looking both ways, without need to turn round the clock as the shark circled around us. He came closer and closer, and I gripped my knife with failing courage, ready to give him the gentle prod Goatskin had told me about. I hoped that if any prodding had to be done he would do it first, but most of all I hoped and prayed that there would be no prodding at all.

My prayer was not granted. I knew something was about to happen when I saw his frogman's feet flap rapidly and vanish. I turned round and saw the shark's white belly pass right overhead at about an arm's length. I saw the little sucking fish very close by, they seemed to be dragged across my mask. Then Goatskin shot up beside me, his right arm with the knife stretched out, and he stabbed the white belly as it slid past again.

At that moment something seemed to explode. I turned over several times in a whirlpool of violent currents; when I had found my sense of direction again Goatskin was circling underneath me, and the shark was nowhere to be seen. What hit me must have been the backwash of its tail, when it fled at the sting of the knife.

I had no idea any more at what height we were, but I hovered on, my heart pounding and my knees trembling, until Goatskin joined me. We floated hand in hand over the ruins, the wreck, and the flowers; two children in a dream. Then, at last, he nudged me, and pointed upward, and we rose.

∽

When we climbed back on board and told Mr. Astanasia what we had seen, he was very pleased and offered us a drink which we took in the sunlight, shivering, while our harnesses were taken off. Although the water had been warm, we were very cold now. We told about the shark too, and Goatskin sounded very confident about it. Just a big dumb animal, he said. Nobody had ever been attacked by a shark in the Mediterranean. They were the harmless kind, only very curious. I said I was quite willing to believe that, but hoped he wouldn't be there next time. "No hope," said Goatskin, "we have aroused his curiosity, now he'll be there every time we go down."

I said, "I see."

252

We didn't go down again that day. Mr. Astanasia thought it better not to hang around the spot too long. We sailed back into the open and lay in the sun and slept, while Bernard and Jacques and Pjotr went out to hunt the dinner.

That night, after everybody had gone to bed, I chatted with the old bosun. We were just idly drifting, so for once he could forget about the wheel and talk. When we came to our diving he said, "Yes, that temple is a lovely sight, with that old wreck on top. I saw it when I was a boy."

I thought that was extraordinary, and told him so. But he laughed. "I think every sailor boy in the Mediterranean has seen it," he said. "Whenever we were around these corners we always went to have a look, through a little glass case, you know, that we held outside the boat in the water. The number of people that have been going down there with masks and diving bells and scaphanders, my, they must have been at it for centuries. That wreck has been picked as clean as a skeleton in the desert."

I thought at first that this was just another Mediterranean fantasy; but as I thought about it, looking at the stars, I found a lot of sense in his story. The wreck and the ruins were so close to the surface, and could so easily be seen, that it seemed unlikely that nobody had ever bothered to go down before. Mr. Astanasia's expedition became a bit of a mystery.

"What did the old gent come here for?" the bosun asked. "To take photographs or something?"

I thought there was no harm in telling him the truth. "No, he's looking for antiques," I said.

The old man laughed. "Antiques?" he asked. "The only antiques left to take away down there will be those stone wheels. I wonder who sold him that idea. The Greek?" I said I didn't know.

When I went to call Goatskin for the changing of the watch I told him about the bosun's story, and, for once, he reacted reasonably. He too must have realized that the ruins were much too close to the surface to have remained untouched for three thousand years.

"Well," he said. "I don't know. Either the old boy has been

sold a dud by Captain Perpendiculous, or he's looking for something else that he hasn't told us yet. We'll soon know."

Four hours later, toward sunrise, when I had just come back to the poop after my four hours' sleep and Goatskin was about to go down, Mr. Astanasia rose silently from the hatch in his Roman senator's gown, smoking one of his long cigarettes. He said, "Good morning," and "Well, this looks like the beginning of another glorious day," and then, with a smile at the old bosun, "Surely there is no need to keep the crew out of their beds? We are just drifting, aren't we?" I could take a hint, so I told the bosun to go back to his bunk. He was delighted.

When we were alone on the poop Mr. Astanasia offered us a cigarette each, and after he had even lit them for us with an aristocratic hand, he said, "I think it's time, gentlemen, that we had a little talk in private."

Goatskin, who never looked before he jumped, said, "Yes, I think so. We heard—"

Mr. Astanasia lifted his hand, a cultured gesture of interruption. "There's no need to tell me what you heard," he said. "My portholes were open."

"Right," said Goatskin. "Well then, what are we looking for?"

"For something that may be found one plateau lower down," Mr. Astanasia replied. "And if it isn't there, you may have to go down one step deeper."

"How deep will that be?" I asked.

"A hundred and forty meters."

"So we can forget about the second step," Goatskin said.

Mr. Astanasia smiled and shrugged his shoulders. "If you prefer," he said. Goatskin was about to say something hearty; I put my hand on his arm before he shot his mouth off. I wanted to know what the dear old gentleman was up to. "Then what are we looking for?" I asked, and Mr. Astanasia answered, "You'll see when you find it."

"What do you want us to do if we find it?" Goatskin asked.

"We'll cross that bridge when we get to it," the old gentleman said, tersely. "You find it first. Good night."

As he turned and went down the stairs Goatskin said, "Good morning." Then he grinned at me in the blue light that preceded

254

sunrise. "For our next private conversation," he said loudly, "we'll climb the foremast." I beckoned him to follow me, and we went along the deck as far forward as we could go. Then we leaned over the rail, and looked at the bow of our ship, slowly rising and sinking in the limpid water with the long, slow swell. We talked about the mysterious order and agreed that it was all very fishy and were sure it was gold he was after, or bags of diamonds, or something, and that the temple business had been a device to get us out here without a share in the profit. Goatskin said we should insist on a share before we started risking our necks by going down deeper; I was in favor of locating the mystery thing first if we could, there was no need to kick up a row before his appetite had been whetted.

As we stood there, whispering, we had our backs to the ship, so we didn't see her coming. When she said, "So, sweet old Mr. Astanasia has shed his mask?" she gave us quite a shock.

Goatskin didn't even bother to look round. I said, "Good morning. Yes, he has. Did you know him, by any chance?" She was wearing the thin pink dressing gown and, although there was no sunlight yet, her dark glasses.

"No," she said. "I'd never seen him in my life, before he sat down with us on the terrace."

"So when you offered to come with us it was only a pretext, your saying that you wanted to look after him?" I asked.

"That's right," she said. "I didn't like the look of him. I wanted to be around."

Goatskin snorted, with his back to her. "I never thought I'd sink so deep," he said, "that one day I would set out for a diving expedition with a bodyguard of whores."

I said, "What if you went to bed?"

"Want to pick another fight?" he asked. "I'm your man, you know."

I said, "Go to bed."

He stood up, stretched, and yawned; then he said, "If you want to be a sucker, I don't suppose anyone can stop you. But if I may give you a piece of sound advice as a friend, put her— there." At that he pointed overboard, walked away, and went down the ladder to the fo'c'sle.

255

We had become used to this, so I wasn't amazed any more that she should take it so calmly. She took his place by my side, and we leaned over the rail again, looking at the sea and the orange clouds of sunrise.

"It looks as if you and the old Captain were the only ones the old crook didn't take in," I said.

She shrugged her shoulders. "He is quite a common type on the coast. If you had been living in the South of France as long as I have, you would have seen through him too."

"Well," I said. "I don't think there is anything seriously wrong. I only hope that that bloody fool won't get one of his fits of bragging and go down to a hundred meters or worse."

"So do I," she said. "That's why I came."

It was the closest she got to the confession that she was in love with him since I had first met her. I wanted to say something, but I didn't. "It isn't so much the danger of going down," I said. "I think that theoretically we can go down as deep as we like with those bottles. It's the danger of coming up. I had a look at the list of depths and hovering times. With two bottles we can go down to ninety meters, cast one look round and then we have to start coming back. By the time we arrive at our last decompression stage we'll have to open our spare tanks. So if the thing is lying at eighty or below, we might as well forget about it, for we won't have the time to do any work on it."

"I don't like this," she said. "I hope there will be nothing."

I said, "So do I," and then, after a silence, "There's something else I don't like, and that's the sharks. Not so much because they frighten me, but because I'll have to frighten them, and that will make me use my air too fast. If we go down deeper, we'll have to sink as quietly as we can, hardly moving, to eke out our air; the moment a shark turns up, you start breathing like a steam engine."

"What about those anti-shark tablets?" she asked. "Somebody told me they existed."

I said, "Yes, we had them during the war in our lifebelts. 'Shark chasers,' they were called. Big tablets, the size of a cigarette box, sown into the linen. If you found yourself afloat in the tropics you ripped them out and they dissolved in the water and made a black cloud around you like an octopus. They are no

256

good under water. You can't take that cloud with you as you move."

"I thought there were other ones," she said. "An American invention, tablets that when they dissolve give off the smell of a decomposing shark's corpse. It seems they stay away from that."

"Maybe," I said. "But I've never heard of them. And even if they exist, we haven't got them on board. No, all we can hope for is that our friend stays away."

"He won't," she said. "Everybody says so. He'll stay around here for weeks now he has seen you."

I said, "So I gather."

It had become lighter, the sun was about to rise, the world looked very beautiful. I felt far away from everything; I didn't worry about today, this morning was lovely. I said, "He told me in La Ciotat that you had some oriental theory about the mirror of the sea being the dividing line between life and death. Is that true?"

"Yes," she said.

"He also said that once he had dived with the Cousteau you wouldn't let him touch you anymore. Is that true too?"

She answered, after a silence, "I never let him touch me, not even before he dived."

I don't know what it was, perhaps the peace of the sunrise, the beauty of the sea, but it was as if I could hear her thoughts whisper in the silence. I said, "There is no need to lie to me about him. We have got beyond the point where he matters. If you don't want to talk about him, say so, but don't lie. It spoils things."

"All right," she said, "I don't want to talk about him."

I said, "That's fair enough," and we stood silently looking at the sun rising until it blinded us.

༄

As we stood by the wheelhouse with our harnesses on, Goatskin said, "I think the best plan is that we dive together until we get into the blue. As soon as you feel that you have gone deep enough, stay where you are and wait for me. Don't think you're God's brother-in-law, the dark is pretty frightening, and I don't

257

expect you to go down with me all the way. If you get into a panic at a depth of eighty, we'd find ourselves in an awkward situation."

I said, "All right. I'll put my safety before my honor."

"But I think it's more likely," he said, "that you'll have to stay at a pretty low depth anyhow, because of the shark. If it turns up again, I'll leave it to you. You stay at the depth where we meet it, and play around with it a bit. Then I can sneak into the purple without it following me. There's no need to be frightened."

I said, "I suppose there isn't, but I am."

It irritated him. "Don't be silly," he said. "You know now that they aren't dangerous, just curious. If you meet it again today, you'll see it looks like an old friend."

I said, "I know it won't attack me, but yesterday I was knocked for six by just the backwash of its tail. I hate to think what would happen if it gave me a wallop with that thing while we are playing."

"Then take a harpoon with you," he said. "It's six times as long as your knife and you can keep at a safe distance while prodding."

I said, "All right. Let's go and see."

We went down the pilot's ladder and dived. Mr. Astanasia was not standing at the rail this time to wish us good luck. He was standing on the poop, with the spider. The others shouted jocular greetings as we clumsily lowered ourselves into the water. The bosun called, "Daddy, bring back a little monkey for me!" It wasn't funny, but under the circumstances it made me laugh—hysterically. I had difficulty checking myself by remembering that I was using precious air with this nonsense.

We were slightly farther away from the wreck and the temple than we had been yesterday; we descended in a slant and didn't catch sight of the flowery mountain slope until we were at about twenty meters. After we had made our fourth ceiling, we swam horizontally toward the wreck until we found ourselves in about the same spot where the shark had been when we first saw it slide past behind the pillars. I looked round for it, but it wasn't there. Only swarms of smaller fish, of wonderful colors, who hovered round us in a glittering cloud.

Once we had reached the pillars underneath the wreck, we

258

went down deeper into the blue, descending along them. It was the first time I had entered the blue and although it was very beautiful, like floating in an evening sky, I didn't like it, it restricted my field of vision to about six meters. It began to remind me of La Ciotat harbor.

We went down deeper still. I followed Goatskin and saw his color change below me from orange to brown, then from brown to dark green. Beyond him, the blue became purplish; there was nothing else in view. We had passed the base of the pillars now and slid down sideways along what seemed to be steps. The steps continued down into the blue, darker and darker, until I saw a vague dividing line, quite straight, that seemed to be the edge of a precipice. Goatskin got darker and darker, although I stayed very close to him. The blue changed to deep purple. I didn't like the sight of that purple; the gathering darkness began to terrify me. And then, quite suddenly, as I went deeper with my hand stretched out, I felt something cold, as if I had dipped my hand into the water from a boat.

I slid into the coldness, then I stopped. This was too much for me. I hovered for a moment, getting very cold, and I saw Goatskin's shadow vanish in the darkness below. Only his bubbles went on rising past me in little clusters, joining and separating, big round ones into myriads of small ones, glistening like foam. I rose a couple of meters and when I rose I slid into the warmth again, like stepping out of the shadow on a hot summer's day. The bubbles went on floating past me, glistening, and I rose higher to get back to the light. As I rose, I felt very confident. I timed my periods of hovering with a feeling of familiarity. I was an expert now. I thought I must be at fifty meters, so I had to wait a long time before I went higher up. It was a pity I hadn't got a waterproof wristwatch, for I wasn't sure whether I had the right idea of time. Goatskin's bubbles rose slowly, regularly. I counted the periods between them. Three seconds one time, four the next, then four and a half, then three again. It was no use counting them. I just had to trust my common sense.

I thought I had hovered on the edge of the steps for at least a quarter of an hour and decided to rise to the next ceiling. It got lighter as I rose, I could make out the steps again. As I had

259

nothing to do but to hang around until this decompression period was over, I got closer to the steps to see what they were made of. They were thickly overgrown with weeds and a sort of moss, and full of little animals, crawling, flitting, and jumping. I thought I saw a sea star and prodded it gently with my harpoon. It shot up and vanished in the dusk with a few spasmodic movements.

Now I was hovering, the crowd of fish around me got thicker. There were a few that were almost as big as I was, and they came very close. I knew there was no reason to be afraid, they were just curious; but then I saw an eye staring at me, luminous like a cat's at night when it catches a light. I didn't like that; I waved at it with my harpoon. The eye blinked and vanished. I thought there would be no harm now in going up to my next stage, for the dusk didn't get lighter as I hung on. It seemed to darken.

I rose another five meters or so, and all the fish rose with me. I began to get irritated by their silent curiosity. I did silly things in my lonely boredom: I pointed at one and followed it with my finger, I shook my fist and blew a burst of angry bubbles by calling "Boo." As a particularly stupid one advanced on me, stopped at about a yard's distance from my mask, and gaped like a village idiot, I put my thumbs on my temples and twiddled my fingers. His face was so stupid that I burst out laughing. I had to stop that, the air was much too precious. I tried to put my mind off what I had done, for everytime my thoughts skirted it, I began to giggle again. So I began to hum. At first I just hummed, while breathing out. It sounded deep and sonorous, like a church organ. I had a beautiful voice under water. I started playing a tune on the organ with one finger, "Sometimes I feel like a motherless child." It sounded so beautiful and sad that it brought tears to my eyes, which would run down my cheeks and start filling my mask if I went on humming this heart-breaking tune. I had to find something gayer. I tried "Daisy," but that sounded out of place. I suddenly became conscious of the situation: an orange creature hovering on the steps of a temple no human feet had trod on for three thousand years, humming "Daisy." Goat-skin's bubbles were still rising from the depth, but they didn't

260

rise like soap suds any more. They rose like puffs of foam. He must be very deep. I began to get worried. It was high time that he was on his way back. I wondered whether he had lost his sense of depth, or perhaps he had got stuck down there. I decided that I must put my mind off thoughts like those, for they set my heart pounding and that made me breathe too quickly. I rose another ten meters, back into the light.

I was halfway up the pillars now, the wreck rested somewhere above me. I wanted to look up but thought I had better not turn on my back, every unnecessary movement was a waste. The crowd of fish had followed me; there must be hundreds of thousands of them around me by now, and as they caught the sunlight they began to glitter and get color, and I floated, dazed, in a whirlpool of diamonds and rubies. They were the most beautiful creatures I had ever seen; and now that I remained so still for so long they came closer and closer, throngs of them, swerving around and below me, changing from silver to green and from blue to gold in whole sheets, like starlings swarming. Goatskin's bubbles rose through them, clusters of silver dust blown up, and whole swarms of little fish rose with them. Then suddenly, as if swept away by a gust of wind, they vanished, all of them, blown into the blue. I looked round, alarmed, and felt a shadow pass over me. Then I saw the shadow pass, a slanting tunnel into the blue. I turned on my back and saw the shark, the three suckling fish hanging limply from his belly.

I thought, "Well, here we go again," and giggled, and my knees started trembling. Goatskin's bubbles were still rising, but they had got bigger now. They weren't silver foam any longer; little round suds glistened in the sunlight, changing color as they rose. The shark turned round in the distance and came back. I rose another five meters; I wanted to have a clear view and so I hovered at the level of the wreck's deck. It was at about six meters to my left. The shark came straight at me and I pointed at it with my harpoon, like an old lady with an umbrella. That thought made me giggle again, and I prayed, with a feeling of panic, "God, don't let me giggle, don't let me giggle, dear God."

I thought the shark with its myopic eyes was going to run into my harpoon and I dived again, foolishly, and turned on my back

261

once more; my bubbles rose in two bursts by the side of my face. The shark passed overhead and dropped something. It was as big as a horse's, and I darted aside to avoid it. Then I saw that something had attracted its attention.

It had turned around, looking for me, and was suddenly distracted by something else: Goatskin's bubbles. It seemed to be fascinated by them. It advanced on a little cluster, rose with it, as if it were sniffing, then it dived again, circled, and advanced on the next lot. At the fourth cluster of bubbles it did something that set my heart pounding. It sniffed, made a full swerve very fast, during which it turned on its back. I saw it open its mouth, which was much bigger than I had thought, and flash through the cluster of bubbles, catching them.

I suppose it was all part of the play, but I didn't like it. I wanted to get back to the surface, before it should start playing with my bubbles and follow them down to their source. But it had forgotten me; it stuck to Goatskin's bubbles, playing with them again and again, swerving round, turning on its back, opening its mouth, swallowing them. And then, abruptly, it hung quite still in the air, as if listening to something, seemed to be shaken by a convulsion and I saw a spurt of bubbles burst out of its mouth. I heard a deep rumbling sound. It shot backward and flashed away at high speed. As it vanished in the blue, I understood that it had belched. Its own belch had terrified it out of its wits. It must have been the first.

I didn't know how much time passed before I saw Goatskin emerge again, but practically the instant I saw him hover below me, my air stopped and I had to open my spare tank. I was alarmed, because at the depth where he was now, he couldn't come up straight away. I rose almost to the surface and watched him for awhile; then I had to go to the ship. My air gave out at two meters' distance from the pilot's ladder.

He didn't come up until a quarter of an hour later. I felt a bit ashamed. I had breathed very regularly and sparingly, I thought, and he had been down much deeper; yet I had used my air a lot quicker than he. When he came up the pilot's ladder I got a shock. His mask seemed rusty inside, I could hardly see his face.

262

As he took out his mouthpiece he spat angrily, and his spittle was red. "Ugh!" he said. "What a mess! I'll have to wash those damn tubes out before I use them again." Then he took his mask off and I saw that underneath it his face was covered with blood. It looked horrible. "Christ," I said. "What happened?" He answered, "Nothing. My nose started bleeding. I pushed up my mask against my nostrils to block them. Then I had to swallow the blood and kept on blowing it into the tube. Give me a drink quick. I'm as sick as a cat."

Pjotr hurried to get him a drink and Bernard washed his face. While he sat on a wine barrel, shivering, having his face washed, he asked, "Seen the shark at all?"

I told him about the shark chasing the bubbles, as he sat sipping his drink. When I told him that it had swallowed them and been chased by its own belch he looked up. I said it had been very funny and he said, "Yes, it must have been," and then suddenly he went to the rail and vomited. Nicole was by his side in a flash and wanted to put her hand on his forehead but he snarled, "Bugger off, you Goddam bitch," and hung over the rail, retching. I led her away.

She was very calm and composed, but she trembled. Although I was getting cold despite the sun, I didn't want to leave her to get a towel. I took her to the foredeck where we sat down on the bowsprit. She looked as if she would break down any moment. Her face had gone a curious green, the color it had been as she sat underneath the blue parasol in Saint Tropez. Then I had thought it had been the blue shadow, now I realized it must have been something else. "I don't think it's anything serious," I said. "It's swallowing the blood that made him sick."

She looked at me and smiled. "You're sweet," she said. "But would you mind just leaving me alone for a bit?"

I said, "Sorry," and went down to get my towel. I was very chilled and felt rather lonely, which I hadn't for some time. I wondered how deep he had been and if he had seen something.

When I came back on deck after having put on some clothes she was still sitting in the same place. I wanted to go to the midships but she called me. I went back to her, smiling formally, like a nurse.

263

"Sorry," she said. "It wasn't because of you. It was because I —I didn't feel well."

I said, "I see."

"Sharks aren't dangerous until they smell blood," she said. "If you hadn't frightened it away, he would never have come back."

I felt my cheeks go cold. "It wasn't me who frightened it away," I said. "It was the sound it made itself."

"I know," she said. "I . . ." and then she covered her face with her hands.

I thought of putting my hand on her shoulder but then I didn't. I said, "Don't worry, I'll see to it that he doesn't go down again." Then I went to the poop.

Goatskin was lying in the sun, a rolled up blanket under his head, smoking a long cigarette. I sat down beside him and asked, "Feeling better?"

He said, "Yes."

"Seen anything?"

"No."

I looked at him. His eyes were closed and his face was pale, but his thin lips seemed to be smiling. I didn't like that smile and I didn't like that cigarette. I knew he had seen something. I sat by his side for a while but we didn't talk. The bosun sang *"Les jeunes filles de Camaret se disent toutes vierges."* I jumped when there was a loud clatter behind my back; two crutches had been thrown out of the hatch. Captain Perpendiculous' head appeared above the threshold as he climbed the stairs on his knees. When he saw me he grinned and said, "Good morning, Captain!"

Then I knew for certain that Goatskin had seen something. The pirate had never greeted me before.

Chapter XIII

THAT NIGHT I TRIED TO KEEP HIM FROM DIVING AGAIN THE NEXT day. I didn't ask what he had seen, I didn't mention the purpose of his diving at all. I just talked about the shark, saying that if he went down again as deep as he had done, his nose would

264

certainly start bleeding again and this time the shark might not frighten itself away.

He listened to me calmly, his thin lips smiling, and when I had finished, he asked, "Are you by any chance speaking on behalf of Nicole?"

"I'm speaking on behalf of every sane person on board this ship."

He laughed. It was an unpleasant little laugh. So far I had thought he wanted to go down again to get what he had seen; after that little laugh I began to suspect that he was back on the stage once more in the role of a tight-lipped, cynical desperado, at the end of his tether, about to commit suicide in a daring exploit that would end his life with a flourish. It made me angry. I suddenly realized that both Nicole and I had been playing up to him by our worrying, and now I was again acting the perfect stooge. "All right," I said, "if that's the way you want it, go and have yourself torn to pieces by a shark. But I can tell you this much: even if you had found Aladdin's cave in the purple, I am not coming with you tomorrow. Let your Mr. Astanasia put on the Cousteau and have a romp with the shark himself. I'm through."

"I am glad you have realized at last that you won't get anywhere with that Chinese whore while I'm alive," he said.

I said nothing. I told myself that it was unfair to slap the face of a man who was recovering from a bleeding nose.

"If I told you what I found, would that make any difference?" he asked, with his stage voice.

I said, "No."

He put his hand in his trouser pocket, brought out a smart oblong box, opened it and selected a cigarette. He had never selected a cigarette before, on the sound principle that they were all the same. This conception of smartness came straight out of English detective novels, the only place where people selected cigarettes. I knew for certain now that he was play acting. I knew for certain too that, whatever he had found, Mr. Astanasia had been very pleased with him.

"Want one?" he asked.

I said, "No, thanks," and then, "I must say things have changed.

I never would have thought, when we sailed the Northeast Passage together, that the time would come when some night-club crook would make you feel pleased with yourself by giving you a box of cigarettes for risking your neck." It was quite a little speech. It sounded as if I was getting onto the stage too.

He answered, "That's right, Skipper. Things have changed. If I don't come back tomorrow that will be the logical ending to a lot of things."

I suppose he expected me to oblige him with some more, but I didn't. I said, "Good night, Hamlet," and went to the wheelhouse.

Nicole was lying on her bunk, I thought she was asleep, and I started undressing quietly so as not to wake her up. She asked from the darkness, "Did you talk to him?"

"Yes."

"Any good?"

"No."

I went on undressing. Then I lit a cigarette and sat down on the chart table and looked at my shadow, moving on the ceiling in the faint light of the compass.

"So you are going down tomorrow?" she asked.

I said, "He is, but I am not. I won't do any good, and I hate to see a human being torn to shreds by a shark."

"Don't talk like that," she said, "please."

I sat smoking for a while in silence, feeling rotten. I knew he would go and I would go, and I wished it was all over. I stubbed out my cigarette, said, "Good night," and climbed into my bunk. I lay awake for a long time, waiting for her voice to call softly, "Skipper," and then I'd go down and lie down beside her and she'd put her head on my shoulder and tell me everything: that she loved him and he loved her, that she had seen him go to hell and known he would commit suicide one day if he went on diving, that she had feebly tried to wake him up from the spell the sea had thrown over him by refusing to let him touch her unless he gave up diving. She must have been torn between her love and her urge for self-preservation until she was frantic. I thought I understood it all now, and I was sure I could help her, if only she opened her mouth and called me.

266

But she didn't. I lay awake, waiting, until the bosun came to call me for the day watch.

∽

The next morning, after he had put on his bottles, his frogman's feet, and his mask, he stood ready to go down in the wheelhouse and saw me fully dressed. He said, "Well, Skipper, it's been nice knowing you."

I said, "Don't be a Goddamned fool. Kick that old bastard in the arse and be your age."

He smiled his maddening smile and said, "I've only got one thing to ask you. Either I come back or I don't, either way suits me, but I don't want to come back as a cripple. Do you understand?"

I said, "No."

"I am serious," he said, "it's the last favor I ask you for old times' sake. You have made up your mind to stay where you are, all right, stick it. If for some reason you find that I got into trouble, don't act the little hero and pull me out. I'd rather drown than spend the rest of my life in a wheelchair, babbling nonsense."

He was so completely in his role that I couldn't think of anything to say that would sound real. In the end I said, "Don't worry, I'm through with you," and turned to go. As I heard him laugh behind me I couldn't help looking round. He stood grinning at me, his blue eyes were cruel and mad. "Don't think," he said, "that you'll ever be alone in bed with her. There will be a ghost between you."

I said, "Jesus, you make me sick," and went away.

As I went to the fo'c'sle I heard a voice ask, "Captain?" and saw Mr. Astanasia in his Roman bathrobe advance on me. "Aren't you going down?" he asked.

I said, "No sir."

His old-world politeness waned as he said, "This is a surprise. I thought we had agreed that both of you would do your best to make this expedition worth while for me. I am afraid I must insist that you go."

Suddenly all my pent-up rage concentrated on the old man.

267

"Sir," I said, "I don't know what you are after and I don't care, but I warn you: if anything should happen to that boy you'll be sorry for a long, long time. Understand?"

His face hardened until it looked as if it had been cast in bronze. He looked at me like a sphinx, who had been watching the vermin at its feet for over three thousand years, and was resigned to watch some more. "I have never been impressed by threats, young man," he said in a bored voice; then he turned on his heels and went away.

I had decided not to be on deck when he dived. I was going to lie in my bunk in the fo'c'sle and read. But while looking for a book in the mess behind Bernard's bunk I couldn't help glancing out of the porthole.

I could not see him go down without putting my head out, but I heard him. I heard the crunching of the rungs of the ladder as he descended, the spluttering of the bubbles as he put his head under water; then I saw an orange patch slide past below me and I followed the trail of the bubbles with my eyes as he swam away. We were very near the wreck, he went almost straight down. The bubbles went on rising in the same spot after a while. Then the ship slowly swung round on the swell, and I lost sight of the spot. I went to the wheelhouse.

Nicole was still lying on her bunk, her eyes closed. I took the old captain's binoculars and watched the spot. The bubbles went on rising, regularly. I glanced at the clock, it was a quarter to eight. He had been in the water for five minutes; he should be well into the blue by now, making his seventh ceiling. I went on watching the bubbles and saw them change gradually to patches of milky foam. He must be at about eighty meters now, the bubbles would go on coming up like foam even if he went down to a hundred or more. I looked at Nicole; she hadn't moved but her face had the same greenish paleness that I had seen twice before. It was the only thing she couldn't control with her will.

The ship was very silent. I looked at the deck and saw them all lined up at the rail, watching the bubbles. I also saw my bottles, my mask and my frogman's feet, lying ready beside the wheelhouse. I wondered who had put them there.

268

He had been under water for nearly half an hour now; at the depth where he was his bottles would not last longer than an hour. He should be on his way back, but the foam still rose in milk-white patches. I counted the periods between them. Three seconds. Four and a half. Three. Four. Three. I had hardly let them out of my sight since the moment he had gone down; they had been coming up regularly like this for over half an hour. This meant he was either still going down or searching in the purple. He had not worked yet, or I would have seen it. The periods between the bubbles would have been a lot shorter if he had.

My mouth was very dry. I realized it as I swallowed. If he was still at his lowest depth by this time, without having done anything, it meant that he was very late rising. He should have been on his way back, but I was sure he wasn't. I fumbled in my pockets and took out a crumpled pack of cigarettes. Without looking away from the bubbles I put one in my mouth, searched my pockets for my lighter, counting the periods all the time. Three. Three. Three and a half. And then suddenly: One. One. A half. One. . . . This was it.

I couldn't stick it in that wheelhouse, I went outside, stood beside Pjotr at the rail, staring at the bubbles. One. A half. A half. Three. Five. Five. . . . I felt something hot on my arm; it was Pjotr's hand, squeezing. One. A half. A half. Five. And then the bubbles changed. They rose to the surface differently, much weaker, as if he was breathing very little. One and a half. One and a half. One. One. One. I said, "All right."

Pjtor jumped at my bottles, and not he alone. Jacques, Bernard, the old bosun, all the men who had stood leaning on the rail, staring at the bubbles, rushed toward my diving set at that one word. They put the bottles on me in a matter of seconds. I put on my frogman's feet while they were adjusting the harness and strapping the ballast belt round my waist. I put them on the wrong feet, but left them as they were; I went down the pilot's ladder without blowing in my mask to try it. I had wanted to jump into the water from the deck, but checked myself in time. If I had, the mask would have been ripped off at the impact. I remembered to blow in my mask when my feet were already dangling. There was an air leak on the left hand side. While I was adjusting it a voice called, "Look!"

I saw a great commotion in the water on the spot where the bubbles had risen, bits of seaweed came to the surface, and then a limp, round thing. I thought, feeling suddenly sick, that it was he. I dived and swam toward it. The moment I was under water I saw it was dust and bits of seaweed. There was no living fish in sight. The brown thing was an old lifebelt.

I dived; as soon as I saw the wreck and the pillars I went down seven or eight meters, then I had to make a ceiling because of the pain in my ears. I was looking for his bubbles rising, and I thought I saw them, very faintly, floating up, with the dirt that went on rising in clouds. I had my harpoon with me; as it flickered in the sunlight I thought it was something else and started breathing faster, fear tightened the skin on my thighs. I dived again until the pain forced me to make a new ceiling, and then I heard a weak tapping sound, very close.

This tapping gave me a sudden courage. Perhaps it wasn't courage but something else. It just made me realize that he knew I was there, and was calling me. I forgot about the shark, I forgot about the terror of the purple, I went down deeper and deeper in reckless plunges, making ceilings only when I had to bite in my mouthpiece for excruciating pain. Then, on the verge of the darkness, I saw him.

He was rising slowly out of the night. Weak foam spiraled out of his neck. His arms hung limply by his side. But what gave me that feeling of sickness again was that the foam coming from his neck was red. As I got to him I saw his mask had turned into a dark, opaque disc.

He was rising limply, on his side. I thought he had lost consciousness, but when I touched his shoulder he threw his arms around my waist and tightened them, desperately. I knew I had to get him back to the surface as quickly as I could, but if we rose straight without hovering it would be suicide. I had to decide for him, and I knew there was only one decision I could make: to stick to our decompression periods, even if he died with his arms around me. I rose back to seventy meters, trailing him as the shark had trailed the little fish hanging from its belly.

When I thought of the shark I realized that I had lost my harpoon.

In the heart of the blue, at fifty meters, I saw the faint red foam that rose from his neck stop. I thought he was dead, but his arms that were still round my waist suddenly tightened in spasmodic convulsions. I groped hastily for the gauge of his spare tank and opened it. The foam started rising again. He was still alive, but he had only got ten minutes left. I rose to forty; it was much too soon, but I had to risk it. The blue got lighter, I saw the flowered slope again and somewhere above us on the left the dark shadow of the wreck on the pillars. Then I saw it move. It wasn't the wreck, but another shadow, circling.

I didn't know what to do. We were at forty meters. We needed at least one more hovering period, at twenty-five. Then my air stopped and I opened my spare tank. Only as my hand went toward it I discovered that all the time I had been stroking his arm, the way he had done to me after the shelling. For some reason this decided it. I took a deep breath, pushed down my feet like a frog, and we shot upward, out of the blue, toward the sky.

I saw the white belly of the shark streak over us and gripped his arm tightly and shut my eyes, while my ears began to hammer and scream. I swallowed my saliva to release the pressure and the thought flickered through my mind how futile this was. Then, just as my eardrums had recovered, I heard the sharp click of a report, and then two more, in rapid succession. I recognized that sound. Harpoon guns, discharging.

I opened my eyes, saw we were very close to the surface, saw three orange creatures with diving respirators swim above me, blue guns gleamed along their outstretched arms. I saw the harpoons dangle at the end of the lines, grazed off the shark's skin that was as hard as armor. I saw the shark speed toward them, back from a swerve into the blue, its mouth open, its teeth glistening in the slanting sunlight. Then I reached the surface.

❧

We were all pulled into the longboat, one by one, by frantic people.

The moment we were out of the water, I took off his mask.

271

Blood fell out of it like a soggy cake. He was horrible to see; his skin was blue, his legs were scratched, he felt stone cold and didn't seem to breathe any more. Pjotr was weeping in the boat with long heaving sobs; Jacques comforted him mechanically and went on staring at the sea. Bernard sat quietly smiling, but he shivered all the time. I felt numb and dizzy, and sat sick and motionless with Goatskin in my arms, while the bosun and the boy rowed us back to the ship. He was hauled on board in the boat and lifted out of it when it was on the level of the deck.

I had only one wish: to lie down on my back in the sun and sleep and forget it all, but I couldn't. I had to make decisions, arrange for him to be taken to a hospital, make a report of what had happened and have it signed by witnesses. I would get into no end of trouble once we arrived in the civilized world; everything the old Captain had forgotten would now fall back on me: there was no logbook on board and they would certainly ask for it, I should have written my report in it. Goatskin was carried into the wheelhouse and put on Nicole's bunk. She washed him and nursed him, covered him with blankets and hot water bottles and tried to make him drink cognac; if someone else wanted to get near him she almost snarled.

I woke up out of my dazedness because Mr. Astanasia asked me where we were going, after I had started the engine and given the bosun the course. When I said we were going to Athens he became very nasty. He said he could under no circumstances agree to that, he commanded me to proceed to an Italian port. I said Goatskin was dying and I was going to take him to the nearest hospital that was any good, and that was Athens. He dropped all his old-world charm as he screamed that he would not let me, that he commanded me to go to an Italian port, that I was responsible for the consequences; Captain Perpendiculous threw his crutches onto the deck when he heard the row and joined in, shaking his fists, hollering Greek curses. I called Pjotr and Jacques and told them to take these people away and lock them up in their cabins. When Mr. Astanasia heard this he changed his tune; he started wheedling and wringing his hands. He said that if we went to Greece he would get into the most terrible trouble, would I please, please go to an Italian port. I

272

said that if we met a fishing smack we would hail it and perhaps they would take him and his Greek on board and sail them to an Italian port at a price. He tried to make it Goatskin who would be taken to Athens by a fishing smack, but he didn't succeed. He sat on the foredeck for hours in the hot sun in his white bath-robe, smoking one long cigarette after the other, watching the horizon. Captain Perpendiculous watched the horizon too, pacing up and down on the poop on his crutches, pockmarking the deck.

We met a small fishing smack toward four o'clock and I hailed it. There was a long conversation in Greek between the Skipper and the two passengers. In the end they hurried down the stairs and got their luggage. When he wanted to leave I said I'd like some money. He went mad and started hissing foul language. I said, "You are wasting your time. I want some money, and I won't let you off this ship until I have got it." He looked as if he was going to strike me, then the Skipper of the fishing smack called from below, and he pulled out a wallet and took out some bank notes and threw them on the deck; the bosun had to jump on all fours to prevent them being blown away. When I counted them I saw it was quite a lot, but I didn't know the value of Greek money. When we arrived in Piraeus the next morning I found out that it would just pay our mooring charge and a thousand liters of water.

In Piraeus Goatskin was carried off the ship on a stretcher by two orderlies, who had come with the ambulance. The ambulance looked clean and white in the dark confusion of the quay. Mili-tary and police swarmed over the deck, I had forgotten that in Greece the war was still on. It took a long time to fend off all those wasps; then I went with Pjotr and Jacques to the French consul. There, in a cool office with antiblast strips pasted to the window, I made my report and signed the declarations. We had agreed to leave Mr. Astanasia out of it, so as not to complicate things. If indeed he was wanted by the police here it would mean that we wouldn't get out of this place for weeks, answering questions.

We lay in Piraeus for weeks all the same, waiting for Goatskin to die. Nicole had gone with him to the hospital and she stayed with him all the time. She wasn't allowed to see him for more

273

than two half hours per day, but she sat on the bench in the hall all day, and when she was put outside at night she sat on a bench in the courtyard. We brought her food and a blanket, when she didn't want to come back to the ship; we agreed that we would take watches by her side at night. We could not let her sit there alone.

During a fortnight, when it still seemed a matter of hours before Goatskin should die, she didn't say a word all night. She just sat, the blanket round her knees, and occasionally she dozed, her head on the shoulder of whoever was sitting beside her. Then, the message came that he would live, but the left side of his body would remain paralyzed. When Nicole heard this she broke down and cried. I led her away with my arm round her shoulders to the bench in the courtyard, where we sat down in the sun. I talked to her, and so did Pjotr and Jacques and Bernard, but she wouldn't listen, she just cried. We didn't quite know why, whether from joy or horror, or just exhaustion. We all said to each other how lucky he was to have pulled through, but we lied. Every one of us knew that this was the worst that could have happened, and not only to him, to all of us.

That was the curious thing. We took it as a matter of course that we should stay with him and nurse him and look after him. I only realized this when I was allowed to see him for the first time, that night we were told that he would live. He was lying in a small white room; his face and his hands were dark patches in the gathering dusk. He could hardly move his lips. We talked only for a few minutes. I didn't understand all he said, but I gathered that he was telling me what had happened. He talked about the wreck of a plane at the depth of a hundred meters, of a steel box on the lap of a skeleton, and how the plane had suddenly started moving and slid off the edge on which it was resting, and sunk into the darkness. He seemed to think it was funny, for he laughed; then I realized that the gasping sound he was making wasn't laughter. He gabbled, "Skipper," and "old times" and "living corpse" and "don't leave me alone" and wept. I said, "Don't worry, old boy, we'll stay with you." Then a nurse touched my shoulder and gestured that I had to go. He waved at me weakly with his left hand as she opened the door to let me out.

274

A week later he and Nicole went to Nice by plane. The consul paid for the tickets, saying he would get the money back from the insurance. The insurance seemed indeed to be well arranged, the old Captain had done it. He had insured the crew against accidents, and this meant that Goatskin would probably have a pension for the rest of his life. If that old Captain hadn't been there, I hate to think of what would have happened. I thought of the many times Goatskin had wanted to strangle or drown him or lash him to the mast. Now, he owed his living to him.

On the first night of our homeward trip I remained on deck to keep an eye on the navigation, as the Cyclades were a tricky water. I hadn't been able to think clearly ashore, but now we were sailing slowly under the stars, heeling in a soft night breeze, a fog seemed to lift in my brain. It was the first time that I remembered clearly what had happened, from the moment that I lay on my bunk, awake, waiting for Nicole to call me, the night before he dived to his death. For the first time I realized how odd it had been, us two, lying one above the other, staring in the darkness, waiting for what we knew would happen and not making a move to prevent it. Not only we, the hunters too, the crew, everybody: all of us had waited, without doing anything, for the drama to take its course. We had all dumbly accepted as inevitable that he should go down the second time, as if we had been taking part in a tragedy of Fate. But it had not been a tragedy of Fate at all, just a desperate boy imagining things. If, the next morning, I had knocked him down I would have saved him. And if he had wanted to go down all the same, even after he had woken up, I should have broken his leg or locked him up in a cabin; but whatever I should have done, I hadn't done it. I had just said theatrically, "I won't go," and lain on my bunk, staring in the darkness, knowing that he would go and that I would go after him, a victim of forces stronger than I, and I hadn't woken up to reality before it was too late.

And then I thought of Nicole, who had made a mess of things too. She should have got up, quietly gone to the deck and thrown the bottles overboard, then we would have sailed back to the South of France the way we had left, a jolly crowd of youngsters on a crazy ship, with a piano on the poop.

275

I leaned on the rail and looked down at the dark mirror of the sea. Occasionally a shimmer of luminous green rippled past from the bow of the ship. I thought of the dream landscape lying below, and hated Goatskin for taking me away from it. For now we would have to nurse him and stay around him and feel guilty and let ourselves be insulted and pestered by this cripple, who had never had such power before, who was the only one among us whose philosophy of life had remained unchallenged: that we were jetsam washed ashore by the war, a few useless creatures left over from the massacre of youth that was World War II.

And suddenly, as I thought this, I knew it wasn't true. This conception of ourselves as a lost generation was false, a mystification that had sprung from Goatskin's warped mind. I had been lost and lonely for a while after the war, but that was only natural. Everybody who had gone through it needed a period of readjustment. He had imposed that conception upon me; it had started in Antwerp. I had known he was play acting all the time, and yet he had convinced me. And not only me, but Jacques and Pjotr and Bernard too.

When I thought this I had a curious feeling. A spell was taken away from me in those mements, a spell that had started long ago, when I had lain awake on my bunk in room 77 in the Grand Hotel in Westport, and listened to the others wheezing and snoring around me, and read the poem on the wall. All of them were now on that distant shore, except me. Even Goatskin was there, and I suddenly knew that he had always been.

Suddenly I understood what had bound us together and at the same time made me hate him: he lived with the dead, and he had wanted me to live with them too. To him the distant shore was the jungle under water, the bottom of the sea, where they all were.

It was a romantic thought, but it liberated me. When the sun rose over the Cyclades I felt as if I had conquered the terrible pull of the dead, of the war.

I wanted to do something that would save us, something that would liberate us from the war and make us take up a new life, in peace. Only, I had no idea what.

276

Chapter XIV

IT WAS JUNE SIMMONS WHO MADE ME THINK OF IT. IN SAINT TROPEZ
I found her letter. It had been waiting for me at the harbor master's office for over a month. She wrote a lot of amusing nonsense
but again at the very end of her letter she almost blushingly
wrote in a hurry a few serious lines: "You said that you didn't
know what to do with yourself because there is no room for you
with any of the tugboat companies. Surely there is always room
for a rescue tug somewhere, and surely there are lots of old war-
surplus tugboats around. Couldn't you try to interest somebody
with a little money in manning a tugboat with an ex-war crew,
and get a fair chance of a good profit in the gale season? I hope
all this doesn't sound too amateurish, but you told me so much
about ocean-going tugboats when we were sitting on that bench
under the palm trees that I feel a bit of an expert now. If it is
silly what I have said, don't judge me too harshly. It is so nice to
think about you and the sea in an English vicarage garden."

I thought the plan over for a while, then I decided to tell
Goatskin.

He had recovered as far as he probably ever would recover. He was a plump pink body in a wheel chair with one side
of his face still and resigned in a weird half-smiling melancholy.
The other side, that was alive, was devilish. He could form words
with only half a mouth but whatever he said was destructive.
Nicole, who pushed his chair, fed him, washed him, put him to
bed and helped him on the toilet, got the worst of it. His entire
mumbled conversation to her consisted of insults. He called her
"Chinese whore" several times an hour, urged her to bugger off,
to leave him alone instead of using him to attain holiness, why
the hell didn't she go to a nunnery and do some useful work if
that was the way she felt, instead of wasting her time on a useless piece of meat that had been kept alive against his will by a
lot of sadists and good-for-nothings? He knew why we had fished
him and nursed him past the death he had longed for: to profit

277

from the insurance. If not, could we please tell him what money we were living on? He was just a paralyzed pig, being fattened by a lot of bums who made hay with the money he earned by having turned into a cripple. His metaphors got mixed up whenever he talked about himself, and he exaggerated so shamelessly that no one among us took it seriously and told him to shut up. Yet in all this exaggeration there was a core of truth that went on secretly nagging our consciences: we were all guilty, because we had let ourselves be paralyzed into inactivity by his one-man drama until it was too late.

When I told him about our plan he was sitting in the sun, his eyes closed, sweating. Toward the end of my story he opened his evil eye and the live half of his mouth started grinning. When I had finished he said, "Charming. So you want to drag me onto the bridge of a tugboat now and lash my chair to the rail. Well, well! Aren't you afraid that one day you might kill the pig that lays the golden eggs?" I wanted to argue with him but Nicole, who stood behind him with her sunglasses on, shook her head. She had grown very thin of late; the shape of her skull had become marked in her face which made her look alien and oriental and a bit frightening. Goatskin saw me sigh and turn away. He said, "Don't worry, Skipper, I'm your man. Lash my chair to that rail. I want to see you make a mess of it." I couldn't quite remember what the moral arguments were against slapping the face of a cripple. I got up, said, "You're having quite a time, aren't you?" and went away.

If I wanted to put our plan into practice I would have to go to Le Havre or Brest, the only places where a rescue tug had a chance in the gale season. The sad thing was that the money to pay for this trip had to come from his insurance. I tried to forget about that, but I couldn't. His crooked half-smile traveled with me as I went North.

ᆼᄋ

The pianist was really mad. He had a red face, bulging eyes, bat ears, and his chin stuck out. He played tinny dance tunes of the twenties, kicking the piano, slamming the lid up and down, and he sang with a breathless falsetto to his own accompaniment,

278

"I love my mummy, my mummy loves me, I am only twenty, and she's twenty-three."

He was the only excited person in the café; the rest were stolid, silent tugboat captains, staring at him, their big hands asleep on the marble by the side of their little glasses. They looked exactly like the old captains in Shadwell Basin, nationality didn't seem to make any difference. Only their berets were French, otherwise they looked like Captain Bakker done by different cartoonists.

I had told the landlord that I was looking for Captain Perseil of the tugboat *Jeanne,* the owner of the ship *Brighton Belle,* and he had said he hadn't arrived yet, but he would point him out to me when he came. I sat listening to the mad pianist screaming, banging the piano, making obscene noises with his lips, whispering filthy language between two crashing chords. Then, after an hour or so, the landlord called, "Psst!" and pointed at a man coming in.

He was very tall but looked stocky because his shoulders were as wide as a bull's. He walked with the gait of the sea. On the back of his head was a peaked cap with a dirty white cover. He sat down at one of the marble tables and I got up.

"Monsieur Perseil?"

He looked up. His face was very large; his small black eyes looked at me without interest.

"Are you the owner of the *Brighton Belle?*"

He looked at me for almost a minute. Then he said, "So what?"

I told him I had seen the ship, lying in a dead arm of the harbor. I had asked whom it belonged to, they had given me his name, and said that I probably would meet him if I went to the Café de la Marine around ten o'clock.

"So what?" he asked, after another long silence.

I told him I was looking for a laid-up tugboat, and wanted to interest the owner in putting the ship into the rescue service with a crew of war veterans, who would ask only a very small salary and take the rest in a percentage of the prize money if they brought in a ship.

"I have no money," he said. Then he looked away for the first time and called, "Calva!" at the counter. I thought he would continue the conversation, but he didn't. He sat waiting for his Cal-

279

vados, staring at the counter. The mad pianist hammered and screamed. Captain Perseil seemed to have forgotten I was there.

A fortnight ago I would have left it at that, but this was our last chance. I had seen scores of old tugboats all along the Channel coast, but either the owners hadn't been interested or the ships weren't seaworthy anymore. The *Brighton Belle*, which I had discovered that afternoon in Le Havre, was a wooden ship, but I had been on board and seen that she was in a fair condition with her engines still in and a full equipment. Beachcombers had told me she belonged to the Captain of the tugboat *Jeanne*, who was very rich but very hard to deal with. As to the second definition they had certainly been right.

I went on telling him about our proposition, shouting down the mad pianist, but he didn't listen. He was waiting for his Calvados; when it came he thanked the landlord with a nod and a smile, as if he was quite alone and tried to establish some human contact.

I told him about our experience as a crew, about the Western Approaches, the Northeast Passage, D-day, and the Invasion of the South of France. I thought he had forgotten me altogether and was about to go away, when he asked, "When did you sail the last time?"

I thought the game was lost anyhow, so there was no harm in telling him the truth. "The last time I sailed as a mate on the Dutch tugboat *Texel*," I said, "to the Far East."

He looked at me for the first time with something like interest. "Captain Bakker?" he asked.

"Yes."

"All right," he said, "come back here tomorrow morning at eleven. Good night."

I said, "Good night, sir," and went back to my table. The mad pianist was in a frenzy. He spat between his legs, turned on his stool, glowered at the motionless sea captains with his bulging eyes, and mumbled, "Bombs. Air raids. Sirens. Blood. God damn it, give me sensation. What the hell am I doing here, in this fish pond?" Then he turned round again and played a boogy-woogy version of "Silent Night, Holy Night," kicking the piano, howling blood-curdling screams, ramming his elbows down

280

on the keys. I thought he was going to have a fit; to see all those stolid faces gaze at him without mercy became a revolting spectacle. Then, as he began to get hoarse in a paroxysm of obscenities, they got up, one after another, put money underneath their empty glasses and filed out.

After they had gone the landlord patted the pianist on the shoulder and said, "All right, all right, stop it." The pianist couldn't stop, he went on playing, sniggering madly. The landlord slapped his hands and slammed the lid shut. "Go home," he said. "Tell Celina to give you an injection." The pianist got up, mumbling about blood and air raids, and shuffled out.

"Wonderful boy," the landlord said to me, as he was stacking the chairs. "The best barometer in town. If he carries on like that you can be sure there's a gale brewing."

I said, "How extraordinary."

"Haven't you seen them run?" the landlord asked. "They've all gone to rake their fires and round up their crews. He is a full six hours ahead of the meteorological office, and he has never been wrong yet. Where are you from?"

I told him that I was a Dutchman, and that I came from the South of France, to look for a ship.

"Tugboat?"

"Yes."

He asked me what my rank was, and when I told him that I was a captain with a crew who wanted to sail on the rescue service he understood that I was after the *Brighton Belle*. A lovely ship, a pity she was made of wood. Wartime job. He had seen Captain Perseil talk to me, so he must be very interested. "If you can sail for him," he said, "you'll find he is as straight as a die and as hard as nails. His yes is yes, but if he says no, not even an earthquake will rattle him. Are you staying in a hotel? You can have a room upstairs, if you like. It's small, but the sheets are dry."

The room was indeed very small. I had to bend down to get through the door, and to undress stooping. But the sheets were dry; they seemed to be the only dry things in the world as I lay listening to the rain lashing the little window, and sweeping the roof in waves.

281

I wished June Simmons were here, for I felt so homesick for the sea and the jungle of silence that it frightened me.

෴

The next morning at eleven o'clock a gale was rattling the windows of Café de la Marine. Every time a customer opened the door a whirl of sawdust was blown up from the floor, and those inside put their hands over their glasses to protect them.

Captain Perseil wasn't there; when I told the landlord that I was waiting for him he said, "In that case you might as well go for a walk. He left at three o'clock last night for an S.O.S." I asked him where the S.O.S. had come from, but he didn't know. He was proud of the gale because of his pianist. "What did I tell you last night?" he asked. "Not a cloud in the sky there was, not a breeze, and now listen to it."

The wind whined under the door and hurled itself against the façade in shuddering bursts, like blast. I sat in the Café de la Marine sipping sour red wine for the rest of the morning, and talked about the war with the landlord. He said Le Havre had been badly bombed; I had seen that for myself when I arrived. Never in my life had I set eyes on a town that looked more desolate, even Westport had been gay compared to this. We also talked about Perseil and the other captains who came to the Café de la Marine each night. He told me that the *Jeanne* was the only ocean-going tug on rescue service; the others were harbor tugs that would meet incoming vessels in a gale but never ventured beyond the pierheads if the wind got above its nines. The only other rescue tug between the Scheldt and Cherbourg was the *Texel* in Flushing; Perseil and Bakker were constantly in each other's hair if there was an S.O.S. between them.

I hadn't known Bakker was in rescue service this season; for some reason I liked the idea. I walked along the quays that night, my pipe upside down in my mouth against the rain, leaning against the wind that occasionally knocked the breath out of me. As I staggered along the barges crunching against their poles, in the wild light of arc lamps swinging with a sound of iron, I imagined how gratifying it would be to meet old Bakker in a gale and snatch a wreck from under his nose, the old bastard. I

282

wondered whether Captian Perseil hoped I'd know some of the old man's tricks, to beat him with his own weapons.

As I had nothing to do I went to see the *Brighton Belle* once more. The wind had risen to such fury that it blew the spray off the surface of the harbor and sent it careering through the rain; I had to clutch a lamppost occasionally not to be blown off the crown of the dike. The *Brighton Belle* lay tugging at her moorings and I had some difficulty getting on board for she veered away from the quay all the time. After a gust had pushed her stern in I jumped, and as I landed on her wooden deck I was surprised at the softness of the impact. Water spurted up my trouser legs as my heels struck the wood; it was so rotten that it had become spongy. I hadn't noticed this when I had my quick look at her yesterday; the weather had been dry.

It was the first of a series of alarming things I came to notice during my second visit. As I slowly made the round through her insides, striking matches, I saw how old she was and how tired, although she was only five years old. Like all wartime vessels she had been intended to last four years only and been constructed like an M.T.B. or an M.L.; two layers of wood diagonally put, with linen between them. Now her outer skin had cracked, water had soaked between the linen and the wood and set it rotting. As I stood on deck once more, my back to the rain, and looked at her, I knew that we would be lucky if she didn't spring a major leak the first time we ventured out with her in a gale.

That was the reason why I wasn't so delighted with Captain Perseil's acceptance of my offer as I had expected. He had come in the morning after, towing a Finn with a list of twenty degrees and the splintered remains of a deckload of timber. He looked pleased when he entered the Café de la Marine: he greeted me almost jocularly, called me *mon gars* and offered me a Calvados. Then he said, "I have considered your offer and I'm interested. Tell me the details."

I told him all the details. I said I hadn't got a crew yet, apart from a mate, but that I was sure I would have a first class one together within a fortnight if he gave the word. They would all be war veterans used to the rescue service; we had been doing nothing else for over a year on the Western Approaches.

What he was interested in most, I found, was whether I knew Bakker well. He put me some leading questions about what I would do under certain circumstances with a wreck in a strong gale. My answers seemed to satisfy him. When I told him that I had sailed as opposite number on the same boat with Captain Van Dam during the war, he seemed quite delighted, this obviously settled it. It was clear that he wanted to beat the Dutch with one of their own pupils; old Bakker must have kept him awake nights. "All right," he said, "it's a deal. I'll fit out the ship and I'll advance you some money to pay your crew a week's salary each. How much do they get?"

I made the calculations in the margin of a newspaper. Each salary he halved, without listening to reason. I tried to stick my ground but I might as well have tried to haggle with a statue. He wouldn't pay more than half of whatever I suggested; when I arrived at the mate's salary and my own I doubled the amount I had in mind, but he didn't fall for it. "Nonsense," he said, "I'll pay you a quarter of that." He certainly knew what he was talking about.

I expected him to be as stingy when I came to my calculations for fitting out the ship, but I was mistaken. He was so generous with the hawsers, the overhaul of the engines, and the paint that I dared to say I had the impression she was rotting. "Of course," he said. "What do you think? That I'd have left her lying there with a hood on her funnel if she wasn't? In that case I would have manned her with an A-one crew long ago, instead of with a lot of bums." I tried to be a little gentleman and said, "Thank you, sir," but he wasn't impressed. He was a realist.

That same afternoon I wired to Saint Tropez for Goatskin and Nicole to come, and I telephoned Sparks in his Paris office. They told me he was no longer with the company, but they gave me his address. I sent him a wire, saying that I had found a ship for the season to be stationed in Le Havre in rescue service, and would he be interested in a post as a wireless operator on a co-operative basis. I had little hope that he would, but it was worth spending money on trying. In the rescue service the wireless operator is the most important member of the crew, if he is a bungler you might as well stay at the quay.

284

To my surprise he sent back a wire: ARRIVE LE HAVRE NINETEEN FIFTEEN PLEASE MEET. It seemed I had caught him at the right moment. When he got out of the train I saw at first glance that he hadn't been doing well. He acted breezy and confident, but his clothes were shabby. I told him about our plan, on our way to the Café de la Marine. He had difficulty with the wind on corners with his cardboard suitcase. At first he tried to be choosy and aloof about the whole thing, but when we went on board to have a look at the transmitter toward nightfall he dropped all pretense. He inspected the set in the dark cubicle, striking matches all the time, and giving soft whistles of admiration. It was a lovely wartime job, he said, full of gadgets to play with. The only thing that would take a lot of money to get repaired was the radar set, which had been half dismantled.

We had a meal in the Café de la Marine. He ate ravenously and gulped down the red wine, with his Adam's apple sliding up and down his scraggy neck. I asked how Françoise was; he shrugged his shoulders and said he had got bored with her, but he was obviously lying. She must have left him when his luck gave out. I suspected he had slept under the bridges for quite a while with that cardboard suitcase.

Later on, when the wine had done its work and mellowed the months between us, it felt as if we had come closer to one another than ever since the war, closer than last time in Paris. I was happy to have him with us, for he was a wonderful wireless operator, one of the best.

∾

Goatskin arrived three days later. I went to meet him with Sparks at the station. Sparks was very good at mastering his surprise when he saw him sit in a corner seat of a third-class compartment, grinning half-wittedly behind the steamed window. He talked with him quite normally, while we were waiting for the wheel chair to be taken out of the van. Nicole was looking after that. He said, "Well, well," and "How are you, old scoundrel," and made a move to slap his knee, but his hand stopped in mid-air. Goatskin was obviously very pleased to see him, but he couldn't help being nasty. He gabbled, "You look very rich and healthy. How's your millionaire's daughter?" Sparks was casual and airy about it, but I saw him blush.

Nicole came trotting along the platform with the chair on its squeaking little wheels; we lifted Goatskin out of the compartment and put him in it. The gale was still blowing, Nicole wrapped him up in his coat and his muffler, he was wheeled to the Café de la Marine like a sack of potatoes. My heart sank as I saw this; I imagined what he would be like on the bridge in that chair, with the spray coming over in torrents.

When we arrived at the café and Nicole unwrapped him he was dazed and shaken. He sat blinking with his one live eye and had difficulty breathing. When he got a glass of red wine he spilled half of it down his shirt and snarled at Nicole when she wanted to mop it up with her handkerchief. The landlord did it with a towel.

After we had carried him to his room, Sparks looked at me, horrified, and asked, "God, how did that happen?" I told him; he listened shaking his head and muttering "God" all the time. I was surprised to find that he reacted to the idea of diving as to a horrible, unnatural thing. I didn't try to tell him; I didn't want to get more homesick than I was.

When Goatskin came down again for dinner he had picked up. At first he was cross and silent, but after several glasses of red wine he became lively; when the mad pianist started kicking and slamming the piano he became gay for the first time. It was the first time I saw him forget that he was a wreck now, the live half of his body seemed to have conquered the other at last. He laughed and babbled and began to sweat; if I had held up my hand and looked at him with one eye shut, covering his right half, I could have believed the old days had come back.

He seemed to believe it. After he had sent Nicole to bed, he put his hand on Sparks's, and said, "Good old Sparks! God, am I glad we came through it alive." He sighed a sick man's happy sigh, then he looked at me like old Goatskin again, for the first time since the last morning he dived. "All right, Skipper," he said, "tell us about the ship you found."

I told him, but I wasn't thinking of what I was saying. I was

286

looking at his happy face, his broken youth, and felt like crying. If ever there was a motherless child, far away from home, it was he.

∽

To get a crew we put a small advertisement in a Dutch weekly: "Tugboat company wants experienced officers and crew, ex-war, for ship in rescue service, one season only." We had decided on the advertisement because to travel to Holland and round them up would have cost much more. We hoped we would get some replies but doubted it.

Within a week we received over a hundred letters. We had never suspected there were so many of us left. We had a choice of mates, engineers, wireless operators, and cooks; our old cook was among them. He wrote a flowery letter on yellow stationery, with the name of his restaurant printed on it in glossy lettering. He gave a truthful report of his experience during the war, but exaggerated the size of his restaurant shamelessly. I had hoped that the Chief would reply, but there was no letter from him among the hundred. I wrote him specially, and he answered that he would have loved to come but that his wife was expecting a baby and that his shop was getting into its stride at last, so he couldn't, but he knew of a very good first engineer who had nothing to do, a man called Baas who had sailed with him as a second. Baas was among the letters, so we asked him to come. He arrived with Cook, a second engineer, a bosun, and three sailors. They had joined forces in Amsterdam at Sparks's suggestion, and taken an excursion ticket together.

When we met them at the station we found that we knew them all, but during the war we hadn't known their names. They were all delighted to find that they knew us too and our first communal meal in Café de la Marine was happy and quite like old times.

Goatskin was delighted to see them. As long as he was in a room without a draft, where he could remain seated like everybody else, he seemed almost normal apart from the stillness of half his face and the fact that he couldn't use his right hand. He had become very adroit eating with his left hand. After the first few glasses of wine nobody seemed to remember that there was something the matter with him.

287

It was extraordinary how little time we needed to recapture the old wartime atmosphere; by the time the coffee was served it seemed as if we had not been separated at all. Cook still wore his blue ring, but he lost his peacetime refinement when we started singing. The only one who liked our singing was the mad pianist. He jumped up and down like a frog, clawing the piano and screaming high mad squeals of brotherhood. Every night he had been mumbling about air raids and blood and sensation and wished the war would come; now he seemed to think that it had indeed come, that we had brought it with us; he wasn't bright enough to realize it wasn't the new one yet but the old one revived. Cook was drunk first. He started singing New Year's Eve psalms that were very gloomy, about man being like grass and our footsteps being wiped out by the wind of time. We sat listening to his sentimental tenor with a feeling of drunken sadness. Then Goatskin began to tell stories. He was quite drunk too, but his words came easier than when he was sober. He would have talked exactly like this if he had just been drunk and not half paralyzed. He told us about the most wonderful woman he had ever met, the woman of his life. She was much older than he, much older than any of us, but yet eternally young. Five thousand years ago a Greek had seen her, after climbing a sand dune, and he had stretched out his arms toward her and cried, "Thalassa!" Millions of men had tried to possess her since, but he had been one of the few who had succeeded. Perhaps it was because we were all drunk, but when he told his story of love with Thalassa, the sea, we listened with a feeling of beauty and wonder; even the mad pianist, who didn't understand a word of Dutch, sat watching him spellbound. Nicole was sitting behind him. She couldn't know what he was talking about, I thought, but I had forgotten that she knew Greek; she had told me about the Victory of Samothrace, so she probably knew what Thalassa stood for. As I was listening to Goatskin's drunken fairy tale of love I began to understand that she had always known this. She had refused to let him touch her as long as he made love to that other woman, the sea, and although he would never make love to that other woman again, she still would never get him back.

Goatskin told the listening crew about the world under water for hours on end, and he gave the sea a curious bewitching personality, calling her Thalassa all the time. It was the story I had thought of when I had looked down on the magic jungle for the second time: the forbidden door, the opening of it, the land of dazzling beauty and mystery, the ending in a nightmare of horror. "That's why," he said, suddenly, "I suggest that we change the ship's name." He took his glass in his shaky left hand, lifted it solemnly, and his live eye glistened when he said, "I christen her Thalassa."

The mad pianist understood him. He raised his glass too, and said, "Thalassa, *à-Dieu-vat*."

When he looked round our circle and asked, "Agreed, boys, dear boys?" we mumbled, "Yes," and drank to her.

ᵔᵔ

Looking at it from Captain Perseil's point of view I couldn't blame him. He was an unimaginative man, a black-eyed Bakker. When we told him the next morning that we wanted to rechristen the ship, he was angry. "Nonsense," he said, "the ship has been registered under her proper name and I'm certainly not going to the trouble of having it changed. And who the hell do you think you are? The ship is mine, you are just a crew of bums whom I want to give a chance. I begin to regret it."

He was right. Every sailor knows that it brings bad luck to change a ship's name; we had aroused his suspicions. So far he had left us entirely alone, now he began to ask for our licenses, because of the insurance, he said. He took our licenses with him and came back with the message that the mate and the second engineer had been turned down by the insurance. The mate because he was a cripple, the second engineer because he had no license at all. When the war started he had been a donkeyman who had been promoted after the second engineer on his ship had been killed in action. As the tugboat captains had a complete freedom of action during the war his Captain had promoted him without bothering about examinations. It was a nasty shock to us, mainly because of Goatskin. We had all, without talking about it, behaved as if there was nothing the matter with him; I had planned to take the bosun on the bridge to take the watch with him, and if we went into action I would be there myself anyhow.

Now I was forced to find an official mate. I decided to talk it over with him first, before I sent for another one.

When I told him the live half of his face remained calm and smiling. I had expected him to get one of his fits of rage; for once he would have been justified. But he listened as quietly as when I had told him I was to take over the command of his ship in Westport. When I had finished he said, "I can't blame him. I know I am finished and I don't mind. When I dived that last time I knew what I was doing. My only regret is that you didn't do what I asked you to do."

"If you had really wanted that," I asked, "why did you tap for help? I heard you."

"Weakness," he said, "a last fear, which I suppose is natural. But I was quite ready to go. I had been playing with the idea for a long time. You should have let me."

I didn't say anything. He frightened me a bit, he sat there so calmly. I knew there was something coming.

"If this tugboat plan should fail," he said, "I want you to do something for me. If you promise me that, the whole thing will be bearable, a last mad adventure. Even if we fail I'll like it, for I like mad adventures. But what I don't like is that desert in front of me. I can't spend the rest of my life in this wheel chair. Skipper, I just can't. You must promise."

"What?"

"If we fail you must come back with me to Saint Tropez. There we'll take a twenty-foot cutter, one of those little fishing smacks, and go, the two of us, to the Bay of Port Cros. There, one morning, you'll put the Cousteau on me and one frogman's foot. One is enough, because under water I can walk on one leg. I'll walk among the white rocks, the banks of flowers, past the wood that you have seen, near the wreck we went to on the first day. In it I know a little open space, where the bottom is almost blue. It is full of sea stars and anemones, and there's a little cave with a colony of *mérous* that I have never disturbed. It's the only spot under the sea where I have never felt the urge to hunt. I have sat there often, watching the *mérous* at play, and one day, just before I went to Antwerp, I went there again and lay on my back in the sunlight. I must have fallen asleep, for I woke up because my air

290

gave out. I woke up with an odd feeling of drunkenness, and I wanted to stay there. It cost me a tremendous effort to open my spare tank, and surface. For days after I had to fight the urge to go back there and lie down again in the sunlight and fall asleep. That's why I went to Antwerp. I wanted to see whether I could still get away. When I left you that night, after that game of chess we left unfinished, I told you I had to go back because there was a girl waiting for me. You asked me who she was, and I told you. Do you remember?"

I did.

∽

I got a proper mate, who was rather young but had very good references. His name was Middag. I met him at the station and explained the situation to him: he would be the mate only in name, the moment we left the harbor he would be third officer. He understood it all without much explanation and when he met Goatskin he called him "sir," which was clever and put our minds at ease. The new second engineer was in reality a chief; Chief Baas and he got on well, after the first day when they turned round each other like suspicious dogs.

Just before we made our trial run with the *Brighton Belle* Sparks received a letter from Flushing. It was from a friend of his who was now the wireless operator on the *Texel*. He wrote that the news had reached Flushing; everybody had been tickled by it except Captain Bakker; he had taken the news grimly and said that it was shocking because we were undermining the reputation of the Dutch tugboat service. He had called us "bloody amateurs" and "warm water sailors with megalomania" so we shouldn't expect any help or mercy from him, if ever we found ourselves fighting over a wreck.

When Sparks read the letter aloud everybody laughed and said silly things about old Bakker, but I didn't like it. God knew I didn't worship the man, but I had sailed with him and one thing nobody could deny: he was about the best tugboat captain alive. When I said this, Goatskin made a little speech: "The trouble with you, Skipper," he said, "is that you have no self-confidence. You have been like that ever since you came to Westport; any old

291

man who told you that you were an amateur always had you on his side. I think it's about time you got out of that. You won't be much good in the rescue service if you don't."

I thought about this and found that he was right. It had started in Westport, before I sailed on my first operation. When I went to see Van Dam he had regarded me as an amateur and I had felt he had reason to. I had quickly taken up the routine of our work on the Western Approaches, but I had never quite rid myself of the notion that I was a wartime emergency. Probably I was wrong, for I hadn't done badly since, but the feeling was still there, and it became acute on hearing that letter.

Our trial run was successful; the ship was old but she held the sea well and her speed was really something. When I tried her it was a choppy day; she rolled a lot cross-seas, but the moment I turned her in the wind she took the waves like a race horse. If we were lucky we would get our first S.O.S. from a direction in the wind, head on she could take anything and would remain very fast, much faster than the old *Texel*, who was forced to slow down to half speed sailing head on as soon as the seas became steep.

When we came back from our trial run we were very pleased with ourselves and with the ship, but Captain Perscil, who had been watching us on the pierhead through a pair of binoculars, looked gloomy when he came on board after we had moored. He didn't say anything about our maneuvering; he just looked gloomy and said he wanted a word with me. I took him to the chartroom, and there he put down an unexpected ultimatum. "I've been watching you boys," he said, "and I want to tell you something. I'll give you one chance, a fair one. If we get a gale with a lot of S.O.S.'s I'll take the one that is farthest away. You needn't sail unless there's something near home, the kind of thing your compatriot from Flushing will jump on. If you bring that in I'll give you a contract for the season. If you lose it to him, you're through."

I wanted to argue with him at first, but he wasn't the man to argue with, and I also couldn't help thinking that his point was reasonable. The others didn't agree with me; there was a lot of bad language in the messroom addressed at Captain Perseil.

292

Goatskin and I didn't take part in the general slandering. We sat smoking in silence, listening to the boys, and then he looked at me with his live eye, and smiled.

Chapter XV

OUR FIRST GALE CAME THREE WEEKS LATER. WE HAD BEEN WAITING for it nervously, congregating in the Café de la Marine every night around nine o'clock to listen to the weather forecast on the radio and the mad pianist, like the other captains. The mad pianist was indeed six hours ahead of the meteorological office with his forecast. That night he screamed and kicked the piano and spat between his knees and slammed the lid up and down, howling like a banshee and hissing obscenities; I was embarrassed because June Simmons was there.

She had arrived that afternoon, and I had met her at the station. I hadn't arranged her coming. She had just written me a postcard saying that she had a week's holiday and taken her ticket. When I stood on the draughty platform, waiting for the train to arrive, I was worried. Our crowd wasn't very wholesome for an English girl to mix with; the wartime vocabulary had come back, and after it the wartime habits, our table manners had dwindled with the rest of our social graces and by now we were as we had been on the Northeast Passage: a bunch of pirates whose entire conversation was made up of curses and anatomical discussions about the female body. But when I saw her get out of the train with the same red bonnet on, I was unexpectedly delighted. She had stayed exactly the same, as if it was only yesterday that we had said good-by and she had gone on waving until the bus turned the corner. She said, "Hello, Skipper, how are you?" and shook me by the hand. I carried her suitcase on my shoulder to the Café de la Marine, leaning against the wind, and she chatted all the time, with her tassel fluttering behind her. The boys were waiting in the café; Sparks kissed her on both cheeks in a very French fashion. I had forgotten that he knew her from the Invasion. She also knew Goatskin, of course, and said, "Well, well, how's chess?" He grinned, looking very pleased, and said,

"How are you, nurse?" She was introduced to the others as "Nurse Simmons" and she sat down with us for a meal, chatting all the time and laughing. It was miraculous to see how well mannered everybody got in her presence, a bit hard on Nicole who hadn't been able to keep us decent during the past weeks. She and Nicole hardly exchanged a word, but whenever someone else was talking they sat secretly watching each other and smiled politely whenever their glances crossed. I wondered how they would get on.

The evening seemed to be a great success until the mad pianist went berserk. Of course June Simmons knew perfect French, after the years she had spent in the Midi, so there was no hope that the nature of the lunatic's screams would remain hidden to her. She didn't betray with a single remark, or even as much as a silence, that she understood what he was hollering. It was we who were embarrassed. Sparks explained to her that the man was a human barometer, trying to make it a joke; but never before had I heard the madman go so far in his frenzy. As the other captains began to get up and leave it was a relief that I could do the same. I told her that I'd be back after the ship had been put ready, and she said, "All right, Skipper, I'll wait for you." Then she smiled at me, and that was the moment in which I realized what I should have known months before.

It was quite a discovery, and I thought about it on our way to the ship, pushing Goatskin's wheel chair against the strong gusty wind together with Sparks and the boy Middag. I had been full of apprehension for this gale that had come at last; it was odd how this apprehension had been taken away from me by her smile. It was all still very indistinct, just a feeling of warmth and a boyish happiness, but I didn't mind sailing into the teeth of old Captain Bakker any longer, now she was there to come back to.

We made the ship ready for sailing. Sparks sat down at his receiver and it was agreed that if anything came up I'd be sent for at the Café de la Marine. I suggested, rather feebly, that I should stay on board, but Sparks patted my shoulder and said, "Off you go, Skipper, and good luck." When I opened the door and let in a whirl of wind he called after me, "I'll do my damnedest to hold them off until the morning!"

When I came back to the café the landlord was stacking the chairs; as I opened the door I sent a cloud of sawdust spiraling off the floor and Nicole, who was used to this by now, quickly covered her glass with her hand. June didn't; when I got to their table she was busy fishing sawdust out of her wine. They seemed to have broken the ice; Nicole got up after quickly finishing her wine and said, "Good night, June, see you in the morning. I'll give you a knock at eight." Then she went away.

I felt ill at ease hanging on downstairs because of the landlord, but being French he loved the situation. He brought us a new bottle of wine and asked, "You are sitting up for an S.O.S., I suppose?" I said, "Yes, I don't think I'll go to bed." He stuck a candle in a bottle, lit it, and put it on our table. Then he said, "Good night, *Commandant, bonne chance*," turned out the lights and left us alone.

I had looked forward to this, but now we found ourselves alone in the empty café with the rain lashing the dark windows, the candle flame fluttering in the draft, and the shadows of the stacked chairs dancing on the walls, I felt uncomfortable, at a loss what to say. She looked at me in the candlelight with her dark eyes, the silly tassel hanging over one ear, and smiled and said, "Well, here we are."

I said, "Yes."

"I am glad you came north," she said, after a silence, "I didn't like your letters from the South of France."

"So?" I said. "What was wrong with them?"

"I didn't like your descriptions of the diving."

"Why not?"

"You said it was like a dream, and I could quite see it was. I thought that to go to sleep and dream is all right as long as you wake up in the morning, refreshed. I had a feeling you didn't."

"I can hear you have been talking to Nicole," I said.

"I have," she answered. "But I have known it for a long time. When I sat looking at your friend tonight, I couldn't help thinking how lucky I was that it wasn't you."

I didn't say anything to that. I sat looking at the candle flame, fluttering in the draft. It was courageous of her to say so frankly that she was in love with me. She had done it before, when we stood waiting for the bus. Yet, this time like the other, I felt uneasy. The warmth and the happiness after her smile an hour ago began to wane. Perhaps I had been imagining things. I had been lonely ever since Stella. It was only natural that I should have been looking for someone to fall in love with. It was a pity she had said that; it gave me the feeling that she was after me. I wanted to take the initiative myself.

She must have felt this, for she said, "I know it's bad tactics to throw myself at you, but I think that we owe it to each other to be frank. I'm in love with you, and if you are not with me that's just too bad. But I think you are. Only there is something else. Someone else, if you like."

I couldn't help smiling, for she had said it so solemnly.

"Thalassa, I suppose?"

She met my smile without flinching. Her dark eyes were kind and full of understanding, but very strong. It was a gentle strength, that gave me a feeling of warmth and happiness once more, faintly, like a first hint of sunrise.

"You don't know it yourself," she said, "but you are further gone than you think." Then she sat watching the candle flame too; the wind hurled itself against the windowpanes and set the reflection of the candle flame trembling. "Nicole is worried, in case this tugboat venture should not come off," she said. "He asked you to help him to commit suicide, didn't he?"

I didn't know what to answer. In the end I said, "Yes."

Then she put her hand on mine. We sat looking at the candle flame, not saying anything, when a ghost appeared behind the glass door and banged on it. I got up to open, the wind blew out the candle. It was the boy Middag. "S.O.S., Captain," he said.

I wanted to turn round to tell her, but she was by my side. "Good luck," she said, and then she put her arms round my neck and we kissed. It was as if the gentle strength she had quietly radiated during all these years went inside me during that kiss. Then she said, "Good-by."

∽

While I had been sitting in the candlelight, things had been moving fast outside. The boy Middag tried to tell me, shouting, on our way to the ship; when I came on board Sparks was very excited. Lots of S.O.S.'s had come in, one from a Dutchman in the Gulf of Biscay for whom Captain Perseil with the *Jeanne* had left an hour ago. Now he had contact with a Greek, who had lost his rudder due west of Ostende; he had already arranged with him that we would come to his assistance and we had better be quick about it, for his signals were getting very weak. Obviously his transmitter was folding up. While he was telling me this, his right hand went on nervously tapping a calling-up signal; I thought it was the Greek, but suddenly he said, "Hush, there he is," stopped tapping away, then he listened, intently. I watched the words his right hand pieced together, "Leaving—this—minute —for—Greek—Ostende—sorry—no—more—old—man—watching."

"Who was that?" I asked.

"The *Texel*," he said.

He gave me the markings of the Greek's position and the boy Middag and I set out the course. Goatskin wasn't with us in the chartroom, he had already been lashed to the bridge rail in his bath chair. I found him when I came up; he was wrapped in a tarpaulin as if he was a piece of cargo made sea-fast, with ropes crosswise across the parcel. He was wearing a southwester, tied up under his chin; I could scarcely hear him when he shouted, "Good luck, Skipper!" from underneath his wrappings.

We sailed at once. The wind had livened to fury. When we stuck our head into the outer harbor and passed the shelter of the quay, we heeled sharply under the impact and I had to give ten degrees of rudder to keep her on her course. When we cast off I had still felt confident and calm, the whole thing seemed an exciting adventure. But the moment the wind got us not only my breath was knocked out of me, but my self-confidence too. It was incredible that I had never realized it before: this was the first full-scale gale into which I sailed as a captain. On the Western Approaches, whenever the wind had got over eight, we had stayed in port enjoying a well-earned rest, for if the weather was bad, there were no planes or U-boats; the convoys could sail at their ease. On the Northeast Passage we had known a gale or two, but then all I had to do was to follow the taillight of the merchantman ahead of us. The only gale I had ever sailed into with

297

a ship under my command had been the one on D-day, but that had only been a half-grown one, and the ships had been so thick on the sea that my main worry had been not to crash into my neighbor. Now, for the first time in my life, I was sailing into the open, asking to have the hell beaten out of me, with no one to rely on but myself. It was only a moment, I dismissed the thought as soon as it came up; but during that moment I knew the truth.

When the full force of the gale hit us smack on the nose as we swung out of the harbor, the *Brighton Belle* rammed her head in with such force that the spray flew above her funnel and I had to duck behind the shield to protect myself, as the water clattered down and lashed the windows of the wheelhouse with a sound of hail. I was worried because of Goatskin, but he had ducked inside his tarpaulin like a turtle.

The beating the *Brighton Belle* took from the sea was terrifying. Like an old bird, out for the first time in years, her feathers were sent flying in all directions. First we lost the starboard navigation light; it was swept clean off its brackets. Then the tarpaulin covering of the starboard boat was sent flying, an hour later the starboard boat itself. The rail of our foredeck caved in after an hour and a half; then the boy Middag came running up, drowning in the spray, and hollered in my ear that the door to the chartroom had been ripped off and the water was playing inside, washing things away. I decided to keep her head on the course; while I stood on the bridge trying to see a landmark, a horizon, a star in the swirling darkness ahead of us, I realized that this indeed was our last chance and I was grimly determined to take it or drown.

What the crew did during that trip was impressive. Others would have abandoned the effort within an hour after we had left the harbor, for the ship was obviously breaking up. She, like we, had not been intended to outlast the war. During the six hours we were ploughing away toward the Greek I expected, at almost every white horse that came storming toward us out of the total darkness, that she would stick her head in never to rise again.

But she didn't. Every time she rose, foam streaming from her

298

nostrils, and every time she rammed her head in again, sending up explosions of spray, her propeller turning wild, setting her whole ramshackle body aquiver. I had no idea what speed we were making, but even if we made only five or six knots we should be very near the spot where the Greek had sent his last signal. Sparks came to the bridge several times and said he went on calling him, but that there was no answer. I asked him if he had heard any of Bakker's signals but he hadn't. The *Texel* had been as silent as a grave.

I knew the *Texel*, I knew her better than my own ship. She was sturdy and would remain afloat under any circumstances short of the great flood, riding the waves like a duck, but she couldn't make any speed. Even though she had the wind on her hind quarters right now, it would take old Bakker at least three more hours to reach the spot of the Greek's last position. He was ours, only in this turmoil of heaving darkness and crashing avalanches of water I couldn't see a thing, so I told Sparks to send out a last signal to the Greek, hoping his receiver was still working although his transmitter had packed up; a signal asking him to send up a flare to mark his position. During a quarter of an hour after Sparks had palmed himself hand over hand back to his cubicle to transmit the signal, the boy Middag and I stood peering in the darkness, due north, waiting. Then suddenly, far away, a faint red light shot up into the sky and we slapped each other's shoulders and cursed with joy and I hollered when Sparks appeared, "Make answer! We have seen your flare and will change our course accordingly!"

The flare had been very far away, much farther north than I had expected, but I didn't know the *Brighton Belle* yet. I didn't know how much she would drift in a wind like this. I changed our course and we lunged ahead, the waves came in over our portside now and started stripping the last of the feathers off her. I had forgotten about Goatskin until I suddenly heard a scream and jumped aside just in time to avoid a dark object being hurled at me from the darkness down the slope of the heeling bridge. It was the wheel chair. The sea had smashed the port rail of the bridge. If we heeled over the other side the bath-chair would roll back and vanish overboard.

It happened. The boy Middag and I both threw ourselves onto the dark parcel hurtling down at us, its little wheels screeching. We were dragged all the way down the bridge but we wouldn't let go. We wouldn't have let go of it even if it had meant that we would have been washed overboard; but when we were nearing the dark edge of nothing, the ship heeled over once more and we were hurled back to starboard, dragged by the chair, our boots scratching the planking, vainly trying to get hold of it. The chair crashed into the starboard rail with a sickening thud and a howl of pain. Then it started rolling down the glistening slope toward the open portside once more. But the helmsman jumped out of the wheelhouse and managed to throw a rope under the wheels that acted as a brake. It took us a long time, wrestling, panting in the darkness, lashed by the spray, but we managed to get hold of the thing and to fasten it to the front rail. I tried to look under the tarpaulin, shining into it with a torch. All I saw was a pale still face hanging limp, its eyes closed. I shouted, "Are you all right?!" but he didn't answer. He had passed out. I wanted to take him down and put him on the bunk, but the chartroom was open to the wind and the waves and it wouldn't be long before the communicating door to the cabin would cave in as well. There was no other solution than to leave him where he was. I called the Cook and asked for brandy; Cook tried to pour it into his mouth, but he wouldn't take it. At first I thought he was dead, but he moaned and tried to lift his hand. He couldn't. He tried some more; in the end he took a gulp of brandy and there was no other solution than to leave him like that. The ordeal would soon be over.

It should have been. After we had been sailing on our new course for four hours I began to worry. I had the bosun standing by at the line gun for over three hours now, ready to shoot the hawser line over the Greek's deck the moment we spotted him. But wherever we peered in the darkness we saw nothing. In the end I asked Sparks to send a new message asking for one more flare, hoping his receiver would still be working.

We waited for Sparks to come back; he took a long time. I went down to his cubicle myself. He sat cramped in his chair, lashed to the table, listening. When I came in I was flung against

300

the bunk and held on to its side with all my strength. The ship rolled as I had never known a ship to roll before. "Any answer?" I shouted, and he made a gesture silencing me. I saw his right hand scribble; I let go of the bunk, slid down to his chair and grabbed it, my legs spread out. Then I read over his shoulder: "Sorry — tried — to — warn — you — but — the — bastard — was — sitting — in — my — cabin — watching — me — stop — we — got — hold — of — the — Greek — one — hour — ago — after — you — changed — your — course — because — of — flare — which — Bakker — let — off — himself — stop — the — old — crook — you — break — his — skull — when — we — meet — in — Le — Havre — where — we — are —towing — this — duck — stop — I — wish — sorry — there — he — is — again."

Sparks turned round in his chair and looked up at me. There were tears in his eyes. "Well," he said, "there goes our future."

I went to the bridge and wheeled her round for home.

∼

When we entered the harbor in the dull gray light of the storm-swept morning, the *Texel* was mooring her Greek at the main quay. All the boys were on deck and looked at her. All of them had only one thought: to get hold of that old bastard's neck and wring it. To have let off that flare, making us believe it was the Greek, was such a callous miserable deed that the only revenge could be physical violence. No words could express that depth of mean play. He had known it was our last chance, he had known that if this time we failed there would be no hope left for us ever to come back in the tugboat service, unless we signed as sailors and stokers. Yet he had done it. He had snatched that Greek away from us, who had been so near, and he had snatched him away not because of his superior seamanship but by means of a dirty trick.

The only one who thought it funny was Goatskin. When we unwrapped him so soon as we entered the calm water between the piers, he was dizzy and very pale but conscious. "What happened?" he asked, and when I told him he laughed. He laughed

301

so much that the tears ran down his cheeks. I thought, with an odd feeling of disgust, that the only thing his dead eye could still do was weep.

When we moored in our home berth the two girls stood waiting on the quay. They must have seen us come in and ran round the harbor to meet us as we moored. They came on board the moment the gangplank was out. Nicole climbed the bridge, panting, and when she saw Goatskin she gave a curious animal sound, fell on her knees beside him and hid her face in the tarpaulin that covered his legs. I felt very tense and clenched my fists to keep down the blind rage that urged me to go ashore and run round the harbor to the *Texel* and jump on board and rip open that communicating door and go for Bakker with all the violence of the seven arid years that surged behind me.

I met June at the bottom of the bridge steps. She looked very pale. "God," she said, "what happened to the ship?" The old *Brighton Belle* was indeed a gruesome sight. Even without Captain Perseil's ultimatum we would never have sailed her again, for to get her repaired would cost several months in dock.

I said, "Yes, we took quite a beating." Then I saw the faces of my crew, silently staring at me almost in reproach. I said, "Don't worry, boys, that's exactly where I am going now," brushed past June and went ashore.

She caught up with me when I was walking round the harbor, very fast, cursing under my breath. "Where are you going?" she asked. I said, "I am going to settle an account." "No," she said, trying to hold me back by my arm, "no, please." I pulled myself free, and said, "Leave me alone," but she went on running beside me, imploring me not to do anything silly. I had my whole life before me, I was a wonderful sailor, there was nothing wrong with me, the ship had been old and rotten, please, please, darling, don't do it, please. I stopped at the *Texel*'s gangway. June looked quite haggard; she had lost her red bonnet and her hair was blown across her face. She grabbed my arms with both hands and looked at me with such despair in her eyes that I felt my rage sink down, like a wave retiring. I said, "Sorry, I didn't mean to be rude."

302

She looked at me and I saw her face change. She managed a smile, then she said, "All right, darling, go ahead," and she turned me round herself until I faced that gangway.

When I crossed it I tried to recapture the fury I had felt since Sparks and I had looked at each other after that message about the flare. But I couldn't any more. I felt tired and hopeless, when I stepped down on the deck and went to the chartroom that I knew so well. I stood for a moment in doubt, my hand on the doorknob. Then I turned it and went in without knocking.

The old man was sitting at the table, writing in his log. When I saw the back of his bald head, his fleshy neck, his short sleeves, his hairy pulses, the rage came back all right. I said, "Captain, I want to talk to you," and my voice was not steady. He looked up. When I saw his blue fish eyes stare at me without any feeling, any expression at all but a cruel, merciless stupidity, I felt like smashing his teeth in. I thought of the twenty-nine young tugboat captains out of the thirty-five that had died during the war, of Dop and Barger and Frankendaal and Daamen, and then of the five fat old men out of six who had come through alive, and of whom this bastard was the worst. In Shadwell Basin we had asked ourselves timidly what had been the magic secret of their survival; now, looking at that stupid cruel mug, I asked myself what had been the curse on us.

"Well?" he asked.

I said, "That flare you let off when you heard us asking the Greek was a dirty trick. I ought to beat the daylight out of you, you Goddam old swindler." He rose slowly to his feet, menacing like a bull, and my voice rose in fury when I said, "You knew it was our last chance. We have sailed this whole Goddam war together and yet you rubbed our face in the shit."

"Yes," he said, and his voice growled deeper than I had ever heard it. "And do you want to know why, young man? Because if our country wants to get back on its feet after the beating we took, we have to give the best we have got. As long as I can help it, the tugboat business shall not fall into the hands of a lot of amateurs, like you and your beachcombers."

At that moment I knew I was going to strike him. I talked on only to postpone the blow that I felt quivering in my fists. "You call us amateurs, but you needed a dirty trick to get ahead of us!" I cried.

He gave a deep sigh through the nose, and looked at me almost with pity when he said, "You go somewhere quiet and think out the answer to this question: how come that I have found that Greek in the dark, whereas you have not?"

Then he sat down and continued his writing.

∾

When I came off the ship, dazed, June was there. She didn't ask any questions, she just put her arm through mine. We walked along the quay, down the pier, until we sat down on a bollard behind the fishing smacks, because we couldn't go any further.

I hadn't noticed where I was going. I had been trying to recover from the blow, but there was no recovery possible unless I accepted the truth that stared me in the face. At last I had discovered the magic secret of the old captains: they had known their job.

As I sat there, staring at the ships and the harbor, I forgot about her, until she asked, "Well?"

I put my hand on hers and said, "Well, I have just heard the verdict." Then I looked at her and tried to smile. But I felt at the end of my tether.

"And what is that?" she asked.

I bit my lip, for my eyes went hot, and said, "I am no good. Old Bakker found that Greek in the dark. I didn't. God knows how he found him, but there you are."

"He must be a wonderful captain," she said calmly, almost cheerfully. I felt very alien to her. She couldn't know what this meant to me. I think that that moment, sitting close to her on that bollard, hand in hand, was the loneliest moment in my life.

"There was a time when I thought I was a wonderful captain too," I said, trying to make it sound like a joke.

She pressed my hand. "And I thought I was a wonderful nurse."

I looked at her, smiling at me, at her dark eyes full of gentleness and understanding. I remembered her with her Dagenham

Girl Pipers' cap on her eyebrows, sticking that thermometer in my mouth. "Well," I said, "you weren't."

I looked at the masts again, the ragged clouds blown low across the sky, and I felt nothing, I felt empty. But she went on quietly talking as if all this was quite normal, as if we were as common as the sparrows on the quay.

"I think that we all have to learn a lesson after this war," she said. "Whatever we may think we have done in the emergency isn't solid. If we really want to start the peace we have to pick up our life at the point where we left it when the war started, because peace isn't just the fact that the guns have stopped firing, it is something in ourselves."

"That sounds lovely," I said, "but what the hell am I to do with myself, if I am not a good captain?"

She pressed my hand again, smiling. "Could it be that you are a very good mate?" she asked.

I looked at her, with a song rising inside me, and then I kissed her, her head in my hands. I kissed her like mad, my eyes tightly closed, with the song thundering in my ears like the surf, and then I said, "God, June! You are right!"

We got up and walked back to the city.

∽

When I told Goatskin that I was going to look for a post as a mate on a tugboat again, he didn't look surprised. He just asked quietly, "Why?" and I said, "Because I want to learn the job."

He looked at me with his one live eye as he had looked only once before: on the deck of our schooner, in the harbor of La Ciotat, after I had come up, shaken, from my first dive with the Cousteau. Then he said, "You lucky bugger," and called for a bottle of wine.

Our farewell dinner was very gay, if one took into consideration that to all of us except to me this meant the end, and perhaps to me too. But I didn't care any more; it wasn't my future I had been worrying about, but my past. We raised our glasses for the last time and the mad pianist played "Auld Lang Syne." Goatskin was very cheerful, and that was a lucky thing; if he had been depressed we would all have been.

After the others had left, Nicole and June hung on. Goatskin said, "What if you girls went to bed? I would like to have a word with the Skipper." They were very good; they finished their glasses and went, arm in arm.

"Well," he said, after they had left, "now tell me what happened."

I told him, all of it. Never before had I felt so close to him. It was as if I was talking to myself. I told him how I had gone to the *Texel* to break old Bakker's skull, how he had put me that question in the nick of time, how I had ended up at the end of the quay with June and sat down on that bollard, and what she had said. "The funny thing is," I said, "that I don't mind not being a captain. I always felt like an impostor, ever since I first sailed with the *Zeeland* in Westport with old Van Dam as my opposite number. He was a professional all right. If he hadn't been killed in that air raid he'd still be sailing, like the others."

"Good old Skipper," said Goatskin, and then he drained his glass and looked at me sentimentally with his live eye. He looked as if he was getting drunk. "Self-confidence has never been one of your vices."

"Take it easy," I said. "As a mate, I don't think anybody could wish himself a better one than I."

"Hear, hear," he said, and then he poured out another glass. He sat with it in his hand looking at the sparkle of the light in the wine when he asked, "So you won't come with me in that twenty-foot cutter, will you?"

I said, "No," and when he smiled, I added, "I am sorry."

After that we sat in silence. There were so many things we wanted to say, so much feeling that waited to be expressed, that we just sat and looked at the landlord stacking the chairs. Then he said, "O.K., Skipper, take me upstairs."

I lifted him out of his wheel chair and carried him up the stairs. The landlord wanted to help but I said I could manage. Nicole heard us come up and she opened the door. June was there. I put him down on the bed.

"Good night," I said. "Good night, Nicole."

Nicole said good night, and then he asked, "Are you leaving in the morning?"

306

I said, "Yes."

"All right," he said. "God bless, Skipper. See you on that distant shore."

June took my hand on the dark landing.

Chapter XVI

I TRIED TO FIND A JOB AS A MATE DURING THE REST OF THAT WINTER. Nobody wanted me, mates came thirteen to a dozen. I would have given up after a fortnight, if June hadn't been there. I found odd jobs ashore to keep going; none of them lasted longer than a couple of weeks. Then one night in early spring I heard in a pub on the Amsterdam harbor that old Captain Bakker was looking for a mate. He had fired three in rapid succession and there were no applications any more, because those three had told stories that made your hair stand on end.

June came with me when I went to Flushing. The *Texel* lay riding on her moorings, the tide was strong. As we approached the ship, that lay quite alone at the empty quay. I heard the old man bellow curses to his bosun, ordering him to slacken the mooring ropes, telling him he was a Goddam bungler who ought to be drowned with his head in a bucket of his own blood. June mumbled, "Charming," and kissed me and said, "All right, darling, this is it. Here comes the best mate of the fleet."

When I appeared on the quayside I saw him standing in the doorway of the chartroom. He said: "Jesus Christ, there he is again. Haven't you stopped following me about, you bungler?"

I said, "No, sir," and went on board. When I entered the chartroom he glowered at me as if we were still facing each other, that morning in Le Havre. "What do you want?" he growled.

"I heard you are looking for a mate," I said.

He stared at me, and I saw something dawn on his face that I had never expected I would see there: incredulity. "You want to sail as a mate?" he asked.

I said, "Yes, sir."

"With me?"

"Yes, sir."

The incredulity changed into suspicion as he went on staring at me, narrowing his fish eyes. "Why?" he asked.

And then I said, with a feeling as if it were the marriage vow, "Because I want to learn the job."

He looked at me a few seconds longer. Then he said, "High time too," and turned away.

"Does that mean that I am accepted?" I asked.

"Yes," he said, "one bloody bungler or the other, it's all the same to me. We sail at six, to Hammerfest, so you'd better get some warm underwear."

I said, "Yes, sir," and turned away to go.

His voice stopped me in the doorway. "But I warn you!" he cried. "On board my ship the war is over!"

I said, "Yes, sir"; and after stepping over the threshold onto the deck I turned round once more and said, "Thank you, sir." But by that time he had vanished in his cabin.

∽

June stood waiting on the quay. I said: "Yes. We leave at six for Hammerfest."

"Congratulations," she said, "Mate."

We walked along the quay in silence. Then I said, "You'd better take a hotel room if you want to see me off."

"I will," she said.

We walked some more. Then I said, "I don't think we can marry until I'm a captain."

Then she laughed and kissed me in full view of everybody, which was very un-English, and said, "But darling, that may be never!"

I said, "You're right," and we walked arm in arm to the station restaurant where we ordered the full menu.

Later that night, in her hotel, we spent our last money on a whim. We rang up Saint Tropez to tell Goatskin and Nicole that we were going to be married when I came back from this trip.

I rang up the harbor master and when I asked him to call Maurice to the phone the old man shouted that I was two days

308

too late. Maurice and the Chinese girl had left for a cruise in a cutter they had hired, just the two of them. When I asked whether by any chance he knew their destination, he answered that he wasn't sure, but that he had heard them mention the island of Port Cros.